C

Benny has lived her life in the shadows, avoiding the public eye. Her life as a recipe blogger pays the bills and lets her socialise, but she is about to get the assignment of a lifetime.

Her boss orders her into a one-week ride-along with agents of the XIA, the eXtranormal Investigation Agency. It is the anniversary of the agency, and they need to improve their exposure with the general public.

Against her objections, she is paired with a standard set of agents—a vampire, a shifter and a fey. They are willing to work with her, and it is only when she signs the waivers that she learns why. They all read her column.

A week doesn't seem like much time to learn about an organisation that deals with things most folk don't enjoy thinking about, but it whips past when the assignments go from casual crime to murders that have one pivot point. Benny.

Two Parts Demon

Benny has completed the XIA course that will let her work with the agents she became close to while hunting a serial killer. It will take effect the moment they are cleared of demonic influence. Nothing like knowing that your blood is despised to make a girl feel wanted.

After a night on the town with Freddy, Benny runs into the agents, and they are not only hogging her favourite taco joint, but they are interested in her social status. She is about to say yes to whatever they can come up with when she gets a call from her house, and the night goes downhill from there.

Karaoke, kidnapping and binding spells make up the rest of the night when Benny must head to the demon zone and Argyle, Smith and Tremble refuse to let her go alone.

Nothing like jumping into a dimensional prison to lock in a first date.

Three Parts Fey

With her binding to her partners, Benny feels safe and settled. She wants to start her career in the XIA and make a place in that organisation. The past rears up and has other ideas.

The binding has its own issues. Their group has to meet and greet each family they are attached to and try to gain approval for their union. A different technique is required for each species, and they have to be ready for anything.

True love might win the day, but politics is a pain in the butt.

The characters and events in this book are fictitious. Any similarity to real persons, living or dead, is coincidental and not intended by the author.

Copyright © 2016 by Viola Grace
ISBN: 978-1-987969-12-2

©Cover Design by Cora Graphics

©Cover photography by
© *BigStockPhotos.com/* leksandr Doodko
© *Depositphotos.com/* mppriv

All rights reserved. With the exception of review, the reproduction or utilization of this work in whole or in part in any form by electronic, mechanical or other means, now known or hereafter invented, is forbidden without the express permission of the publisher.

Published by Viola Grace

Look for me online at violagrace.com, amazon, kobo, B&N and other eBook sellers.

One Part Human
An Obscure Magic Book 1

By

Viola Grace

Chapter One

Benny hated assignment meetings. They were intolerable, as those selected for the lacklustre jobs tried to squirm out of them. Today was no exception.

"I don't see why I am up for this particular assignment, Julian. Doing a week of ride-alongs with the XIA is not my idea of scintillating reporting. What am I going to do? Get stuck in a black van for a week?"

The gathered reporters were all staring at her with amusement and relief that it wasn't them.

"Benny, you have basic magic senses and two years of mage studies at the university. You are the most capable of seeing if the XIA is actually worth the money we have put in over the last fifty years or if the anniversary is celebrating mediocrity." Julian rubbed his green-scaled hands together. "Add to that the fact that you are human and it makes you the perfect foil to the extranatural officers that you will be dealing with."

Benny scrubbed her hands through her hair. "This isn't a good idea. I just want to write the recipe articles and information on how to carve pumpkins for the best light distribution at Halloween."

Julian drummed his nails on the table, and he let out a gust of air. "Do you want me to spell this out?"

"Please."

He waved at the selection of reporters in the room and on displays. "None of us can pass for human, and therefore, the XIA would consider us a suspect if they forgot we were there for the article."

Benny covered her eyes with one hand for a moment before glaring at the occupants of the room. "They don't do that."

Freddy was next to her, and she nodded. "They do think we are up to no good."

Benny gave her friend a sideways look. "In your case, they are right."

Freddy shrugged. "I have to be me."

"Freddy, it is when you take someone else's identification that you have a problem." Julian sighed. "Right. Settled. Benny, you are on the XIA, and they are expecting you for the nightshift. Go home, get some sleep and take notes on everything you can. They aren't allowing photos, but that is to be expected. I trust your memory and your common sense. Everyone else. As we have stated, get to it."

He pushed himself to his feet and walked over to Benny, she turned so he was staring at her face. "Take care and don't do anything that Freddy would do."

From behind her, Benny heard, "Hey!"

"For a full week?"

"It is the fiftieth year of the XIA. It needs a full week of examination, and we are the only news agency they are willing to deal with. More to the point, you are the only reporter they are willing to deal with. Apparently, they like food."

Benny nodded, grabbed her notepad and her tablet and got to her feet, topping the goblin by close to two feet. He didn't have a problem being even with her boobs, and she didn't even notice it after a few years.

Freddy linked arms with her and asked, "So, did you want to start happy hour a little early?"

"No. I have to run this past Mom and Dad. You know how they feel about the XIA."

Freddy let out a gusty sigh. "Did you want me to come with you?"

"Nope, but thanks for the offer. I will keep you posted on anything interesting that you can investigate for the gossip column."

"Appreciate it, Benny. Have a good night and don't forget to write down anything interesting about the officers you are with." Freddy wagged her eyebrows suggestively, and Benny sighed.

"I will consider it if there is anything noteworthy. I have never actually been in the XIA offices before."

"Few humans have."

Benny snickered and headed to her desk, leaving Freddy flirting with the copy guy.

She stuffed everything she needed into her bag and headed for the door. It was just past eleven, so her parents should be getting ready for lunch.

She called her father and warned him that she was on her way.

"Do you want some lunch?"

Benny smiled evilly, "Only if it is no trouble."

"No trouble. See you in half an hour."

"Love you, Dad."

"Love you, Benny."

She hung up and did a little dance. Her mother's lunches were nothing to be sneered at.

Benny's stomach was groaning happily as she finished her third course. Soup, salad and half a roast chicken had gone to the next life via her plate.

"You had better have room for dessert, Beneficia." Her mother was smiling as she made the warning.

"I will be able to manage something." She grinned, and her father grinned back while her mother went to get coffee. Her mom stared at her across the expanse of the counter. "Now, why are you here today, darling?"

"Now, before I say anything that will upset you, know that I am not pregnant, this isn't about a boy and I am not being arrested."

Her father sat back and drummed his fingers on the table. "I would be in favour of all but the last. You need to meet someone, pet."

"I know, Dad."

She cleared her throat and took the coffee her mother handed to her. "I will be spending a week in a ride-along with the XIA. I can't get out of it and still keep my job."

Both of her parents turned to stone in that moment. Two heads turned to look at her with horror in their gazes.

"You know how dangerous that will be for you, Benny." Her father took her hand.

She gripped his calloused fingers. "I know. But it should be fine. I am just writing about their protocols and the division of departments."

Her mother put a strawberry shortcake in front of her. "The

eXtranormal Intervention Agency is not safe for you, darling."

"I know, Mom, but I won't be spending a lot of time in the office. I will be with them in a vehicle."

Her dad leaned forward. "And if the shifter can smell your blood?"

Her mom scowled. "Or the fey or the vampire."

"Then, they smell that I have a complicated family tree. I figured that out when I was six."

It had been a school project that her father had lit on fire, and he had spoken with her teacher, and the woman had allowed little Benny to paint a portrait of her mother instead.

Benny continued. "Lots of people have mixed family trees nowadays."

Her mother shook her head. "Not like you, pet." Her mom came over and stroked her hair.

Benny hugged her with one arm and let her mom stroke her hair a little more. She shared a look with her father, happy to be in her mother's arms and he smiled briefly, the memory of their near brush with sadness flickering in his eyes. It had been fifteen years, and they still felt the panic of those first weeks of her mom's diagnosis any time she touched them. Cancer sucked.

Smiling brightly, Benny sat up straight and attacked her dessert. "I will be fine. I will make some concealer and get through the next week with all the grace and style you two gave me."

Her father nodded. "Good thinking. Better safe than sorry. I will help you."

They all sat around and finished dessert. Her father did the dishes, and when all was tidy, they headed to the herb garden for the ingredients they needed to craft a draught that would keep Benny's blend of ancestors from rising and being noticed.

It was just another kind of cooking, and Benny had gained her passion for it honestly.

The taste of strawberry kept coming up as Benny walked up the steps of the XIA. At the door, she showed her credentials and let her bag be searched. The scanner was what she was worried about.

She went through the glyph-covered archway, and it glowed softly. The officer monitoring it smacked the side of the terminal he was looking at and smiled. "Go on in, Miss Ganger, it is always going off."

She was given her visitor's pass and sent past the final checkpoint into the offices of the XIA by an officer with the focused stare of a shifter.

She nodded and followed his quick direction to the briefing room where her agents were waiting to meet her.

The plaques on the wall gave her clear direction through the maze, and she could see the magical glyphs on all doorways and at even spacing throughout the hall. This place was protected against violence and demonic interference from the ground to the highest level. There were no shenanigans of an extranatural nature here.

When she got to the briefing room, she knocked and waited until she heard the call to come in.

She wished she was nervous. She should be nervous, but nervous never came to her easily. Curiosity was her motivating emotional factor.

She identified the lawyer first, the captain second and the three agents that she would be riding with were lined up and visually taking her in.

"Miss Ganger. Welcome. I am Captain Matheson. This is the primary counsel for the XIA, Ms. Wingart. She has a release form for you to sign as well as additional waivers that you need to go over."

"Of course."

The winged fey captain smiled at her. "Please, have a seat. The sooner we can get you signed in, the sooner we can release the men for their rounds. And yourself of course."

"Oh, of course."

A few of the glyphs on the wall glowed, and Benny realised that the lawyer was trying to glamour her.

She settled down and looked over the first page quickly. "You can keep the glamour. I am trying to get this over with as much as you are. Making your skin shiny and your boobs perky isn't really something I care about."

She heard the lawyer gasp, and she signed the first document after striking out the segment that indicated her family would not be alerted to the reasons for her injury.

She flipped on to the second and third forms and signed away her right to photograph the details. She crossed out the inability to report on anything that she had seen, writing in that she would respect the privacy of the officers and those witnessed through the ride-along. No proper names or addresses would be used.

She signed off on it with those changes and slid it back to the five-foot pixie.

The woman flicked her a look through heavily made-up lashes. "You have some magical training."

"Just enough to keep me from doing anything stupid."

"These terms are acceptable." The fey put her own signature to them, and the captain followed suit.

The counsellor picked up her paperwork and headed out of the room. The moment she cleared it, the three agents applauded.

The captain shook his head. "Knock it off, guys. Miss Ganger, these are the agents you will be riding with. Agent Tremble, Smith and Argyle. This is Miss Ganger of the Redbird City News."

Agent Tremble was the elf, and he inclined his head. "You are the one with the delightful cooking articles."

"Apparently."

Agent Smith was the shifter. He had lovely golden eyes that smiled when he said, "They really are good."

Agent Argyle had deep red hair and chalk-white skin. He was some sort of undead, or she would eat her laptop.

"I don't know about food, but I will trust their judgment. It isn't that they jerk off to your articles, but they come pretty close."

"Argyle!" The captain rolled his eyes.

The undead showed his fangs as he grinned. "Apologies, sir."

"Be polite; Miss Ganger has agreed to the ride-along under duress. It is the XIA's fiftieth anniversary, and we need to make a good impression. Be on your best behaviour."

They snapped to their feet and saluted sharply.

Benny blinked and backed up in her chair when they moved. She had seen images of the XIA. Height was a factor. If they could intimidate a perpetrator, they were ahead of the game. You couldn't be weak and take down a shifter or a fey or one of the undead. They were all in good physical form, and she had to stop herself from staring.

They seemed to get taller as she stared, but that was only because they approached and each shook her hand.

"Pleased to meet you, Miss Ganger," was said by each one.

Somehow, she got to her feet and looked at them one by one. "So, when do we get going?"

Agent Smith grinned. "That would be now."

Chapter Two

Benny sat in the back with Agent Tremble. She was strapped in while he and the others were not. It was part of her contract.

"So, Miss Ganger, where did you get the recipe for mini-mushroom quiches?" Agent Smith asked her from the front passenger seat. Argyle was driving.

"My mother is an excellent cook, and she and my father used to entertain frequently. She hosted a number of different species at the dinner parties, and I would help her."

"Used to?" Agent Tremble raised his eyebrows, the pale, graceful lines rising toward the platinum blond of his hair.

His hair, as well as that of the other two, was fastened tightly at the base of his neck with only two long tendrils falling to either side of his very elegant features.

"Yes, my mother was ill several years ago, and since then, my family has drawn in on itself. She helps me work out the recipes and change things to keep them modern and doable for today's cooks."

"Well, if my mother cooked half as good as you did, I never would have left home." Agent Smith grinned. "I wouldn't have been able to; I would weigh nine hundred pounds."

"His pride would have eaten him." Agent Tremble laughed.

Well, that settled it. She was with an elf, a vampire and a lion. Her chance of surviving the night was pretty good.

A call came in, and Smith took it. He keyed in the address and Argyle turned their SUV and they spun off into the night.

The shift she was on began at eight and ended at four in the morning. It was eight thirty right now. Seven and a half hours of holding on for dear life as they whipped through the night. At least they weren't on horseback.

Argyle grinned at her in the mirror. "We don't have a siren;

she is on desk duty."

Benny smiled and giggled.

Tremble chuckled. "It is an old joke, but we like it."

Smith turned his head. "We are heading to a fey-fey altercation. We won't ask you to stay in the car, but don't stray too far from it. You are here to see us operate, but we don't want you in danger, Miss Ganger."

"Call me Benny."

Tremble looked over at her with surprise. "Benny?"

"Yes." She didn't tell him what it was short for. Beneficia was not a common first name. Benny was socially acceptable just about anywhere.

"That wasn't the name we were given when we were first briefed."

She wrinkled her nose. "Probably not, but it is the one that I will answer to."

"Fair enough."

Their vehicle was travelling at high speed through an exceptionally wealthy neighbourhood. They approached a gate, and Argyle flipped a switch. The gates swung open and let them through.

Benny could hear screaming and see flares of fey magic from where she was sitting. She leaned back as Argyle brought the vehicle to a sudden halt. The other three were out their doors and heading for the altercation without a word.

She unbuckled her seatbelt and slipped out of the SUV. It wasn't hard to follow the others. The shrieking fight between the fey was impossible to miss.

Benny was surprised by the two clumps of dazed humans, seven in all. Tremble grabbed the male fey, Argyle grabbed the female and Smith called for a pickup van and medical assistance.

Tremble spoke calmly as he forced his prisoner to his knees. The female suffered the same fate from Argyle.

"Now, what is the cause of all this?"

The man snarled, "It was my day with the pool and hot tub. She had it last night."

The female with deep-blue hair that seemed quite natural, based on the colour of her pubic hair glowing through the gauzy gown she was wearing, hissed. "It is still my turn. They are the same lovers."

Argyle closed his eyes slowly, and he was obviously counting to ten. "Smith, did you call for medical?"

"I did."

"Have them bring some iron supplements. Those humans need restoration and protection. They are fey locked."

Benny stared with her eyes wide. The male fey looked over at her and said, "Hello, beautiful. When this lot is hauled off, would you care to stay and play?"

His erection tented his loose trousers, and she felt the pull of his glamour.

His wife caught on and smiled slyly at her. "Yes, lovely. Stay and play."

The amount of magic being used on her was obscene, as were the images they were casting at her. She blinked and smiled weakly. "You know, that sounds like so much fun."

She steeled her voice. "Except that parasites like you two make me sick, and preying on deliberately chosen, powerless humans throws you right into that category, making you subject to the magical abduction, assault and confinement charges. Seven counts by my guess, because even if they wanted it, they couldn't legally want it."

She flicked their power back at them, and both of them were out cold in an instant.

The humans collapsed a moment later.

Smith looked at her in surprise with a grin on his lips. "Can we keep you?"

She blushed and stood back while they cuffed the fey and carried the humans to the front of the expansive home.

Tremble came to her side as their backup took away the two fey in the prisoner transport. "We aren't all like that."

She patted his arm. "I know you aren't. This isn't the first round of fey I have met. My parents used to socialise, remember?"

"Ah. You do seem very resistant to mental seduction."

She grinned. "They should have bought me nachos and a hotdog. I roll over for that."

Smith passed her and made a quick note, muttering, "Nachos and a hot dog."

She blushed again, but got back in the vehicle while they completed checking on the humans and making sure that there were none left in the house. Smith did the check.

Benny sat down and made notes about the evening so far.

When the medical attendants arrived, there were three ambulances, and they divided the victims relatively evenly, putting IVs in several and urging them into the vehicles. They were on their way in six minutes.

Her privacy disappeared in the next moment, because the guys climbed into the car, and they were off again.

She sat for three minutes before asking. "So, what do you guys think of the use of the term extranatural instead of supernatural?"

Argyle shrugged. "It is more appropriate. We are more than we were."

Tremble laughed, "And the fey don't care. Extranatural, extranormal. We are both."

"Extra-ego." Smith smirked.

Argyle looked at her in the rear-view. "You have a little extranatural in your nature, don't you, Benny?"

She shrugged. "I suppose, but since the great wave two hundred years ago, we all have bits of magical creatures in us, even if we don't know it."

Tremble smiled, "If you had a magical creature in you, you would know it."

It took her two seconds to blush.

Smith shot back, "Not if it was you. She would need an enlargement enchantment and a magnifying glass."

Argyle ducked and focused on the driving as Smith and Tremble had a slap fight. A second call broke it up, and Smith had to take it.

It was amazing to see them shut down and resume their business as agents. They went from teen boys to adults in under a second.

She stared out the window as they swung from the elegant neighbourhood to one far more middle class.

Smith turned, "We have been called out for a disorderly werewolf. I suspect first shift, but I won't know until I meet him."

Tremble snorted. "We are doing backup."

"Where should I be?"

Smith sighed, "For this one, remain in the vehicle. We don't know where he is or how his thoughts are processing at the moment."

Argyle was sombre. "I will lock the doors."

It was as much of a warning as they could give her. She knew what happened to those who ran afoul of newly shifted weres. They usually ended up in the emergency room with permanent scarring, if someone got to them fast enough.

She sat in the vehicle with the lights off, making notes. The agents went to the home that the call had emanated from, and Smith and Argyle began tracking the shifter.

Benny really wanted to be out there with them, because inside the vehicle, she felt like a staked goat.

Smith shifted his head, and his lion's mane was glaringly obvious even in the darkness. He took off down an alleyway toward a back lane, and Argyle followed while Tremble stayed on alert.

Benny froze when a shadow moved close to the vehicle. She heard the light scratching of claws on asphalt and the ticking as it paced closer. Benny had been around enough shifters to know when one was hunting.

She unclasped the seatbelt as quietly as she could and eased it away from her, holding it so it didn't make a sound as it rested in place. She shifted herself to the centre of the vehicle while he wasn't looking, but every time she moved, he lifted his head.

Tremble hadn't caught on to his proximity. He was on the wrong side of the vehicle for his patchy and fluffy body to be visible to the elf.

He sniffed along the doorframe next to her original seat. She was fascinating to some species; it came from her blended family tree. According to her grandmother, many species wanted to get in on that kind of power. They would do what it took to be part of the next generation.

She watched his half-shifted back hunch down, and then, his head snapped up, his jaws parted and his gleaming tongue came out. The orange of his eyes was hot with a combination of lust and fury. Yup, he was a teenager.

Benny tried not to flinch as he flicked at the handle of the door, trying to get it to open. He would only work with his human instincts for so long, and then, he was coming through that door.

She whispered a repelling charm and one to reinforce the door.

He blinked and stumbled back as the first charm struck him.

The roar in the darkness was a relief. There was nothing like the bellow of a lion to make a young dog cower.

The young man submitted immediately. Smith cuffed him and hauled him off down the street.

Argyle and Tremble met with the initial caller and then returned to the SUV.

Tremble grinned, and she scooted away from his seat and back to her spot behind the driver.

"It was your little charm that got my attention. You repelled him very well."

Benny smiled weakly. "He was trying to get into the car, so it seemed the best course of action."

Tremble put his hand on her shoulder, and Argyle hissed, "No contact, Tremble. Those are the rules."

"She's upset, Argyle."

"Rules are rules, and we are on duty."

Tremble pulled his hand away with a sigh. "Sorry. Our job does take us to places where a lone female is endangered."

"Only because most races refuse to teach their females to hunt and kill for fear of the men being thought obsolete."

She buckled up, and they drove the SUV to follow Smith to the house where the young lad had made his escape from. His family was in the yard, and lights streamed out. Smith brought him home as they pulled up, and the youngling was alternately hugged and struck in the head with the back of a hand by other shifters.

When Smith had finished admonishing the family on how to get their son into therapy for his change, he returned to their vehicle and resumed his human visage.

"Well, done, Benny. You kept calm and let him remain next to your window until he tried to get in. That was enough time for me to come around. After this is over, I am going to file a request to get you assigned to us."

The other guys laughed, and they were called to their next mission. There was an undead committing petty crimes, and they were now free to chase it down. Argyle was going to have to take point on this one.

Chapter Three

Three petty extranormal robberies, followed by a hooker with no actual genitalia and two disgruntled customers.

Benny had never seen a mer-woman as a hooker before, but she made a convincing argument for never intending to furnish the half-elves with sexual services. She was trading her magic and the touch of her mouth.

They locked her up for unlawful spell peddling. Magic—you could give it away, but if you wanted to charge for it, you needed a license.

"Why do you turn your prisoners over to the other agents?"

The hooker was on her way to booking. Smith entered the details of the arrest into the computer in the SUV, and he grimaced. "We separate it to speed the process along. As agents, it is our job to investigate, not to continue the interrogation. The prisoners will be interrogated at the office and processed according to what they have been charged with."

Tremble smiled. "Argyle and Smith are the best agents to do the data entry. I am not comfortable with technology."

Smith muttered, "He means he can't type."

Argyle snickered as they rolled out again, "Or spell."

Tremble flipped them off and turned to her, "So, Benny, are you finding this ride-along educational?"

"So far, it is very interesting. I had no idea of the range of the calls you were sent out on."

Tremble laughed. "You haven't seen anything. We also do speeches for the Changeling Guides and Scouts, the newly undead and the Fey Integration Association. We go out, speak and then get back to work."

"What about the Mage Guides and Scouts?"

"They are on their own. Human officers deal with them."

She nodded. "Right."

She had never fit in in the Mage Guides, but it had been the only option for her. She didn't appear to be anything other than human, but the magic was in her blood. Her sash still hung proudly on the wall of her parents' study.

Smith looked up from his keyboard, "Were you in the Guides?"

She blinked. "Uh, yeah."

Tremble smiled and a wicked gleam came to his eyes. "I bet you looked adorable in that uniform."

She gave him a bland look. "From time to time I still do."

Argyle's shoulders shook as he chortled.

Tremble sighed and smiled blissfully. "Well, my dreams are set for the next week."

Benny grinned, and she settled into her place as pervert mascot to this gathering of officers.

"So, when do we eat?"

Smith smiled. "Thank goodness. Someone else with an appetite...for food. Argyle, tacos!"

Argyle muttered about basic human necessities, and he pulled a U-turn, heading for Benny's part of town.

Taco! Taco! Taco! was her favourite haunt when she went out with Freddy, but she had never been there in the wee hours. It was after midnight and not yet dawn, so she was on new territory with a bunch of XIA agents.

Dem-rah was the chef on duty, and he waved at Benny cheerfully, all four arms waving. "Benny, darling. What can I get for you?"

"Three chicken, two beef and plenty of hot sauce." She looked over and nodded. "And a coke."

He got her order, took her money and turned to her companions with a cold face. "Agents, what can I get for you?"

Smith and Tremble ordered, their food was served, but it didn't look anything like Benny's.

Argyle sat at a picnic table and sipped at a thermos. Apparently, he brought his own.

She looked at Dem-rah as she wrestled for a straw. "While the agents seem willing to eat anything, please give them the same calibre of food that you serve to me and my friends."

"They are with you?" He raised his brows and snatched the food back before the agents could grab it. Smith looked like he wanted to cry.

"I am doing a ride-along for the article. One week for the XIA anniversary." She smiled. "It is really very interesting so far."

She munched one of the tacos and groaned happily. "I might have to start waking Freddy up before dawn and hauling her over here. It is worth it."

Dem-rah beamed. "Gratitude for the compliment. It means much coming from you."

She winked and joined Argyle at the table. She worked her way through her delightfully spicy tacos in soft shells and sighed happily when she was done.

Smith looked at the food suspiciously, but Tremble dived in. He moaned and sauce covered his pearly skin. Smith took the hint, and he was halfway through his platter of ten when he picked the mass up and went back to order another ten tacos.

When he came back, he smiled at his new treasures. "When this is over, do you mind if I wake you up in the middle of the night to act as my food liaison?"

She laughed. "Probably. Dem-rah is an excellent cook, but his brother had two arms broken by overzealous XIA agents twenty years ago and spider goblins hold a grudge. You were getting the health-code special. It met all the codes...barely."

Smith sighed. "It still tasted damned good."

Tremble daintily cleaned his face with a napkin. His lips were slightly swollen from the chili sauce, but he looked happy.

Smith destroyed the second set of ten, and Argyle looked at them wistfully. "I never ate a taco."

Benny acted on reflex, and she extended her arm. "Here you go. It is still active in the bloodstream."

He blinked. "Are you sure?"

"Just a taste. I am sure the others would help pry you off if necessary."

"They might have to."

"I heal quickly so I digest quickly. If you want to taste taco, you had better bite now."

He flashed his teeth and bit her wrist. She focused on providing him with the taste of dinner and downplaying what was all in her bloodstream.

She counted to five before she tapped his cheek. After that, she clenched her fist and put pressure on her vein to remove the flow.

He lifted his head drowsily. "So, that is a taco. There was a lot more going on in there than human magic, but thank you. Few folk realise that a little donation does not bind them to a vamp."

"I had a decent education. My parents raised me right."

She pressed the puncture wounds and tried to get them to stop.

Smith sighed and took her forearm, licking his tongue across the wounds. They sealed up, and she was soon back to fighting form.

"Thank you." She smiled.

Argyle was looking at her with a sober expression. "Thank you. It was an honour to have tasted you."

"I would have to second Argyle's statement. I could get drunk on the taste of your skin, Benny."

"Not an option. We are on business. I was just upset that Argyle had not experienced Dem-rah's tacos."

Argyle looked at her with assessment in his gaze. "You are not afraid of any of us, are you?"

She shrugged. "Nope. I have met people from most species and guilds over my life. My parents used to entertain a lot."

"Politicians?" Tremble arched his brows.

She shook her head. "No. Academics."

He chuckled. "That would explain it. You have a self-contained manner that I usually associate with humans in their fifth or sixth decade."

She smiled and inclined her head. "I will take that as a compliment."

"You should. A woman who cannot appreciate the past holds little appeal for most men with family histories."

Argyle chuckled and licked his lips again, "Or personal ones."

Tremble chuckled. "That, too."

Benny clutched her hands to her chest and said on a breathy gasp. "So I might be good enough for a man one day? Oh, joy! I never thought such a thing would be possible. Butt-heads."

Smith's shoulders were shaking as he covered his mouth with one hand. Finally, he said, "Keep your compliments, Tremble. The lady neither needs nor wants your approval."

Benny waggled her eyebrows as she finished her soda. With

a last slurp, she tossed the cup to the garbage can. A hand shot out and pulled the trash inside.

Tremble blinked his pretty eyes.

Smith chuckled. "Trash troll?"

"Yup. One of the best recyclers in the last ten years. That can probably weigh around four hundred pounds."

Argyle turned his head to look over the street. "Anything else lurking around that we should know about?"

"Nothing out of the ordinary. Same old, same old." She got to her feet and headed over to Dem-rah. "Any chance that I can get your spice mix recipe out of you tonight?"

"Ah, Benny, only if you were my wife. So, I am afraid that it will not happen. Your father would kill me if I tried." He winked.

"Yes, in an extremely unpleasant manner. Ah well, it was worth asking."

He winked and got back to cleaning. "It is always worth asking."

She returned to the XIA agents with a series of hand wipes, and she distributed them with a smile. "What happens next?"

Smith straightened, "We get back in our vehicle and wait for the next call."

They got to their feet and headed for their transport. Benny followed along and settled into her spot, buckling the seatbelt and waiting.

Argyle drove down the street at a normal speed, and when a call came through, they were off.

Chapter Four

A pugnacious zombie was refusing to accept last call, so Argyle took their group to The Hyde.

Benny had been to the nightclub twice in her life, and neither time was particularly memorable. This one definitely made it one for the books.

Tremble ordered her to stay in the car. "Lock the doors. This time of the morning, most things out here are hungry."

She nodded and stayed in the dark of the SUV.

The XIA agents went into the club, and it was six silent minutes before the doors burst open and Smith tumbled out with what she hoped was their target.

The lion shifter was beating the undead into the pavement, and Argyle and Tremble came out after them.

She saw Tremble calling in a pickup, and then, she turned her attention back to the zombie giving as good as he was getting.

There was snarling and gnashing of teeth on both parts. Two minutes later, the hauler arrived, and Tremble stepped forward, wrapping the zombie in bands of fey magic. Argyle stepped in and loaded the zombie into the storage case that had been brought out for him. He would remain boxed up until he calmed down. That would probably be sometime after Friday night. Zombies were notoriously vulnerable to alcohol and caffeine.

Argyle held him in the case while Tremble locked him down. To Benny's surprise, they were wearing black gloves that they stripped off and dumped in the biohazard container inside the transport vehicle. Even Smith was wearing the gloves, and he peeled them off, tossing them with distaste.

The drivers of the pickup vehicle handed Smith some wipes, and he rubbed every part of himself with them to remove the zombie smell.

Benny hid her smirk as they joined her again. At least they got to get physical on their shift. She had the feeling that she was holding them back a bit.

It was the last bit of excitement on her first night.

Two more hours of hashing the events of the evening for her article and she was ready to go home. They pulled into the XIA lot, and the moment they were parked, she hopped out of their vehicle.

After the zombie fight, the air had been a little thick in the SUV, so breathing fresh air became a luxury.

She stepped away from the vehicle and made sure she had her notes and her purse.

Tremble leaned against their SUV. "So, Miss Benny, same time tomorrow?"

She chuckled. "You mean later today? Yes. I will be here. Four more shifts with you guys before the anniversary. I have more research to do."

Smith looked at her with concern. "Are you all right to drive home?"

"Aw, how sweet. Yes, of course I am. All I have done tonight is hang out in the car."

Argyle inclined his head. "It was an entertaining first evening."

She bowed to them all. "Thank you for improving my education."

With her shoulders back, she headed to her car, starting it up with a flick of her keychain.

She opened the door and chucked her purse into the passenger seat. She slid behind the wheel, and the car roared with excitement before she even put the key in.

"Down boy. We are going." She stroked her dashboard and checked the mirrors. Everything was clear, so she got underway to get herself home.

Driving an enchanted car was not for everyone, but Benny was confident enough in the car to take it anywhere and let it take over if it needed to. She called it Pooky, but it used to be a pukha.

The earliest touches of dawn were sparking, threatening to bloom. Benny drove back to her home and sighed happily when she parked next to the dower house.

She dragged herself and her stuff into the house. "Morning, Jessamine."

The house's ghost smiled and whispered. "How did it go?"

"I need a shower and sleep. The agents were fine."

"Just fine? That isn't the chatter in the spectrum. I have heard that the agent teams are fine physical specimens."

"They are, and I will talk to you about them when I wake up."

"Fair enough. Your room is ready."

Benny removed her jacket and hung it up. Her shoes went flying, and she peeled off her clothing on the way to her shower. Jessamine was her housekeeper and companion, and she liked the cleaning. Benny was in no mood to stop her.

Half an hour later, she was wrapped in a towel with another on her head, flipping through her notes and transcribing them onto her computer in a rough outline.

Jessamine blacked out the coming dawn and edged the computer away from her until Benny caught the hint. "Good night, Jess."

"Good morning, Benny. Have a nice rest."

The room was dim and quiet. Benny leaned back and pulled the sheets over her, trying to rest before she had to go back.

The moment she closed her eyes, images of her agents danced through her mind. Their dancing eventually slowed, and her mind slowed enough to sleep.

Benny glared at the sunset and checked her phone. "Jess, did you change my wallpaper again?"

Jessamine floated over. "No. Why do you ask?"

Benny turned it to face her. "Because I have never seen a picture of a kitten in a sailor suit on my phone before now."

"Maybe he just crawled in there." Jessamine smiled.

"I doubt it. It isn't Fleet Week. No sailors should be creeping around in my phone." She tapped the back of her phone with her finger. "Put the starscape back."

"I don't have time. Your parents would like to see you at the big house."

"When?"

"As soon as you woke up?" Jessamine wrinkled her nose. "Sorry. I forgot."

"Damn, damn, damn." She raced to her room and put on her

clothing for the evening of sitting in a car.

The black button-down shirt would hide any stains if anything happened to smack into her. She didn't know if they were hitting Dem-rah's joint again, but she was willing to take that chance.

Her bag, phone, wallet and notebook were with her as she got into her car and blazed a path the two kilometres to her parents' very large abode.

Gravel flew as she braked and threw her car into park. She grabbed her bag and headed into the place she had grown up.

Her mother greeted her in the hallway. "Oh, sweetie. You didn't brush your hair."

Benny muttered a quick spell, and her hair sorted and tidied itself, wrapping up into a professional bun.

"Much better, darling. He has been waiting all day. There was an omen yesterday, and he has been eager to speak with you."

Benny hugged her mother and headed to the study. The door opened and closed silently as she entered the largest collection of magical books in the state, possibly the country.

Her father was leaning over his work desk and eyeing a vial of blue liquid.

He looked up and smiled. "Ah, Beneficia. I am glad that you made it before heading out tonight. Drink this."

She took it and tossed it back. "What was that?" The taste left on her tongue was hot strawberries and fungus.

Benny handed him the vial, and he tucked it onto a rack next to four other doses of the same liquid.

"It is a protection and concealment spell. I also want you to take the charm that your uncle Magnus left you."

She winced. "It is so heavy."

"There was an omen last night. Something is stirring around you, Beneficia. Your safety might be in the hands of the XIA, but they do not know what you are. They can't guess at how valuable you could be in the wrong hands."

Benny sighed, and she went to her section of the library. The shelves were filled with some of the most powerful charms ever crafted, and they were all hers. Each one was given to her on a birthday or graduation. The charm that her uncle Magnus had given her was the size of her open hand, but at least it was flat. The weight she hated was actually the magical protection that coated her skin.

She found the case and opened it, sighing as she draped the chain around her neck and settled it under her shirt.

"There we go, Dad. Happy?"

He smiled, his bright eyes tired. "I will be happier when I know that you are safe."

"Would you feel better if I didn't go on this assignment?"

"No, it has nothing to do with where you are. Something is coming for you, and it doesn't matter where you are or who you are with. Some events cannot be avoided."

Benny blinked at the sober look on his face. "You are really worried."

He came over and stroked her cheek. The magic of her defenses crackled.

"I am very worried. I have been fielding calls all day. All of your aunts and uncles with a bit of precognition are worried about you."

She blinked. That was a lot of magical academics. Her childhood had been filled with folk she called aunt or uncle who were unrelated to her. Her family consisted of a long line of only children.

"I will be extra careful. I promise. You know me; I am not going to do anything stupid."

He smiled. "I know that you are careful, but when this kind of darkness pursues you, you have to meet it head on with as much armament as you can muster. Once we know what we are up against, we can create a battle plan."

"Like at Easter?" The long-standing making of maps of the grounds and segmenting the areas for maximum egg retrieval never failed to frustrate her mother's attempts to make it challenging.

Her father laughed. "Exactly like Easter. Now, your mother has some dinner for us. Let's go."

He offered her his arm, and she took it out of long habit. They left the library and followed the scent of one of her mother's dinners. Benny wished that she had inherited the cooking gene, but she would have to be content with the ability to find food.

Before they tucked into the meal, she asked her dad, "Why do I still taste strawberries?"

Her mother portioned out the mashed potatoes. "It is to cover up the taste of troll, Beneficia. It was one of the strongest flavours we could find."

Benny swallowed and reached for her glass of juice. She gulped it and put it down. "For future reference, nothing covers up the taste of troll."

Her mother chuckled and her father grinned. It was a normal family dinner at the Ganger house.

She pulled Pooky into the parking lot and locked it behind her while she hustled to the vehicle where her team was waiting for her. "Sorry. Am I late?"

They stood in their dark uniforms and badges, smiling.

Tremble chuckled. "We were afraid we had scared you off yesterday."

Argyle smiled slowly. "If you are ready, we will go."

Smith moved around and opened her door for her. "I have been ready to go for an hour."

Benny rolled her eyes and settled into the SUV with her notepad and pen at the ready.

They climbed in with Smith at the wheel and Argyle on the computer. They really did take turns.

Tremble was next to her, and they left the parking lot with a smooth glide of the wheels.

Day two was underway.

Chapter Five

Breaking up bar fights was not normally an XIA duty, but when it was a newly transformed stone giant causing the fuss, it definitely called for additional help for the bouncers.

Benny stared at the familiar logo of Syren's Karaoke Club. It was not the sort of place that she had ever seen a giant before.

"Stay in the car, Benny." Tremble muttered it on his way out.

"No. Witnessing this is within my agreement. I just have to stay out of the danger zone, which is about twenty feet for a giant. I won't get that close, but I need to see how you guys handle these situations."

"Twenty feet?"

"Yes. Twenty feet away." She smiled.

He watched the flow of traffic out of the club and jerked his head. "Stay safe."

She followed him into the club and stuck to the wall. This was her hangout on weekends with Freddy and a few other friends.

When she eased into the main room, she could see the problem. The giant had a group of partiers pinned up against the stage, and the XIA agents were joining another team in surrounding him.

She watched as one attempt from the other team failed. Claws didn't work. Strength didn't work and magic bounced off. Benny wondered how they were going to solve this and stayed as close to the wall as she could. When the giant spotted her, a light came to his eyes.

"Sing!"

Benny blinked. "What?"

"You! Sing!" He pointed right at her.

She squinted at his features and tried to see the human that had been inside him. "Holy shit."

Her mind pasted a picture of a young, gangly man who participated in every week's competitions and who enjoyed nothing more than to sit and listen to song after song warbled by other contestants.

He brought his fist down on a table shattering it to chunks. "Sing!"

Kobar was crouched near the precious equipment, and he waved at her. "What do you want, Benny?"

"Bring me life."

Argyle nodded slightly, and Benny took that as permission. She stayed out of the smashing range and eased up onto the stage.

Kobar handed her the mic and brought up the music and display. She didn't need it. She knew this one song backward and forward.

The lyrics began slowly as the song explained a normal human existence and the longing to be exceptional.

Benny watched, and the giant turned toward her, lumbering to the foot of the stage.

She sang about waking up in a body that wasn't hers. Breaking her mirror because she had become something new, something dangerous that she couldn't accept.

The agents got the hostages out.

The song changed to accepting the magic that had lodged inside and the new family, new friends and new life, which blossomed out of the change.

The giant looked at her dreamily, and Benny put as much of her inner siren as she could into that song.

Another officer rushed in on silent feet with headphones. Argyle and Tremble took the headset and eased up to the giant just as the song was ending. The man shook himself out of his stupor and yelled, "Sing."

She turned to Kobar. "Bring me the power."

He swiftly moved his hands over the keyboard and the song roared to life. Benny didn't like singing it first, but it should to a good job of disguising what the officers were up to.

She was halfway through the first chorus when they got the headphones on him. Pure siren song locked him in his own mind, and he fell backward with a tremendous thud.

Benny waved at Kobar, and he cut the music. She put the mic

down and crept out to the SUV while the others bodily hauled the giant out of the club.

Smith was the first one back to the car, and he handed her a bottle of water. "I think you need this. You did well. He might have hurt someone before the headset arrived if you hadn't been there. How did he know you could sing?"

She sipped at the water. "Before his change, he was a regular at the club. He would sing and he had an okay voice, but he would listen to each and every performer. I hang out there on the weekends, and he recognised me."

"And you recognised him."

"It took some doing. He must have had a latent shift some time in the last month or so." She remembered the look in his white eyes and shivered.

"His community officer will deal with him at the station. For now, we got him under control and no one got hurt."

She looked at the heavily armoured collection van and the four men carrying the giant between them. "I am glad no one got hurt, but he is still trying to fit himself back into the human world. He is in for a rough time."

The others returned to the vehicle, and Argyle's fingers moved rapidly over the computer terminal while they all settled in.

Tremble smiled at her. "You have a good voice."

She swallowed more water and nodded. She had pitched her voice to enthrall the giant, an old siren's trick that she had gotten from one of her great grandparents. Her dad was right; her life was suddenly getting dangerous.

Her blend of magic could be explained, but not all in the same body.

She sat back and quietly noted the next few stops. They checked on some apothecaries and then drove off to arrest an unlicensed precog who was selling slivers of the future.

The young man looked at the officers with contempt, right up until the point where Smith put the cuffs on him. Fear trickled through his expression.

That draining of colour got her attention. He didn't seem inclined to share his information with Smith, but with her father's warning in her mind, Benny wanted to know.

She angled to intercept him as he was led to the transport. "What did you just see?"

He leaned back and stared at her. He got a sly look in his eyes. "Why should I tell you?"

"Because I know something that you don't about your skills."

He snorted. "I can see the future."

The officer holding him raised his eyebrows in an indication to make it fast.

"Tell me what you saw and I will tell you what might get you out by the end of the evening."

The young man mulled it over for a second before leaning forward and whispering in her ear. Benny kept her face impassive, which turned into a grin when he touched his cheek to hers.

He blinked. "What the hell?"

She laughed. "I am warded against casual intrusion. Now, when you get to the agency, ask them to test you for seer focus. That is all you need to do."

"What?"

"Your talent for foresight is directional. You have options for your vision, and you are choosing the most traumatic."

He blinked. "How do you know that?"

"It is a natural instinct in your kind. You want to see the worst in order to prepare for it. Unfortunately, you charge people for what you see and that is what has gotten you into this situation."

"My kind?" He looked both intrigued and offended.

"Human seers. So, ask them to test you for seer focus. It can't hurt, and it might keep you from being arrested." She waggled her eyebrows.

He frowned and headed to the transport with the officer behind him.

When Benny turned toward the SUV, her agents were all lined up and watching her. "What?"

Smith grinned, "Is there something you want to tell us?"

"Yes, Argyle needs to drive for the rest of the night." She sighed. "I will explain more in the car."

Smith looked at Argyle. "I am okay with it if you are."

Argyle shrugged. "Sure. But you get to do double tomorrow and Thursday."

They shook on it, and everyone resumed their position in the vehicle.

When Argyle had pulled away from the curb, Smith turned to her. "So?"

"He saw an accident in which we get a spike through the window on the driver's side. Argyle could survive the damage, you couldn't. Argyle also has faster reflexes, so we probably won't get into the accident anyway."

Argyle looked up to the rear-view mirror. "Thanks for that."

She smiled. "If you are injured, you can use me for repair."

Benny could swear that he licked his lips, but she *knew* that he winked as the next call came in.

Smith gave the address to Argyle, and they were on their way.

The location was a cemetery, and flares of magic had been felt, but the magic users at the dispatch centre had determined that the magic wasn't human. It meant the XIA had to come in.

Argyle opened his window and shut the lights down as their vehicle glided on the paved pathway of the Heartway Cemetery.

"What are we doing?" She whispered it to Smith because Tremble was focusing, his hands cupped in front of him.

"Tremble is looking for the source of the energy pattern."

Argyle cruised through the dark space between the glowing white and grey stones.

Tremble opened his hands, and a small orb of light floated up and toward Argyle. The light moved to the left side of the steering wheel.

At the next turn, they went left.

They cruised through a number of turns, and finally, the light lowered. Argyle stopped the vehicle, and a number of hand signals went through the car. Benny could barely make them out; her night vision was her one weak point.

They slipped out of the car, and she took the hint and stayed inside the vehicle.

With no one around her, she reached out with her own senses and picked up on the crackling energy of a communication spell. Someone was trying to talk to a dead person and that person was not using human magic; there was the definite taste of trees in the air.

The spell was interrupted, leaving a lot of power hanging in the air.

Benny made notes as she felt what was going on with the

change of attitude in the energy. She finally gave in to her curiosity and followed the power signature out of the vehicle to the group standing around and discussing communicating with the dead without a permit.

Tremble came to stand next to her. Benny whispered, "Is she going to drain the spell?"

He cocked his head. "She said she did."

"It is still here. I was top of my class in spell identification. The power is in the air."

Tremble nodded. "Right. Well, I will speak with her."

Tremble went to speak with the woman who was obviously a dryad. The woman got angry and the power surged.

The grass on the grave that she had set the spell on began to grow rapidly.

Tremble and Smith held her. Argyle called out. "Benny, is there anything you can do?"

She sighed and approached the grave while the woman shrieked and fought with the strength of an ancient oak.

The headstone was that of a man who died in his early forties. He was either a son or a lover. Either way, his connection to her was his link to the world.

The spell was simple and had a few ingredients. Benny took the water vessel that had been left on the grave and scooted all the energy back together, embedding it in the water.

Benny stood and turned to face the furious dryad. "Gentlemen, let her go."

The woman lunged, and Benny struck her with the water of her own power. She was overwhelmed and passed out.

Benny sighed and broke up the small items that she had needed to fire off the spell. All were readily available within twenty metres of the grave, so it wasn't destroying vital evidence.

Tremble eyed her as Smith and Argyle cuffed their catch.

"How did you do that?"

"Simple spell cancelling. I put the power into the water and threw the water at the dryad. She is tree based, and her skin absorbs water on reflex." Benny got to her feet, dusting her hands off.

"How did you know how to do that?" Tremble walked back toward the SUV with her.

"Practice. I did take spell work at university. I just happened to major in journalism." She smiled.

"I am guessing that your transcripts from school would make for fascinating reading."

She shrugged as the lights of the transport approached. "They were part of the reason I am here on this ride-along."

"That and your knack for recipes."

"How could I possibly forget?" Benny laughed and got back in the SUV.

Chapter Six

When the accident came, the SUV spun to the side as the pipes shot through the driver's side and pierced Argyle.

The vehicle that had lost its load of pipes was stopped a few feet away, and Smith was staring at the end of the metal that would have ended his life.

Argyle hissed. "Get me out of here."

Smith called the emergency services, and Tremble got out of the vehicle.

He grabbed for a kit in the back of the vehicle and came around the side. Benny went out his door; hers was pinned by the same pipes that were running through Argyle.

Smith was out of the SUV, and he had the driver pinned to the vehicle while he watched Tremble hacksaw off the following edge of tubing.

Benny grabbed the window striker, and she crawled into the front seat where Argyle was holding terribly still. "I am just going to break the window so we can get you away from the door."

He nodded slightly. She struck the window, and the glass shattered into a sheet that folded when she pushed at it with her forearm.

The object had entered below his arm and punched down to the spot just above his hip. The blood was dripping sluggishly, but he could survive it. Smith would have had no chance.

Tremble sliced through the outer pipe and reached inside to make quick work of the inner section. The moment that he was free, Tremble came around and pulled Argyle out of the vehicle through the passenger side.

Without saying anything, Argyle pulled the pipe out of his body and threw it to clatter on the street.

Benny was a woman of her word. She offered her arm, and he bit down without hesitation. Her protection amulet heated, but it responded to ill will and bodily injury. It would stop Argyle if he got carried away.

Her head spun after a few minutes, but thankfully, the emergency services arrived with bags of blood for him.

She tapped on Argyle's cheek, and he looked at her. "They have blood for you, Argyle. Let go or I will make you let go."

He slowed his draw on her skin and released her forearm from his deadly grip.

Smith took her by the arm and licked the wounds closed once again.

"Thanks for asking about that warning."

She smiled and swayed. "Sorry, I am a little dizzy. He took quite a bit."

"I think you need something to eat, and our group is done for the night. The car is totalled." He smiled and put his arm around her.

"I have blood on me."

"Well, you were fairly close to him. It is natural for you to have blood on you."

She touched her ribs. "Nope. My blood. Can I see a medic please?"

Tremble must have been listening, because he grabbed her and carried her to the medics who examined the graze along her ribs. The young woman smiled. "It is a small cut. Two stitches. May I?"

Smith stepped forward. "I can heal her without the stitches. I would have if my partner hadn't hauled her off."

The medic raised her hands and stepped away. "Go ahead. I will be nearby if you need help."

Smith knelt at her side. "I know this wasn't covered in your authorisations, so may I?"

She looked into his eyes and nodded. "Yes, please. This isn't really comfortable."

Benny held the shirt away from her skin and left the area clear. Tremble moved behind her and took over holding the fabric as well as pulling her against him to support her.

She leaned back, and when she was comfortable, Smith leaned forward and applied his tongue to her wound. She wouldn't have said that an alpha would be out as an XIA operative, but only the alphas gained the ability to heal. It was a means of keeping the other shifters subservient. They had to surrender to the alpha in order to be healed.

When Smith applied his tongue to her, she tried not to hiss. He lapped around the edges and finally dragged the rough pad over her wound.

Tremble tried to distract her. "You know, the average young lady would not be so calm in the face of having a wound licked closed."

She gave him a narrow-eyed look. "You still think I am average? How sweet."

Smith chuckled.

Argyle came toward them and sat on the edge of the emergency vehicle with one blood bag clamped in his jaws and two more in his hand.

Benny looked at him. "Oh shit. I forgot. How are you doing?"

He grinned—a weird and bloody grin, "I am doing well. Your immediate help was invaluable."

She could see him sparkling with energy and hoped that he came down from his high before he tried to drive or before he lifted the SUV from the wreckage.

Smith kept lapping at her skin, and she shivered. The pain was gone, and the healing had turned to a hot wave of interest that got the attention of all three men with her.

She blushed. "Sorry about that. That particular area is a bit sensitive."

Smith dragged his tongue along her skin, but when she realised he was outside the scope of her injury, she grumbled and flicked a finger against his forehead. "I am not an all-day sucker. If there is no more wound, you can stop now. Thank you for your help."

He sighed and ran his tongue across her one final time before lowering her shirt back into place. "That is the most fun I have had on shift in years."

Argyle grumbled. "Speak for yourself."

Tremble chuckled and helped Benny sit up. "It isn't the worst night we have had, but it does become one of the most memorable."

Benny sighed. "I am just glad that it didn't become a pissing contest when I mentioned what the seer had said."

Smith and Argyle shrugged. Smith said, "If it was true, it

would save my life, and if not, I would just have to drive for the next two days."

Argyle shrugged and prepared to switch bags. "Driving isn't an issue for me. I don't mind, so it wasn't a big deal."

Tremble chuckled. "We aren't here because we are set in our ways. Each of us joined the XIA because we wanted to protect our communities and the extranatural community at large. We are flexible."

She blinked and tried to ignore the subtle invitation in his voice. "Right, well, what happens now? We obviously can't continue tonight."

Tremble looked at her with surprise. "Why not? A change of uniforms and a new vehicle and we are on our way."

"Seriously?"

Smith nodded. "Let's not be crazy, we will take a break and have dinner. But yeah, we keep going."

Benny wanted to go home and change her shirt, but that wasn't an option...or was it. "Can we swing by my house, so I can change my shirt?"

Argyle shrugged. "I don't see why not. Where do you live?"

"Anchor Lane. It's about ten minutes from here."

"Well, our ride just arrived, so we can get going as soon as I change." Argyle opened the buttons of his dark shirt and peeled it off.

Benny quickly found anywhere else to look. Argyle had been in amazing shape before he had become a vampire. He still had a golden tone to his skin over the grey base colour. The ridges of his abs were a work of art, and only the stripes of the injury marred the view.

He was oblivious to her admiration as he returned to their SUV where he grabbed a bag out of the back and he flicked out a new shirt.

"Pull your eyes back in your head, Benny." Tremble was amused.

She blushed hot and Smith laughed.

"Sorry. The extranormals I hang around with are usually not humanoid shaped. They tend to have extra limbs and such." She looked at her bloodstained hands. "Sorry."

Tremble put his hand on hers, and Smith echoed him.

Tremble said, "I did not mean to cause you any issue or embarrassment. I forget that humans are subject to that kind of thing."

She swallowed and nodded, trying to pretend that he was right in his assessment. He wasn't. She had been imagining pinning Argyle up against the SUV and having her way with him while the other two watched, but that was what happened when you had an alternative upbringing. The colour in her cheeks had been excitement.

Smith gave her a curious look, and she tried to put a frown on her face. This was the hardest part of being what she was; pretending to be what she looked like.

He helped her stand up, and she swayed.

They walked toward the new vehicle, and she locked up. "My notes, my bag."

Tremble patted her arm. "I will get them. You go and have a seat."

Smith kept supporting her until he was tucking her in the new vehicle that Argyle was signing for. "You aren't what you seem, are you?"

She blinked. "What do you mean?"

"I have tasted magic users before, and while I taste magic in your blood, there is a whole lot more." His head bent toward hers, and the warm scent of him swamped her.

"Most girls are more than what they seem. You are reading more into me than there is."

"You are also skilled at evasion. That comes with practice. You are not saying no, but you are not saying yes. It is quite the dance."

She gave him a narrow-eyed look. "Why does it matter?"

"I am an investigator. I despise a mystery. I will solve you before this is over."

"Is that a threat?"

He grinned. "I am an excellent investigator."

Tremble brought all of the bags and equipment to the new SUV. The delivery woman grinned. "Take care of this one."

Argyle growled and moved the car seat back into a driveable position.

Their group settled in their new vehicle, and Argyle didn't move until she put on her seat belt.

"So, where am I going?"

"Seventeen Anchor Lane. It is a small house off the gravel drive. It is just off Aspen Parkway."

He nodded, and they were on their way to her house.

She was nervous. She had never had anyone over to the dower house, at least not anyone male. Jessamine was going to get into such a flap over this.

The door opened like it normally did when she approached, but today, she had three XIA agents watching out for her.

"No, I swear it is fine, and I live alone for all intents and purposes." She tried to push through the wall of backs in front of her, but they insisted on clearing her house.

She thought it was just an excuse for them to rifle through her stuff.

Benny walked in and called out, "Hello, Jessamine."

Her companion came to her through the refrigerator. "Benny, did you know that there are men here?"

"Yes, I know. They are the XIA agents that I am shadowing for the week. When you opened the door, they used it as an excuse to charge in here."

"You look tired. There is something in your workroom for that."

She wrinkled her nose. "I will try to grab it if I have time. I need to change my shirt. I was in a bit of an accident."

Jessamine shot upward and then returned to Benny's side. "Two of them are in your bedroom. Shall I get them out?"

"Go ahead and spook them. I will be up in a moment."

Tremble was on the main floor, in the living room. Benny followed him.

"What are you looking at?"

"There are no pictures of you and your parents after puberty. You talk of them fondly, so I assume they are still alive."

Benny smiled slightly. "They are. I still see them nearly every day. They live just down the road."

"Why no pictures? They looked so blissfully normal."

She followed his gaze to the picture on the mantel with her parents cuddled together, her father's amber eyes smiling and her mother's brown eyes filled with love.

"They still look the same to me, but life isn't always kind. Anyway, you are on duty and I need to get Smith and Argyle out of my underwear drawer."

A shout sounded from upstairs followed by a thud.

Benny chuckled. "And that is my cue."

She sprinted upstairs while Tremble asked her if she kept mousetraps in her underwear. It didn't deserve a reply.

Chapter Seven

Jessamine was guarding her lingerie, and the other two were standing back against her bed.

"Gentlemen, this is my housemate, Jessamine. Jessamine, the elf downstairs is Tremble; this is Agent Smith and Agent Argyle. I will be down in a moment, guys. Shoo."

She flapped her hands at them, and the moment they were out, she opened her shirt, dropping it in the fireplace.

"What happened?"

"Car accident. Pipes punched through the car door. Argyle got the worst of it; I just got grazed."

"You are wearing a protection glyph."

"I am, but it protects against people, not hardware." Benny rummaged around and grabbed a dark-grey button-down shirt.

She quickly scrubbed her hands and headed back downstairs where the investigative team was analysing her photos and trophies.

"You have won several karaoke tournaments." Smith raised his brows in surprise.

"Yes. I cheated. Can we go now? I need to eat."

Tremble held up another. "Battle of the Bands?"

It was cheap, horrible and manipulative, but she began to shake, and she descended to the floor in a faint.

Argyle caught her before she made contact with the hardwood, and Jessamine flapped her hands.

"You have to get her something to eat. I would do it, but I can't touch anything around here. Well, not with witnesses around."

Benny fought a grin as she continued to fake weakness. It was Jessamine's greatest point of irritation that she could only be a poltergeist when there were no witnesses. When Benny was away, she could touch everything. The moment Benny returned, it was back to haunting only.

"There is some juice in the fridge. That should perk her up."

Benny glared at Jessamine through narrow eyes. Her mother made her freshly blended juices and stashed them in her fridge while she was gone. Drinking one would definitely perk her up, but she would be grossed out for hours.

The bottle of bright orange juice emerged with Smith sniffing it cautiously. Argyle sat her up, and she took the bottle with genuinely shaking hands. It was one of her favourites. Carrot, orange and ginger with just a hint of parsley. She was relieved to be able to actually get half the bottle down.

She shuddered slightly as she capped the bottle. "That should do."

She shifted to her knees before getting to her feet. Argyle stood and steadied her as he helped her back to the kitchen. She put the bottle in the nearly empty fridge with finality.

She inhaled and boomed out, "Everybody in the car! You can rifle through my house the next time you are in the neighbourhood."

Argyle grinned, "I had no idea you had a voice like that."

"They don't give those karaoke awards to just anyone." She chuckled.

She locked the house though it wasn't necessary. If threatened, Jessamine would remain invisible and beat the crap out of any intruder.

The night air was crisp, and it was past midnight. Benny could feel the wild magic building all around them. It was one of the selling points of Anchor Lane; the magic was heady and heavy all around them. The perfect place for spell work.

Smith inhaled sharply and glanced over at her. "The air is heavy."

"Very."

"Is it always like this?" He looked up at the waning moon.

"Of course not." She climbed into the SUV and buckled in. Benny smiled. "Normally, it is far stronger."

Argyle laughed and reversed out of her driveway before heading back to the parkway. "So, where shall we head next?"

They were on their way back to Dem-rah's taco stand when an urgent call came through. Benny made notes on the evening's activities until the radio crackled.

All XIA units in the area were asked to report, and Benny's

note taking took on an urgency.

She saw the collection of vehicles accumulating near the park, and she swallowed nervously. The coroner's van was an indicator that this was not going to be an amusing anecdote for the blog.

The normally cheerful guys were solemn as they left the vehicle. She checked that her pass was clipped on her belt, and she eased out of the SUV and trailed behind them, staying outside the tape that had been hastily erected.

She put her hand over her mouth when the woman who was floating in the air suddenly dropped. It wasn't a woman anymore; it was a body.

Benny looked closely and watched for the departing spirit. There was nothing. She stared and frowned, concern growing. There should have been something. There should have been a soul.

She let her features go blank and went looking. Nothing. No whiff of a soul and a dark hole where it should have been. Whatever killed her did it by ripping her life force out and pulling it through her soul until the ragged piece left behind had gone with the flame of existence. First, her battery had been drained and then someone pulled the plug.

Benny watched her XIA agents mingle with others of their rank before they moved in an organised wave, seeking clues.

Benny crouched and focused on the young woman. She was about Benny's age and was dressed for work.

There were no marks on her wrists or ankles or around her neck. Either whatever had taken her had convinced her to go along or it had sedated her with magic and transported her here.

The fact that she was dressed for work was strange. If she was out in the evening, she should either be in casual or party clothing. The suit and sensible pumps didn't match the passage of time. Even working overtime, she should have been home hours ago.

She watched the men meticulously picking up and bagging every bit of evidence after photos had been taken. She took note of the gloves that appeared from every pocket and the care with which the scene was examined. Lights were blazing bright, and the scene lit the park up. If the centrepiece had been anything other than a dead body, it would have been beautiful.

When the challenge came, it was from the coroner's people. "Who are you?"

She stood and showed her badge. "I am a special observer with the XIA."

The young woman with the grey cast to her skin sniffed at her. "You smell like blood."

"There was a car accident earlier. I am sure that my jeans and shoes are covered in it."

"There is none on your shirt."

"I changed my shirt, but I had three XIA agents rifling through my living room, so I left it at that. Tomorrow, I will bring a full change of clothing, though I have no idea where I would change."

The woman suddenly smiled. Benny jerked back in shock. The medic assistant went from a cold vampire to a stunning woman. The transformation was reversed when the woman resumed her calm face and headed to where the coroner was examining the body and checking the temperature.

Argyle spoke from next to her. Benny jumped again; she hadn't heard him approach. She was just not on her game today.

"She is the mayor's new assistant."

"A new vampire?"

"Oh, she isn't a vampire...not yet. She is his assistant."

"But she has the same presence I am used to in vampires."

He grinned, his fangs flashing. "I know, but Miss Wicks is still in possession of a beating heart. She appears when there is something that he needs to concern himself with."

The woman in question returned. "It was pleasant meeting you, Beneficia Ganger. Agent Argyle, there will be a mage team going over this place with seers. Make sure that it isn't compromised."

He nodded. "Yes, Miss Wicks."

The woman pulled her calm face into a grimace and stuck out her tongue.

Benny chuckled. "It was nice to meet you, Miss Wicks."

"Call me Leo. It is short for Leonora. I am sure I will see you again, Miss Ganger."

She didn't say good night as she walked away. Benny looked at the body and knew why.

"We are going to be stuck here for the rest of the night. Did you want to catch a ride back with the coroner?"

Benny looked over at the body and nodded. "If they wouldn't mind."

She needed to get a little closer to the woman to determine where the soul had been ripped out, but if she was actually a human, there shouldn't be any way for her to know that the soul was missing. No one had mentioned it, but the coroner would figure it out. They were usually in the undead spectrum, and locating souls was part of their business.

Argyle asked the coroner's assistant, and she nodded and spoke quickly.

Argyle came back. "You will have to ride with the body bag in the back."

"That is fine. I am really exhausted by the events of the night. Some peace and quiet in the back of the van won't hurt me."

He gave her a piercing look, but didn't comment.

Benny winced as she realised that she should be upset at the thought of sharing space with a dead woman. Dang, she really was tired.

She waited while the preliminary exam was made and the woman was bagged up. When the gurney was tucked away, the assistant beckoned to Benny, so Benny waved good night to the others.

She settled in the back of the van, introduced herself to the assistants who were in the only two seats in the vehicle, and she looked at the body bag, closing her eyes as she looked for hints of magic or other energies.

"I apologise for the lack of seating, but we don't often transport the living." The woman smiled shyly.

"It is fine. I was just thinking that she looked so normal. Like she had just left work."

The passenger turned more fully to her. "I know. It is usually difficult to see them like that. The lack of blood is disturbing though."

"I didn't see any wounds."

"There aren't any. That is what is so weird. Did you want to sit in on the autopsy?" The young woman was eager. She wasn't a vampire, wasn't a zombie. Benny guessed ghoul, but it was impolite to ask.

"Molly, that is up to Dr. Tanner." The driver sighed.

"He will say yes. I promise." The young ghoul smiled widely, showing a tremendous array of yellowed fangs.

"I would love to if he authorises it."

Molly beamed and turned to face the dashboard. "He will."

Benny kept her senses running across the body next to her for the rest of the ride. She really doubted that she would be allowed in the autopsy room.

Chapter Eight

Benny put on the disposable tunic and the facial shield as well as the rubber gloves and booties. Dr. Tanner had said yes.

It was unusual for a zombie to show this level of animation, but Dr. Tanner waved his arms and explained every point in the process.

They began by photographing every inch of the woman before they undressed her, putting the clothing into evidence bags. Dr. Tanner looked for any unusual markings, and he was thorough, examining her from the toes up. When he finished his visual examination, he took a few photos of the area around her mouth.

He and his assistant turned her over, and they examined her back. With his fingers, he parted the hair, and there must have been something there, because he shaved the back of the head.

"Found it. She was branded. Get that camera around here."

The assistant handed Dr. Tanner the camera, and the doctor went to work.

"Miss Ganger, come here and look at this." He smiled and pointed out the icon that had been burned into the scalp.

"Why wasn't it visible before?"

"My guess is that it was applied after she had been levitated. They flipped her over, lifted her hair, marked her and then put her back and drained her. You can see here on her mouth that she had some internal bleeding. Whatever removed her soul also took her blood."

Benny blinked innocently. "Removed her soul?"

"Yes, we usually see that sort of thing in demon attacks, but there hasn't been one of those in the city for fifteen years, and the demons don't take blood. This is something new."

Dr. Tanner went to work opening the woman up, but there

was no blood. All the organs revealed were pale, and it was exceptionally sad.

Benny watched the autopsy, and he completed his findings of soul death by magical means by person or persons unknown.

She swayed and remembered that she had lost a lot of blood and hadn't had anything to eat all night. Benny excused herself and headed for the parking lot and her car.

Pooky did most of the driving, but he didn't take her home, he took her to her parents' house with the sun trumpeting noon above her.

Benny stumbled into the hall and headed for the library. Her father lifted his head from his desk, and she raised her hand. "Soul consumption with branding and blood consumption."

Three books came soaring out of the stacks and landed on her desk.

"Benny, what happened?"

"A woman is dead in the park, no soul; it was scooped out like a melon, and then, some son of a bitch drained her blood after he branded her."

"Can I help?"

"They think it might be a demon attack, so you can help me look."

Benny grabbed a pen and paper; she drew the glyph carefully, leaving an opening in the mark in case it had the power to summon.

She and her father went through the huge tomes, page by page, atrocity by atrocity.

Her mother came in with a tray and cleared her throat. "Enough!"

They both looked up. Her father gave his wife a slow smile of welcome.

"What is it, Mom?"

"Benny, you need to eat, and if you are going back to work tonight, you need to change your clothing. Jessamine brought some clothes over earlier. Take a shower, eat and drink this tonic. It will keep you going until morning. You know how you get with no sleep."

"I need to find this, Mom."

"So, let me and Dad look. You go and refresh yourself. I made your favourite. Cream tea."

Benny stepped away from the demonology tome. "Fine. But there had better be a chocolate tart in there or I will be cranky."

Her mother let her go, but Benny heard, "How will I be able to spot that with your normal cheery demeanour?"

"I heard that!"

Benny was on the stairs when she heard, "You were meant to!"

Benny ran up to her old room, and the folded fabric was sitting in the centre of her bed, right down to sneakers.

She got into the shower as fast as she could, hoping that the rush of water would drown out the sound of her father and mother having a quickie. It was in his bloodline, just as it was in Benny's, and her mother was remarkably tolerant of both of them.

Her parents' physical needs were one of the primary reasons for her moving out. There were some things that defied explanation to a date or one's girlfriends.

She noted the pink tinge to the water and guessed that she had been wearing more blood in her clothing than she thought. It was hard to tell, both her jeans and the vampire blood had been black.

When she was warm, clean and definitely refreshed, she wrapped herself in a towel and scrubbed at her hair. It felt good to be home; everything was where it was supposed to be. She brushed her hair out and whipped it into a ponytail before she put on her underwear and the jeans and t-shirt.

The shoes were her favourites and not at all appropriate for being with the XIA. They were white, silver, blue and had a streak of pink that tied the look together. Benny really hoped that she wasn't going to step in any blood tonight.

She trotted down the stairs to the library with her protective charm between her breasts again.

Her parents were decent, but the windows were open and the candles were burning. Telltale signs of their recent intimacy.

Her mother had one of the tomes in front of her, and she tapped her finger. "I found it, and it isn't good. Now, Benny, eat."

The table in the centre of the room was set with tea and the three-tiered tray full of sandwiches and treats.

"Can you read it out loud while I eat?"

"Of course."

Benny went over and kissed her mother's cheek before she scampered over to the tea.

Her mother intoned the description of the ritual, and finally, she set up the important bit, it was an exorcism for soul transfer, but it would only work with a demon soul.

Benny paused with a salmon sandwich at her lips. "Demons don't have souls. That is what makes them demons."

"That is what it says. This is to be used if you have a demon with a soul and you want to sell the soul as a commodity. It has to have happened before or this spell would not be here."

Benny nodded and ate her narrow sandwich with as much enjoyment as she could. She went for the blueberries with clotted cream next.

With deliberate focus, Benny made her way through the tower of sandwiches, cakes and tarts. No bad news was going to put her off her love of the teeny sandwiches.

She sat back with her tea, and her mom reached into her apron, withdrawing two vials. One was the blue protective vial and the other was the energising vial. Benny made a face. "You couldn't have reminded me before I ate the last cream puff?"

Her mom smirked. "No. I need to get my fun where I can."

Benny got up and took the vials. "I still love you, Mom."

"Not for the next ten minutes, but I know your heart is in it."

Benny gulped the energiser first, shuddered and gagged, and then scarfed down the enhanced identity protection potion. Strawberries and fungus. *Yum.*

As fast as she could, she returned to the table and slugged down her Earl Grey Tea.

She poured another cup and scooped honey into it, drinking the hot mix as fast as she could. The flavour lingered, and she prayed that she didn't start belching.

Benny faced her parents across the room. "Now, who would want to pull a soul that wasn't a demon? Why did they kill that woman?"

Her father shook his head. "That is what the XIA has to investigate."

Benny sighed. "Abiding by the law is hard."

"Oh, sweetie, you are only beginning to understand. You have lived your life as a human, and I am delighted that you could, but there are prejudices out there that extranormals are all subject to, and your family bloodlines blend most of the dangerous races. How you ended up looking so human is a blessing that your mother passed along; it certainly didn't come from my side of the family."

She looked at her father and sighed. His sacrifice had put him in a situation of house arrest. Their friends and family came to them, and it was those tolerant people that had given Benny her start in life. Now, she was dealing daily with those who had not faced that kind of threat to their existence because of their appearance. They just didn't understand.

Benny was in her car and heading for the agency when her phone rang. She pulled over at the side of Anchor Lane and answered. "Hello?"

"Benny? This is Tremble. There has been another victim and the pathologist has seen some demonological symbols."

She cleared her throat. "Really?"

"Yes, the expert refused to meet with the day shift, so we are on our way there. He is located on Anchor Lane, so I thought we could pick you up this evening."

She looked toward her house. "Um, sure, when will you be here?"

"We are just pulling onto Anchor Lane."

"See you."

She dropped her phone and quickly drove forward to park her car. She threw her bag with her soiled clothing into the house and took the duffel that Jessamine had prepared for her. A moment later, she was waiting for them as they pulled into her drive.

She hopped into the car. They all looked a little the worse for wear. "Where are we going?"

"Thirteen Anchor Lane. Your neighbour. Apparently Dr. Emile is the local expert on demonology."

She fought the urge to cover her eyes. "Yes, I have heard that."

They drove to her family home, and she got out of the car with them. The agents put themselves between her and the unknown. *How sweet.*

Argyle knocked on the door, and Benny watched her mother

open it.

"Good evening, madam. We are here to speak with Dr. Emile. We are agents with the XIA."

Her mother spotted her. "Beneficia dear, go make some tea. I will show them into the library."

"I will make the tea after they meet Dad." Benny weaseled between them and beckoned them inside. "Please come in."

Once everyone was inside the foyer, Benny made the introductions. "Agents Tremble, Argyle and Smith, this is my mother, Lenora Ganger. Dr. Lenora Ganger, master magus."

The men greeted her mother, but they were looking at her like she had grown another head.

Benny led them to the library, and she paused to let them take in her father's emerald skin, the wide curving horns, slit pupils in his amber eyes and the claw-like nails at the end of his fingertips.

"Agents Tremble, Argyle and Smith, this is my father, Dr. Harcourt Emile Ganger."

Tremble looked at her. "Your father was human."

She rocked her hand. "He was. Sort of. It is a long story. I will go and make the tea."

Benny escaped the library with a whoosh of relief.

Her mom was nearby. "You did well. Very professional. They had no idea?"

"They might have. Two out of three have tasted my blood." She blinked, shook her head and made her way to the kitchen.

The water boiled in two minutes, and she carried the tray of steeping tea into the library. Her mom brought another tray of sandwiches.

The agents were still standing at a distance from her father. She set the tray down on the table and went to hug her dad. He held her carefully as he always did. "Do you need anything, Benny?"

"Just a hug. I was so busy before I didn't hug you hello."

"Missed you, too, Benny."

When Benny turned, the agents had relaxed, and she gestured to the tray. "We found out why he did what he did. The ritual requires some explanation. Have a seat."

Confronted by her family, they sat.

The agents were silent. All three stared at her father as if he was a spectre.

Benny rubbed her forehead. She looked at her dad and he nodded. "Gentlemen, do you want me to explain?"

Argyle nodded. "Please."

Her dad picked up one of the tomes and kept flipping through the pages so they could stare at him without feeling awkward.

"Fine. My great grandmother was a succubus summoned to bear the heir of a wizard. That would be my grandfather. Once she had completed her contracted obligation to bear a human-looking heir, she returned to the demon zone. My grandfather grew up, married a werewolf and had a son. He became a professor of arcane studies, and at the turn of the last century, he met my mom."

Her mother went over and wrapped her arms around her emerald mate. "It was love at first sight on my part, but his nose was so stuck in his books, I had to peel down to my corset and chemise before he would look my way."

Her father laughed. "And at that point, I could not look away."

Benny rolled her eyes and continued. "They got married and lived happily with my father and mother sharing their lives and their interest in magic. Mom aged slowly and her pregnancy with me took six years. She says it was worth it for the stares alone. Anyway, when I was ten, my mother got cancer. She was dying and she was doing it quickly."

Benny watched her dad put his arm around his wife protectively. She cleared her throat to get rid of the emotional wobble and sighed. "He waited until the moment she died, and he healed her body then transferred his human soul into her before she could completely pass on. They now share the one soul, but it was all that was keeping my father's parentage from being really obvious."

Smith cocked his head. "So that makes you part demon?"

Benny wrinkled her nose. "Well, not that it matters, but given my parentage and ancestors, I am really only one part human. The rest is a much longer story, and we have a killer to catch."

Her father slammed the tome shut and nodded. "Now that introductions and explanations have been made, let's get to work. This is time sensitive."

Chapter Nine

Tremble was staring at her with intense focus. "You are not human?"

She lifted the book with the initial explanation of the ritual and opened it to the ritual. "No. I look human, but that is a trick of my genes. If you look at my mom's ears, you can see the point and a slight ridge from a siren ancestor; there are signs of troll and fey around her. I think there is even some shifter in there."

Argyle wandered over and looked at the books. "I can't read that."

She pinched the bridge of her nose. "You can't. There are reasons that few people are capable of being demonology experts. Demon blood is a requisite for being able to read the script. I will translate if you like, or my dad can do it."

Her father grinned, flashing his deadly and shark-like teeth.

Smith nodded. "We trust your translation, Benny. Please proceed."

She squinched her eyes shut for a moment and then began. "All right. Well, the suspect is looking for a demon, a very specific demon."

Argyle was suddenly all business. "What demon?"

"A demon with a soul. The question is why that woman?"

Smith lifted his head. "She isn't the first. She is the seventh woman born on the same day to be killed in that particular way. The others were out of our jurisdiction, so it took most of the day to find them. The ladies were all the same age, within one week."

Benny whirled when she heard her father growl. "No."

Her mother placed her hand on his, but he continued to flex his muscles in agitation and the fan-like crest rose out of his dark hair.

Tremble whispered, "What is he doing?"

Benny scowled. "He is angry, but I don't know why."

Through clenched teeth, her father asked, "All born here thirty years ago in the ninth month on the twenty-third day, give or take?"

Her mother gasped. "Harcourt, you didn't!"

He nodded grimly. "I did. I mirrored Benny's soul on the other eight girls in the nursery."

Benny felt sick. "You have to be kidding."

Her father came to her and held her tight. "I wanted to protect you and that was the only way I knew how. Your power signature was distinctive, even when you were a baby."

Smith asked, "You are thirty? You don't look thirty."

The sound he made immediately afterward indicated one of the others had struck him.

"Why not just a shield?" She mumbled it against his chest.

"Magic is too noticeable. The other girls were all healthy with young parents, so the likelihood of them moving was strong."

"They died because of me."

His hand stroked her hair, and he murmured to her as he had when she was a teenager. "No. They died because someone is trying to kill you, or at least part you from what is rightfully yours."

"Ripping a soul from a demon. Why would someone do that?" She let him continue to hold her. It was for his need and not hers. He could not defend her in the wide world, but he could offer her comfort here.

He sighed. "I do not know about other demons, but if they took your soul, you would have to attach yourself to a more powerful demon of the zone for protection. You would become a slave."

"We will not let that happen." Tremble's voice was determined.

Argyle pitched in. "Do you know who the other woman is?"

Benny eased away from her father. He shook his head.

She swallowed. "I can find her. If she is carrying a mirror of my soul, I can get a location."

Her mother nodded and got a map. She flipped it out on one of the long tables and moved around the room collecting scrying equipment.

Smith asked softly. "What is she doing?"

"She is setting up a search map."

Her mother laid out the tools and beckoned for her to come close. "All right, sweetie. First, you know what to do."

Sighing, Benny took the bucket that her mother handed her and walked away from the crowd. Throwing up before working was an important part of scrying. She literally had to be hungry in order to track her prey. Her mother's bloodline had some creepy hunters in it, and her talent for all magic came from the maternal side of the family. Raw energy and power came from her dad's ancestors.

Once she had completed her purge, she rinsed out her mouth, washed her hands and face, and she glared at herself in the mirror before coming to a conclusion. This was going to take a lot of power, so she was going to have to drop a minor bit of glamour that she had been using since she was in kindergarten.

It took more effort to pull the glamour off than it did to keep it in place, but she needed every bit of access to her soul in able to create the template to search for.

Her left eye glowed slightly and she sighed. The cat was out of the bag, the agents were going to see her as she was. Here was hoping that it didn't wreck the friendships she had been starting.

Benny kept her head high, but she was watching carefully for any signs of disturbance in the agents. There was a mild bit of blinking, but nothing major.

Smith quirked his lips. "You look a little pale."

She snorted. "Right. You see how you look when you have to puke on behalf of a tracking spell."

Tremble nodded as if he had figured it out, and Argyle sat still as stone.

Her mother had assembled all the implements, and she stood aside as Benny approached.

Benny closed her eyes and moved her hands over the assembled objects. Two items jumped into her hand. A heavy charm embossed with serpents and books joined a long black crystal bound with silver. Benny transferred them both to the same hand at the same distance from her palm and she exhaled slowly.

The map was of the entire continent, and she would work in

narrowing areas until she pinpointed the target.

She held the pendants out and watched them pull from one side to the other as she focused on herself. Both located her hometown, so Lenora moved the large map aside and pulled out one with local streets and surrounding areas.

When the pendants pulled toward her home, she blocked that and continued to move her hand until there was a second indicator. She followed the new location to a charming suburb.

Her mother subbed out the maps again for a satellite view, and Benny focused and indicated a house on the left side of a cul-de-sac.

"Bowl and knife." Benny kept her focus, and when her mother put the small bowl on top of the house image, Benny cut her finger and dripped six drops into the bowl. The blood swirled and took form.

"Jennifer Langstrom. Nineteen Yarrow Path." Benny staggered back, and her father helped with the first aid.

The agents were staring at her. She stared back. With her eye unglamored, she could see them for what they were, and it was an interesting sight.

Smith's body had a healthy golden glow, his hair nearly waved in the energy he was putting out, Argyle's eyes were sunken and his skin was chalky, but sparking with light from the inside out, and Tremble was a confusion of power and nature. His power was going in all directions all the time.

Smith blinked slowly. "Is your eye going to stay like that?"

She lifted her hand toward her face and could see the reflected light. "I am sorry, but it is. I can't put it away and then whip it out when I need it."

Out of reflex, she lifted the scry bowl to her lips and drank the water and blood drops. Tremble made a face, but the other two watched the bowl like it contained a treat.

Lenora tidied up. "Well, you have the address, you had better get going."

Smith paused. "Where did you get all those maps?"

Benny chuckled. "I will explain the idea of having friends on the planning committee, as well as being an official city archive in the car."

Tremble stiffened. "You cannot come along."

Benny crossed her arms. "I have to. There is no one else who can stop the spell work. It is an easy fix, but no one can manage it unless they have mage training with demon control as a primary field of study."

Argyle smirked. "You have studied it?"

Her father cleared his throat. "It was necessary. She had to use it for the first time when she was fifteen. She is very good at it."

The agents looked over at her father with his claws, bright eyes and evil fangs. They looked to her mother, and she merely smiled cheerfully.

"Benny is very good at doing what she feels is necessary. She isn't one to put herself in danger. She will keep herself as safe as she can." Lenora finished putting the maps away and neatly tidied the tools that had been used in the scrying.

Benny stood and drummed her fingers on her bicep with her arms crossed. "Jennifer is in danger right now. She was still at home, but I can track her if she is taken. Now that I know what I am looking for, she will leave a trail."

They nodded and took their leave of her parents. Benny was in the car and buckled up in under a minute and they were on their way to talk to Jennifer.

She wished that there was less silence in the car, and suddenly, there was.

"So, dating must have been awkward." Argyle chuckled.

Benny grinned. "You have no idea."

Smith chipped in, "Did you get asked out by normals?"

She wrinkled her nose. "Yes. Their families encouraged them because my parents were and are on the boards of five local universities. A relationship with me meant an increase in their choices for a higher education."

Two dates. She had had two dates before her father fully turned into what he was now. After that, all introductions to her parents had been short and to the point, and heavily glamoured. Glamour was hard to stick on a demon, but as long as her father stayed calm, he looked just like he used to.

Tremble cocked his head. "You introduced all of your prospective mates to your parents?"

She looked at him and raised her eyebrows. "You have met my parents; do you think I had a choice?"

The men in the car chuckled. Tremble grinned. "I suppose

not. It must have made for a fascinating adolescence."

"That is one way of putting it. Mind you, in all those years of dating, I only had one bad experience." She chuckled.

Smith started to ask her about that one experience, but they arrived at Jennifer's home.

Tremble opened his door and looked at her.

Benny held up her hands. "I know. Stay in the car."

The agents left, and Benny kept her senses wide and looking for any signs of trouble.

Benny couldn't sense anything and that was when she got agitated. Jennifer was gone, and there was only the slightest hint of where she had been.

Chapter Ten

The moment the agents returned to the SUV, she said, "Down the block to the left."

The night air was cool and bracing, but Benny was stuck next to a closed window. She had to settle for the view she was getting through her mage's eye.

They were at the turning point in under a minute, and she tried to focus. "Okay, I am not trying to be difficult, but I can't sense her from inside the car."

Smith nodded. "Right. I am going to shift, and I will stay with you while you follow the trail."

They parked and left the vehicle. Tremble and Argyle were ready to move, but Smith had to strip.

Benny blushed and focused her vision and senses on the trail left by her mirror.

The sound of flesh flexing, tendons snapping and claws scraping the pavement caused her to peek a little. Smith twisted and arched into his lion form, and he was huge.

The actual full shift of a shifter was always something that creeped her out. She could face anyone in a body that didn't conform to normal standards and see their true beauty, but the twist of a body from its natural state into another beast made her a little queasy. It was probably the snapping tendons and rippling flesh.

The lion came up to her and sniffed her, chuffing softly.

Argyle nodded. "He's ready. You are consulting here, but you are also observing. Do not involve yourself directly."

Benny focused, and she started to run. The men were behind her, and Smith was at her side.

Jennifer was up ahead, and there was other magic, human magic, involved.

The faster they moved, the further away the soul seemed.

Benny growled and started to run faster. The moment she got within a hundred yards, she felt the separation of soul and body. She grunted and put her power around the soul.

She staggered when something tried to crack through the protection. There was a shout of frustration, and heat was the next thing to strike her energy.

Benny and her followers burst through the hedges, and a horrifying sight greeted them.

A man wearing a shadowed cloak was hunched over the floating body of his victim.

Smith sleeked into an attack mode and charged the man.

Energy sparked as the pentacle halted Smith's advance.

Benny stumbled through the energy field and fought for air as she said, "Get away from her."

Confronting someone was not normally in her nature, but she could feel the pressure he was putting on her shields, and it was not comfortable. If she left him alone, he would crack through it and that would be the end of the woman in front of her.

The cowled head turned toward her. "Stay out of this, mage. You don't know what you are dealing with."

The agents were up against the warding and shouting at the attacker.

Benny stood straight and hit him with attacks spells she hadn't used in a decade. With her hands held a foot apart, she pelted him with balls of burning moonlight. The first few had no effect, but as she increased her speed, she knocked him away from Jennifer.

She kept firing at him, pushing him back toward the edge of his circle. If she could get him past it, the agents could get him.

Thud, thud, thud. The energy balls struck over and over until it was a solid stream of power that edged his foot into the circle.

The agents stumbled in, and the mage looked at her in shocked horror. "Bitch!"

A swirl of dark power wrapped him, and he disappeared.

Benny stumbled and shook her hands as the power had nowhere to go. It was time to put the soul back in the body.

Argyle looked at Benny. "What is wrong with her?"

She blinked, lifted her hands and grabbed the protective orb that she had cast. "Her soul is here, but she needs a healing before I put it back. Her body has been primed for blood loss. If I put her back in before the healers get here, she's dead."

Tremble was speaking on his phone, and he finished the call. "I called them when we first hit the barrier. They are driving in across the green."

He wasn't wrong. Benny could hear the approaching sirens and see the lights.

Smith came up behind her and supported her. She hadn't realised that she had been swaying. His lion form smelled of sunshine and musk. "Thanks, Smith."

He grunted and remained behind her while they waited for the healers to stabilise the victim.

Tremble marked out the transport site that the attacker had used. Argyle asked her, "Did you get a look at him?"

She nodded. "He was completely average with the exception of the twisted expression of greed and panic on his features."

"Could you describe him to an artist?"

Benny held out her hand, put an orb of energy into it and she printed the face from her mind onto the energy. "Here. Put this on some twigs and leaves and you can take a photo of it."

Tremble went to the shrubs and broke off a branch, bringing it back to carry the fey globe. "So, fey blood, too?"

"After this is over, I will invite you guys over and take you through the portrait gallery. The only thing I don't really have in me is a lot of normal human." She shrugged and eased the orb onto the leaves that would support it and give it energy for a few hours.

The medics started to load Jennifer onto a gurney.

Benny moved around Tremble. "Is she stable?"

"Non-responsive. We stopped the haemorrhaging. We will be able to treat her at hospital."

Benny nodded, grabbed the soul and she pushed it back into Jennifer's body without the mirroring of her own.

Jennifer started moaning and shifting, and the medics got into high gear.

Benny staggered backward, and Smith was there to support her.

Argyle caught her elbow and he frowned. "Are you all right?"

"I have just cast more magic in ten minutes than I have in ten years. I had forgotten what kind of an energy rush it is." She rubbed her forehead.

Tremble handed the orb over to some uniformed officers, and they carefully carried it to their vehicle before they taped off the scene.

Benny sighed. "What happens now?"

Argyle cocked his head. "You are interviewed, and we have to begin looking for the mage who was draining the victim."

She yawned and leaned against Smith, lounging on him as she lost focus. "Whomever is going to interview me had better work fast."

Another XIA vehicle pulled up, parking on the grass. The trio emerged up and stalked toward their team.

Argyle muttered, "I should get the SUV."

She reached out and grabbed his arm. "Not until I am sure that they are not going to arrest me."

He chuckled. "Right."

The three agents were cordial enough to her team, but Smith got a little bit of ribbing for his current shape.

The elf of their team, named Frond, brought out a notepad and smiled at Benny. "Now, can you tell us what you saw once you entered the circle?"

She explained the levitation, the man trying to drain the woman of her soul and his escape when she attacked.

"Are you a registered mage?" He raised a brow.

She blushed. "No. I am afraid I am home schooled. I am a registered Mage Guide, but that is about it."

He nodded. "You are that journalist that the XIA was asked to host."

"Correct. Benny Ganger."

He grinned. "I love your recipes."

"Thank you."

"What spells did you use to repel the assailant?"

"I used a moonlight repulsion spell in the form of rapid snowballs, and to protect Jennifer, I encased her psyche in a heavy warding with a starlight base and used my own body as a power source to maintain it."

He made frantic notes. "All mage-based?"

"Um, no. The light attack was fey. The protection was part mage and part fey." She smiled, and Smith rumbled behind her.

She took his sound to mean she should shut up.

"How can you master fey magic?" Frond raised his pale green brows.

"I never said I was a master; I said I was home schooled in magic. My parents are both academics. The books were all there."

He nodded and continued to make notes.

He opened his mouth to ask another question, but Smith shifted his position and pushed Benny away from the elf with his huge paw. He huffed and moved his head.

"You are kidding."

He made the motion again, and she boosted herself onto his back. Lion riding was not comfortable; they were made entirely of shoulder blade.

Her XIA team made their way back to their vehicle in silence. They all had been interviewed before being released.

At the SUV, Tremble helped Benny off her mount.

"Thanks, Smith."

He huffed and wandered around the vehicle before shifting back to human.

Argyle tucked her into the SUV and buckled her in place. "Call your parents. I managed to grab a soil sample for analysis. That power wasn't human, so it might give us a clue."

Benny sent her mother a text before she listed to one side as they started moving. Smith still tucking in his shirt. Tremble moved next to her and put his arm around her. "You did well, Benny. You saved a life tonight."

She gave a weak thumbs-up and drifted into a daze as they headed to her parents' home.

When they arrived, Argyle carried her out and into her family home.

Lenora came out and asked, "What is wrong with her?"

"She used a lot of energy tonight, and she has been weak since."

Her mother touched her cheek and looked Benny in the eye. With a rueful sigh, she touched Benny's neck and then jerked her hand sharply. "Rule one of spellcasting, Benny?"

Benny felt her strength return in a rush. "Remove all protections and dampeners. Argyle, you can put me down now. I am an idiot."

Argyle held on to her for a few more moments until her father growled in the background.

Smith grinned. "You forgot to remove a dampener?"

She shrugged. "I wear one most of the time. I don't do magic in public, so it never occurred to me."

He chuckled. "Same reason I remove all the clothing. I can still shift, but it gets in the way."

Benny giggled and rubbed her arm against his in camaraderie.

Argyle took her left side and Tremble guarded her back.

"Mom, we got a soil sample from a transport site. It is less than an hour old, so there should still be something traceable."

Argyle handed the sample to her mother, and her father took it with a sharp plucking of his clawed fingers.

Benny's stomach growled. "Come on. While he works on that, I will make something to eat. You are still entitled to meals."

Her mother nodded with a smile and went into the lab with her father.

Benny led the other three to the kitchen and the huge butcher-block table. "Have a seat. Do you want something hot or cold?"

"Hot."

"Hot."

"Hot."

She chuckled and started a pot of water. "Soup it is."

They looked a little doubtful, but they remained quiet until the ingredients started to line the table while the water began to bubble. Their expressions turned to happy anticipation when she got the stock heating and the smell filled the kitchen. Her mother might do most of the cooking, but Benny was pretty fair when it came to feeding family and friends. She glanced at the attentive agents who were watching her with hope every time she touched ingredients. Yeah, they counted as friends.

Chapter Eleven

They blinked at her as she set the huge empty bowls in front of them. Argyle looked a little nervous.

"Don't worry. My mom keeps a fully stocked pantry. Demon diets vary greatly depending on their exertions and the time of year."

Smith looked impressed.

The noodles were done and drained, so she divided the tangle into four large bowls and two clamp jars. The meat went on in layers, the vegetables went on next, herbs and finally the broth was ready to add to the bowls.

She kept Argyle's bowl to the side. It had the regular mix of meats plus some blood sausage. She went to the fridge and got the ceramic pitcher of blood, pouring a dollop into the bowl. Once that was done, she parcelled out the broth in the bowls and set out the chopsticks and spoons. The un-brothed clamp jars were tucked into the fridge for later.

A final touch was the selection of sauces, and she settled at the table with them. "Have at it."

She dug in and slurped at the noodles.

After a few seconds of hesitation, they all followed suit.

The slurping and flicking of broth was tremendous.

Smith blinked. "This is nice. Really nice. I watched everything, and I still don't know what you all put into it."

Argyle was smiling happily. "It is settling nicely. You have cooked for vampires before?"

Benny slurped. "Yes. For the given, not the taken."

He paused. "You really do have a complete education."

Tremble snorted. "You are just cluing into that now?"

Smith wasn't speaking, he was just slogging through his bowl as if afraid that the soup would disappear if he stopped touching it.

For Benny, it was a recipe that her great aunt had taught her on her seventeenth birthday. Since she wasn't really allowed to go out, it was a better idea to make her friends and family comfortable and happy. It was an old-fashioned idea, but her aunt was an old-fashioned woman. Three hundred years old and no relation to her at all.

Most of her relations were no relations. It was a fact of life that when you came from a line with this much power that you either spread your family wide or it boiled down to a single line. Each generation on either side had one child and that line culminated in Beneficia.

When Smith finished his meal, he picked up the dishes and washed them, putting them on the draining board with efficiency.

"So, Benny, what kind of shifters are in your bloodline?"

She sighed. "I only had two. My grandmother was a wolf shifter, and her father was a human multi-shifter."

"And some demon, a bit of human. How much fey?" Tremble smiled.

She shrugged. "They pop up now and then. Even some vampire makes itself known on my mother's side."

Argyle perked up. "Given or taken?"

"Given."

He looked relieved. "Do you know the sire?"

She chuckled. "Rumour is that she was a true given. No one knows for sure. She rarely returns for a visit."

Smith scowled. "What?"

Argyle looked at him. "Didn't you ever take vampire studies?"

Smith narrowed his eyes. "Pretend I didn't and refresh me."

"Two types of vampires. Those who come from a line that took immortality by violence and those who had it given to them. It is a very long and sad story, but that is the basis of it. I am a given vampire. I was offered this as a choice, and it does not come with the territory bindings or hierarchy that the taken vampires love."

Tremble sighed. "Smith knows; he just likes to make Argyle explain things. It is his personal form of entertainment."

Smith grinned. "It really is. These two constantly remind me that I am the youngest, so I make them over-explain things. It amuses me and irritates them, so we all win."

Benny chuckled and finished her soup. "If anyone needs to freshen up, there is a restroom down the hall and to the left. My parents will be occupied for another twenty minutes, so I think I will work on dessert."

Tremble arched his brow. "How do you know that it will take them twenty minutes?"

She looked at the clock. "It is time for them to have sex. My father's exposed nature increased his sex drive, so they have sex at regular intervals throughout the day, which allows him to keep his focus and continue his research."

Argyle blinked. "Sex?"

Benny pulled cupcakes out of the freezer and set them for a thaw cycle in the microwave. She fired up the coffee maker and got things underway. "Of course. My great grandmother was a succubus. The sex drive comes with the species."

The three agents looked at each other nervously.

She snorted and pulled out ice cream and fruit. "You three shouldn't look so shocked. There hasn't been a shy and sheltered human in this house for the last twenty years."

They looked at each other and Smith nodded. "Since your mother got ill."

"Right. During her recovery and my father's change, there was a house full of folk to protect me from my own parents as they adapted to their new status." She peeled the paper cups off the cupcakes, set them in bowls and piled three different scoops of ice cream on each one before topping them with berries in sauce.

She slid the bowls in front of her guests and got the coffee. "It has been a long night, drink up."

They sat in surprise and grabbed for the spoons she put in front of them. Her instincts for dessert had not abandoned her. She hoped to have hit every craving that the three had.

Smith paused and mumbled around his treat. "So, right now, your parents are having sex?"

"Yup. All the rooms are soundproofed, but it is pretty much guaranteed with the stress of the last few days." She poked at her own cupcake.

Tremble arched his eyebrows. "Stress?"

He had a smear of blueberry on his cheek.

Benny grinned. "Yes, stress. It is hard enough for my parents to have me living outside their home without knowing that I would be exposed to danger. They have hidden me from the world, and suddenly, I was getting into a car with the same men who are duty-bound to throw me in custody for my bloodline the moment that my control slips."

She reached out and rubbed the blueberry off his cheek. She sucked the syrup off her thumb.

Argyle was staring at her, and Smith swallowed hard. She gathered their dishes and quickly washed everything. "Why are you guys boring a hole in my spine with your eyes?"

Tremble cleared his throat. "We have never arrested a demon blood before. I do not think that any of us put you in that category."

Benny kept washing and snorted. "You need to. It is what I am. With the mirror of my soul now off Jennifer, I am the last target. If I am attacked, my instincts will rise past my training and I will defend myself against the assault, no matter what you are doing."

When everything was on the draining board, she settled at the table and met their gazes, one by one. "So, which one of you likes to play with cuffs? I am pretty sure you are going to need them before this is over."

Lenora chuckled. "Benny, stop scaring them. None of them are used to aggression in females."

Her mother had a well-satisfied glow, and the agents suddenly didn't know where to look.

Her mother came up to her and kissed her forehead. "You told them."

Benny grinned. "Never be ashamed of what you are or how you were raised."

"Right. Well, your father is just about done on the sample. He has identified the classification of sponsoring demons, and with a little bit of help, you should be able to get a name."

The agents were on their feet in a heartbeat.

Lenora looked into the pot on the stove. "Noodles?"

"In the fridge."

"Thanks. I will make a tray for Harcourt. He has been worrying, and you know what that does for his appetites."

Benny nodded. "I know. I will distract him. The agents

should do wonders."

Her mother's laughter rippled after them as they left the kitchen and headed for the lab.

"Your family seems peculiarly jovial given your circumstances." Tremble muttered.

"My mother and my father are bound for life, however long that is. The day that one dies, the other will pass so that neither will know the pain of living alone. I have grown up in that love as part of it. When they do pass, I may have preceded them or I may remain alone, but I will have the memory of their love around me. It is a pretty good feeling."

She pushed the door to the lab open, and she paused, "Arms in, gentlemen. Don't touch anything. There are things in here I would not advise even the lightest of contacts with."

They all nodded, and she led the way to the active workspace. Her father was focusing on what appeared to be a PH strip with black boxes. He was measuring the tip of a glass rod covered with an inky substance.

His crest rose as he found his answer. "Son-of-a-two-headed-scum-sucking-bitch!"

Benny blinked. "Hiya, Dad. So, you found out what is doing this?"

He looked at her, and his pupils were completely black with fury. "I have to make a call."

He pushed past the agents, and Benny scrambled after him. "Dad? What is it?"

They converged in the library where her father was, indeed, making a call. The huge copper bowl filled with mercury swirled, and her grandfather's face was hovering above it.

"Where is she, father?"

Her grandfather, Zephyr Luciver Ganger, scowled. "What is it, son?"

"Kyria's father. He is after Benny."

Her grandfather had the urbane look of a studying magus. At four hundred eighty, he didn't look a day over fifty. His features were completely human if you didn't look at his slightly pointed ears and teeth, as well as the flickering shape of his pupils behind the reading glasses.

The mercury began to swirl. "After Benny? He cannot have her. She is not bound to him."

If Zephyr was getting agitated enough to effect the communication, his local weather must have been going haywire.

"Have you talked to your grandmother?" Zephyr's demon features were becoming more apparent as he got angry.

"No, if she is in the zone, they could track the call. I wanted to know if you have had recent communication with her. You are her son; you can speak without all the extra magework."

Her grandfather nodded. Benny waved from behind her dad. His expression softened for a moment before it hardened with determination. "I will get in touch with her and find out why Yomra is trying to come after Benny."

"It is worse than that, Dad. They are trying to strip her soul. There is a human agent who has been doing the work for him, but Yomra's signature is there for anyone to see."

"I trust your work, son. I will return your call within the hour or Kyria will. No one is touching Benny." Her grandfather disappeared.

The XIA agents looked at each other before Argyle asked, "Who is Yomra?"

Benny rubbed her forehead. "A whole new batch of trouble."

Chapter Twelve

They sat in the library. The agents called in, and Jennifer was stable, but there were no further leads on the case. What they learned here would show them their new direction.

Harcourt pulled up a chair, and they gathered around a book of demons. Benny flipped to her ancestor's page and she turned it around.

"Yomra. Demon high king, one of a dozen or so. He had dozens of children, but my great grandmother was supposedly his favourite."

The agents took in the etching of the demon king. Rich blue leathery skin, yellow eyes and spikes running down his spine made the biggest impression. The raging erection was also hard to miss.

"His deal was that he fathered children on human women for favours, and when they had born his heirs, he granted them their wishes until they passed on. Few, if any, survived childbirth. My great grandmother was one of those babies."

Benny picked up a book of succubi and flipped to her great grandmother's page. "Kyria worked for her father in demon tradition, carrying out the deals and seducing the weak-willed. My great grandfather traded some dark spell work for an heir by Kyria. Yomra agreed and was amused as hell. Succubi cannot breed with humans. Yomra had no clue as to how much Milton wanted to be with Kyria. He put all of his magic into their joining, and it produced my grandfather. Zephyr. The moment she was a mother, demon law broke her ties with Yomra. Kyria was free, and Yomra was down one seducer. That was nearly five hundred years ago."

Her father nodded. "Benny is the first daughter born since then to our family line."

She turned Kyria's page to them, and she watched their gazes flick from her to the picture and back again. "I know. There is a resemblance."

Argyle nodded. "More than a resemblance. The eyes are the only difference."

Benny snorted. "I am four inches taller."

The house shook and the temperature spiked. "Only when you are wearing heels, kitten."

Benny grinned and ran to the other woman. "Gamma!"

Kyria held her and twirled her in her arms. "I hear that bad things are happening here."

It was like looking into a skewed mirror. Benny heard her mother sigh. "Hello, Kyria."

Her gamma looked over at Benny's mom. "Lenora. I see you have managed to hang onto my grandson."

Benny stepped away. "Mom and Dad are soul bonded, and it was his soul that did the bonding. Be nice, Gamma."

Kyria sighed and stroked Benny's cheek. "I like the eye. It looks good on you. You should be proud of what you are. Folks need to see it."

Benny sighed. "Gamma, these are XIA agents. Agent Smith, Agent Tremble and Agent Argyle. Agents, this is my great grandmother, Kyria Luciver."

The agents moved forward and shook her hand, one by one. Kyria's expression turned from amused to delight.

"Kitten, who knew you had so many men mooning after you. I confess that I am practically dizzy with admiration." Kyria stroked their hands and forearms with focus.

Benny pinched the bridge of her nose. "They are not admirers. I am writing a piece for work. They volunteered to haul me around for a week. That is all."

Kyria shook her head, "Oh, kitten. You can be so blind when you want to be."

"I haven't been a kitten for ten years." Benny scowled.

"You will always be a kitten to me. Now, what do we think is going on here?"

Harcourt came over and greeted his grandmother with a kiss on the cheek. "I think someone is trying to hand Benny over to Yomra."

Kyria leaned back and hissed. "He has no claim over her. She is of his bloodline, but she has a soul."

It all snapped together in that moment. Benny looked to her mother, and Lenora nodded grimly. "The soul stripping spell."

"That one hasn't been used in eons." Kyria frowned.

Argyle nodded. "Until the last few months. Eight women across the country have had their souls and blood pulled out. They were all born the same week as Benny and in the same hospital."

Kyria nodded. "Right. The ninth?"

The agents homed in on that. Tremble asked, "How did you know there were nine?"

Kyria smiled. "Demons love numbers. If they didn't find what they needed in the first eight, they will need the ninth."

Benny nodded. "That is me now. Jennifer is out of the game. She is safe now."

Smith gave her a look. "That power surge..."

"Her soul is locked in her body now. There is no way that a separation can occur while she lives." She smirked. "Anyone who tries is going to blast their own consciousness twenty feet straight back."

"Way to go, kitten." Kyria chuckled and then sobered. "Now, Harcourt. Show me what you have found."

Benny stepped back and let the two demons in the room work on finding the third.

Argyle looked at her. "Should we be arresting someone?"

She chuckled. "Letter of the law is that a demon can only be arrested or detained while off their own territory or out of the demon zone and only then if they are found to be tampering with a human in an unseemly way. It does leave a lot of room for flexibility of the arresting officers."

Smith snorted. "You seem to be very aware of the laws."

She gave him a wry look. "What is the damage threshold before a shifter can be charged?"

"Four hundred thirty-four dollars."

Benny grinned. "It looks like you are very aware of the laws."

Colour tinted his cheeks. "Okay. Fair enough."

Argyle murmured. "What are they looking for?"

Lenora came over and whispered, "Kyria can locate her father, but I doubt he will actually be dumb enough to leave the zone. Kyria will be able to sense Yomra's energy and provide you with a tracking device."

Smith chuckled. "She doesn't appear to like you much, Mrs. Ganger."

Lenora laughed, "It has been fifty years since I stole her grandson into a life of academia and lust. The lust she could forgive, the life of study went beyond the pale. She dreamed of a life of success in the public eye for her grandson. With me, he glowed in the shadows."

Benny turned to her mother and beckoned for a moment. They crossed the room and bent their heads together in the hallway.

"What did Gamma mean about the agents and me?"

Lenora chuckled and hugged her. "Don't worry about it. These things reveal themselves in time. Demons live in the moment and pursue them, but you are more than that. Let your moments come to you."

Benny read the truth in her mother's eyes. There was something on the side of the agents, but she didn't know which ones. "Do I have to pick one?"

Lenora laughed. "Baby, in this family, you have the right to choose whatever blend of love makes you happy. Don't force it to be one-size-fits-all."

Benny hugged her mom and felt better about the diagnosis. She liked the agents and having seen one of them completely naked and a pretty good idea about the other two, the idea of trying them on for size held a certain appeal.

She returned to the library to find Kyria between Smith and Argyle, rubbing their arms.

"Gamma! Hands off."

Kyria sighed and released the men. They turned to Benny with dazed expressions.

She sighed and pulled them away from her seductive grandmother. A light tap on the cheek was enough to bring each one around. Tremble was wisely giving Kyria a wide berth.

Benny's father finally announced. "Grandmother, please put the tracking charm into place. They need to find this man."

"It is already dawn. They cannot use the charm until the evening." She cast the enchantment anyway.

Benny perked up. "Oh, they are off duty now."

Harcourt put the charm in a box and handed it to Tremble. "Here you go. This will take you directly to the man with Yomra's energy. It has been dulled to our family, so that should not cause interference."

Tremble took it.

Benny noted that even the ageless fey looked exhausted. "Why don't you guys go to bed? You can drop me at my house, and Jessamine is more than enough to warn me of any incoming weirdness."

Smith raised his hand. "I will stay at your home. You are the last option for a victim, and Argyle sleeps too heavily to be a good guardian."

Benny nodded. "Right. Well, it was great seeing you, Gamma."

She hugged her grandmother, gave her dad a hug and kissed and hugged her mother before heading out the door with the XIA.

Quiet exhaustion reigned in the vehicle as Argyle drove back to her place. Smith and Benny got out with Smith pausing for a moment to get some kind of order from the other two.

Benny headed inside. "Jess, we have company."

Jessamine floated in, and she wrinkled her spectral forehead. "Really?"

"Yes. One of the Agents is staying with me over the course of the day. I am being hunted."

Jess nodded. "I will make something for when you wake. Water is already in your room, and the moment you lie down, I will dim the lights."

"Thanks, Jess."

Smith came in with a small bag. "So, where are we sleeping?"

Jess floated toward him. "Benny's is the only room with a bed, so you will have to share."

Benny gave her a dark look. It would only take seconds to make up one of the guestrooms.

Smith nodded. "Right. Meet you there."

He headed past her and up the stairs.

Benny glared at her intangible roommate and swatted her furiously. "Really? Really?"

"He's cute. Besides, he is still on duty. Nothing is going to happen. You need to relax and let folks enjoy you for the multifaceted being that you are, Benny."

Benny suddenly felt her exhaustion, every moment of being

awake, the running, the accidents, every instance of the last two days. "Can you have my owl jammies meet me in the bathroom?"

"Will do. Go on. I will watch over you."

She headed upstairs with her limbs collecting lead with every step. Smith had removed his shirt, and the sight perked her up enough to head directly into the bathroom. She got ready for bed and put on her owl jammies before she stumbled out into the bedroom.

He was wearing boxer briefs and nothing else. "What side do you sleep on?"

She yawned. "Right side. Closest to the bathroom."

He nodded and grinned. "Nice pajamas."

She blushed a little and climbed into bed. Smith did the same on the left side, and she felt a moment of concern. That moment faded as the room darkened and her body felt its fatigue. Using magic to avoid sleep resulted in a coma-like event. With Smith and Jessamine on duty, she was as safe as she could be.

Benny snuggled under her sheets and muttered, "Jess, get us up one hour before sundown."

A cool hand smoothed her hair, and she heard, "Rest, kitten. I will keep you safe."

Benny tried to fight the wave of sleep when she heard Kyria's voice, but she was too tired. Darkness pulled in tight around her.

Chapter Thirteen

Harcourt watched as his grandmother reappeared. Kyria smiled. "She is safe."

He exhaled and took his wife's hand, pressing a kiss to the back of it. "The wards are in place?"

"He would have to be driving a tank to get through them." Kyria smiled. "I used the vial Lenora gave me. The house is guarded by nature. No demon magic is visible."

Harcourt smiled. "Good. Yomra is arrogant. He will be expecting us to fight magic to magic. Benny has so much more to battle with, and if she lets herself, she is able to use all of it."

He looked to his wife and saw her worry. "She will come out of this alive, Lenora."

She stroked his head and neck in an absent way. "I know she will, Harcourt, but I believe that other things are going to rise."

"You mean..."

"Yes." She glanced at the Kyria and didn't say anything else.

Kyria poured tea for them and smiled. "You mean when the little bastard who tried to rape Benny mysteriously died from having his soul inverted? It was the last demon attack in this town and the only one for a hundred years before that. It got attention."

Harcourt smiled grimly. "He had assaulted four other girls, but Benny got away with a broken wrist and some scratches. She didn't want to return to school with him there, so I managed the situation."

Kyria smirked. "And you did as any good father would do if he had the skills."

Lenora was quiet. Harcourt kissed the back of her hand again. The killing haunted her for reasons Kyria did not need to know.

"I would do it again. He was a rabid parasite, living on the pain he inflicted." Harcourt nodded. "Now, what do we do about finding your father?"

Kyria shrugged. "I have carried out what I could. The rest is up to you. He is bound by demon laws to stay away from me. I will watch to see what happens, but I have offered all the help I can. The rest is up to you and those born free from the touch of the zone."

Harcourt was astonished when his grandmother disappeared.

Lenora sighed. "I thought she would pull that move. Speak to Zephyr and bring him up to date. Perhaps your mother would have an opinion of the matter."

He chuckled. "She is very opinionated for one in her situation."

"Gender equality began long after she died. She is looking forward to learning and seeing Benny do more with her life than Lettice ever dreamed of."

He wrinkled his nose. His mother had already passed on when Benny was born, but that had not stopped her from being involved in her granddaughter's life.

"Right. I'll speak to my mother. She will have some insight into this matter."

Harcourt went to the desk, and he pulled out a glossy brown case. Inside the carefully crafted case was a velvet bag, and inside the bag was a medallion with two of his mother's fangs and one of her claws from when she shifted. She had donated the implements when she had begun her decline, and Zephyr had woven them into the medallion as a gift for his son.

Harcourt held the medallion in his hand and smiled. "Mother?"

Lettice Ganger flowed out of the medallion and stood next to her son. "Harcourt. It is so good to see you again. You have grown."

He chuckled. "I have not."

Lenora smiled. "Good morning, Lettice."

Lettice beamed, "Lenora. You are looking well. Where is little Benny?"

Lenora chuckled. "Little Benny is thirty years old, and she is in danger."

Harcourt watched his mother glide across the floor and sit in a chair, her Edwardian clothing as precise as it always had been.

"Explain what is going on, and I will tell you what my opinion is on the matter." Lettice drummed her spectral fingers on the table and waited.

Harcourt and Lenora sat with her and explained the situation. After an hour, Lettice made her comment.

"This isn't good. Benny is going to have to run this out, but this isn't good. Lenora, call your family and have them on standby. If anything goes sideways, we are going to need to hide her and do it quickly. An untethered demon is a danger to society, and they know it." Lettice frowned. "Damn, I wish I could have a cup of tea."

Harcourt watched as Lenora focused on her palm, and she wove a cup of tea out of ectoplasm.

With a smile, Lenora handed the tea to her mother-in-law.

Lettice beamed and sipped at the cup. "Oh, that is lovely. You learned that spell for me?"

Lenora smiled. "I have been holding onto it just in case."

"Now, can you do the same trick with a nice rare steak?"

Lenora laughed. "I can, but it will take about an hour."

"Well, I am a shifter and not a magic user, but life with Zephyr taught me a lot. If Benny has you backing her and family ready to gather around her, she can survive this."

Lenora scowled. "What do you mean? I am sure she will weather the assassin."

Lettice waved that away. "I am speaking of the public exposure of her family and bloodlines. There is no avoiding that now. She will be exposed as a blend of species that no one thought could even breed. She will go from being sheltered to a publicly acknowledged freak. That is why she will need family and friends. Her life is about to shift, and it will never be the same, no matter the outcome."

Harcourt let his mother's words sink in, and he nodded. "Lenora, get on the phone. We need to be ready."

He glanced at his wife and smiled, she was already on the phone, and she was making a list with her free hand. Lenora's grasp of modern technology was one of the things he loved about her, one of the things out of thousands. He could not imagine life without her and Benny in it, and it was that love that kept him in touch with the part of him that was born human.

Having a man wrapped around her was definitely a novel way

to wake up. Benny tried to ease free of Smith's body, but he tightened his arms the moment she moved.

She had to pee.

She sighed and pried his arms away, slipping out from under the covers and making her way to the bathroom. After she relieved herself, she washed her hands, scrubbed her face and brushed her teeth again. As she crept into the bedroom, she checked the time, and it was only just turning eleven. She still had four hours to sleep at the minimum.

Benny flipped back the covers, and Smith had taken up the available space. She huffed. With a determined focus, she rolled him to his other side and scooted into the bed, bracing her back against his.

She felt him trembling slightly, and she turned her head as she tucked herself in. "Are you laughing, Smith?"

"Maybe. I did not expect you to flip me over." He got out of bed and headed for the bathroom.

She chuckled and wormed her way back under the bedding, pulling the covers up and over her ears. When he returned, he wrapped his arms around her again, and he made a happy grunt when he pulled her against him.

"This is a little odd considering that as far as I know your first name is Agent."

He chuckled and sighed against her neck. "William. My first name is William. Argyle's is James, and Tremble's name is Hurias."

She smiled. "Nice to meet you, William. Hands stay in neutral territory."

He sighed. "You are no fun."

"Fun comes after stopping the guy trying to psychically rip me to pieces. For now, I will settle for a bit more sleep." She squirmed against him for a moment before she settled in to sleep.

Her squirming had made sure that his sleep was a little further away than hers, but that was what he got for hogging the bed.

The scent of breakfast for dinner got Benny out of bed a few hours later. She got dressed and tiptoed down the stairs.

"Jessamine?" The whisper shouldn't carry, but while Benny

could smell food, she couldn't hear any of the noises that she associated with breakfast.

She stood in the kitchen and called out, "Jess?"

There was no answer and that was unusual. Jess was always available even if she was doing double duty down at the main house.

She looked around, but it was when she spotted the portrait of her and her parents that she knew something had gone wrong. Her father was his dapper green self and that was not the portrait in her home, it was the one in her mind.

Benny ran upstairs, and she tried to wake Smith, but he was still wrapped around her. She had been disembodied.

Snarling, Benny jumped on top of her body, and she thrashed around. Smith snorted and Benny looked at him with narrowed eyes. She slowly and carefully eased into him, hiding inside his larger form. His aura shuddered as she made room for herself, but when the shadows crept up the stairs, she was glad that she had hidden.

Gremlins crawled along the walls, chittering to themselves as they sought her out. She had been pulled into the space between worlds. When the gremlins ran their hands through her body and came up empty, the chittering took on a panicked tone.

She watched as they avoided touching Smith, and when he moved, she rolled with him. Keeping inside him was paramount.

The gremlins searched every inch of her bedroom before they started to crackle and explode, one by one.

She counted down from the dozen she had witnessed until the twelfth gremlin exploded. It was not the right number. Demons didn't use even numbers.

Three minutes passed until the final gremlin crept from beneath the bed. He was larger than the rest and looked like he had accumulated the bodies of his fallen brethren.

The aura she was nestled in snapped tight around her. It was in defense rather than attack so she held still.

The gremlin looked at her body, and he ran his hand down her cheek, over her breasts in a lewd gesture.

Smith's aura sat up, and he flexed his claws. He slashed at the gremlin, and the beast staggered back. The roar that Smith let out caused the gremlin's entire body to ripple. They locked together in combat, and Benny was along for the ride.

They slashed, hacked and clawed at each other on the psychic plane. Benny could feel the protective anger that Smith was channelling, and it drove him forward until their attacker was carved into strips by the lion's claws.

When the gremlin was gone, the room itself lightened.

Benny's body stirred and sat up, and just like that, she was pulled out of Smith and back where she belonged.

She sat up, still in her pajamas. She prodded Smith in the shoulder, and he shot out of bed.

His half-shift was impressive, but his tail had to be uncomfortable in those shorts.

"What the hell was that?"

Benny rubbed her forehead and felt a trace of oil that was more than natural. "Soul separation. Kyria came to me as I was falling asleep, and I felt her touch my forehead. I need a shower."

"Is it safe?"

"To take a shower? Yes. To keep the mark on my skin? No."

She headed into the bathroom and started the water. Her clothing went flying, and she turned to step into the shower when she realised that she had left the door open and Smith was an interested audience.

She kicked the door mostly closed and stepped under the spray, soaping up and scrubbing her forehead. Gamma had some explaining to do.

Chapter Fourteen

They entered the main house, and Benny flicked one of the portraits on the wall. The lockdown was immediate.

Kyria was sitting with her grandson, and she paled when Benny entered the room.

"Why, Gamma, you look surprised to see me."

The obvious attempt to teleport stretched space around the succubus.

Harcourt got to his feet, glaring at his grandmother. "What did you do?"

Kyria looked around with wild eyes and tried to find an exit.

Lenora muttered quickly, and bands of power wrapped around her grandmother-in-law.

Kyria was suspended in midair and unable to do anything. Every bit of her was confined, Lenora made sure of it.

Benny explained the sleep visit to her father and mother. Her father's crest came up, and her mother seethed. "It is fine. Thanks to Agent Smith, I am perfectly fine."

She walked up to her genetic twin and asked, "I just don't know why."

Kyria tried to speak, but Lenora had her all wrapped up.

Benny threw a translation orb into the air.

I want another child, but my mate is a demon. He is also beholden to Yomra, and if we have a child, I will be back where I started five centuries ago. I want another child, so Yomra offered a compromise. I could provide another female born of my flesh to take my place.

You are the only daughter of my blood, kitten. Kyria's eyes begged for understanding.

Benny tightened her fist and the orb shattered. "Don't call me kitten."

Smith put his hands on her shoulders. "Easy, Benny. It is

over."

She turned to look at him with astonishment. "It isn't her that has been killing across the country. Yomra took her suggestion and decided to go around her. If he can get two females of his bloodline to do his will, he would increase his power exponentially. He convinced a gullible human to do his work for him, and they have been following the power lines until it led to me."

"If they knew where you were, why didn't they come here?"

She closed her eyes. "They were leaving me with nowhere to run."

"So, before, you could have put your mind into anyone of those bodies?" Smith's fingers were tight on her shoulders.

"Yes, but only if this one was coopted. It explains the blood portion of the ritual. They are destroying the bodies so I can't use them."

Smith nodded. "Right, so this is more than personal, this is high demonology."

Lenora flicked her fingers and Grandma Lettice appeared.

Benny smiled. "Grandma!"

Lettice floated over and wrapped her arms around Benny. "I am so sorry that Kyria is such a selfish bitch, but she is a demoness and that must be remembered."

"I know. It is why she was the first one that I suspected. Dad's altered portrait was my big clue. He was more demony than even I could imagine. It is how she sees him, or how she wants to see him."

A knock at the door got Benny's attention. "I will get it. Keep the bindings up."

Tremble and Argyle were at the door. Argyle was wearing a heavy set of shades and his hood was up, but he looked rested.

Benny grabbed them and pulled them through the ward before resetting it again. "There have been developments."

"Where is the amulet?"

Argyle frowned. "I left it in the car."

She sighed. "Thank goodness."

"Why?"

"I am pretty sure that Kyria spiked it."

She beckoned them inside. "We will explain."

They gathered in the library, and everyone was brought up to speed.

Benny smiled at the agents. "You get to see why it is so seldom that folks arrest demons."

Smith growled. "She attacked you."

"Did she? She manipulated a member of her family and used gremlins to investigate the world between in search of me. To anyone from the outside, it would look like she was concerned."

Smith opened and closed his mouth. "Can't we get her for targeting you and removing you from your body?"

"Why? I am fine now. If you hadn't been holding me as we slept, you would never have known what happened."

Tremble and Argyle glared at Smith. Benny saw her parents give her amused glances, and Lettice stared at the three agents before smiling.

"Oh, gentlemen, this is my grandmother, Lettice."

Lettice smiled. "I am pleased to meet you. I have been working with Harcourt and Lenora to create a more reliable tracking device. I have designed something that should work."

Kyria tried to squirm free of her bonds, but Lenora tightened the restraints.

Benny kept glancing at her great grandmother. She was about to demon out, and it was something that the agents needed to see.

Lettice and Harcourt went to the workbench, and Benny joined them.

A few drops of the soil sample, some oil of rabbit's foot, a dash of snake venom for focus and finding the path, a drop of Benny's blood to bring it all together and enough magic to hold it around a crystal. The luck was an extra touch that Benny added. She felt she could use it.

Benny held up the new charm and nodded. "Perfect. I just have to go to the lab to get something."

She wound the chain around her fingers and smiled brightly. Kyria got to her frustration mark, and the agents backed away. Vivid purple-scaled skin, three head waves, black on black eyes and a set of fangs that didn't look like blow jobs should be on the menu.

She waved her hand from the agents to the very angry demoness near the ceiling. "And that is why you don't cast a demon sex spell. That is what lies beneath."

They stood with their eyes wide, and she went to the lab to get the aerosol nullifier as well as a vial of liquid. She tucked the liquid container into her cleavage and held the spray in the hand opposite her new tracking charm.

She returned to the library and hugged her parents. "This should be enough to settle things tonight."

Her father held her tight. "Take care, and if anything happens, come home immediately. We will take care of you."

Her mother whispered, "What your father said. You can always come home, Beneficia."

Benny nodded and headed to the door. "Keep an eye on Kyria. She might try to run when we break the warding."

Harcourt nodded. "We will be watching her."

The agents followed her to the car, and she smiled at Argyle. "Can you bring the other charm out?"

He nodded and reached into the car, careful not to touch the surface of the metal. He looked at her. "Now what?"

She kicked over a stone edging the drive and smoothed it clean with her foot. She sprayed the neutraliser on the rock and nodded. "Put it down there."

He set it down on the rock, and a sizzle came from the charm. When he stepped back, she worked the spray over the charm from the bottom to the top, including the chain. It sizzled and crackled as the coating magic covered and blanked out the demon magic.

The charm burst into flame, and it confirmed that there wasn't simply benign tracking magic involved.

Never trust a charm you don't make yourself. Her mother had chanted it over and over. Benny never imagined that she wouldn't be able to trust family.

With the new charm in her fist, she looked at the agents. "Do you want to call for backup?"

They looked at each other and shook their heads. Smith added, "Not unless we can't handle what happens. We don't want you exposed or endangered."

She quirked her lips. "Gentlemen, the moment that we get a heading, I will want all the backup you can call. My life is immaterial, catching the man who would make a deal with a demon by killing eight women and attempting to kill a ninth, all for some power we don't know about, is paramount."

Benny opened her door in the SUV and looked at them. "What if the demon in question shows up?"

Argyle got behind the wheel, Smith at the computer and Tremble was in the back with her once again. Benny put the neutraliser spray down with the safety on and switched the charm to her right hand. From her seat, she leaned forward and sent power through the chain. The charm lifted and swung back toward the main road.

Argyle nodded and said, "Tremble, you keep on the directions. Watch the charm and tell me which way to go. Benny, stay buckled in and keep behind me."

She chuckled. "To think, only a few days ago, we were after psychic hookers selling magical seduction, and today, we are trying to stop someone working for one of my relatives from ripping my guts out. Ah, evolution."

Tremble raised his brows and chuckled. "I thought that I had problems with my family."

Benny sighed. "The more races you add, the more possibilities for problems. This is just one part of my bloodline. The rest can be better or worse depending on where you are standing."

Argyle smiled at her in the rear-view mirror. "That sounds like a series of stories."

Night embraced the interior of the car, and Tremble's low voice droned the directions.

"It is quite entertaining. Some species shouldn't be in the same room together." She chuckled.

They continued on their way until Tremble asked, "What does it mean when it is twirling?"

"We are here."

They were next to a cemetery, and it was obvious where they needed to go.

Once outside the car, each of the agents got a weapon from the back of the vehicle. This was serious. They were not going in alone.

"Call for backup." Benny insisted.

Smith sighed and reported that hostile figures had been sighted in the cemetery along with stray magic. Backup was nine minutes away.

Benny nodded. "Right. Now, we can do this."

She lifted the charm, and it lifted straightforward, leading them to the gates. "Now or never."

Tremble flicked two long butterfly knives open. "I vote never."

Smith clenched his fists around the studded and bladed grips that covered his hands. "Voting never as well."

Argyle shrugged. "I vote now so that Benny can get on with her life."

Benny grinned. "And I vote now, and I get two votes because I am a woman."

Smith looked like he wanted to argue, but Tremble put his hand on the lion's shoulder. "Don't contradict her."

Snickering, Benny led the way.

The rich smell of loam mixed with the green scent of oaks and the tang of pine. There were no fresh graves in the cemetery, which was very odd given the amount of empty spaces available.

Benny watched as the crystal lead them right into one of those vacant expanses.

She held her hand up and the other three paused. "Something's wrong."

She put more power into the crystal, and shadows began to shift in the open space. The shadows collected and coalesced into a single figure. It was the man who had taken Jennifer.

"Finally, you have come to me." He smiled, and it was not a good smile.

She could see the twenty-foot circle around him.

Benny quickly extended her arms to either side. "Bite me."

The dark figure laughed, but Argyle and Smith followed her orders. She winced as the teeth went in and each man took in her blood. She turned her head to Tremble and whispered, "Kiss me."

He took in the hint and threaded his fingers through her hair, pulling her head back and kissing her.

She exhaled her power, and Tremble's kiss became possessive. As Argyle and Smith released her, she had to press her hands to the elf's to get him to let her go.

When Tremble staggered back, his eyes were glowing. Argyle and Smith were doing the same.

Benny chuckled. "Now, gentlemen. Please come with me."

The shadow man had watched with amusement, but when all four of them passed the edge of his circle, he freaked.

"Not possible! Only demon energy can pass that circle." He brandished a rod, and it glowed bright.

She recognised the symbol branded into the first woman and Jennifer.

She didn't bother explaining blood and power transfers. He didn't need to know.

He lunged at her, and Tremble moved between them. When the man raised his rod and attacked, the elf nimbly danced to one side, bringing both blades down into the back of the shadow's wrist.

The scream shook the trees. The branding rod rolled across the grass. The agents surrounded the shadow and went after him, pummelling and slashing at him. Benny went for the branding iron.

She tore off her sleeve and wrapped it around the handle. She didn't want to touch it if she didn't have to.

The shadow was still fighting, but it was slowing.

"Can you hold his head?"

They shifted, and she moved behind the shadow man, pressing the glowing glyph to the back of his head. He screamed and began to float. Well, he tried to float. The agents still had control of him.

Benny whispered, "Let him go. I have marked him with his owner's sign. He is about to be reclaimed."

The agents stumbled back just as backup arrived. The man soared up, and shadows emerged from around him, taking his body apart inch by inch.

Benny pulled out the nullifier from between her breasts, and she poured it over the branding iron from the still-smouldering head to the handle. She coated it and watched it writhe and twist on the ground as the enchantment that it held crumbled to dust.

She staggered out of the circle with the agents and collapsed on the ground.

A vampire XIA agent walked up to her and said, "Beneficia Ganger?"

She nodded. She knew what was coming. "I am."

"You are under arrest for twisting the loyalties of the XIA

agents assigned to your ride-along."

She held out her wrists, and the cuffs went on. At least she could get some sleep in a nice safe cell. "Take me away."

Chapter Fifteen

Benny sat in processing while they tried to cleanse Smith, Argyle and Tremble of her influence.

She was fingerprinted, had ocular scans run and had to provide a blood sample. "This is a little involved, isn't it?"

The woman doing the processing sneered. "Demon spawn need to be watched at all times. We need to know what you are and where you are at every moment of the day so that you won't spread your influence."

Benny sighed. "Of course not."

"Why did you physically contaminate the agents?"

"So that they could make it through the protective circle this time. The first time we tracked the killer, they were blocked by the spell."

"How was it that you were able to make it through?" Officer Rorik sneered at her.

"It was keyed for demon frequencies."

"How did you know that?"

Benny snorted. "I didn't. I thought that the agents would get there before I did. I am not a hero."

"Of course you aren't."

Benny pinched the bridge of her nose. "I am a journalist, and I write recipes for a blog. That is it. I don't have any weapons or attack training. I don't know what to do when someone takes a swing at me. I avoid confrontation at all costs."

"So, how did someone as cowardly as you come to be ripping apart a demon's avatar?"

Benny blinked. "Is that what that was? I thought it was a seduced soul being used. It was an actual projection?"

"Answer the question."

"I simply did to the shadow man what he did to the victims. I thought it would create a hole by which the soul would be pulled to the one yanking on his strings."

"Because you thought that it was a projected soul and not the actual demon."

"Correct." Benny lifted both hands and drank some truly horrible coffee. Her cuffs clanked as she moved.

"Why didn't you resist arrest?"

"I knew you were coming. Sort of. I knew that one way or another, the demons would move to put me in custody."

Officer Rorik stared at her with wide eyes. "What?"

"Out of the last nine generations, I am only one part human, two parts demon and the rest is something else. The demons are pernicious, but they are part of me. I can't do anything about that, but I can keep that part of me under control. Every. Day. Of. My. Life."

The officer was staring at her, mouth open.

Benny flexed her wrists but didn't try to release herself.

The officer got to her feet. "Just a moment."

Benny waited with her senses banked and her mind quiet. The agents would be fine the moment that her blood left their systems after a good meal. Tremble just had to exhale near a tree and he would be clear. She hadn't harmed anyone and there wasn't really anything to charge her with other than unlawful seduction. The last time she checked, seducing a man without sleeping with him wasn't a crime if she didn't use magic. It wasn't even a crime if she did use magic. This was racism pure and simple.

After twenty minutes of quiet, the door opened and Captain Matheson and the XIA attorney, Ms. Wingart, came through the open doorway.

"Ms. Ganger, can you please come with us?" The captain was serious.

She lifted her hands and the chains clanged. "I would love to, but I need a little help."

Ms. Wingart turned to the officer. "Chains off. Now."

Officer Rorik paused, "But she is a demon."

"Chains. Now."

The officer walked over and slowly unlocked the cuffs. She was glaring at Benny the entire time.

Benny rubbed her wrists and got to her feet. She knew she was hardly intimidating, but the woman flinched away.

Benny looked at the captain. "Be honest. It is the eye, isn't it?"

The captain chuckled. "Of course. Please come with us. We have a proposal for you."

The lawyer took her by the arm and walked out with her as friendly as could be. She was escorted out of the Magic Enforcement Unit and down the underground tunnel to the XIA.

Ms. Wingart said, "You have to pardon the ME Unit. They suffer from a lack of imagination and even less humour."

"I am aware of it. I didn't want to undo the cuffs and break her sense of security, but their spell work is exceptionally sloppy."

The lawyer laughed. "I know. I think they like to attack our kind when they run. I have no idea why you were there to begin with."

Benny shrugged. "I am not a shifter and I look human. I was exhausted after a very trying few days."

Captain Matheson smiled. "I have read the reports. Despite what the ME Unit would have you believe, our agents were keeping us informed of their growing attachment to you. I have spoken with your parents, and the spectrum of attraction has now been explained to my satisfaction."

The lawyer cleared her throat. "We will continue this discussion in our offices."

The rest of their walk was silent. When they got to the scanner, Benny walked through it without any trouble. Her demon side was well and truly tamped down.

The captain raised his eyebrows, but didn't say a word until they got to his office.

He held a chair for her, and she dropped into the comfortable leather with a groan. Ms. Wingart got her some water and a pastry from a sideboard and put them on the desk within easy reach.

"Smith, Tremble and Argyle have been given clean bills of health on all scores. They are still infatuated by you and that brings me to the reason you are here."

Benny leaned back with the pastry cradled in her palms. "What?"

"I want you to take agent training and join their team as a magical specialist. The agents speak highly of your skills with spellcasting and your ability to think on your feet."

She nodded and worked through the Danish. "Wha abou duh demong fing?"

Ms. Wingart chuckled. "For the days when you slip up, we will get you a special pass. We think you would be a valued member of our team, and we are willing to back you in whatever court proceedings are going to shake loose from this."

Benny knew what she meant. "Jennifer."

"Correct. There is no suit pending, but there is the potential for one. It all depends on her."

Benny blinked. "I would like to speak with her. I have to explain what happened to her."

"That is not advisable."

She finished her pastry and grabbed for the water. "If I had been cursed my entire life, and then, it had been lifted, leaving me floating around with no clue as to what I really was, I would really like to know it."

The captain nodded. "We will investigate her state of mind. If she is considered stable, you will be allowed to meet with her with legal representation present."

Benny yawned. "Can I think about the offer?"

Ms. Wingart nodded, but she produced a simple contract. "Here is the offer to train you as an agent with a probationary period of six months beginning after your two weeks of protocol briefing."

Benny scanned the contract and blinked. "There is a provision in here allowing me to date members of my team in direct contradiction of the standard agent regulations."

Ms. Wingart nodded, and her head shifted into that of an eagle before returning to human. "We thought it would ease tensions if you could act on your impulses."

She had a brief image of the agents naked and quickly shook her head. "I do not feel that it is a good idea."

Ms. Wingart smiled and got her briefcase. "Fine. Stroke out the clause."

She left the room, and Benny and the captain were on their own.

Captain Matheson smiled. "If I were in Smith's pride, I would have ordered him to court you. I am not. If I were in Tremble's clan, I would have ordered the same. In Argyle's case, I would have talked to Mathias and gotten him to tell Argyle to take his head out of his ass. The problem lies in that I can't encourage one without encouraging all three. It would be bad for morale."

Benny blinked. "All three? I am supposed to take all three?"

Matheson blushed. "Not at the same time, but I believe that each of them offers you something unique. Two can even act as your mate if you want to start a family. I normally don't butt into the affairs of my people, but this is an exceptional situation and you are all exceptional beings."

Benny held up her hand. "Spare me. My ancestors have been down this road before. I don't have lions in my bloodline, so Smith is viable. All of my fey ancestors are powerful, but lower grade, so a high-grade fey is desirable. This is a conversation my family has been throwing my way for a decade. Are we related?"

He chuckled. "No, but I know your aunt, Reedana. She is a persuasive woman."

Her aunt Reedana was more siren than woman, but she did have a powerful way of speaking. If she wanted something, she could argue until you simply surrendered. The woman had stamina.

"Are you dating her?"

He laughed. "I am not that stupid. She is a friend of my wife's."

Benny chuckled, and she continued looking over the contract. Aside from the free rein to date her coworkers, there was nothing objectionable in the document.

She looked up at the captain and debated her options. In the end, there was only one.

"Can I have a pen?"

He handed it over to her with a flourish. When she signed her name, he did the same and grinned. "Welcome to the team, Agent-in-Training Ganger."

Benny smiled. "It sounds weird, but I have been called worse."

"That's the spirit. Now, let's get you a uniform." He rose to his feet and offered her his hand when he was next to her.

With a sense of finality, she put her hand in his and let him guide her through the halls and down to get an ID badge created with a demon-scan override. It was a solid start.

Chapter Sixteen

With her ID, uniform, bag and orientation textbooks, Benny stumbled into the parking lot outside XIA headquarters.

Pooky was waiting for her with his motor running. Freddy was in the passenger's seat.

Benny put her stuff in the trunk, and Pooky opened the driver's door for her. Grinning at her friend, she first greeted the car. "Thanks for the lift, Pooky."

Freddy was trying to look perturbed and failing miserably. "Well, since you won't come to the mountain, my wonderful self came to you."

"Hiya, Freddy. I would hug you, but Pooky is trying to look like a car." She reached out and squeezed her friend's hand.

"So, you have had a helluva week."

Benny began to giggle and then howl at the understatement. "I am nearly done with the article for Julian. It should be ready to upload in about an hour."

"He will be delighted, but he really wants to ask you to write a column about XIA training."

"Sorry. I just signed a confidentiality agreement."

Freddy laughed. "Damn."

"I can hear your disappointment."

Pooky drove them safely and sedately back to the Ganger house. Benny just enjoyed hanging onto her friend as a solid link to normality.

It was funny what a few days with the XIA made her think of as normal.

Her homecoming was warm, full of friends, food and drink. Her mother had called in all of her relatives, and they were there to greet Benny when she returned from her adventures.

When Benny got her parents alone, she asked softly. "So what did you do with her?"

Lenora smiled. "We mailed her back home. She will have to explain her failure to her father and her proposed mate. We can only hope they were not one and the same."

Benny shuddered, and her father squeezed her shoulders. "Bleah."

"I have felt a greatly reduced pressure on my own demonic tendencies, so I believe she has been trying to urge me into some sort of action in order to endanger you." Harcourt was solemn.

Benny nodded. "It is possible. I know that you two are going to have difficulty dealing with my news."

Lenora smiled. "What news?"

"I have been invited to train as an agent with the XIA. I have accepted."

The hands on her shoulders tightened, but then relaxed. "It is the right thing for you, Benny. Even I can sense it, and I have little to no empathy."

Lenora chuckled. "I am pleased for you. It is the first decision you have made for yourself to propel your skills forward. I am just surprised it took this long."

She shared a moment with her parents before the cheerful chatter of the party went quiet.

Benny looked toward the door where the three agents were standing with nervous determination. She went forward to make the introductions, but Freddy got there before her.

"Everybody, these are Benny's XIA agents. She will be working with them. Be nice."

Benny grinned and made the introduction that mattered. "Smith, Argyle and Tremble, this is Freddy. Freddy and I have been friends since we were children."

Freddy preened. "Play your cards right and I know all her secrets. I am amenable to bribery."

Argyle smiled, Smith chuckled and Tremble kissed Freddy's hand.

The tension was broken, and the party returned to its happy chatter.

Smith looked around the room, and he whistled softly. "I recognise a lot of the faces here. Is that a dragon?"

Benny smiled and hauled them through the party and out onto the balcony. She pulled up an aura of silence around them and sighed. "Thank you for coming, but why are you here?"

Smith chuckled. "Well, after the day we spent in bed together..."

She gave him a droll look. "Oh, shut up. Now, there are a lot of people inside that you will recognise from television and movies, as well as activists and academics. Be nice and remember you are not on duty. That said, thank you for coming."

She went up on her toes and kissed Smith softly. Benny stepped away and kissed Tremble, sliding her hand up behind his head and pulling him down to her. Tremble held her gently as if he was afraid he would spook her.

She smiled at him as she drew back.

Argyle didn't wait. The moment she turned to him, he wrapped his arms around her, dipped her and pressed his lips to hers.

Benny caught a glimpse of the crowd staring at them through the windows. Freddy flared up and shooed them away, shot her a thumbs-up and kept guard.

Argyle's skin was cool, but it warmed rapidly where she touched him. When he set her back on her feet, her senses were spinning.

"Wow. Um, okay. I was just welcoming you to the gathering, but that took it to a whole new level." She patted her hair and the agents were laughing at her.

Smith smiled. "Well, now that we have been officially welcomed, I saw a delightful buffet inside and I really want to meet that dragon."

Benny patted his arm. "Stay away from Zora. Regick is really protective of her right now."

Argyle looked toward the room. "I saw a gargoyle in there, and I have always wanted to meet one."

Tremble straightened his shoulders and looked toward the gathering. "There are some high-court fey in there."

Benny laughed. "Go. Socialise. Have fun. Try and find out which guests are toxic and which are not."

Smith slid his arm around her waist, Argyle took the other side and Tremble put his hand on the vampire's shoulder. They returned to the party en masse, and the joy wrapped around them and pulled them in.

The ghosts sat out on a spectral balcony and had their own party.

Lettice poured for Jessamine and smiled. "I am so proud of how Benny has come through this."

Jess nodded at the other ghost. "It isn't over, but she has done well so far."

Lettice smirked. "Even dead, you seers can suck all the fun out of life."

Jess laughed. "I had to pull a lot of strings to get my remains assigned to the Ganger household. The mages didn't want to let me that close to this kind of power."

Lettice chuckled. "You are handling it well, and we have more than enough accumulated power from the family to rein you in if necessary."

Jess smiled brightly, and the other deceased family members raised their teacups.

Their party included ice giants, two fey that had died during childbirth and a few mages in the direct family. The rest of the invited dead were family friends and ancient teachers.

Jess looked out over those assembled and Benny shining like a bright star in their midst. Three hundred years ago, Jess had known that she was destined to be the companion of a melded being, she just didn't know how.

Her death at the hands of a lightning strike had escaped her precognition, but it had given her the charge to retain consciousness in the afterlife. The arrangements had already been made, and her transfer into a spectral being had been surprisingly natural. After that, she just had to wait until Benny entered the world.

In the strictest of senses, Benny was a relation. Across four generations and several removals, Benny was her cousin.

"Do you have any more directions for Benny?" Lettice smiled.

Jess looked over the party and saw the three men causally arranging themselves in a protective detail that was only visible to the trained eye. Benny didn't have anything to worry about, and soon, she would be authorised to use all that she knew to defend those around her.

Jessamine Turing raised her teacup. "Nope. She is doing just fine on her own."

Two Parts Demon
An Obscure Magic Book 2

By

Viola Grace

Chapter One

Benny grunted as she was struck from above and continued crawling through the obstacle course.

"Come on, demon. Lose it!"

Benny gritted her teeth and continued to pull herself forward, arm by arm. She really hated control training, but today was her last day. One way or another.

She scraped her belly on the rough ground of the course; her tank top was no protection against the gravel and dirt. She hissed as a boot connected with her ribs and another kick sent her tumbling. She held in her pain and kept moving until she could get to her feet and run through the swinging, weighted bags.

Benny gritted her teeth as curses and insults to her bloodline were spewed at her. This was practice for being in the field and dealing with those who were not too keen to be subdued. She wanted nothing more than to finish her training and get into the SUV with her agents, if only to get away from the trainers.

She grunted as one of the bags made impact, but kept going. She could see the end of the course.

It had been decided that the best way to prove her worth to the XIA was to go through endless rounds of stress testing. If she could keep her cool under every circumstance they could come up with, she was safe to be in public.

Her ability to use magic was not in question. She was physically capable of managing the tasks that made up the bare minimum of the staffing skills for the eXtranormal Investigation Agency. She could apply for additional training later on, but the course designed to test her skills and tolerances was her first step.

Her impulses wanted her to burn a pathway through the course, but her self-control kept her doing things the hard way.

Benny grunted and heard a distant voice call her a scaly bitch. She sighed and poured on the speed while her bruised body screamed silently.

When she stumbled across the finish line, it was time for the final task. Benny whispered and moved the pegs into the properly sized holes using tightly controlled magic.

The light turned green when the last peg hit the slot, and she dropped to the ground.

Her trainers applauded wildly and cheers sounded around the workout yard.

Benny looked around and nodded wearily. "So, did I pass?"

Agent Tafnor chuckled and pulled her to her feet. "You did. Time for the final photos, and then, you are officially cleared by the training centre."

Benny nodded and headed toward the imaging booth. She had been photographed every day for the last two weeks. The bruises and damage to her body were tracked for a very specific reason—she needed to know how a victim felt. She needed to know how easy it was to damage evidence on her own body, and she had to feel the exposure of the photographs.

All agents were subjected to a rape kit at some point during training. She had opted to get that out of the way on the first day. Today, it was just the indignity of stripping down in front of the camera.

A cold voice greeted her when she entered the space. "Take off your shirt."

She flinched at the aggression in the tone. Benny pulled her tank top off, exposing the damage to her upper torso. The camera flashed, and she winced at the light.

"Hold still."

The camera flashed again.

She was ordered to turn to the side and then face the back of the photo area.

"Now remove your pants."

She hesitated.

"Now!"

Benny got angrier than she had been while she had been physically attacked. The camera flashed, and she flipped her middle finger at the shadows before she removed her trousers and pushed them to her ankles, leaving her bra and panties as the only things covering her.

The cameraman got closer, but she still couldn't see him. He took close photos of her thighs, back and ribs.

"Remove your bra."

"No. You can see the damage around it. This is my body, and I am saying no."

"This is an order."

"No. This is a courtesy. This exercise is to make me feel like a victim or a suspect, and in either situation, I would ram that camera through your jaw." She pulled her cargo pants back up and pulled on her top.

"You are already healing. We needed to document the pattern."

She snorted. "I heal the same as a shifter does. I just don't match any blood types that they do. I have to be faster or I die."

Benny tucked her shirt into her pants, and she lit the interior of the photo booth with a ball of soft light. No hands required.

The goblin in the XIA uniform grimaced. "Can you turn that down?"

She dimmed the light. "You need to use manners when you deal with either suspect or victim. You were very close to breaking my control."

He chuckled. "I know. Check this out."

He turned the camera to her and showed her an image of her glaring at the camera, her eyes were poisonous green and very demonic.

"Oops."

His finger slipped and the image disappeared.

She frowned. "Why did you do that?"

"They are looking for reasons to restrict your movements. Let's not give them an excuse."

Benny cocked her head. "I will not lie about seeing my own demon in the mirror."

He inclined his head. "And so I will lie for you."

His fingers moved over the back of the camera. "Sent. Your training is now complete."

She patted him on the shoulder, a move that caught him by surprise.

Benny sighed. She knew that most of the XIA did not touch the goblins, but she didn't have any hang-ups in that regard.

Their magic and transformation came from the same energy that ran in her veins. There was no difference.

Benny double-checked her clothing and left the photo area. "Thank you."

He was so stunned by her thanks that he didn't respond.

She returned to the training area and accepted congratulations for successfully making it through the course without biting her trainers. Apparently, that was a thing.

Benny just wanted to go home. Her parents had started some kind of extension on the dower house, so Benny was stuck in her old room at the big house with Jessamine haunting her day in and day out. With nowhere to be alone, she was closer to cracking at home than she was having the crap kicked out of her at work.

After the congratulations, she hit the showers and grabbed her bag. If she could manage to get changed, Freddy had asked her out for a karaoke night. Howling into a microphone was right up her current mood.

Pooky was waiting for her, and he revved up the moment she entered the parking lot. Benny flexed her swollen knuckles around the steering wheel and whispered, "Take me home."

Pooky did as he was told. He took her home at a safe and sedate speed. Her muscles were alternately tensing and twitching, so it was better that she wasn't driving.

The shower had been nice, but she was going to run around in the greenhouse the moment she got home. She was healing fast, but not fast enough to go out in a tank top. She would have enough time to administer a healing draught, but she would not be able to drink when she went out with Freddy. Given her friend's penchant for getting her into trouble, it was better that when Benny went out, she stayed sober.

Benny and Freddy leaned in close to the mic and howled along with a full-moon love song. Freddy's other form was canine, so she thought she could hit the right notes. Benny could hear Freddy's voice swing and miss over and over again.

Some of the members of the crowd had their hands over their ears, but others were listening with rapt attention. Those enjoying the music were usually of goblin descent. They enjoyed the notes that were up beyond standard hearing.

As the song concluded, Benny laughed and leaned back, heading for a glass of water. She sat to the side as the next singer took the stage.

"Well, your voice hasn't suffered now that you are all official and stuff." Freddy grinned and slugged down her cocktail.

"I have done a lot of shouting and grunting this week. It is a bit more physically challenging than I am used to, but it keeps me busy. I think I am going to enjoy this." Benny shrugged and nodded to the waitress for another glass of water.

"We miss you at work. You used to bring in samples. The new food writer doesn't bring in samples." Freddy pouted.

It hurt to think that she had been replaced already. "That is too bad."

"You are telling me. I have had to start *paying* for food. It is horrifying."

The water and another cocktail arrived. Benny tipped the waitress and gulped down the water. It was all she had been drinking for the past week. When she needed to heal, it was water or nothing.

"So, are you still going to be driving around with those agents? The photos in the articles were extremely frustrating."

Benny grinned and sipped at her water. "Why was that, Freddy?" She already knew the answer.

"They were fully clothed."

They sat giggling as a baritone crooned a classic from the forties.

Freddy turned to her. "Do you want to do another?"

"Want to? Yes. Should I? No. I have been getting plenty of attention this week. I don't need to jump on stage."

"How are you dealing with that?"

"The freak trying to rip away my humanity or the fact that my great grandmother was behind it?"

"Both."

She didn't mention the role her parents had played. That was something that was going to be dealt with later.

"I am dealing with it. The training has helped."

Kobar came up to the table, and he slipped Benny a piece of paper. He whispered, "Please."

She looked at the song on the slip and listened to the warbling of the current singer and nodded. He walked away in relief.

Freddy looked at her with a raised eyebrow. "What was that?"

"Folks are starting to leave. He has a request."

"Well, I will leave you to it. I believe this calls for a solo." Freddy flapped her hand and waved her toward the stage.

Benny got up as the last of the song died away and took her place behind the microphone. The watchers perked up, and she began to sing a vampire love song about love and death, blood and pain, all coming together to haunt the new vampire for eternity. *Love Never Dies* was always a classic.

The few vampires in the audience were crying tears of blood by the time she finished her song.

Benny felt the same rush that she always did when the applause followed her off the stage. She finished the water that Freddy had guarded, and she waved her hand at her friend. "Come on, time to get something to eat."

"Yay!" Freddy bounced to her feet and clapped her hands.

They made their way through the crowd listening to a mage with quite a good voice. It was time to hunt down a food truck.

Chapter Two

"So, what do you feel like? Pizza? Tacos? That weird noodle thing?" Benny drove through the streets on the lookout for something edible.

"Well, you know I am always up for that weird noodle thing, but I think that tacos are our best bet tonight."

"Tacos it is. Pooky, you know the way."

The car did a quick U-turn, and Benny sat back while they were driven to the taco truck.

When they arrived and got out of the car, Benny snickered. "Well, it seems I have created addicts."

Freddy leaned against her arm. "Do tell."

Benny linked arms with her friend and hauled her toward the picnic table occupied by Smith, Argyle and Tremble.

Two of the three men were covered in taco grease and not at their best. Benny made the introductions anyway.

"Gentlemen, you remember my best friend, Freddy. Freddy, you remember that these are the agents that turned my life upside down, Smith, Argyle and Tremble."

Freddy shook their hands and licked her palm clean afterward. Benny didn't explain, she just headed to the truck and ordered for herself and Freddy with a bright smile and a wink for Dem-rah behind the counter.

With her hands laden with tacos and juggling sodas, she headed for the table where Freddy was flirting madly with the three XIA agents.

Benny settled, and Smith pressed his thigh against hers. "It is good to see you, Benny."

She nodded as she doused one of her victims with hot sauce. "You too, Smith. 'scuse me."

She tilted her head and found four pairs of eyes watching her. She shrugged and dived in. The spice hit her before the flavour did, and she closed her eyes and kept eating. Sweat prickled on her upper lip, but she kept going.

She opened one eye a crack when she heard Freddy starting on her own meal. Having a best friend that was part hellhound was definitely interesting. Her table manners were always lacking, but her enthusiasm could not be denied.

Benny finished her tacos and wiped her face. Her lips throbbed with a steady beat. She daintily sipped at her soda, and the sugar sent her senses reeling.

She sat up and looked at the agents. "So, you have been declared demon free?"

Smith grinned. "Relatively. We are fit for duty."

Argyle folded his hands on the table. "How did you do in your training, Benny?"

She smirked. "I passed, though it was less training and more stress testing. They were trying to make me freak out on them."

Tremble blinked. "That is unusual. What was the purpose?"

"They seem to think that my bloodline makes me unstable. The trainers used every method they could to make me manifest my demon side. It wasn't comfortable, but I didn't flip out."

Smith chuckled. "At least it was only stress testing. They didn't hurt you."

She paused, and it was long enough for him to sprout claws and mark the table. Tremble looked shocked, but Argyle patted his friend on the shoulder and nodded. "I thought as much."

Benny chuckled. "I am glad one of us knew I would have the crap kicked out of me. They used pain, exhaustion and verbal abuse to try and make me lash out. I am happy to say that it didn't work."

Argyle nodded. "When do you report for duty?"

Benny grinned. "I have no idea. They are going to assign me as a fourth to a team. I am cleared to work, but I don't know when I start. When do you guys get to go back?"

Tremble smiled. "We are still on leave, though we have been cleared of all demon influence."

Argyle smirked. "Feel free to influence us anytime."

Benny snorted. "I am dealing with my change in circumstance. Kyria has been banned from my home, and my parents are waiting for the investigation to get to them."

Smith frowned. "Does that bother you?"

"Having to lock out one of my oldest ancestors? Yes. She was part of me, part of my family. She was the origin of the demon blood in my bloodline. It hurts to have her separate from us, but she was acting as a demon. She was focused on her wants and desires and pursuing them." Benny couldn't believe that she was having this conversation in a vacant lot next to a taco truck, but there it was.

Smith cocked his head. "Is that what the fuss was about? Is that demon influence?"

Freddy chimed in. "You don't get it. If a demoness wants to get some sleep and her baby is crying, she will kill it. If a demon male sees a woman he wants and she is with her husband or family, he will kill them to clear the path. The emotions of their victims never even enter their reckoning. They simply don't see anything but themselves."

Argyle cleared his throat. "I have wondered how it works with your parents, Benny."

Benny made a face. "Well, Dad manifested as an incubus, and he is in love with my mother. She provides him with everything he needs, and he is satisfied. His blood binds them, so he would never stray, but he does get sexually frustrated very easily, which did mean that I couldn't have sleepovers. They created a schedule that worked for all of us, and I learned to reheat things in the microwave. Eventually, I learned to cook."

Tremble leaned in, "What do you mean *manifested as an incubus*?"

"No demon is a copy of their parents. It is a random assignment of genetics and magic. Kyria is a succubus, her child was a book demon and his child was an incubus. Kyria's father is a demon king, and she definitely is not one of the ruling demon classes."

Tremble was genuinely curious. "How do you know?"

Benny smirked. "The horns. The kings have large racks like deer do. They are born with those as their crown."

Smith chimed in, "So they are automatically in charge?"

"No. They have to take down another king. It just gives them the right to pick the fight." Freddy mumbled around her taco.

Argyle glanced at Freddy. "How do you know about it?"

Freddy snorted. "One, I am Benny's best friend and have been since we were six. Two, my family has had some occupational exposure to demons in the past."

Tremble cocked his head. "Why?"

Benny took the glance that Freddy threw her. "Okay, I can see that they are more annoying than decorative. How do I get out of this?"

"Tell them if you want to and tell them it is none of their business if you don't." It was fun to see someone else on the interrogation end after the week she had had.

Freddy sighed. "My dad is a hellhound."

The guys just blinked in surprise. Benny sipped at her soda, revelling in the sugar and carbonation. She had really missed it.

Smith dived in. "So, are you a hellhound?"

Benny started snickering, and Freddy kicked her under the table. "Shut up, Benny."

Benny finally decided to pity her friend. "Can I describe it?"

Freddy slumped in relief and nodded.

"She has a canine form with access to the energies of the demon zone. Most of the time, she just reports on sports for the same company I used to write for."

Freddy looked relieved. It was the truth without being the whole truth. It made her other form sound exceptionally impressive, which is why Benny had phrased it that way. Freddy needed more respect than she got.

Benny scooted toward Smith, pressing more firmly against him. "What are the odds of me starting next week?"

He shrugged. "They will probably take a week to work out the paperwork. The mage council has to sign off on your participation as you are a registered mage, not an extranatural."

Tremble chuckled. "Smith is the only one of us who thrives on paperwork. If he says it is so, it is so."

Benny sighed. "It has been a while since I took a week off."

She got up and headed for another round of food. A crowd was starting to gather, and she wanted to fill up before she headed home.

She nodded and held up four fingers when it was her turn at the window. She got a wink and a nod in return as he called the order back in a harsh and guttural tone.

She paid, went to wait with the others and grabbed a handful of sauce packets before she returned to the table, her arms laden with food.

When Benny returned to the table, she had to ask, "So, do you guys normally hang out together, or is this like a time-off thing?"

The agents looked at each other and shrugged.

Tremble said, "We just all wanted tacos tonight, so I called Smith and he got Argyle to drive."

Freddy leaned forward and pointed to Smith, "So, you don't live with your pride." She moved her finger to Argyle, "You don't live with your master, and you, Tremble, don't live with your clan."

The men all nodded, and Benny wondered where she was going with this.

"So, none of you really have a place in the world, according to your own people." Freddy seemed intent on nailing that down.

Benny whispered, "What are you getting at?"

Her friend snorted. "They have been staring at you like they were hoping that you would put as much enthusiasm into wrapping your mouth around them as you have the tacos. I think I need to know if they can put their focus on you or if they will have split loyalties."

Benny blinked. "Their first loyalty is to the XIA, same as mine will be."

The men looked from one of them to the other. Tremble finally spoke. "Our loyalty is to the XIA, of course."

Argyle leaned in and cleared his throat. "Though, from what your parents have told us, you might be amenable to having all three of us in a relationship."

Freddy gasped, but Benny cocked her head. "I have considered it, but while it is culturally fine for me and my family wouldn't have an issue with it, I think yours might."

Benny worked on finishing her second order while everyone at the table was in shock. Freddy grabbed one of them, and before Benny could warn her, she bit into it.

Freddy's eyes flared blood red as she fought the heat in her mouth. She gasped and reached for the soda, but Benny shook her head.

"Damn it, what was in there?" Freddy grabbed one of the sodas from the agents and slugged it down.

"Uh, four spicy hot?" Benny felt apologetic.

"And your soda?"

"The same. I needed a bit of a kick today."

The flame in Freddy's eyes faded, and she sat down, eyeing the remaining taco warily. Benny was reaching for it when her phone went off.

She paused. Everyone that would have called her was here at the table. Who the hell could be calling her?

Chapter Three

"Benny, this is the manor. Please come home." The flat voice of the house she lived in came through the call. The phone was on speaker, and she disconnected the call as it finished speaking.

Benny wadded up her remaining food. "Sorry, folks, I have to go."

Argyle got to his feet, his pale features serious. "We can drive you."

"Pooky will drive me. Freddy, I can drop you on the way home."

"Fuck that, I am coming with you. Get in the car."

The men got up and cleared the table at the same time.

Benny tossed her garbage into the troll-occupied trashcan and headed for the car. The last time she had been called home by the house, one of her school friends had seen her father without his glamour. An investigation had been pending, but her mother passed it off as a demon glamour that she had cast on her husband. It had been a heart-pounding moment.

Pooky opened his door, and she slid into the driver seat. To her shock, Tremble sat in the passenger side. "Freddy is coming with the others."

"Home, Pooky. Quick as you can within legal limits."

The seatbelts snapped into place on both of them, and the car reversed into the lot before taking off on the way home.

"Um, Benny?"

"Yes, Tremble?"

"Who is driving?" He was very polite about it, but she could tell he was nervous.

"Pooky. He's my car or any other type of conveyance I need. I got him when I was fourteen." She smiled and stroked the dashboard as the car danced with traffic.

"It is enchanted?"

She snickered. "Not specifically. It is a living being that has specific shapeshifting categories. It tends to end up as a vehicle, so Mom and Dad asked if he would be my ride, and he agreed."

"I see. It is an excellent driver."

Benny smiled softly, "He really is. He is also a great designated driver."

"Did I misunderstand earlier, or did you say that you would have a relationship with all three of us?"

Benny blinked at the sudden change of topic. "Um, well, yeah. It wouldn't be right to pick one and leave the other two out of it. So, since you three are partners, I would have to take all three of you on, naturally."

"Some would say there is nothing natural about it. Our species do not blend in nature."

"You work fine in the field. I have seen you three in action. It is a solid balance of teamwork, and I wouldn't put my oar in to knock any of you out. I respect the team, so if I date one, I date the team."

His eyes were wide and his ears were quivering with shock. "That is...that is a very interesting way of thinking of it."

"You have met my parents. I understand that what is required for one relationship is not for another. When you care for someone, you adapt to what they need as long as it doesn't change who you are. You have to know yourself to be able to give that to someone else."

He threaded a hand in her hair and leaned forward. She gave in and kissed him, but when his tongue touched her lips, he jerked back. "What the hell is that?"

She blushed. "Spectre peppers. They were in my soda and my taco. Sorry."

Pooky turned and pulled up to the house, two Mage Guild cars were parked in the drive. Benny got out of the car the moment that the seatbelt released.

She ran in and yelled at the mages who were firing spells at the library. "Hey!"

The spellcasters paused.

A woman with dark hair asked, "Do you live here?"

"Yes. What is the issue?" Benny asked.

"There is a demon on the premises, and we have to take him

into custody."

"May I look?" There was no reason not to ask to see what they were trying to pry out of the library. It might actually be a demon.

"Be careful, miss."

Benny glanced over, and her friends were arriving. "They are with me. I was out when I got the call."

She stepped into the group of mages and looked into the library. Her mother and father were floating in the air, and between them was an actual demon—Yomra the demon high king, her great-great grandfather.

Huge antlers sprung from his head, his clawed hands and dark-blue skin gleamed wetly; the spikes down his back were almost as intimidating as the club between his legs.

An oily voice in her mind knocked her to her knees. *Ah, little Beneficia, just as lovely as Kyria with far less wear and tear. I will strike a deal with you. Your parents can return to their lives if you agree to come and work for me. I think you would make an excellent succubus.*

The distended erection he sported made her gag. Benny shook her head. *No. I will not work for you, but I will come for them.*

I give you a week to change your mind, pet. You will be mine. If you don't come to me, I will call you by blood and that is not going to be a comfortable moment for you. Remember, it is my blood in your veins. I own it, and I will own you.

A thunderclap of power and they were gone.

Benny was still on the floor, and the moment the pressure on her mind disappeared, she fainted.

Waking with her friends around her confused her; it took her seconds before she realised what had just happened. "He took them."

Freddy nodded. "That is what the mages say. They are waiting to interview you. I am guessing that they are pissing themselves at having seen an actual demon for the first time in their lives."

Smith leaned forward. "Why did he take them?"

She cast a silencing spell on the area around them and whispered, "He wants me. He wants me to take over for Kyria. If I don't agree, he will pull me in by blood and that won't be good for me."

Tremble took her hand. "What does that mean?"

"Blood call will take my free will and imprison my soul. You can't normally have a soul and be summoned by blood, but if anyone could find a way, he would." She shivered. "My brain still feels oily."

A thud on her silence spell told her they weren't alone anymore. She dismissed the spell, and the four mages surged in.

Argyle got to his feet and held up his hand. "Our teammate has just had a nasty shock. Not only were her parents kidnapped, but there were mages in her home."

The woman that had first spoken smiled, "I am Agent Wells. I need to ask you some questions about the intruder."

"Do you have access to the records of the Ganger family? The recent ones?"

Agent Wells looked uncomfortable discussing it in mixed company. "Yes, there is some demon in the bloodline?"

"That demon is where the blood originated. His name is Yomra. He has kidnapped my parents."

"Do you know why?"

"Because he is a fucking demon. He was a contributing factor in the women who were murdered two weeks ago. These officers of the XIA stopped those plans." She gestured to the men around her.

Freddy smiled and waved.

"Ah, and Freddy is my best friend. She is familiar with my family dynamic."

Freddy nodded, "I have known the Gangers for years. They are good citizens, excellent teachers and Lenora is a great cook."

"Why would he come to you?"

Benny sighed. "Blood binding. He can do a lot with the blood of two of the strongest mages of our current age. Either I turn my blood over or he will capture me and hurt my parents."

"Why not just take you?"

Argyle snorted. "Blood taken from the unwilling loses power. It can still be useful for a purpose, but you cannot build on its strength. He needs her cooperation."

That he was supporting her in her lie was a relief. She tried to look pale and shaken. It wasn't too difficult.

Agent Wells stared at her, but nodded. "You have had a

rough time. We will begin negotiations with the demon zone and see what we can find out. I am afraid that your father's bloodline might make that awkward for him, but your mother should be fine."

"Thank you, Agent Wells. I will be here or you can get me through the XIA. I have just been cleared to be mage liaison for this XIA team."

Her chair shifted, and to her shock, she was sitting on Smith's lap. No wonder she had been so comfortable.

Benny looked up at him, and he smiled down at her, looping his arms around her waist. It wasn't the most professional appearance, but it made Agent Wells uncomfortable enough to quickly take down her contact information before mentioning that there would be a car out front until they had answers about the origin of the demon.

Benny asked a question. "How did you find out about the demon?"

Agent Wells flicked through her notes. "Someone named Manor called it in."

Benny nodded. With the suspension spell, it would have had to have been the house itself. "Thanks."

"Do you know Manor?"

"I do. He lives in the area." She suddenly had a thought. "Jessamine!"

Benny jumped out of Smith's lap and ran for the alcove where Jessamine's remains were stored. Benny opened the box and sighed with relief. In a tiny portrait, her friend and housemate was sobbing softly, claw marks and blood stained her clothing, but she was still in one piece. "Jess. Oh thank goodness."

Jess looked up and sobbed with relief. "Oh, Benny. He was here and through the wards in no time. He used some of Kyria's blood to break in."

"Do you need help?"

"Please."

Benny whispered a spell to heal ectoplasm and watched the claw marks fade. Jessamine manifested near her, and she looked devastated.

"I couldn't do anything."

"Mom and Dad couldn't either. Don't worry about it. We are going to get through this."

Agent Wells was staring in shock. "You have a ghost?"

Jessamine stiffened and floated up to the woman. "Hey, Benny, you have an idiot?"

Benny snorted. "Jessamine was a friend of the family a few centuries ago. She is now a companion and my roommate. I normally live at the dower house at the end of the lane, but my parents are doing renovations, so I am staying at the manor until the renos are done."

Agent Wells nodded. "Well, I have your information, so I will be on my way. Take this and keep it on you in case you need anything."

Benny took the card the woman handed her, ignoring the zing of tracking magic embedded in it.

When the mages were gone, her ghost was back, the agents were staring at her and Freddy was eating cookies. Benny got ready to go and rescue her parents from the demon zone.

Chapter Four

Benny took a deep breath and muttered, "Just like Easter." Freddy explained the comment to the men. "She means it is time to make a battle plan."

She walked to the library, put her hands on either side of the doorway and sent a cleaning spell through it to remove every trace of blood. When the nine popping flames finally confirmed that she had found them all, she mentally cursed her great grandmother and headed into the best magical library for several hundred miles.

"You might want to keep your heads down." She called out the warning before she set up a summoning spell. The spell was specific. She wanted a way to expunge the link to the living demon in her bloodline. With her growing power, there was no way that Yomra wasn't going to try to get his hands on her, now that he was aware of her.

Books flew toward her, and she caught them, stacking them on the table one by one. The books would get her close, but she might have to get help.

"Can any of you read spell books?"

Her four companions shook their heads.

Benny fished her phone out of her pocket and flipped through her contacts. She hoped it wasn't too early.

The phone rang three times before a scratchy voice answered. "Hello?"

"Minerva?"

"Yes. Is this Benny?"

Benny sighed with relief. "Yes. I need help."

"What do you need?"

"You. I need someone who can read spells and intuit a new option."

"At your place or the manor?"

"The manor."

"I am on my way."

Benny felt tears running down her cheeks. "Thank you. You don't know how much this means to me."

"No problem. Now, let me hang up so I can get dressed. I will be there in five."

Benny nodded but the call was over. She put her phone back in her pocket and smiled. "You guys don't have to hang around. I am going to get going on this today."

Freddy snorted. "Right. I will make some coffee; you start whatever you were going to do."

Benny kept a polite smile on her face while Freddy headed into the kitchen. She grabbed Smith's arm. "Do *not* let her make the coffee unless you want to be able to see into next week."

He nodded and went to rescue the coffee.

"Argyle, we keep a guest room upstairs with no windows if you want to lie down for a while."

Argyle came up to her and kissed her softly. "We will get your parents back."

She stroked the blood-red silk of his hair. "I know, I just want to do it before Yomra hurts them. Demons are not known for their self-control."

Her eye was glowing. She could see it when Argyle headed up the stairs and Tremble walked up to her. It glowed against his skin, and she felt the silk of his hair against her face when he kissed her.

She wanted to curl up in his arms and sob, but this wasn't the time. Just outside the manor, she felt Minerva's arrival. "She's arrived. I have to let her in."

Benny made her way to the door and opened it before the agents outside could notice the mage in the archway. Minerva was standing on the steps with a bandolier of tubes and vials around her and two large bags over her shoulders. "Let's figure this out."

Benny hugged her and invited her inside.

Minerva stepped in and her breathing was a little shallow.

"There are three XIA agents here and Freddy. They are making coffee and biscuits to keep us up and running."

"Thanks, it takes a lot of effort to maintain this figure." Minerva quirked her lips.

Minerva was plus sized in all the right places. She was nearly six feet tall, had wicked curves and a lush body that made other women envious, though she would never see it. Minerva was used to being an amazon amongst Victorian ladies. She was designed for battle and had no idea how lovely she truly was.

Minerva rubbed her hands together. "What do you need and where do you want me to start?"

Benny drew her friend into the library, and she walked over to the tomes that her spell had pulled out.

"Minerva, I need your help to locate or create a spell that can cut the ties between a demon and his children."

Her friend whistled long and low. The magic in the sound vibrated in the air. "That is quite the complicated arrangement. Why are we doing this?"

Benny sat and looked up at her with her exhaustion showing in her body. "My great-great grandfather took my father and mother and is holding them hostage for my cooperation as his newest succubus."

Minerva's lip curled. "That is revolting."

"I just want to get my parents back here and keep Yomra from pulling the whole blood-link thing. To do that, we need to find a way to break the connection that all demons share with their sire."

Minerva tapped her lips. "Maybe not all demons. Is your family a straight line?"

"Pretty much. One child to one child and so on."

Minerva grinned. "Excellent. I think I know of a way to do this."

"I summoned all the books that might have a base spell to what we need."

Minerva gestured to the table and the near dozen tomes stacked up. "Can I get started?"

"You can."

"Go and get some rest, Benny. I will have one of your crew call you if I find anything." Minerva cracked the first book open and settled at the table, flipping quickly with her eyes glowing bright.

Mage sight was a rare gift, and it was one of a dozen or more that Minerva possessed. Benny got to her feet, wavered and smiled at her friend. "Anything at all, get them to call me."

"Go. Sleep. I will keep you posted."

Benny nodded and put her hand on Minerva's shoulder. "Thanks, Minerva."

"Anytime. It is the Mage Guide oath."

Benny chuckled. "Right up there with the defense of chocolate act."

"You've got it. Now go. I got this."

It was a dismissal given with a pat on her hand before Minerva shifted her focus back to the tome in front of her.

Benny headed out of the library and toward the stairs. To her surprise, Tremble followed her from his post in the doorway.

"What are you doing?"

"Benny, you are in danger, and we are fully trained to help with your situation. You are going to be guarded until you are no longer in jeopardy. That includes when you sleep."

Since he wasn't on duty, his hair was hanging loose, and as she glanced back at him, the curtain swung and caught the light. *Damn, he's pretty.*

She passed the blackout room and the door was open a crack, letting her see that Argyle was on the bed and watching television.

He called out, "Come on in."

Benny looked back at Tremble, and he shrugged that he didn't mind.

She walked into the dimness and looked at the vampire wearing nothing but his shorts and a sheet. "I have been ordered to nap."

"I am willing to share space if you are. Even the big fairy can come on in."

Benny yawned and kicked her shoes off, skinning out of her jeans, tossing her shirt and unsnapping her bra.

Argyle was staring at her, and Tremble was draped in her tank top. With another yawn, she climbed onto the bed and yanked the sheets up around her.

"You are very nonchalant about sharing the bed with two men."

Benny sighed. "My parents have been kidnapped by a demon who wants me to screw mages for a living, so being in bed with two men I can trust is definitely something I want to enjoy while I can."

Argyle scooted down in the bed and pulled her against him, rubbing her back. Tremble joined them, and with her body protected front and back, she slept.

Benny felt the change in the energy of the room, and she sat up, staring at Jessamine. The ghost was waving at her, and Benny slipped out from between the two men. Argyle was in his restorative state, and Tremble was just snoring lightly.

Benny pulled her shirt on and slipped into her jeans, tiptoeing out of the room and down to the library.

Minerva was scribbling in a twenty-five-cent notebook. She had a cup of coffee next to her and a small stack of crescent rolls.

When Benny followed Jessamine into the room, Minerva looked up and smiled with her eyes glowing brightly. "I think I have it. You are going to need some very specific things, and they will not be easy to acquire, but the magic is sound."

"You think?"

Minerva stretched, her ink-stained fingers reached for the sky. "Pretty sure."

"How sure?"

"If I help you...about ninety-three percent sure." She smiled. "The next full moon is Wednesday, so we are going to have to do it by then."

Benny felt a chill in her stomach. "Why the time constraint?"

"I have a date to act as a proxy in a negotiation with a dragon. I have to be in Sumac Heart City by the full moon."

Benny sat down and put her head in her hands. "Okay. Tell me what we need."

"Well, knowing your mother, we have access to the first two dozen ingredients. The unicorn horn and dragon skin will be tricky."

Benny shook her head. "We have some. Show me the list."

Minerva quickly jotted down the list and divided it into animal and herbal matter. "Here you go. I have the ones I ticked off here." She pointed to a pile of herbs and vials in the centre of the table.

"Are the quantities enough?"

"Oh yeah. Most of this only requires a token of the herb to act as a focus. As you know, my magic focuses on intent, not in strong arming the result."

"It's why you were the first person I thought of. Thank you so much for helping."

"It is fine. I love a good puzzle, and I love your parents. They were the first folks to not bat an eye at my growth spurt. Your mom just gave me an extra serving of everything." Minerva's eyes got a little misty as she smiled at the memory.

Benny put her hand on Minerva's arm. She rested her head on her friend's shoulder. Minerva had gone from the smallest in the class to the tallest in the class in the course of eighteen months. Her body had been wracked with pain, and she ate constantly. Minerva's mother had come to Benny's in search of help for her daughter. Lenora had worked up a daily dose that would help Minerva's body grow to its full potential. No one had any idea that there was any extranatural in the bloodline until she finished growing.

"Well, Benny, if you are up for it, let's go into the greenhouse and pick out what we need from your mother's stores."

Benny nodded, looked down and made a face. "Let me change."

She cast a quick spell and cleaned herself up as well as put on a bra and new shirt from her room.

Smith came in with Freddy, and they paused. "Benny, you look..."

Freddy winced. "Eyes, Benny."

With a deep breath, she pushed her demon back inside and brushed her hands on her thighs. "Better?"

Smith nodded. "Better. Where are the others?"

"Argyle is restoring himself and Tremble is snoring. I snuck out while they were unconscious."

Smith scowled. "You were in bed with both of them?"

Minerva blushed and cleared her throat. "I will be waiting outside the greenhouse."

Freddy grinned. "Come on, Benny, tell all."

"Argyle feels like cool sheets, and Tremble starts as a snuggler who rolls to his back the moment he is out. All we did was sleep. Tremble wanted to start something, but even he wouldn't make a move in front of Argyle." She sighed and patted Smith on the cheek. "We slept. I needed it."

He pressed his forehead to hers and inhaled. "Fair enough."

"You just sniffed me to see if I had had sex with your partners." She whispered it against his cheek.

"Yes. You didn't." He sighed. "How is this going to work?"

"We are going to take turns. I will be with you, with them, and I promise to keep all things equal while we are together." She smiled and patted his shoulder.

"Seriously? All of us?" He looked so hopeful.

She sighed. "Not at the same time, but yes. I don't play favourites, and as Freddy can tell you, I have a knack for knowing what I need. I need all of you."

Freddy's hand was over her mouth, but she nodded and mumbled, "She does know what she needs."

Benny stroked his cheek and gave him a quick peck. "I will see you later. Now, we have to get my parents back. You go for a nap and I will be with Minerva. Freddy can watch me. She doesn't need sleep."

Freddy saluted sharply. "I have this covered, Smith. Get going. There are a dozen rooms upstairs. Take one and sleep. We need to be at our best."

Benny smiled softly as Smith headed up the stairs. "Speaking of being at our best. Thanks for staying for this, Freddy."

"No problem. I know where this is taking us, and I am with you all the way."

Benny teared up as they headed to the greenhouse. It wasn't every friend that would follow you into the demon zone.

Chapter Five

Minerva was wisely waiting and rearranging her lists. No one wanted to go into Lenora's greenhouse if they didn't know what they were looking for.

Benny grabbed the handles on the doors and felt the magic of the house recognise her. She opened the greenhouse, and Minerva followed her.

Freddy waved, "I am going to wait out here."

Benny gave her a thumbs-up and led Minerva through the temperature lock before opening the inner doors. "Remember. Elbows in and let me know if anything grabs you."

"Yes, ma'am. You want the list?"

"Yup. You take the basket." Benny reached over and took her mother's collection basket.

Minerva clutched the woven bark with both arms and followed faithfully in Benny's footsteps.

Benny looked down at the list, and they started shopping.

Snipping carefully to take only what she needed, Benny followed the recipe to a tee. "What the heck are tears of the gorgon?"

"Rocks. Tiny pieces of marble. Your mom has them in the lab."

"Why don't you just say marble chips?"

"Because it doesn't sound fancy." Minerva chuckled. "No, they are really tears of a gorgon. Their transformation and ability to transform others makes them weep for the first two weeks during their adulthood. Their tears are those of a lost past and a fixed future alone."

Benny paused. "That is so sad."

"That is why they cry. It plays the part of finality in the spell and mourns the loss of the past even if you do not feel regret."

It made sense, and Benny clipped the last clinging vine that she needed. It writhed disturbingly in the bottom of the basket.

"We are good. Everything else is a in the dry-storage cupboard in the lab."

Minerva nodded, her elbows carefully tucked in. "You go first."

Benny chuckled and headed for the entrance, past the deadly plants that Minerva found so unsettling. She extended her personal aura, and the plants drew back, giving them a wide berth while they exited the greenhouse.

Minerva was right behind her when Benny opened the temperature lock. Her friend sighed with relief when they were out in the hall and on the way to the lab.

Benny remembered weekends with Minerva, sitting on a stool while her friend and her mother were lost in their herbs and powdered whatsits. She had sat and looked over cupcake recipes while Minerva learned what Benny took for granted—the mechanics of magic.

The lab was far less dangerous to walk through, but Benny still moved carefully. She checked the recipe and got the burner and the bowl made of raw iron.

Minerva found the cutting board, and she carefully picked her knife. Without speaking, she got to work.

Benny got the rest of the immediate ingredients together and stood near Minerva. "What should I be doing?"

"Make a binding spell. You can't go in alone, but I can't track anyone but you when you enter the zone."

"I will have Freddy with me."

"You will need more. Freddy is great, but she can be controlled by a demon king."

Freddy poked her head in. "She isn't wrong."

Benny chuckled, but then she sighed. "I don't want to haul anyone into my mess."

Freddy snickered, "The boys are coming along. You don't even have to ask. As soon as I explained what you were going to be up against, Smith told me they were in. Make the binding potion."

Minerva chuckled. "It will give you something to do and keep you occupied until your sleeping beauties wake up. If you don't use it, you only waste time and a few ingredients."

Benny sighed and went to the recipe book on the wall, hauling it down and flipping through the pages. "Fine."

She got to the segment of sharing spells and paused when she saw her father's handwriting correcting one of the lists. She traced the writing and blinked at the date. It was her birthday.

She stared at the notes and confusion ran through her. According to this, she was supposed to be bound to her parents and living grandparents. They were to hold her soul. This was not the spell to shatter her soul and bind her to strangers of the same age; it wasn't even close.

Benny flipped through the pages and a folded sheet fell out. She read the notes and tears rushed to her eyes. She breathed in through her nose and out through her mouth, controlling her emotions until she could continue looking for the binding spell she needed. She carefully tucked the small note back where she found it. It wasn't for her; it was a note for her father. She had never realised that this book was his.

Minerva glanced at her. "Is something wrong?"

"No, I just never realised that my father had been the primary herbalist until he changed. Mom had been into the raw energy spellcasting and natural magic."

Minerva paused with her pestle raised. "I didn't know that."

Freddy piped in. "It makes sense. Demon magic makes it hard to concentrate on things like time-consuming herbals and spells. They are much more instinctive and aggressive when it comes to magic."

Benny nodded, that described what her father had been doing since she was ten. She found the recipe she needed and checked the basket. All the herbs were out of it. "Can I take the basket?"

"Please. I have taken every crumb."

Benny grabbed the basket and headed back into her own private jungle. She inhaled the bright, rich scents of the herbs essential to spellcasting. For this spell, she needed vines and plants with sticky sap. She took the special non-stick blades out of their drawer and got to work.

The sap leaves had to be lined up just so in the basket or they would dribble their contents everywhere. The creeping vines that tried to hang onto her were a hazard to the balance in the basket, so she had to keep an eye on them.

When she returned to the lab, she felt like she had her mother with her. She got herself a wooden bowl bound with silver and got to work. First, the vines went in and the sap was poured over top. She got a crystal pestle and went to work.

Since it was binding for tracking, she added a werewolf's claw and the mucus of a snail for a trail. The other ingredients were ground into the sap, and then, it was time to put magic in it.

Freddy perked up, this was her favourite part. Benny smiled, put her hands over the bowl and pulled magic out of her to transform the contents. Benny opted for orange-soda flavour.

"There. All done but the blood."

Minerva was still grinding away, sweat on her brow. "Good. Go and drop it in."

Benny shook her head. "Nope. This is a four-way binding spell. It will attach me to them and them to me, as well as each other. I am going to have to make damned sure that they want that or this is going nowhere."

"Why didn't you use a standard spell?"

"Because this has to be equal all the way around or nothing. My binding them to me would be selfish in the extreme."

Minerva shook her head. "It isn't selfish, it is destiny. You have always known what you needed in life, and whom you needed around you. That is some of your fey blood. You must have a seer on your mother's side somewhere."

Benny used a funnel to get the binding potion into a flask. It was glass bound with silver and had the engraving of her mother's and father's initials. It was a wedding gift, and she felt it was appropriate to use it for this particular potion.

Minerva whistled softly. "Is that an Eckerhart?"

"I don't know. It has always been around, and my mom told me it was only for potions that revolved around the family. This definitely counts."

Minerva rummaged through the vials on the bandolier and brought out a small gold capsule. "Add all of this to the binding spell. You need it there more than I do on the outside."

Benny took the small, engraved capsule with reverence. She pried open the vial and sniffed. Wild green, open air, a love song in the distance and the battering of the ocean against rocks. "What is it?"

"Luck. The luck of life. One thousand shamrocks distilled in the bright sunlight and ground with the purest salt from the sea. One grain is enough for a normal being to bless them for a lifetime. You are going to need it."

Benny tapped the crystals out of the vial one at a time until all twenty-three had spilled into the orange, swirling liquid, and it changed to silver with flecks of gold.

She made sure that the gold vial was empty, and she pressed it back into Minerva's hand. "Thank you."

"You are welcome. It needs to be shared, and I can't think of anyone more deserving than you of some bright, new luck."

Freddy looked up, "What about me?"

Benny chuckled. "You will be with me, and your summoner is not in the zone right now."

Freddy perked up. "You know that?"

"I always keep tabs on her. I know where she is every moment of every day. Right now, she is across the world." Benny patted her friend on the shoulder, rubbing in the small crystal of luck she had kept behind.

Freddy blinked, and her eyes flared red for a moment. She nodded and smiled. "Good. The less I hear from her, the better."

Being bound to a mage came with being a hellhound. When Freddy was born, across the world, her mage came into the world. They met when the mage was a teenager, and she chose Freddy's form. The first summoning had pulled Freddy out of the mall and across the globe. When the need was over, Freddy was back in the seat she had been taken from, in the lap of the new occupant. Freddy was stuck with the hound first chosen. The form was set and the connection was made.

Benny might be bound to her family, but Freddy was bound to a stranger who never took her wellbeing into account. It was all about what her mage wanted and the hound was never consulted.

She corked the flask and looked at the silver and gold swirl. "I really hope this works."

The sound of approaching footsteps brought the Y-chromosome into the room in the form of Argyle and Tremble. Smith stumbled in a moment later, rubbing his eyes and looking delightfully sexy.

Argyle asked, "Why are all the ladies in here?"

Minerva chuckled. "We are cooking...sort of. Can you guys go and fix dinner? We have been working all day."

Smith nodded and saluted her. "Yes, ma'am."

The three agents filed out of the lab and clanging could be heard in the kitchen.

Benny cleaned up her workstation and sent all the residue of the spell into the catch basin under the house. Everything was scrubbed and put back where it was supposed to be.

Minerva was still working on her spell, but based on the steam bubbling up from the vessel, it was nearly complete.

Benny asked, "Do you want me to keep you company?"

Minerva shook her head. "Nope. Go on and keep an eye on your men. You can explain the binding spell to them using the paper cup and straws analogy."

"Yes, ma'am." Benny bowed and took the flask.

Freddy piped up, "I will keep her company."

Minerva grinned. "Bring in dinner. I still have an hour to go."

"Yay and yes." Benny gave her a thumbs-up and went to rescue her kitchen. It sounded like it was in distress.

Chapter Six

The surprisingly graceful ballet of chopping, mixing and flipping was taking place in her kitchen.

She was surprised that Argyle was involved, but he was boiling pasta with an eye for it approaching the precise doneness.

Tremble glanced over his shoulder. "What were you working on?"

"Minerva is getting a spell ready to sever the family connections with a demon. I was working on a binding spell in case anyone wants to come with me." She put that out in the open.

Three men turned to her, but Argyle turned the stove down first. The vampire crossed his arms. "Of course we are coming with you. You are not going into the demon zone alone."

She cocked her head. "It isn't that easy. To get into the zone, you need demon blood. To get that blood, you need to have it in you and bound to you. It would contaminate your bloodlines, possibly permanently."

"What would we be bound to?" Tremble cocked his head.

"Me. Well, not just me, but to each other. It would be an equivalent sharing of power and awareness with everyone involved in the spell. So, whoever were involved would be bound together, not just by demon blood, but by whatever was in the mix."

Tremble picked up on the ramifications. "So, I would have links to vampire, shifter and demon?"

"As well as the fey and mage bloodlines I bring to the mix."

They paused together. Benny smirked. "Do you want to discuss it without me here?"

Tremble shook his head. "No. We are coming with you, and if the binding spell is what it takes, then we are willing to bind to you and each other."

Argyle and Smith nodded.

Argyle said, "I am good with it."

Smith grinned, "My mom will be so impressed."

She laughed. "Well, did you want to do this before dinner or after?"

Tremble asked, "What do you need us to do?"

"Four drops of blood into the flask, drawn with a knife. No teeth. You don't want saliva getting in here." She patted the flask.

Smith went to the cutlery drawer and pulled out four steak knives before handing them out.

Everyone gathered around the kitchen island, and she opened the flask. With a quick motion, she stabbed her pinky and dropped the knife, squeezing four drops out without difficulty.

Argyle went next. It took him a while to get the vampire blood to drip, but after a minute, he finished.

Smith was quick, and Tremble's blood looked like it was loaded with glitter.

Benny corked the flask and tipped it to get the blood drops from the sides. The liquid turned to a molten bronze; four cups appeared on a chain around the flask.

"That is different. Well, here goes."

She unhooked the cups and lined them up, pouring an equal measure of the spell into each vessel. She set the flask down and lifted her cup to the men standing with her. They each picked up a cup, and all of them brought the cups together.

"Let's hope this works. I am a little rusty on my potion making."

Benny brought her cup to her lips, and the orange was still there, along with the wild taste of the luck and the pungent flavour of blood. She drained the cup. The power hit her a moment later.

Benny slammed her hands down to the table, watching as her skin changed shape, texture and claws appeared and disappeared. The other three were in the same condition. Ears pointed and reset, eyes flicked and skins changed colour.

It took several minutes, and they were all covered with sweat when the magic had linked them from the inside out.

Smith shook his head. "That was...wow."

Argyle looked at his hands. "My heart started beating for a moment."

Tremble was blinking rapidly. "I felt so much."

Benny took a deep breath. "You will be able to access the power of the others as needed, even my power, though you guys don't have the training to work the human magic."

Smith looked at her. "Why do I feel like I can bench press a cow?"

Benny pointed at Argyle. "That comes from him. You will all experience flashes of instincts that belong to the others. That is normal."

Tremble focused. "What about you; won't you experience a change?"

She shrugged. "I already have all three of your races in my bloodline. I deal with all of those instincts every day. What you need to watch out for is the trickle of demon blood. If one of you asserts that, they can take control; the others need to smack him. The constant urge to dominate others with aggression is one of the signs. Enforcing your will with levitated objects is another."

Smith looked at her with narrowed eyes. "You would not have handed uncontrollable power to us."

"You are right. I can pull you back if I need to, but it sounds a little bossy." She shrugged.

Tremble blinked, rubbed his eyes and blinked again. "I keep seeing a face overlapping yours."

"The demon blood gives you another presence, and if it is strong enough, another form completely. You will see me wearing that other form when we go to the demon zone. I won't have a choice. The magic that binds the demons into the zone keeps human enchantments from being effective. We will have our bodies and our wits. That is it."

Argyle tilted his head. "What about weapons?"

Benny shook her head. "No. I will explain the details later. Finish cooking, Minerva is going to need her strength."

As if her words released them, they turned and resumed cooking. Benny sighed and took the flask back to the lab for cleaning.

Minerva was putting the salve she had created into a glass jar. "Got it. Just two more ingredients and the spell will be complete."

"And that is blood from Yomra and blood from me."

"Right. It will sever the link between you and ripple down all layers of your family. You will still be of the demon breed, but you will be free."

Benny nodded. "Slice through the demon magic that binds me and Yomra can't call on my family."

"Even Kyria will be loose. Sorry, but Freddy filled me in." Minerva got every drop of the salve into the jar, sealed it, and then, she carefully took the empty raw-iron bowl to the sink and poured in nullifier. Bright sparks flew, and Minerva quickly cleaned out the vessel before drying it and heating it on the small burner once again.

While Minerva worked, Benny used the nullifier in the flask and swished it out before dumping the potion into the sink with the catch basin. After that, she was free to use water.

When it was clean and dry, she set the flask back on the shelf and closed the glass-paned door.

The smells coming from the kitchen were delightful, and with the salve ready, the spellcasting implements washed and a strong hunger, they all trooped out of the lab and into the kitchen. There was just something about pasta when you needed to fill up and prepare to break part of your family tree into a pile of splinters.

Benny watched Argyle when the rest of them started eating. When she took her first bite, his eyes widened and he swallowed. She grinned, and he looked at her in surprise.

"I can taste it. I used too much oregano."

She chuckled and swallowed. "Focus on one of the others."

Tremble drank some wine, and Argyle's eyes fluttered and his lips pressed together.

"Holy..." He smiled as his words trailed off. His fangs were on display while he spoke, and he closed his eyes to savour it.

Tremble blinked. "He is tasting what I eat?"

Benny chuckled. "Of course. We are bound." She smirked. "It works with sex as well if you were wondering."

Minerva coughed wildly. Freddy patted her on the back, but her own cheeks were on fire.

Argyle was grinning and Tremble finally caught on.

"So, that is why you said that being with all three of us wouldn't be a problem. What one feels, the others feel."

Benny kept eating and mumbled, "Only when you concentrate."

Minerva sighed. "Didn't you explain it to them?"

Benny grinned. "Not really."

Minerva took a mouthful of food and got to her feet. She went to the cupboard and got four paper cups and a handful of straws that she snipped in two. "Benny's blood is symbolized by the water in this cup. She could give you each some..." Minerva poured a splash of water into each cup.

"If she did that, the blood would not have a connection to her, and after a while, you would consume it, or it would evaporate."

Minerva set the four cups out, and with a touch of magic, she dyed each one a different colour. "These are all of you, each a different power. If we connect them with the binding spell..." She waved her fingers and the straws bridged around in a spoke pattern and then connections for the agents' cups.

"The powers are stable unless someone injures one of them." Minerva took an ice cube out of her glass, and she dropped it in the Benny cup. The colour moved out of the cup through the straws. "She then gets strength from each of you and you get strength from each other. Usually, it is only done between a maximum of three people, but this one seems to be working quite well."

Minerva waved at the cups, and they floated up and into the sink. "The point of that spell is to keep you equal at all times. Your magic will still be separate for the most part, but it will flow when it needs to."

Benny finished her meal and got up to start the dishes. She scrubbed and smiled as she heard Argyle discussing how food actually tasted. Apparently, he had been craving the taste of food since she let him taste his first taco through her veins.

She blinked away tears. It seemed like so long ago, but it had been less than a month since her world had spun out of her control. So many firsts in that time, and now, her parents were in danger because of her. Her stomach flipped at the thought of what she was about to do. It was only in the security of her home that she had discussed the demon zone. Even her father had never set foot in the place.

Dishes and cutlery started to appear on her left, and she washed, rinsed and set the dishes on the draining board in rapid succession.

"How much time has passed, Freddy?"

"Seventeen hours, Benny. You will have most of the night in the zone."

Benny nodded and dried her hands. "I need to get the map. Someone else can dry the dishes."

Freddy nodded. "I will. I know you hate doing it."

Benny wanted a moment alone. She needed to talk to the house.

She left the group in the kitchen with a tight smile and headed for the library, closing the door behind her.

"Hello, house."

The phone rang.

Smiling, Benny went to pick up the receiver. "Hello, house."

"Hello, Benny."

"You know what I am about to do?"

"It is very dangerous." The calm, masculine tone spoke the truth.

"If we do not return, I want you to welcome Minerva as your new occupant. She will respect you and all that is within you."

"You will return."

"I hope I will, and Mom and Dad too, but I am bracing for the possibility that we will not. I want you taken care of in a manner that you deserve. Minerva knows you. She will respect you and listen to your council."

"I will accept her if the Gangers do not return." The voice was resigned.

There was a moment of silence before he said, "There is a present for you on the desk. I have enjoyed watching you grow, and you deserve the protection that I can offer."

Benny looked around and found a box that gleamed with a black silk ribbon. "Do I open it now?"

"You will need it where you are going. Demon eyes cannot see it. Wear it and be safe." The line went dead.

She put the handset down on the phone and tugged the ribbon loose. She opened the ten-inch box, and tears pricked her eyes again. A knife made of ebony and obsidian was nestled in the box next to a sheath with thigh straps.

She slid the blade into the sheath and looked at it, flicking to her demon vision. She could still feel it, but it was invisible.

Grinning, she flicked back to normal vision and strapped it to her left thigh.

Humming to herself, she got the map and flicked her hand to open the library doors. They swung open, and her entourage stumbled inside.

The map was gross, but keeping an interdimensional diagram on normal parchment wasn't possible. A gargoyle's wing hosted the map, and since it did not dry out, the map was rather lifelike.

She pinned the wing open and whispered over the skin in a language that had no name, but haunted the nightmares of anyone who heard their name spoken in it.

The zone took shape and projected into a three-dimensional drawing of the home of the demons. She whispered, "Yomra."

A light glowed in the centre of the city.

"Harcourt Emile Ganger." A blue light lit in the same building as the yellow.

"Agatha Lenora Ganger." A purple light glowed near the blue one. It was a relief.

"Kyria." Hot pink burned a few buildings away. That was something. At least she wasn't going to have to contend with a demon high king and her great grandmother.

She memorized the map and smiled tightly. "Minerva, do you have a few extra vials?"

Minerva smiled. "Always." She fished a few vials out of her bag and held them out. "They have magnetic flip tops. No magic involved."

Benny carefully arranged the vials around her body, each with the top wedged open. If she had to get close enough to get Yomra's blood, she was going to make damned sure she collected it.

Chapter Seven

Pooky transformed into a van when they left the house. They were all silent as the car drove to the Redbird City Park.

Minerva made a few phone calls during the drive. She was the only one who was going to be alone during the procedure, and they were depending on her to get them out. She called on a few friends of hers to come and watch her back while she worked on keeping them safe, even from a distance.

Benny looked at Minerva as she dialled yet another friend. "I wish I could help you with this."

"This is out of your territory. I need folks who will blend in but have my back. Your friends are not known for blending in." Minerva smirked. "I can call in a few favours."

Smith asked, "How are you going to get us out?"

Minerva put her phone to her ear. "I am going to keep my foot in the door."

She continued calling until they arrived at the park.

Benny parked and asked for a moment alone. When she was with Pooky, she asked him for the same favour that she had the house. To her surprise, Pooky refused.

"Fine, if I do not return, run wild and free until you choose to drive around with another teenager." She chuckled and stroked the dashboard. "It has been an honour to be with you."

He rumbled the engine.

What he was saying was clear. He had enjoyed himself as well.

She stroked the steering wheel. "I hope to see you again in a few hours."

The engine purred and the door opened.

She got out and headed toward her group.

Minerva made a glowing orb, and she had a selection of vials and a folded piece of cloth. Minerva held them out toward her.

"The cloth will open all doors. It is a piece of the gown of Giltine, but it can also summon sudden death."

"I know who she is. Thank you." Benny smiled tightly and put the cloth in a pocket of the courier bag she had across her body.

"These are healing potions. They won't do you a lot of good in the zone, but you can take them the moment I grab you, and they will start working when you hit the threshold."

Benny nodded and stuffed them into her bra and pockets. Her clothing would transform along with everything else, so it was best to keep things as close to the skin as she could.

She checked the height of the moon in the sky and beckoned to Freddy. "If you still want to come, it is show time."

Freddy nodded, her eyes went red and she began to shrink. When she was in her hellhound form, she ran to Benny.

Benny opened the flap of the courier bag, and she scooped the Chihuahua with the glowing red eyes into it. "Thanks, Freddy."

The three XIA agents were staring at the bag and the small head poking out of it. Benny gave them a stern look about ridiculing Freddy for her form.

"Okay, Minerva, can you start?"

Minerva held up her hand as she finished making a glyph in the grass. "And I am ready. Stand on the glyph, and I will wrap you up. Close contact please."

The three men formed an arc, and Benny nestled in the centre. "Whenever you are ready, Minerva."

The mage smiled and sent out tendrils of light that touched their skin and disappeared with the contact. Benny felt the protective covering going over them, the means by which Minerva would track them. Elementals were funny things, but Minerva had taken to the control that Lenora Ganger had taught her. Benny had known from the moment she met Minerva that the young woman needed to learn from her mother. There had been moments of jealousy, of course, but Benny had gained a friend, and Minerva had gained the tutelage of one of the greatest mages of the age. Everybody came out a winner.

When they were wrapped up with the elemental tags, Minerva lowered her hands. "Okay, I have sparked Benny's blood, so I can find you wherever you are. When you see fire and hear singing, that will be me. Clump together and hold on tight."

Argyle asked, "What if we want early extraction?"

"Benny can manage to get you out. That scrap of fabric will open the wall between dimensions."

Benny put her hand on his arm. "I can also call her or my mother can. You will be out before dawn."

Minerva nodded. "All right. You get going. I will watch the gate."

Benny straightened her shoulders. "Okay, gentlemen. You will be transformed into your demon self. That will include clothing and cell phones. Bear with the changes and walk with me at all times. Our group won't cause much of a stir as long as you guys stay close."

They were with her, step by step, while they approached the gate that she could see clearly.

Smith muttered, "How have I never seen that before?"

Benny knew he was referring to the electric-blue gateway that they were approaching. "Demon blood is not just for locking folks up. It has a definite positive side, though the lack of a conscience is something you have to get used to working with." She smiled.

One more step and they would be in the gateway. "All right. Everyone put a hand on me."

One hand gripped her left arm, one her right shoulder and two hands gripped her butt. She was so shocked, she took that last step into the gateway and the human world disappeared around them.

Her companions fell to the ground when they entered the demon zone. Benny smiled smugly as she realised that it was where they belonged.

She stretched her arms to the sides, enjoying the freedom of the leather tabard and belt with thigh-high boots. Her men were wearing rich brown leather that complemented their golden skin, which matched her own.

Benny reached up and touched her horns, smirking at what she discovered. She did not have the stubby horns of her great grandmother or the spikes of her father. She had the majestic horns of a demon high king, and it felt completely right.

Smith got to his feet, a row of short horns running along his skull and his feline features matching his skin tone. He blinked at her, "You look..."

Argyle stood, his pale-gold skin set off by his blood-red hair. He had black sweeping horns that ran along from the front of his skull to the crown where they swept up and away. "She looks splendid."

Tremble spoke from behind her, and she slowly turned. His skin was a metallic sky blue, and his horns curled on either side of his head in a ram's spiral.

Benny smiled. "You all look splendid as well. Now, please get yourselves together. We have a bit of a walk into the city."

Smith kissed her suddenly, running his hand down her back and cupping her against him. When he released her, she staggered free, and Argyle kissed her, stroking her sides, her butt and generally making free with her.

Argyle was shoved backward when Tremble lifted her off her feet and plastered her against him. After his turn, her blood was pounding in her veins, and it was only her tiny human voice in her mind reminding her that her parents needed her that snapped her out of tackling the boys and rolling around with them for her personal satisfaction.

"Come on. We have to get to Yomra's palace."

They shook their heads and adjusted their crotches.

Argyle nodded. "I will take point. Let's go."

Benny took Tremble's arm on one side and Smith's on the other. "Let's go."

The city glowed half a kilometre away; it blazed with light. It was very inviting for a den of those who were destined to be painted with the taint of evil, at least as far as humanity was concerned.

As they walked, Tremble asked, "So, how did you end up with those horns?"

She chuckled. "I am descended from royalty. It is more likely than not that I would end up as high king."

She glanced back over her shoulder, and she could see the entryway that Minerva was holding open for them. They just had to find her parents, get some of Yomra's blood and make it back through that door before dawn. *No problem.*

Chapter Eight

The variety of demons in varying stages of undress was a little startling for her agents, but Benny was used to the sight of demons copulating in the street. Well, she was more used to it happening in the kitchen, but catching your parents doing it for the fiftieth time dulled the shock metre.

She twitched her lips as she watched one acrobatic coupling. "Hey, did anyone end up with a tail?"

Butts were checked and none of her boys had a tail. Too bad. Their leather pants did a lovely job of displaying their assets. Somehow, the magic that had surrounded them on their way in had coordinated their clothing.

Smith asked, "So, demons just have sex out in the open?"

She smiled. "Where would you rather they do it? Behind closed doors and under the sheets? Sex is natural, and they enjoy it when the whim takes them."

She walked with her group through streets that were lined with ancient temples, modern homes and palaces. A few of the demons on the street glanced at them, but once they saw her horns, they quickly looked away and went elsewhere.

The bag with Freddy had turned into a cross-body bag with leather and studwork. Every few blocks, Benny glanced down and met the serious, glowing eyes of the tiny, tiny dog. It kept her from joining any of the groups having sex.

Argyle asked casually, "Is sex the currency here?"

"No. It is the entertainment. They don't get Wi-Fi or cable, and demons are easily bored."

Tremble muttered, "What about laws?"

"Don't pick a fight with anyone bigger or stronger than you. There is the law of might here. It is really the only law." She smiled.

"So, murder is acceptable here?"

"Acceptable and encouraged. Demons breed when their kings allow, so you want to keep the population in control. The new arrivals are actually protected for a month until they get the hang of it."

Smith murmured, "How do you know so much about it?"

"I have studied the rules of the zone. Knowing that my father could be consigned here at any moment over the last decade and a half meant that I was always interested in it. My grandfather helped me learn."

"How is it that he never changed?"

"He kept his soul, and he never entered the demon zone. My father shared his soul with my mother, so he lost his grip on his human shape." She smiled.

Argyle looked at her with his eyes shadowed. "And he lost his humanity."

She shook her head. "No, he kept it. He has only ever sought my mother for sex in the years since the transformation. As you can see by those we have passed, that is not a usual situation."

There was no doubt about it. While the demons were screwing in public, they were also enticing anyone who passed to join them.

The scent of sex was heavy in the air. Even with the coupling taking place outside, there was still little to no air movement to sweep the pheromones away. Blood was also in the air, but it mixed with the sex in a disturbing way.

Smith looked the most uncomfortable. He was getting the full blast of the scents, and his erection pressed against the leather he was wearing.

She dug her claws into his bicep and whispered the promise, "When we get out of here, I promise to roll around with you until you are exhausted."

He perked up. "Just you and me?"

"Well, Argyle and Tremble can listen in, but yes, just you and me."

He nodded, and it seemed to renew his focus.

The basilica that they were approaching gleamed yellow to her eyes. She nodded with her chin. "That is our destination."

Argyle inclined his head, his crimson hair swinging around him. They walked down the dusty streets until they reached the front entryway of the domed basilica.

"I go first now. Demons like to stab you in the back. I am depending on your three to keep me alive." She smiled for a moment before straightening her features. They were about to face the second most dangerous person in her universe.

Two lesser demons were guarding the entryway.

The green one on the left challenged her. "Why are you here, lady?"

It was nice that her horns at least got her a civil question.

"Lord Yomra has issued an invitation, and I have answered it."

The demon looked at her through evil yellow eyes. "Who are you?"

She straightened and glared at him through her own green eyes. "His blood."

The two guards jerked to full attention. The green one nodded sharply. "Just a moment."

He left his post and entered the building through a small door.

It took three minutes for the large doors to swing open. She stiffened her shoulders, and she looked at her companions. "Show time."

They nodded with tiny movements of their head, and she could feel that they were prepared to back her up. This entire thing was about her and her family. They were just here for support.

It had to be the roughest first date in history.

The glowing interior cast a weird glow on their skin as they walked into the building and stepped into a throne room, occupied by Yomra himself.

The deep-blue demon got to his feet. "Beneficia! I am delighted to see you, though you are not the demon I had guessed you would be."

"I am consistently full of surprises." She inclined her antlered head.

"You are indeed. Who are your companions?"

"They are mine. Their identities are no concern of yours."

His serpentine tongue lashed out. "You have invited them into my house."

"They are mine, bound to me." Benny smiled. "They are here to take my parents home."

"Ah, yes. My great grandson and his creature."

Benny stiffened. "That creature is my mother."

"*Was* your mother. She has not been that being for some time." Yomra walked toward her, and she remained in position while he caressed her face with his claws.

He murmured, "Who would have thought that Kyria's spawn would have resulted in this? I should have let her breed more."

He lifted her face to his, and his tongue flicked against her cheek. "You taste of power, little one."

She didn't respond, but she could feel the agents tense. She sent them a calming wave through the binding. Yomra was merely being a demon.

When he put his lips above hers, she said. "My parents?"

He leaned back, his eyes narrowed. "Why in such a hurry, child?"

"Because they do not belong here."

"He belongs to me, and she does as well, through his blood."

"If I am here, they do not belong here." She remained calm.

He smiled. "I will offer you and your companions dinner while we wait for your parents to be brought to us. Come this way."

He led the way through an archway that appeared as he approached the stone wall. They followed, and the skull-decorated dining hall opened up in front of them.

The polished table was large enough to seat twenty, which amused Benny because demons were not that social.

"Sit at my right hand while I summon your parents."

He lifted his hand, and a ball of power zinged from his palm through the wall.

Benny sat, and she gestured for Tremble to sit at her right hand. Smith and Argyle filed in and sat down. Benny settled Freddy's bag in her lap.

"Your men seem singularly quiet for demons." Yomra looked the agents over.

Benny smiled. "I only met them recently. They are acclimating to the demon energy."

His attention was back on her. "And yet, you got them to bind themselves to you? Well done, child."

The food appeared in the centre of the table. Plates appeared seconds later.

Benny sent a feeling of fullness to her agents. If they ate, it would be harder to pull them free of the zone. The car ride to the park had been full of briefings, but she wanted to remind them. Myths about humans in hell were based on them entering the demon zone and consuming items generated from its power. It was akin to swallowing a battery; if you survived, you had to wait until the effects of the acid wore off.

A doorway opened, and her parents staggered through it. Harcourt and Lenora Ganger looked a little worse for wear, but they were whole.

Benny inclined her head to her father. "Dad, Mom, I am glad to see you both alive."

Yomra chuckled. "You had so little trust in me? I am shocked."

"Benny, you shouldn't have come." Her mother shook her head.

"I had to, Mom. You two deserve to live your lives free and clear."

Her father was looking at her companions. "I see you have bound some men to your cause."

Tremble inclined his head. "We volunteered. She would not be safe alone."

Smith smiled. "We would not let her take the risk without us."

Argyle chuckled. "We went into it with open hearts and a single cause."

Yomra's voice was dry. "How sweet. Well, this is the closest thing to a family gathering I have ever had. What is the normal protocol?"

Harcourt Ganger raised his emerald-green head and glared at his great grandfather. "You thank us for coming and send us home."

Yomra laughed loud and long. "Oh, no. Now that I have you all here and see the obvious strength in your daughter, I believe keeping you here is the correct response."

The chairs snapped out cuffs and each and all of her great-great grandfather's guests were bound to their chairs by wrist and ankle.

The chairs elevated slightly, and Benny and her family were whisked away to a large room where there were no doors, no windows and no way out.

Benny's heart was pounding as the chair freed her. She ran to her parents and hugged them both. Her father squeezed her and then held her back with his hands on her shoulders. "A demon king, huh?"

She chuckled. "Did you expect anything else?"

Freddy barked, and Benny's mother picked her out of the bag, laughing as her face was licked frantically.

The tiny three-pound dog greeted both of the Gangers with enthusiasm.

Benny's father smiled slowly. "You brought Freddy here?"

Benny grinned back. "I brought Freddy here."

Freddy wiggled back to Benny, and Benny put her back in the purse. It was nice to have a friend who was portable now and then.

Harcourt looked at her entourage. "So, you have made it official."

Lenora laughed. "It is a binding spell. Well done, Benny."

"Thank you."

Her mother went from one man to another, hugging them in welcome. "Welcome to the family, boys."

Benny grinned when her father went over and shook the hands of her collection of demons.

Her mother whispered, "What is the plan, Benny?"

"Well, when you two were taken, I made a few calls and I chatted with Minny. She is going to start hauling us out of here in the next ten minutes."

Argyle scowled. "We have only been in the zone for three hours."

Lenora shook her head. "Time moves differently here. One hour is three in the normal world. You have been here for nine hours."

"Right. We need blood from Yomra on the way out." Benny rubbed her nose.

Lenora raised her brows in surprise. "Really?"

"Minny figured out a way to keep this from happening again. I think we should take advantage of all her hard work, don't you?"

Harcourt chuckled. "If she worked something out, we would be foolish not to. Her pedigree is nearly as convoluted as yours, Benny."

Benny grinned and turned to the agents. One by one, she kissed them and infused them with her strength. She had enough power with her to transport them all out of the demon zone, but she needed that blood to keep this from happening again.

Lenora held onto her husband and asked Benny, "What is the sign?"

"We are waiting for music and fire."

Her father gave her a serious look. "Do you have a plan for getting out of here?"

"Of course. You will know it when you see it."

Chapter Nine

It was easier to stand with Tremble holding her than by herself. His body heat sank into her, and his fey blood sparked the air with the scent of fresh leaves.

Benny stood with her eyes closed, waiting. The first note rang out, and she started to move.

"It's happening. We need to get ourselves to the street as quickly as we can."

She reached into the pocket of the bag and withdrew the scrap from the gown of the goddess of death. Benny stepped away from Argyle and wiped the wall in a wide arc. She tapped the fabric to the stone, and it shattered. She put the scrap back in her bag and lifted Freddy into her arms.

"Let's go. He will have felt that."

Their group surged out the door and headed for the dining hall. The path to the front door was clear, and the first words of Minerva's song were reaching them.

Yomra charged through the wall toward them, claws out. "You shall not leave."

Freddy growled, and Benny launched her through the air. Freddy went to full hellhound mode, three feet high and all teeth, wreathed with hellfire. She went for his leg and grabbed it, pulling him to the ground.

Argyle and Tremble held his arms down while Benny grabbed for the vial in her cleavage. Smith ushered her parents past them and toward the front doors.

It left her free to do what she needed to do.

Yomra was fighting hard, so she grabbed the knife on her thigh and cut the blue skin at the elbow. His blood was sluggish, but she got a few drops into the vial before his skin closed. She sealed the vial and reached for another.

"Hold him." she stabbed into his side and collected more

blood. "Damn, he heals fast."

Yomra was muttering at her in the demon language, and he hissed when she went in for a third strike. "This is going to have to be enough."

The third vial went into her clothing, and she looked her ancestor in the eyes. "Thank you for your help. I just need you to sleep now."

She held her hand over his nose and mouth, applying a sleep spell that should work on demons. It wouldn't hold him long, but it should give them the time they needed.

She kept her finger on his pulse, but it was his erection flagging that proved he was unconscious. She got to her feet and sheathed her knife. "Let's go."

Argyle smiled. "That was different."

Freddy resumed her more portable form, and Benny scooped her up. "Well done, Freddy."

Freddy yapped excitedly and wiggled in the bag.

Benny, Argyle and Tremble ran for the door. The other three were waiting at the door, and Minerva's song was getting stronger. A heavy rhythmic thudding was also getting closer. There were shouts of confusion and fear, which were not in keeping with the demon zone.

Harcourt opened the door, and he cracked one of the guards in the jaw while kicking the other. Benny had never seen her father in action, and she could see what Lenora saw in him.

The thundering grew louder, and down the street, a wave of horses could be seen, flanked by fire.

Tremble gasped. "Where did those come from?"

Benny blinked. "They live at our place."

The first of the horses skidded to a halt in front of her. It nudged her in the chest, and she didn't waste time. She gripped the withers of its mane and pulled herself up and onto its back. Everyone else was doing the same, and when they were all mounted, the fire gathered them up and kept them from being pursued by demons.

They galloped through the main street, past the shocked demons occasionally visible through the flickering flames.

Yomra's blood was still scalding hot in the vials. Benny shifted, but she didn't move them. The last thing she wanted was to drop the blood that she had risked her life to get.

The pale horse under her had a familiar feel. She moved easily with it as it rounded corners and sped on the straightaways. The walk that had taken hours was accomplished in a matter of minutes with flames guarding their backs.

The gate loomed in front of them, and the horses poured on the speed. She could hear Yomra's howl behind them, and she held her breath as they passed through the gateway, with fire sealing it shut.

Minerva was sitting at a picnic table, sweating with a gargoyle next to her fanning her with his wings.

"Benny, did you get it?"

Benny dismounted and pulled the vial out of her bra. "I got three of them just in case."

"Excellent. Here is the salve." Minerva put it on the table and unlatched the top. She frowned and looked around. She pointed at a tree. "You, I need a stir stick."

A twig snapped off and came flying toward her. She caught it and set it aside. Minerva withdrew an empty vial, and she jerked her head at Benny. "Okay, spill."

Benny pulled the onyx and obsidian dagger, slicing her forearm. She filled the small vial and handed both it and Yomra's to Minerva.

Her friend stirred the two bloods into the salve, and then, she handed it to Benny. "Strip and put it everywhere."

Benny looked at the agents, and they grinned. With care, she set Freddy down on the ground and put the vials in the bag next to her. She used a spell to remove her clothing before smearing the goop all over her.

The tingle of being surrounded by magic was a little weird, but Benny kept going until she had covered everything, including the soles of her feet.

Minerva held her hands out. "From the beginning of this blood to the last vessel and all beyond her, this cuts the ties and leaves the power. None may call upon the binding of bloodline, forward or back."

Benny began to tingle, and she was lifted through the air. To her surprise, she could see the same happening to her father.

Fire burst into being around her, a hot violet that didn't touch her. She was slowly lowered to the ground as the fire flickered and burned out. Her father was sitting on the grass a few feet away.

He looked over at her. "I am free." He laughed and reached for her mom, pulling her down to the grass and covering her face with kisses. "I am finally free."

Benny leaned up on her elbows and giggled. Even naked and covered with salve, she felt good.

Minerva grinned. "You can get dressed now. The fire burned off the salve and your attachment to Yomra."

Argyle was holding his hand out to her, and she smiled when he removed his shirt, draping it around her and doing up the buttons. "I think you have engaged in enough magic for one night."

She smiled and leaned against him. "I would say it was enough for a lifetime, but that is exhaustion talking."

The pale horse shivered and stamped its feet.

Tremble cleared his throat. "The horses say they will take us home. I am guessing they mean the manor."

Benny nodded. "Home sounds really good right now."

She moved away from Argyle and walked to Minerva. She hugged her. "Thank you so much for today."

"That is what friends are for. You can ask anytime. Well, any time after Wednesday. I still have that negotiation to take part in."

Benny squeezed her. "We need to go for coffee soon."

Minerva started to shiver, and soon, she was laughing. "Coffee would be great. I will call you after Wednesday."

"Please." Benny gave her a final squeeze before letting her go.

"Now, get going. You need to lock in that binding spell before dawn tomorrow."

"Or what?"

Minerva grinned. "Ask your mother."

Everyone was already mounted except for her. Freddy was sticking out of the pouch that Lenora was carrying. Benny hauled herself onto the back of the pale horse, and their herd wheeled and galloped out of the park.

Goblins were having cookouts all over the park, each fire a different colour. Benny realised that Minerva had called in a distraction that kept their tinkering with the gate to the demon zone from alarming the locals. It was about the same time that she figured out where she knew her horse from.

She leaned over the pale neck and whispered, "You are looking wonderful, Pooky."

He snorted and poured on the speed.

When she looked back, Tremble's face was glowing with excitement. There was something about this predawn ride that was getting him all worked up.

Argyle kept looking east, and when they finally thundered to a stop in front of the manor, she dismounted to open the door for him as quickly as possible. Light was stroking the ground near the drive, and he made it inside before it struck with full force.

She didn't blame him. Being blinded by the sun wasn't any fun.

Benny stood in Argyle's shirt as the rest of her family made it into the house. The horses reared, plunged and headed for the open space behind the house.

Her parents held hands and headed upstairs for some privacy. Benny padded to the kitchen and made a pot of coffee.

Freddy hopped down the stairs with a wild look in her eyes. She transformed back to human in the doorway to the kitchen. "Dude, I just saw your parents naked...again."

Benny grinned and gestured for her to take a seat next to Smith and Tremble at the counter.

"Okay, who wants breakfast?"

Three hands were raised, and Benny sighed in relief. Things were finally getting back to normal. She scrubbed her hands and started making breakfast.

Freddy got up and grabbed dishes and cutlery. "Do you feel any different?"

"Lighter, if that makes sense, like I just took off really tight underwear. I feel like I can breathe now."

She filled a sheet pan with bacon and slipped it into the oven. She crossed the room and pulled out a loaf of bread, popping four slices into the toaster before heading to the pan she was heating on the stove.

She took the orders for eggs and pulled the bacon out before buttering the toast and stacking it. Once the next batch of toast was in process, she cooked the eggs in rapid succession.

Breakfast was ready in ten minutes, and they were all sitting, sipping coffee and enjoying a well-earned silence.

There was enough bacon left for her parents when they came down, wearing robes and relaxed expressions.

Lenora came over and kissed Benny on the forehead. "How long will the binding last, Benny?"

Benny paused. "I think it is for life. I would have to check the book."

Lenora paused. "The book?"

"Yeah, it has been a while since I had to do any potion making."

Her mother nodded but looked worried. "Which flask did you use?"

It seemed like an odd question. "The one with your initials on it."

Her mother grabbed her, hauled her out of the room and whispered frantically in her ear. When her mother had briefed her as to the ramifications of that particular flask, Benny's palms got sweaty.

There was no problem as long as she consummated the union within a week of drinking the potion. If she went beyond that, they would all experience agonizing pain and be completely useless until the joining was completed. It was better to lock in the union and take the pressure off.

She steeled herself and went to fulfill a promise. "Smith, come with me."

He got to his feet with a curious expression.

She smiled. "I made you a promise."

He was at her side in an instant.

Chapter Ten

"What brought on this sudden decision?" Smith blinked as she unbuttoned his shirt. Her bedroom looked a little weird with a shifter in it but Benny was willing to get used to it.

Benny glanced up at him through her lashes. "First and foremost, I made you a promise in the demon zone. I hold to my word. Second, when you showed your demon, it was an incubus, so sex is high on your personal agenda. Third, my mother just informed me that the vessel I used for the spell was originally designed to enforce arranged marriages. It was the gag gift that they had gotten to make sure that she and my father left their studies long enough to consummate their union. If I don't have sex with all three of you in the next five days, we are all going to suffer."

She unbuckled his belt and stroked him through the fabric of his jeans.

He swallowed. "You seem to know what you are doing."

"My great grandmother is a succubus. I had a far more thorough introduction to sex talk than you could imagine." She stroked his chest and pulled his head down to her, kissing him and nipping lightly at his lips.

He growled, and she felt his hands on the shirt, peeling it away from her until his warm palms were stroking her skin.

She sighed and leaned into his hands as he familiarized himself with her skin. The shirt she wore soon hit the floor, and she was left in bare feet as he started to kiss the side of her neck.

Jessamine floated in, paused with her eyes wide and floated back out again.

Smith lifted his head and made a face. "You still taste like whatever that was you were covered with. I think a shower is in order."

She smiled. "I do believe you need to be naked to properly

shower."

He grinned. "I do believe you are correct."

She grabbed him by a belt loop and hauled him into her en-suite bathroom. The shower was large enough for four of them to stand in.

"All right, furball. Strip."

He chuckled and removed his shoes, socks, jeans and underwear. When all he was clothed in was glorious golden skin, she sighed happily.

She stepped into the shower and scrubbed her hair, her skin and, then, she asked the age-old question, "Will you wash my back?"

He was behind her with a shower puff and a sincere desire to get every inch of her squeaky clean. When her back was clean, he turned her and went over her front with attention to all the details.

When he lifted her and pinned her against the shower wall with his body, she was more than ready for him to join her in the most basic of fashions.

He rocked into her over and over. She clawed at his shoulders when she came. Finally, he roared his own satisfaction a moment before he bit her to hold her still while his hips jerked. She hissed at the pain, but it was part of mating with a shifter.

A need for knowledge of his true name, his soul name, burned with the rest of her, inside and out. The spell caster within her needed the true name for protection and she wanted to protect him. She wanted to protect all of them.

When he let her go, she stroked the wet hair out of his eyes and smiled. "Can I know your true name now?"

He blushed. "Andrew. William Eric Andrew Smith."

"Oh, those are good names for a mom to yell."

He laughed and eased her down the wall until she was on her feet. "They were indeed."

She stood, and she should have been woozy, but her bloodline was a little on the robust side. Kyria had once told her a tale of taking a regiment of warriors without once lying down, and while Benny wasn't proud of the comparison, she was ready for another lover.

She sighed and stroked his chest and neck, enjoying the feeling under her hands. "Okay, towels for everyone, and I will find a guestroom for you to crash in."

He sighed. "Will you join me?"

"Eventually. I want to join with Tremble before I get some rest though. Will that bother you?"

"If you come in smelling of sex and my partner? Surprisingly no." He frowned as if the thought didn't disgust him. The confusion that crossed his face was adorable.

She laughed. "That is the binding spell. It makes you want to do what is best for everyone in the union. Even the other guys."

He wrapped her in a towel and draped another around his hips. He cuddled her against him as they walked back into her bedroom. He sat on the chest at the end of her bed and pulled her onto his lap, inhaling and exhaling against her neck. Being with her seemed to relieve tension in him, so she leaned against him and enjoyed the closeness with her mate.

William Eric Andrew Smith. She wondered what Tremble's name actually was.

An hour later, Andrew was tucked into a guest bedroom, and he was breathing evenly. Demon shifting was exhausting, and it had been his first time. He would sleep for hours.

Sighing softly, she closed the door and went down the hall, searching for Tremble. Her sundress swished around her calves with every move and it felt loud in the silence.

He wasn't upstairs, so she went downstairs and found him in the library talking softly with her father and looking at some of the demon texts.

Her father looked up and smiled. "Benny, you look rested."

She winked. "Close enough."

He walked away from the elf who was raptly poring over the text, and he came over to give her a hug. "Thanks for coming for us, Benny."

"You would have done it for me, Dad. Have you talked to Grandpa yet?"

"I did. He mentioned that he felt something was different. Kyria has not been in touch with him yet, but he feels she will be if she can get out of the zone."

Benny blinked. "Oh, right. She used to leave, propelled by Yomra."

Harcourt shrugged. "She will find a way. She always does."

She leaned back in his arms. "Are you less green?"

He winked. "I am. I feel more like my old self. My father is experiencing the same thing."

Her grandfather had the curled horns of the demon scholar, the same as Tremble did when he was wearing his demon. Well, she supposed it was when he was wearing *her* demon, but it was his manifestation.

"I am glad. I hope that this doesn't screw me up with the XIA. They had just accepted that I was a demon blood with self-control. What are they going to think when I let them know that I have cut our family loose from the influence of the king of our bloodline?"

Tremble looked up from the book and stared at her with vivid dark rainbow eyes with slit pupils. "Don't tell them."

She left her dad and wandered over to him. "Why not?"

"They will re-evaluate you and demand the spell that was used to release you. I do not feel that the spell should fall into the hands of someone who has not been raised with the self-control that your family has embedded into you." He gave her a solemn look.

She blinked. "I get the feeling that you guys are going to be tested for demon influence a little more frequently."

He smiled slowly. "Unless they can prove exposure to a new demon, they have no grounds for testing us."

He closed his book and moved in on her.

Her father cleared his throat. "I will go and check on your mother and Freddy."

Benny was focused on the elf that was crowding her back to the study table. "Uh, Tremble..."

He nuzzled his cheek against hers, whispering, "Yes, Benny?"

"What is your true name?"

He moved his lips and exhaled his name against her mouth. "Gelendor. Gelendor Hurias Tremble. There are a few more names but those are the important ones."

She didn't have a chance to engage in witty banter. He kissed her and lifted her to the surface of the table. He pushed her dress up over her knees and stepped between them while he undid the buttons holding the front of the sundress closed.

When his hand slipped inside her dress and his long fingers closed over her breast, she arched into his palm. His other hand moved between her thighs, and she groaned when he slid two fingers into her, followed by a third a moment later. She was rapidly approaching orgasm when he pulled his fingers free and left her breast so that he could work at the closure of his jeans.

When his cock was free, he pressed her flat to the desk and nudged against her. He planted his hands on the table next to her and slowly thrust forward. When she slid back, he grinned and draped her calves over his forearms while he gripped her hips.

Benny gasped when he finally went as deep as he could, and she reached up to grip his arms as he started to move inside her.

His face was focused, but he was watching her. When she felt a curl of pleasure, he angled his hips and repeated the inner caress. Every time she gasped, he echoed the motion that had made her twitch. It was strange to be analysed while having sex, but she was swept up toward release in a few sweaty minutes. She thought it would soon be over, but Gelendor kept her on the edge of release until she was thrashing on the table and hissing at him. She wanted to wrap her legs around him, but he was keeping her precisely where he wanted her.

Benny concentrated and clasped him with her inner muscles to trigger his own orgasm, but her elf simply paused before resuming the slow, even strokes that kept her on the edge.

When she heard herself begging, he bent forward and kissed her, pushing her legs back and grinding against her with slow circles of his hips that had her shrieking as the pulse of release took over.

The table trembled as he pounded into her rapidly until he held himself against her, jerking and shaking as he came.

He released her legs and lowered himself to her, giving her a sweet kiss.

Benny lifted her head and returned the gesture of affection.

He lifted his head and smiled. "I look forward to taking my time with you."

Benny stroked his pale hair away from his face and tucked it behind his pointed ear. "I look forward to that, too. Thank you for taking the hint."

"There is no reason for us to delay this. We agreed to join with you before we drank the potion, we agreed to work with you at the XIA and we testified that you had not used your demon nature to influence us. Agreeing to have sex with you was implied." He grinned.

She chuckled and ran her hands over his shirt. "Next time, no clothing."

"Deal. And perhaps, I shouldn't have started this in front of your father."

She laughed. "I feel a certain amount of smug revenge. I have had to leave this very room many times for the same reason."

He brushed his lips against her cheek. "Your father has told me that they were hoping for this general outcome, though not specifically one that involved you risking your life."

She arched her hips against him, feeling the delightful presence still inside her. "They hoped for this?"

"For you linking with all three of us. Your pedigree has a number of species that find fidelity a bit awkward. Since we each represent a different branch of magic, it is sensible that you have multiple mates, and each of us has already received release from their own people in regards to social obligation. We were possibly the best choice of agents that you could have been with."

Benny chuckled and slid her fingers through his hair. "I think that is just my luck."

"Then, I am glad for your luck." He kissed her again and slowly rocked against her. It was a hypnotic feeling that she wanted to continue, so she wrapped her legs around him and let her senses take over.

She still had hours before Argyle would be awake enough to mate with, so why not spend some time bonding with another of her partners?

Chapter Eleven

After another meal with her family and Freddy had headed home, Benny crept into Argyle's room two hours before sunset.

She slipped out of her dress and crawled into bed with Argyle, nestling against his cool skin and idly playing with his crimson hair until she was relaxed enough to nap up against him.

Benny woke when cool lips moved over her neck, her shoulder and nipped at her breasts.

She grumbled and heard him laugh as he rolled her to her back and wove his fingers with hers as he continued to taste her. She whimpered when he neared her pussy and thanked foresight for taking a flame bath earlier. When his tongue stroked her, she gritted her teeth and whined.

She felt the cold press of his teeth against her while he lapped at her folds and delved inside. Her breath left her in rapid gasps as his temperature affected her in a way she hadn't anticipated. Most of her lovers to date had been warm blooded and hot when she got them naked. Argyle had the temperature of cool marble, and she wanted to feel him inside her.

His tongue was torture, his fingers slid along hers, caressing and binding at the same time. Her breathing increased in pitch, and she tensed against him, trying to push herself over the edge.

The cool slide of his tongue went on and on. He flicked at her clit and then burrowed himself inside her with gleeful enthusiasm.

When she was arched against him and her breath was caught in short pants, he moved his head and bit her inner thigh. The sharp prick of pain made her scream, but it also set her free. A rush of fire ran through her veins, and Argyle growled and released her limb before he slid over her and sank his cock in to the hilt.

She met him thrust for thrust. To her shock, she felt her teeth sharpening. His eyes glowed, and she leaned up to sink her teeth into his shoulder a moment before he did the same.

She felt a second wave of spasms beginning in her core, gripping him and causing her limbs to clench as she held on and tasted blood. He released her in what she could only imagine was surprise.

She snarled, released him and rolled him to his back with a burst of strength, riding him hard until he gripped her hips and held her to him while he quivered with tension.

His teeth were clenched, his neck distended, and he held her tight for close to a minute before he slowly relaxed.

She flexed her thighs and slid her hands up his chest until she was lying on him with her head on his shoulder. He wrapped his arms around her and stroked the sweaty curve of her back.

"I didn't get the chance, what is your true name?"

"Cairbre. My name is James Cairbre Argyle."

She blinked and leaned up on him. "Charioteer?"

He laughed. "Yes. How did you know?"

"I have a lot of old relatives who are still around today. I have had to take five ancient languages via tutors and have gotten three via spellcasting."

He smoothed his hand down her spine. "So, you are well educated."

"As long as you don't count an actual degree, yes. If you do, I graduated high school."

"Why didn't you complete college?"

She wrinkled her nose. "There was a demon-related incident and the XIA was cracking down on scanning for demons. I didn't have enough control at the time to hide that energy. It was stay home and study or get arrested and dumped into the zone."

"What did the assessors say about you when you finished your training?"

Benny smiled; he was the first one to really ask. "I was given a few bits of information. The first was that if I didn't display any demon characteristics, I would be able to act as the first trained mage on a team. The second was that because of my obviously slutty nature—being a demon and all—that I would be allowed to have intimate relations with my coworkers."

His hand paused. "You are joking."

"Nope. I am allowed to mess around with you and you with me. No one will bat an eye, and there will be no repercussions. We won't have to hide."

He wasn't breathing, but he chuckled. "That is a relief. Work will be work, but it is nice to know that I can grab you the moment the shift is over."

"Sure, as long as you are faster than Smith and Tremble." She chuckled. She stretched. "And with that, I need to go and get some rest."

"You can sleep here."

She shook her head. "No, you are getting up, and I need to be in my own bed."

He sighed. "True. Ah, well. Soon, we will be on the same schedule."

She nuzzled her cheek against him. "I look forward to it."

She gave herself a dozen more contented heartbeats before she levered herself up. "Okay. I have to drag myself to my room. You need to pry Tremble away from the texts. I had no idea he was such a fan of reading."

Argyle moved out from under her, and she tumbled across the bed. It was effective.

"You don't know any of us very well. That will change, but it will be a strange process. Just as I learned about your education restrictions today, we will continue to learn about each other as time marches on." Argyle got up and headed for the shower.

Benny ran the cleansing fire over her skin again, slipped on her dress and left Argyle's room to make her way down the hall.

Her own room looked horribly inviting, and when she entered it and a sleepy Smith rolled over, she closed the door, shucked off her sundress and crawled into bed with Smith curled around her. He tucked her against his body and breathed her in as she slowly relaxed in his arms.

Lions weren't supposed to purr, but a soothing rumble was coming from Smith. She was out in under two minutes.

Smith joined the others downstairs while Lenora Ganger made

dinner with her husband's help.

Argyle looked at him. "She is asleep?"

He nodded. "She is. You two wore her out."

Argyle and Tremble shrugged.

Smith asked Lenora, "Did that satisfy the spell?"

She set a casserole of cheesy potatoes on the table. "It should have. You won't know for sure until next Sunday. Damn. You guys don't have to work tomorrow, do you?"

Argyle shook his head. "We are waiting to be authorised to return to duty. It could be tomorrow, it could be in two weeks."

Tremble cocked his head. "I hope it is later. We need to find somewhere to live. She can't run from one of our homes to the next."

Harcourt cleared his throat. "Lenora and I have already done something about that. The dower house is being expanded and renovated for all four of you to live there. Well, five if you count Jessamine."

Smith blinked. "You are serious?"

The demon shrugged. "As serious as I can be. It should be done by the end of the week."

Smith sniffed. "You are losing your demon scent. It is fading."

Lenora smiled. "It isn't fading; he is just gaining control again. He hasn't had that control since I..."

Harcourt lifted her hand to his lips. "It is a good thing, love. You are here, and I am more me than I have been since you were in hospital."

Smith could see the love between the two, and he admired the example that they had set for Benny. She had gotten used to the forms love could take and chosen to embrace the ones that were not parasitic but built up the partner. He did not doubt that she had seen far more than any child would want to, but she had come through it strong and loving with a great sense of humour.

Tremble asked, "How did she come by the name Beneficia?"

Argyle smiled, "In my community, it is the name of an assassin."

Lenora smiled slowly. "It is my mother's name, and she is still a vampire killer for hire."

If Argyle could have paled any more, he would have. "So, that is Benny's grandmother on your side?"

Lenora smiled. "She is. My grandmother, Sabina, was near to term when she was crushed by a carriage, and she was offered a chance at life in the darkness. My grandfather made her take the offer; he could not bear to watch the life leave her."

Smith looked at her with wide eyes. "Her husband was a vampire?"

"No. Lord Hearther was the vampire that gave her life. She healed and went into labour. My grandfather was a mage who had many friends across many species. He called upon the vampire; my grandmother transformed and had my mother."

Argyle was shaking. "So, you mean to say that I have been bonded to the granddaughter of the Hunting Shadow?"

Lenora smiled. "Do they still call her that? I will have to let my father know. He thought it would blow over after a century or so."

Tremble smiled and tried to change the fixation of Benny's namesake. "So, who is Beneficia's husband?"

Harcourt chuckled. "Welgainer Mills, the forest lord."

Tremble put his head on the desk. "I should not have asked."

Smith chuckled. "Any shifters I should get nervous about?"

Harcourt shook his head. "My mother has passed. She was Lettice Norington Ganger."

Smith swallowed. "The Great Wolf. The one who created a lasting peace between all the clans, packs and prides on this half of the continent. We are so outclassed."

Harcourt shrugged. "You know that Benny comes from exceptional bloodlines. You don't even want to know how extensive her medical education is."

From his head down on the table, Tremble mumbled. "I think I can guess."

Her parents stood proudly.

Smith could see the pride radiating from them. They were the product of a brilliant and terrible family, and they had created a brilliant and dangerous daughter. And he was one of three men who had basically married her. *Ah, hell.*

Benny woke up after two hours of sleep. Her body wanted to be up in the middle of the night, and she blamed Argyle.

She muttered to herself, brushed her hair and put on jeans and a t-shirt, running around barefoot was one of the bonuses to being home.

She brushed her teeth carefully. Blood in the gums was never pleasant to wake up to.

When she was clean and presentable, she headed downstairs. It smelled like meatloaf and cheesy potatoes.

Everyone was eating when she came in, and she quickly took a seat and started filling her plate.

Tremble smiled sheepishly. "Sorry for not waiting for you."

She scooped up some green beans and winked. "This isn't the first meal I have been late for, and it isn't the last. When you get into a spell, you can't stop just because dinner is ready. Well, you can, but it blows up in your face and one of your eyes glow." She chuckled.

Lenora laughed and rubbed Benny's shoulder. "It was terrible and funny at the same time. She nearly blew half her head off and her hair was standing straight up. It was a good thing that demons heal fast. In about an hour, she was fine except for the eye. She got control over it about a month later. It showed up on picture day."

Smith was amused. "How old were you?"

"Nine. I was trying to make a potion to make my spell book glow in the dark so I could work past my bedtime."

Tremble stared. "And you blew your head up?"

"I wanted to peek into the cauldron even though it said it needed to be covered for an hour. Apparently, the part that made it glow was also explosive." She shrugged and finished grabbing for food.

Benny ate with a ferocious appetite, and the guys looked at her uneasily. She chuckled and sipped at her water glass. "You have seen me eat tacos. How is this different?"

Argyle pointed out, "You bit down so hard, you bent your cutlery."

She set down the fork, and she didn't see anything. With a blush, she grabbed the knife and straightened it. "Sorry. I really like meatloaf."

Lenora smiled. "I know, punkin."

Benny finished her food and sighed. She sipped at her water

and looked at her mates. "What would you like to do this evening?"

Argyle looked at her with a smile. "I would like to see the portrait gallery. You apparently have some ancestors I have only heard of in myth and legend."

She looked at her mom. "Do you want help washing the dishes?"

Her dad winked. "I will help her."

There was going to be more than dishes worked on in the kitchen, so Benny bolted to her feet. "Portrait gallery. Right. Come with me, guys."

They were just about around the corner when her mother moaned.

Benny blushed and kept moving. "Damn. Not fast enough."

Chapter Twelve

The double doors pulled open easily, and she stepped forward, triggering the lights.

Argyle was standing next to her, and he stared at the endless line of portraits with wide eyes. "How long does this go back?"

"We start with the most recent and then head back at least five generations. There are more after that, but most of them have passed on."

Smith stared at her. "Most of them? There are some still alive?"

She nodded. "Oh, yeah. I have some going back far past the first wave."

The men looked at her, and she sighed. "What?"

Smith cleared his throat. "We are just wondering what we add to the union. You have an extremely impressive bloodline."

Benny pinched the bridge of her nose. "I am not my parents, my grandparents or my great grandparents. Extrapolate that as far back as you like. I am me, and my instincts told me that you guys are the ones for me. I know the plural is a little off putting, but I know what I need, and I need you, all of you."

She was engulfed in a group hug, and instead of it being smothering, they surrounded her so that she was in the centre of the triangle.

It was the best place she could have thought to be, and she hadn't even known it existed seconds before.

When they let her out, she kissed each of them softly, and then, she inhaled. "Right. Well, you have met my parents. This is the after picture."

She pointed at the image of her father standing behind and holding her mother, all green with his head spikes. The precious nature of their connection was shown in her hands over his and the gentle manner in which he cradled her.

Benny sniffled. "This one always gets me. It is so sweet."

Argyle put his arm around her shoulders, and Smith's was around her waist. Tremble produced a handkerchief.

She blotted at her eyes and smiled. "Right. Sorry. The rest don't make me so weepy."

She stepped with her group to the next picture. "This is them before the change. Oh and that is me."

Smith whispered, "How old were you?"

"I was six when this was done. Mom and Dad had to hold me in that position, but you can tell I wanted to be somewhere else." She looked at little Benny and the hands on her shoulders. One elegant and feminine, one heavier with ink stains.

Tremble smiled. "You were adorable. I have a niece that glares at the camera like that."

Benny filed that away. "I hadn't thought to ask. What will your families think about this?"

Argyle shrugged. "My family is no longer speaking to me, though they do still exist. My clan will eagerly embrace a relationship with your family."

Smith nodded. "I feel certain that my pride will as well. I have three sisters, one of whom is married to the alpha."

Benny blinked. "Oh. Nieces or nephews?"

"Two of each." He grinned. "Hey, you are an aunty."

Benny swayed. She had never considered that she was gaining family aside from the guys.

She looked to Tremble. "You?"

"One sister, one brother. My sister has a daughter and that is the niece I was referring to."

She exhaled. "I am going to need birthdays and preferences for gifts."

They all grinned at her.

She asked, "What?"

Smith chuckled. "You treat family very seriously."

"Of course I do." She straightened her shoulders and turned to the next portrait.

"This is my grandfather Zephyr with his wife, Lettice. Zephyr was half demon, but he could flick back and forth fairly easily. And that is my wee little dad standing there with the serious face. Grandpa is a scholar demon, like you were, Tremble."

The men paused, and she kept going. "Lettice was born a wolf shifter, which was weird because neither of her parents were wolves, but we will get to them later."

Tremble asked, "Pardon me, but did you say I was a scholar demon?"

She stepped to the next portrait. "Yup. You were a scholar, Smith was an incubus and Argyle was a warrior. The horns I was wearing marked me as a high king if I went to the trouble of killing Yomra."

Tremble smiled. "You may have gotten those from Welgainer. I have heard he has an incredible rack of horns when he chooses to show them."

"Funny you should mention him." She pointed to the portrait. "Welgainer and his lovely wife, the dhampir, Beneficia."

Argyle went up to it and looked from Benny to the portrait and back again. "You have her eyes."

"So I have been told. The next portrait has my mom as a little girl."

The men were startled into laughing when they saw Lenora sitting in the antlers of her father's head looking every inch the forest god with a little girl perched on his head.

Beneficia was holding her husband's arm, and they were all laughing. Benny was a little sad that grandmother was wearing deadly weapons, even in the family moment. No wonder she was so stressed out.

"Did she always wear the silver blades?" Argyle asked with genuine curiosity.

"Yeah. She still does. She is not a lady you want to startle." Benny chuckled. "She still looks like that, by the way. She hasn't aged."

He blinked. "I look forward to meeting her one day."

"You will. We have regular family gatherings and even aim for a variety of holidays. Most of the parties are held here at the manor, but if there are too many attendees, we rent out *Ritual Space*."

Tremble asked, "Is that place still around?"

Benny nodded and moved down the gallery. "It is. Neadra Baxter is still the proprietor, and she gives our family preferential treatment. We put in way more magic than we take."

She paused in front of her father's grandparents. "This is Alberta and Andrew Norington. She had no powers, and he was a mage multi-shifter. She was my true one part human. Her and Haggard Mills." She wrinkled her nose. "He is down there a little further."

Tremble raised an eyebrow, "You only have the two humans?"

"Powerless ones, yes. The rest are all mages."

She smiled at her great grandparents. "They were Lettice's parents. Both have passed on, without remaining behind. They left the world together."

The guys were silent as she walked to the next portrait. They looked at the image of Kyria and her mate with surprise.

Smith asked, "Why is she here?"

"She is my great grandparent and my dad's grandmother. Of course she is here."

"She tried to strip you of your soul," He was obviously struggling to understand it.

"But she was a good woman while I was growing up and that was what helped shape me into the very accepting soul that I am today. She taught me about what love could withstand and how there comes a time to surrender to fate." Benny smiled fondly at her mirror image.

She cleared her throat. "Kyria's mate, Milton Ganger, was a mage and alchemist. He lived to the old age of ninety-eight. She was forced to return to the demon zone when he died, but she kept in contact with her son and his son as much as she could. She couldn't stay in the human world if she wasn't bound to a mage."

She twisted her lips. "We don't have a portrait of her parents. I have no idea who produced her, aside from the obvious."

They continued through the portraits that included a pixie, a frost giant, Sabina the vampire with her husband the mage.

Tremble asked, "These go back centuries. How did you get them all?"

Benny smiled. "A spirit painter. This is my gallery. My parents each have their own. They thought it was important to know what I had come from and how blended my history was. There are books that are filled with stories that my parents had a soul copyist create. The history of everything in my veins is in this room."

Tremble cocked his head. "Where are the books?"

She laughed. "In the shadows near the door. They build up with my own activities, so you had better watch the dates on the books."

They finished with the portraits and entered the statue gallery.

Smith smiled at the woman sporting stripes in the arms of a man covered with designs etched into his skin.

"Why did they become statues?"

"They go back over a thousand years. Their names are etched in the base of the statuary. Their blood may be in my veins, but they don't come when we call. They still deserve to be acknowledged." She shrugged.

Argyle looked through the statues and came to a halt. "I know this woman."

Benny followed him through the statues and paused in front of the statue. "Ah, her. She is my godmother, Giltine. Lithuanian snake goddess of death, mistress of the poison of the dead."

Smith cocked his head. "Minerva gave you a scrap of Giltine's gown."

"She did. It opened the doors in the demon zone. Only something that was ancient power could work in the zone. Giltine has been generous with her assistance before. I can only imagine that Minerva got the scrap via polite and honourable means."

She bowed to the statue with her hand over her heart. "Her gift saved seven lives that will eventually come into her embrace."

The stone glowed softly in acknowledgement. Benny sighed in relief. She had called upon her godmother before on a day she didn't like to think about, but it was not something she would ever take for granted. Goddesses did not like to be taken for granted.

The men must have caught onto her mood, because they completed their examination of the statues and then requested that they return to the daylight.

Benny knew a good idea when she heard it, and they walked back past all the generations that led up to her existence and out the doors.

The moment they exited the gallery, her phone rang and she dug it out of her pocket.

Her aunt's number was displayed, and she blinked. "Excuse me while I take this call."

"Hello? Aunty? Just a moment."

Benny walked with her guys to the den and gestured for them to have a seat. She threw a silence spell around her and suddenly remembered why her aunt was calling. *Oh, hell.*

Chapter Thirteen

Benny had completely forgotten about the anniversary party until her aunt Sabina called her and warned her that arrangements were underway.

The ruby anniversary was a big one, and Benny couldn't believe that it had slipped her mind.

"Benny, the entire family knows that you have been busy. This is the beginning of your life and the celebration of theirs. We will handle everything, and you just have to show up with those three agents of yours."

Benny laughed. "Of course, Aunt Sabina. No sampling though. They are mine."

"Ever since Edgar died, I have kept my sampling to the necessary." Her aunt chuckled.

"Where are you now?"

"Over in Bright Larch, doing some clan business."

Benny was flailing around for a notepad with one hand while pinning the phone to her ear with the other. "What kind of clan business?"

"Oh, just touching base with the local king. Gaining permission to pass through his lands. I should be there in a few days. The caterer is booked, music, flowers, wine, beer and all the alternative refreshments are arranged. You just need to keep the secret and prepare to sing."

Benny blinked. "Sing?"

"We talked about this. You were going to sing a tribute to their relationship and their bond as a couple with you as part of their family."

"Right. Right. I wrote the poem, I just haven't set it to music yet. I have a few ideas and will get them hammered out by the party."

Her aunt laughed in low and throaty tones. "You will do fine,

Benny. Beneficia has even arranged leave to come in for the party. It is looking like the majority of your living family will be there."

"Excellent. I look forward to seeing them all. Talking through the portraits just isn't satisfying. I need hugs." Benny grinned.

She had left a small detail out of her tour of the gallery. Talking to her ancestors who were willing to make the connection could most easily be accomplished via the portraits. A phone worked just as well for the living ones, but the dead ones were trickier.

She was delighted that Beneficia was coming to the party. Being the deadliest dhampir in existence, she required special writs to travel from one state to the next. An entire line of vampire kings had to sign off on her travel, and it took a bit of effort. That she was making the effort for her daughter was sweet. She was a loving mother, but she was also tremendously fun at parties.

"I will contact Neadra to confirm *Ritual Space* for the event." Benny crossed her fingers.

"Good. Confirm the address with me, and I will have all the arrangements set. We are running out of time, child. Call Neadra and call me back. The sooner it is arranged, the sooner we can relax."

"Yes, Aunty." Benny blushed.

"So, when will I meet these young men of yours?"

"At the party, but I should warn you that we have already been bound together. Even if you are not a fan of them, I am keeping them all."

Sabina paused. "I see. Well, when are you going to hold your reception?"

"Um, we are going to have to finalize it with all of their clans, prides and folk."

"Fine, but the moment you have locked it all in, I want to hold a party for you. Set a date for the next full moon. Hang on."

Benny heard pages flipping. Her great grandmother still liked the feel of paper.

"Aha! You have eight weeks. The next blue moon. I think it will be appropriate, and it will give you plenty of time to get into your new job."

"How did you know about that?"

"I talked to your mother a few days ago." Sabina chuckled. "Okay, go make that call. I would do it, but Neadra doesn't like vampires."

"Right. I will call you soon, Aunty."

She disconnected the call and waved off the wall of silence.

"Gentlemen, I am about to have my ass handed to me by my aunty." She wrinkled her nose and headed over to the couch, settling between Smith and Tremble.

She scrolled through her contacts until she found the number she wanted. Wincing, she connected the call.

To her relief, the call was answered immediately. "Hello, Benny."

"Neadra, I have an emergency and I need to rent some space."

The low chuckle was extremely amused. "How much?"

"What do you have available for Saturday night?"

"Shockingly enough, it is wide open. You can have the whole place."

Benny blinked. "I will take it. Do you need a deposit or are you content to take my word."

"Do we need transport access available?"

"Please, beginning an hour before sundown until an hour after dawn. Caterers, tents and a sound license please."

"Done. Call me with the details in the morning. I was just on my way to bed."

"Thanks, Neadra, you are a life saver."

"Enjoy it. You lucked out. I just had a rash of cancellations with non-refundable deposits. With your booking, I am in a delightful mood."

Benny grinned. "Thanks again. I will get the details for the caterers and have it faxed to you in the morning."

"Anything for your parents, dear. I know what time of year it is. Good night, Benny."

The line went dead and Benny blinked at her phone for a moment before tucking it into her bra. "That turned out incredibly well."

"You are planning a party?" Argyle was warming his hands by the fire.

"We are. My parents have been together for nearly fifty

years. We normally have a party here for their anniversary, but now, we are going to head out to *Ritual Space* and run around for a night. We will have the entire place to ourselves, so all family is invited no matter how freaky." She grinned.

"Are we invited as well?" Smith smiled a little shyly.

She leaned over and kissed him. "Of course. You are all expected to be there. I will send you the invitations sometime tomorrow...or later today. I am a little muddled right now."

Tremble chuckled. "Since Smith got a personal invitation, it is only fair that you will have to invite me and Argyle the same way."

She pressed her forehead to Smith's and rubbed back and forth for a moment before flipping back and landing in Tremble's lap. His kiss was rough, he held her hair and she responded for a moment before her reaction ceased his incursion.

Benny glared at him and licked her lips. "Will you attend my parents' anniversary surprise party?"

He inclined his head. "I will."

She sighed and boosted herself off his lap, sashaying over to Argyle. "Argyle?"

He grinned. "Yes?"

"Would you attend my parents' anniversary surprise party?"

She placed her hands on his chest and slid up the cool surface of his shirt, even with the fire, he was still cold.

She loved the combination of heat and cold as she went up on her toes and pulled his head down. His lips were soft marble, and she shivered against him. They kissed slowly and softly for several minutes before Smith growled low in his throat.

She leaned back and blinked as she waited.

"Of course I will join you. I will file a request for the night off as soon as you let me go."

Smith and Tremble were already on their phones.

She sighed and let him go.

Benny fished her phone out of her bra, "Fine, you do that and I will call my Aunty Sabina."

Argyle stiffened. "I thought Sabina was your great grandmother."

"She is; she just prefers to be called Aunty, as does Beneficia." She hit her aunty's number and waited while it rang.

Sabina was a vampire; she would be awake.

"Hello?"

"Aunty Sabina, it's Benny. I have booked *Ritual Space* for Saturday night, and she is expecting a fax with the details. Transports will be allowed beginning one hour before sunset and continue to be accessible until one hour after dawn. She is getting the noise waiver, so we are good. We have the entire facility."

"How did you manage that with such short notice? I am not complaining, I am just amazed."

"It was pure luck." Something sparked in her mind about luck, and her eyes went wide.

"Right. Well, hooray for luck. Okay, I will fax her the information, and she can call me after sundown. I am emailing you a copy as well, so check it out and see if I missed anything. Just make sure to have the song ready."

"Yes, Aunty. All the invitations are out?"

"They are. You know the spell?"

Benny smiled. "I do. I will get to it as soon as I hang up."

"Thanks, pet. It was something I could never grasp after Beneficia arrived."

"No problem. Have a good night."

Sabina groaned. "Unlikely. I have to negotiate for possession of a few thralls. They went to a party and the king decided not to release them. My job is so glamorous."

"And you do it well. Good night, Aunty."

"Good night, Benny. See you in a few days."

Benny hung up and sighed.

Her guys beamed at her.

Smith chortled. "We all got the week and weekend off. I have no idea how we got so lucky."

Benny sighed. "I think we have Minerva to thank for that."

They looked at her in surprise.

"She gave us a thousand doses of luck in the binding spell. I think it has officially kicked in, though the first sign may have been the piece of Giltine's robe. The odds of her having that were astronomical."

Tremble put his phone away and walked up to her, wrapping her in his arms. "We are feeling exceptionally lucky, and this is enough proof that you are possessed of a powerful magic."

She sighed and rested her head on his chest. "And it is all

human mage magic, so there will not be issues with you three being tainted by demon magic again."

Tremble chuckled. "They cannot test us for that for another year."

Instead of cuddling her, he spun her away from him and then back.

She went into the patterns of dance on instinct. "Why are we dancing?"

To her surprise, Smith took her hand and twirled her expertly. "If I am not mistaking your invitation, we are going to a party, and I don't think any of us will dance with anyone else."

She let Argyle take her for a spin after that, and then, she stepped back. "I have to write an invitation with addresses and details."

They sighed as one.

She went to the desk in the corner and opened a piece of parchment. The address was in her phone, and she prepared a quill, selected the proper ink and started to work the letters onto the parchment. She was careful with the dates and the spelling of the address. When she had it down and completed, she verified the spelling twice before chanting to wake the ink. When the ink lifted, she leaned in and blew softly on it. The words disappeared with her breath, and they were being printed on every invitation that was sent by Sabina.

When it was done, she capped the ink, put away the parchment and took the quill to the fire. When it flared blue, she relaxed.

Tremble was watching with fascination. "You use the magic so easily."

She shrugged. "I have learned it along with learning to walk. It is my nature."

"I thought you would have more fey magic."

She smiled. "I have that too, but I don't use it in the house. I would blow the roof off by accident. My grandfather taught me, and he is a little heavy handed with the natural powers. I was not taught subtlety."

Smith looked a little unsure. "Is there a chance that I can go for a run?"

She blinked. "Damn. I am sorry. Of course. Come this way."

Benny led them out of the den and to the back of the house,

past the kitchen and out to the grounds. The manicured lawns rolled, and Smith stripped rapidly, shifting into a stunningly proportioned lion that gambolled over the green before dashing to the left.

Benny turned to the other two. "Care to join me on the terrace? We can wait until he finishes chasing the horses."

Argyle grimaced. "Please pardon me, but I need to go and feed."

"Can you drink from me?"

His eyes glowed hotly. "I would love to, but I do not wish to weaken you."

"I am sure you will not take more than you need. You are a given vampire, you don't need much."

He nodded slowly as if afraid she would change her mind. He settled on a chair, and Tremble watched over them as she sat in the vampire's lap.

Argyle held her carefully, and he lifted her forearm to his lips. He licked the skin slowly, and she shivered. When he bit, she felt only a surge of heat and nothing more.

The heat began to build with every stroke of his tongue and each sucking swallow. She was shaking in his embrace, his hand behind her back supported her and the other kept her hand to his lips while he drank.

He drank for ten minutes or so, and then, he carefully licked her punctures closed. If Tremble hadn't been there, she would have stripped naked and jumped him after the first bite.

Her blood was singing, and she was lightheaded. When Argyle looked down at her, she grinned and kissed him, tasting her blood in his mouth.

She sighed when they parted. A moment later, she bolted to her feet at the sight of a lion being chased across the meadow by a herd of horses who looked distinctly unimpressed with the newcomer.

Tremble leaned against the railing. "You know what they are, don't you?"

"The horses and Pooky? Yeah. They are the Wild Hunt. Ancient steeds of the fey, and in alternate mythologies, they are the bearers of the dead." She grinned at his surprise.

"Tremble, my car can change into a van and then into a horsy. I put that together already. Dang, I think I should head down there and calm things down."

With the pursuit heading back in the other direction, she stepped out into the path of the stampede.

Saving one's mate from a herd of horses because he tried to chase them didn't rank high on her dignity metre. The moment the lion passed her, she stepped out, and the herd split, thundering around her and Smith. She could feel his breath on her neck, and she glanced back at him. "You just had to try and grab them, didn't you?"

He rumbled and his tail lashed from side to side. To see a goofy and pleased expression on his features melted her heart. She stroked his nose and rubbed his forehead. "Having fun?"

He rumbled again and nuzzled her with his huge head. Argyle and Tremble came toward them, and she leaned against Smith's huge skull.

They stood around and scratched him behind his ears and under the thick waves of his mane for close to an hour. Smith was boneless with happiness when they finally decided to return to the house. Dawn was approaching and an uneventful sleep was definitely earned.

Chapter Fourteen

Benny woke up smooshed between Smith and Tremble. She didn't remember getting into bed with either of them, but here they were.

She levered herself up and out from between them. Tremble rolled to one side and clutched at his pillow while Smith frowned. With some contortions, she left the bed and headed to the bathroom to attend the call of nature and take a proper shower.

She was unsurprised to feel a pair of hands on her in the shower, but she was taken aback when she turned to see Argyle soaping her back. "Good afternoon."

He pressed a kiss to her shoulder. "Good morning. For some reason, I am wide awake this morning."

She whispered, "What time is it?"

"Eleven in the morning." He was running his hands over her and getting the soap into all the nooks and crannies that had seen so much action the day before.

"Ah. I thought it was closer to four."

He chuckled and ran his hands over all of her curves. "No. You must have some rejuvenating properties in your blood."

"I probably do. There are a lot of extremely long lifespans in my family."

He bent forward and pressed his lips to her neck. She arched back into the shower spray, and his cool mouth mixed with the hot water to make her shiver.

His hand worked between her thighs, and the hot spray, cold skin and precise touch of his hand had her gasping under the flow of the water until she bit her lip and clutched at him with her nails in his shoulders as she enjoyed her first climax of the day.

Dazed, she didn't move when he turned off the water and helped her out of the shower. She was still focused on her swimming senses. He tucked a towel around her, and she wrapped her hands behind his neck, pulling him in for a kiss and playing with his hair. "I do love your hair colour."

He chuckled. "I guessed as much. You play with it every time you are in touching distance, which is not as often as I would like, but that is something that will change as we settle down. I do love the way you taste."

She blinked. "Well, it is probably all the magic."

Argyle whispered in her ear, "That wasn't what I was referring to."

Heat seared her cheeks, and she cleared her throat. "How did you hear I was up, anyway?"

"Jessamine and I were working on the floor plan of the new house. She told me that you were up, and I can move quickly when I need to, though slow is my preferred pace." He winked.

Her blush didn't show any signs of slowing.

Smith and Tremble sat up when they came into the room.

Argyle sighed. "Well, I am going to have to leave you."

She blinked. "What?"

He laughed. "I need clothing, a toothbrush, my laptop. Jessamine said that the house is working on one large bedroom for all of us, but that won't provide me with what I need." He smirked. "Lenora did provide me with a set of sunglasses that will keep the light from blinding me, so I should be good to go."

Smith got up and pulled on his jeans. "Can you take me by my place?"

Tremble nodded. "Me as well. I would like to be back here for dinner."

Argyle nodded. "Come on. Get dressed. I will meet you downstairs."

Benny felt left out, but then, she had all of her stuff around her.

She wandered to her dresser and pulled out some clean underwear and a black t-shirt with a kitten with wings on it. She was going to drop the towel, but she noted the three interested faces.

"You can head downstairs. I will be down in a minute. We are going to have to work on finding a way to each get personal time, or we will drive each other nuts. Namely me." She wrinkled her nose.

Argyle smirked and headed for the door. "Oh, Benny, what is that tattoo on your right hipbone?"

She scowled and put her hand over her towel-clad hip. "A birth-control spell. Regular human drugs don't do much for me, so Minerva helped me design it."

Smith sighed in relief. "So, I don't have to make any awkward announcements to my pride when I introduce you?"

She shook her head. "No. I don't want to have to rush anything, and I will have quite the lifespan to deal with if I don't do anything stupid. I can spare a few years before kids are an issue."

Tremble smiled and came over to give her a kiss. "I would not mind a child."

She looked at him archly. "You would like to quit the XIA to look after the child full time? I have just gotten a job where I can be myself out in public. I am not going to put a cork in that until I have had some life experience that doesn't involve me hiding in the shadows."

He crossed his arms and gave her a bland look, all confidence and buff security. "I would certainly resign my position to take care of my child."

She blinked. "Well, that sucks the air out of my next statement, but good to know."

He gave her a quick kiss on the lips. "Think about it."

Smith pressed a kiss to her cheek a moment later. "I am content to wait a while."

She laughed and gave him a peck on the lips. "Me, too. Off you go."

Argyle didn't mention anything because he couldn't father a child. He merely winked and headed out of her bedroom and toward the stairs.

The other two bowed and left her alone. She sighed and pushed the door closed. With her mind whirling with the mental image of a small person in her arms with pointy ears and her hair, she got dressed and then pulled on a set of denim shorts. She put on her favourite kitten socks and pattered downstairs where her family was, once again, gathered in the kitchen.

She came to a halt when she saw her father. "Dad?"

He turned to her with open arms. "Come here, Benny." He hugged her.

She hadn't hugged her dad as a human for over sixteen years. The lack of scales was weird and his thudding heartbeat was in her ears.

"What happened?"

He grinned. "Now that Yomra has lost his influence, I was able to use a glamour again. It feels solid, but I am testing it out at home."

Her father's hair colour was a shade darker than her own, but his dark-hazel eyes were the same ones she saw in the mirror every morning. He was just as handsome and reassuring as he had been when she was small and he was lecturing at colleges and universities around the country.

"You look..."

He grinned. "I know, sweetie. It feels pretty good, too. My demon form is losing its ferocity, but this will be a better transition for going out in public."

She wiped tears off her cheeks. "It is just so nice to see *you* again."

Benny could see her mom, and Lenora smiled while she finished putting lunch on the table. It appeared that the change to the old was a favourite all the way around.

After lunch, the guys took off and went in search of a change of underwear. Benny was not complaining.

She saw her parents eyeing each other once they had finished the dishes, and Benny chuckled. "I am going to take a walk to the dower house. I will be back later."

Her parents didn't respond, so she left out the back and started walking across the grounds.

Pooky galloped up to her and nudged her with his head. She grinned. "Fine. Let's go for a ride."

She hauled herself astride him, and he galloped off toward the dower house. Whatever was going on there, he was eager to have her see it.

They jumped the creek, crashed through the meadow and, finally, he jogged into what would be her back yard.

"Oh, wow."

The back deck that hadn't been there before had a huge hot tub large enough for all four of them to fit in easily. Benny walked into her home, and she noted that it was three times larger than it had been on the main floor. A gym had been added with heavy-duty machines, a larger kitchen and dining room took up the main floor, complete with a living space and a wide-screen television.

Benny snivelled as she walked up the stairs. Her parents and the house had gone above and beyond. She checked the guest bedroom, the upstairs bathroom and, then, she gingerly made her way into her own bedroom.

Her bedroom now took up two-thirds of the length of the house. Beds for the guys were arranged on one wall, but the focal point of the room was the bed that was wide enough for all of them. "Oh, geez. That is not happening."

The house around her sent a wave of amusement out.

The wardrobes were empty and ready. There were bookshelves waiting for books, footlockers and a pile of pillows on a thick carpet. The bathroom was built for four people to brush their teeth at the same time. It was a home built for her group, and Benny sighed. "Is there a study?"

Silent laughter ran through the walls around her. She headed down the stairs and followed the silent nudging to a flat and nearly invisible seam in the wall under the stairs. It opened at her touch, and a staircase spiralled down under the house.

She followed the spiral down into a space that made her cry like a toddler. In a wood-lined room that felt warm and snug. She had bookshelves, desks and her personal spell books in place. Across the room, a lab was fully set up behind a blast spell. It had the texture of water when she entered it but was bouncy as a marshmallow when she struck it.

There was a modest selection of ingredients and equipment, but it was more than enough for the standard alertness spells and healing potions that she made up for herself. Potions weren't really her thing, but it was nice to have the option to fiddle with it if she had the inclination.

She had her personal space. If she wanted to share it, she could, but if she wanted privacy, she had it.

"Thank you so much." She spoke to the house around her.

Her mom wasn't able to tell her when the family noticed that the homes were alive, but she suspected it had something to do with spellcasting. At home, Benny was fairly relaxed about using magic, as were her parents. That casual power must have seeped into the walls somewhere along the way. It was either that or the wood had been alive when the houses were built.

With one last, wistful look at the space around her, she climbed the stairs and let herself out the back door.

Pooky shook his head and turned, pawing at the ground. A huge stable was visible where an empty field had stood.

"Shall we take a look?"

She walked with Pooky at her side to the barn and looked around at the space for the entire herd as well as a currycomb and brushes.

He nudged her to the care equipment.

"Can't I just run you through the car wash?"

He snorted, so she began the hypnotic process of brushing his hide while he stood with his eyes half closed. Dust and loose hairs flew for a few minutes, and then, it was all about taking care of the pukha who had come into the demon zone with his buddies to save her.

His mane was silky smooth and gleaming, as was his tail, by the time she finished.

She stopped and he stamped. "Dude, there is nothing left to do unless you want me to put braids in it."

Her arms were throbbing, and he looked at her with narrowed eyes for a moment before he nodded.

She put the gear away and asked him. "Take me back to the manor?"

He nodded, and she slipped onto his back; the door to the barn slid shut behind them. She held onto the well-groomed mane as he bolted with the speed of a thoroughbred across the meadow, over the creek and onto the manicured grounds of the manor.

She slipped off his back near the terrace. "Thanks for that." She patted his back.

He butted her chest with his head and then wheeled around to show his pretty hide to the others in the herd.

Benny shook her head and walked into the house, finding both her parents studying in the library. "Thank you, both. That had to have taken a lot of energy."

Her dad looked up. "We did it before the Yomra incident. If I had known what was coming, we still would have done it."

Her mother smiled. "So, you like it?"

"Yes, but how did you know about..." She waved her hand

vaguely to indicate the guys.

Lenora smiled. "Even your father could see the way they looked at you. Hell, even Kyria mentioned it to me."

Benny sighed. "Well, I am exceedingly grateful. I wonder how she is doing."

Lenora got up and came over to give her a hug. "We can wonder, and I think we might one day find out. If she got free of Yomra, she might be with her mage and trying to have that family she has always wanted but been denied."

Benny's dad got up and joined the family hug. For that one moment, they were together with fond memories of the succubus that had gotten them to this moment.

Chapter Fifteen

Moving into the house was going to have to wait until after the party. Benny got dressed and finished fussing with the bow on the gift.

What could a girl get parents that had been together for five decades? The box contained charms that she had put together with Tremble's help. The vines that surrounded the wedding-day images were made of minerals, wood, gems and iron. They were the most powerful protection spells she could manage, and friends and family had donated the materials. The photo of their first kiss as man and wife was in a spiral of magic and love.

Benny slipped the present onto her pocket and prepared to take her parents out for *dinner*.

She came downstairs and smiled at Harcourt and Lenora Ganger. "Are you two ready?"

Her mother was wearing an elegant midnight velvet gown, and her father was wearing a tuxedo that suited him admirably.

"You both look amazing." She brushed at her tears when her mother took her father's arm.

"Thank you. Now, where are the boys?" Lenora insisted on calling them that, even though Argyle and Tremble were older than Lenora was.

"They are finishing moving into the house. They are going to meet us at the restaurant." Benny smiled brightly. "Come along. Pooky has something special for tonight."

They left the manor together, and the stretch SUV in the drive revved the engine.

The door opened, and her father helped her inside where she started the illusion spell.

Her mother smiled brightly, and her father settled next to her in the large space in the back of the vehicle.

"Anytime you are ready, Pooky."

The door closed and the vehicle rolled forward, down the drive and toward the highway.

When they pulled even with the house, there was a flash of magic and Benny asked, "Pooky, can you stop for a minute? I need to get my wrap from the house."

The SUV rolled to a halt, and Benny got out of the car, winking at the gathering of folk who were waiting to surprise her parents.

"Dad, can you come out here?"

He appeared a moment later, and his face was shocked and, then, he grinned. "Lenora, Benny can't remember which shawl matches her dress."

Her mother left the SUV and the gathering shouted, "Surprise!"

Over two hundred people had gathered, and Benny was delighted that she had managed not to blow it.

Lenora was crying and holding onto Harcourt. Benny went up to them and smiled. "Happy anniversary."

Her mother grabbed her in a tight hug and squeezed. "Well done, Benny. I didn't suspect anything until that last flicker."

Benny chuckled. "Come on and meet your friends and family. Fifty years ago today, you two agreed to spend the rest of your lives together. Most of these folks were there."

Her parents grinned and wandered into the crowd, accepting hugs of congratulation and many comments on Harcourt's changed appearance.

Benny sighed and headed toward Argyle. He was looking devastating in a tuxedo, as was Smith. Tremble was rocking a fey formal costume. He was covered in a black tunic, tight black trousers and about three pounds of silver embroidered thread. He looked delightfully sexy.

Benny kissed each of them lightly and smiled. "Have you been having fun?"

Smith grinned. "There are leaders here from nearly every high family on the continent."

Benny shrugged. "My family gets around."

From behind her, she heard, "Benny!"

Benny turned, and a blond with her hair in an elegant twist that belied her appearance of youth immediately hugged her.

"Soph! You look...fourteen."

Soph smiled at her. "Part of the curse. You look great. Are these yours?"

Benny stifled a snort as Soph waved at the guys.

Benny made the introductions. "These are my mates. This is Argyle, Smith and Tremble."

Soph bobbed a curtsey.

"Gentlemen, this is Sophia DeMonstre, the Cursed One." Benny inclined her head.

Soph exhaled. "That is my least favourite part of the curse."

Smith raised his brows. "Curse?"

Benny explained with a grin. "Soph is part of a family that was cursed by a dying monster. She has to hunt and unravel curses that pop up randomly or are cast into objects. Her skill is to see the solution; her curse is to have to deliver it. Slow aging is part of the curse; she is older than I am."

Soph made a face. "Funny. Well, I am here with my parents, and they would love it if you said hi. And I am only older by a month."

Benny hugged her again. "I will be only too happy to say hello when I spot them."

Soph leaned in. "Are you singing?"

"With this crowd? Of course."

Soph bobbed another curtsey to the guys, and she took off, with the bounce in her step that was uniquely her.

Argyle blinked. "There was something very odd about her."

Benny grinned. "With a look from those green eyes, she pulled apart the magic that animates you. She analysed Smith's shifting and took in Tremble's grasp of natural energies. She analysed me once, and then, she got a headache. Minerva made her so dizzy, she vomited."

Tremble smiled, "I thought you had a more diverse bloodline than Minerva does."

"I do, but hers was far more powerful when it intersected with humanity. I am like looking at a starry sky. Minerva is like staring into the sun."

She looked around and linked arms with Tremble and Smith. "Come on, let's mingle."

They met with dragons, gargoyles, vampire kings, her namesake, the forest lord and Sabina. When Benny was ready to introduce them to her grandfather on her father's side, Sabina whispered, "You need to start this now."

Benny blinked. "I am the MC?"

Sabina took her by her shoulders and pushed her toward the stage. "Can you think of anyone better?"

Benny made a face and got up in front of the microphone. Her parents were ushered to a table on an elevated dais so that they could see the festivities.

The band concluded their soft song, and she nodded to them in thanks. She leaned over to the guitarist. "Do you have the song?"

"When you introduce it, we will play it."

She gave him a thumbs-up, and he responded with all four of his. She licked her lips and turned to the microphone.

"Thanks one and all for being here tonight for the fiftieth anniversary of Agatha Lenora Mills Ganger and Harcourt Emile Ganger. Fifty years ago tonight, they pried themselves away from their books and stood up in front of family and friends with a judge officiating, and they swore to be together until death did they part, for better or for worse, in sickness and in health. The richer or poorer thing wasn't an issue."

The crowd laughed. The Ganger family was ruthless when it came to investing, and they had enough money for ten more generations.

"They skipped along together for a few decades before they realised that all of their friends' kids were in college and they hadn't bothered to start a family. I came along as scheduled."

More laughter rippled through the group. Benny watched her parents holding hands and smiling at her.

"There was another decade of lectures, tours, students and a child at home setting fire to dandelions in the yard. That is when the *in sickness and in health* came in. My mother got sick, really sick. Cancer is a bitch, but with all the magic in the world, we couldn't stop it. Harcourt really, really tried."

The crowd was quiet. Most knew what had happened next.

"Mom got sick, and Dad stayed at her side. Even at ten, I knew that death was about to part them. To my surprise, my mom lived and Dad turned into the emerald-green goof most of you are familiar with. They shared a soul, but as any of you realise, who truly know them...they always did. Here is to fifty more years of light, laughter and mayhem that always sees you side by side."

A server brought her a glass of white wine. "To Lenora and Harcourt! Fifty years and counting!"

The toast was carried through the gathering, and everyone raised their glasses to the happy couple. Benny drank, and everyone followed suit.

The conversation rose to a murmur, and Benny got a glass of water. She slugged down the water and faced the mic again. She nodded to the bandleader, and they prepared to get going.

"Mom, Dad, I wrote you a song about your life and the love that you showed me was possible."

She nodded to the band again, and then, she began to sing.

Benny felt the jerk as something pulled her out of her body. Everyone seemed frozen in time, but she could hear her voice singing the song of love and loss and love again.

A figure in white at the edge of the crowd beckoned her over.

Benny felt her astral stomach flip. When she was standing in front of the woman, she curtsied deeply. "Lady Giltine. You honour our gathering."

A touch on her shoulder brought her upright again. "Little Beneficia. I see you didn't tell any of your part in your mother's recovery."

Benny blinked. "I didn't do anything. My father shared his soul."

"Your father shared his soul with your mother the day that he married her. Did you never wonder why I was chosen as your godmother? A goddess of death is not a normal choice."

Benny glanced at the woman in white with the pale-blue eyes that had seen so much. She was the death licker. Master of poisons.

"I did not think about it. I was not consulted at the time."

The woman smiled slightly. It was tiny, but it was there. "True. Your mother had been dying for two years when you were born. They bound you to me in the hope that you would do what you did. You stopped me in the hallway and kept me there until your mother had been revived as a demon thrall with half a soul. Because of our connection, it had to be me to collect Lenora, and with my goddaughter standing in my way,

I could not progress without destroying what I had sworn to protect."

The day came to her. Her father and mother had told her to leave the room and keep everyone out. Benny had agreed and faced down the lady of death who tried to pass. She kept her there until her father had opened the door with her mother, pale but breathing in his arms.

"The demon venom killed the cancer and it killed her, but without a true death, she was able to be revived with magic in a way that should not have been possible."

Benny blinked and looked at the glowing faces of her parents listening to her sing. They both had tears in their eyes, but they were smiling.

Benny steeled her spine. "We are honoured you have come to our party."

"I was invited, but I wished to speak with you. Your men, do you wish to keep them all?"

Benny blinked. "Of course."

"Mark them as yours. Get your friend Minerva to help. She has creation in her blood. Mark them soon. Not all deaths are as easy as mine." She changed the direction of her conversation. "It is a lovely party. Thank Sabina for the invitation." Giltine faded away.

Benny finished the last line of her song, and it hung in the air.

Her parents began clapping frantically, and the crowd followed. She bowed her head for a moment while the noise roared, and when it ebbed, she leaned forward. "I would also like to thank Neadra for hosting this event here in *Ritual Space*. It was pure luck that I managed to get this place to ourselves, so feel free to zap, shift and do what you like as long as you respect the guardian of the property. Now, dance!"

Music kicked into life, and Benny headed down the stairs, across the open space and up to her parents. She handed them the box and smiled. "Here you go."

Her dad opened the box, and he stared in amazement at the charm. "Benny, this is wonderful."

Lenora picked hers up, and she teared up. "Oh, Benny, this is amazing. So much power."

"It is a specific protection charm. It can't be stolen."

Her father helped her mother put her charm on, and then, he put his on.

"Happy anniversary, you two. I love you both."

Her parents rose and came around the table to hug her. Her father whispered, "Thank you, Benny."

Benny looked over the dance floor and found Minerva, fidgeting near the edge. Benny smiled and worked her way through the crowd. "Minerva. I am so glad you could make it. I need to commission you for something."

Minerva looked exhausted.

Benny paused. "Geez, Minerva. Come with me."

Her friend was so tired that she followed.

The buffet was set up, but few folks were indulging. When they were away from the crowd, Benny sat her down on a stone and asked, "What is wrong?"

Minerva rubbed her forehead. "I think I taunted the wrong guy."

"Tell me about it."

"I don't want to, not today." Minerva straightened her shoulders and looked attentive. "What do you need?"

Benny waved it away. "I need a way to mark all of us; I mean me and the guys. Wedding rings won't really cover it. I need a tattoo or something, something that will work on all of us."

Minerva smiled. "I have something in mind, but it might be painful. Small but painful."

"Pain doesn't matter. Pain is fleeting. If it protects them from whatever is coming, I say that I can convince them."

Minerva grinned. "I bet you can. I will bring you the designs in three days. It will take that long to work up the ink, though I have the pattern in my head."

"Tell me what you want in return."

Minerva smiled. "One favour to be granted at a later time that will not cost you life, limb or the affections of your mates."

Benny smiled. "Deal."

They chatted about the guests at the party until the guys came to grab Benny for dancing. The logistics of dancing with all three were difficult, but not impossible. She spun and whirled until she was dizzy, secure in the knowledge that she was safe, her parents were safe and she was loved.

It wasn't a bad haul for a week of vacation. She wondered what the next week of actual work would bring.

Three Parts Fey
An Obscure Magic Book 3

By

Viola Grace

Chapter One

Benny laughed as they staggered into the dower house, leaving her parents the big house for the evening. Benny and Argyle supported Smith, who was distinctly limping from his fall while eluding a handsy gargoyle.

He kept muttering. "She tried to take off with me."

Benny was still giggling, though it wasn't helping. "You are just too adorable for words and probably the only one she felt she could subdue without calling attention to the struggle."

His black look was answer enough. The other two stayed wisely silent, but Benny could see them grinning at each other.

The party had been a riot. Everyone had enjoyed themselves, and her parents were on their way to their house for an anniversary all alone.

Dawn was staining the sky, and the dower house closed the drapes as Argyle made his way into the kitchen.

He looked at her with suspicion. "Benny, was that you?"

"Nope. It's the house. It is structured for us now, and while the arrangement may be a little odd, we should be able to make it work." They hadn't been with her when she examined the new setup that the house had made with their specific union in mind.

He looked around. "Is Jessamine here?"

"Not quite yet, though I imagine she is holed up in her resting box. What my parents are engaging in, no one needs to witness."

Smith grumbled. "Where can I put my foot up?"

"Up the stairs. When you find the bedroom, you will know it. I will make a poultice for that ankle."

Tremble helped Smith up the stairs, and Benny got to work.

Argyle seemed content to keep her company.

"I didn't know you could make a poultice without a lab."

She grinned and got her mortar and pestle. "Folks have been grinding up herbs for healing purposes since they could mash any leaf with antiseptic properties with a rock."

He smiled. "My mom did that while I was growing up. Every bruise, bump and cut got the same treatment."

"How old were you when you were given your vampirism?"

As she spoke, she flicked through the counter herbs and found the ones she needed. She plucked a few medicinal herbs and then bulked the rest of the mortar out with parsley.

"I was twenty-six. Parsley?"

"Sure. It improves just about everything." She winked and started to grind the leaves together. "I will actually use magic to make this more effective, but Smith needs to learn to be lighter on his feet, and a few minutes of pain is a good teacher."

"Shifters heal quickly." He watched her work at the process of making the equivalent of an herbal pressure pack.

"Yes, and magic heals even faster. If he was able to tap into his demon side, he wouldn't have even had to hop away from the party."

"Truly?"

She looked at him and winked. "Yup. But, as he manifests as an incubus, the rest of my night would be shot."

"I am still getting used to that idea. We all have different aspects?"

"Of course. Your demon form is not only dictated by its attachment to you, but also to your personal magic, to what you are at the core. That is why demons are so direct, they hide nothing."

He chuckled. "I gathered as much with the public nudity in the zone. Our clothing was a bit of a jarring note."

She wrinkled her nose and kept working. "Personal touch. You are bound to me, so I dressed myself as I wished to appear, and you and the others were dressed to flatter me."

"Because you are the high king."

She shrugged and checked the mix in the mortar. "Did you ever doubt it?"

He chuckled. "Not for an instant. The first night you were guarded, but there was power behind your choices. You knew what each species would do and how they would do it. Knowledge is power, and you know a lot."

She scraped the contents of the mortar into a plastic container, and she inhaled the scents of mint and parsley. The other herbs were hidden underneath.

Before she could get distracted, she washed her tools and set them on the draining board.

"And now, we go and fix the lion."

She grinned and headed up the stairs. Argyle drew even with her and offered her his arm. She took the support and walked toward their bedroom.

As their footfalls struck, a voice called out. "Argyle, you have to see this place."

The vampire grinned and entered the room; the gauzy curtains closed automatically and the synthetic lighting came on.

Benny released him to let Argyle lead the way, and she trailed after him.

Smith was on his back with his leg propped up on pillows at the edge of her bed. The huge expanse made him look tiny, but he was craning his neck to see everything in the room.

She snorted. "Hike your trouser leg up, Smith."

He grimaced and showed her the swollen joint of his ankle. His shoe had been abandoned on the drive home. She cut his sock off and winced at the break that was visible through the purple skin and white bone pressing at it.

Benny swallowed and carefully applied the paste she had created downstairs.

He sighed and smiled. "It feels cool."

Benny finished covering him in the ground-up herb salad, and she held her hand over his ankle. The demon blood was minute, but still very much inside him. She put it to work and fixed the bones back into alignment before knitting them back into place.

"How bad is the sprain?" He levered himself up on his elbows.

"Hold still. It was a break, not a sprain. Your tendons just held everything in place. I am fixing it, but healing spells are tricky, so I am cheating."

She concentrated and muttered the spells that shaped her focus, and her focus fixed his bone and muscle.

When the last cell clicked into place, she sat back and groaned. "I am way too tired to be doing this."

Argyle and Tremble were next to the bed, watching. Smith was flexing his foot and grinning. "It feels better and smells nice."

She snorted and crawled off the bed. "I am going to wash my hands. You go and wash your foot. I need to sleep."

Argyle asked. "May we join you?"

"That's what the bed is for."

She headed to the bathroom and scrubbed the green off her hands. She washed her face and brushed her hair, unzipping her cocktail dress as she returned to the bedroom.

"If you guys don't like the giant dorm room, I am sure that we can manage something else."

Her men were all in a state of undress. Argyle was wearing his customary shorts to bed; Smith was naked, as was Tremble.

Benny appreciated the view, but she was too tired to do anything about it. "At the foot of each bed is a globe. That globe will create a privacy screen that extends for three feet on either side. You can walk through it, but while you are inside, no visual will enter or leave, the sound is the same."

The dress slid to her feet, and she shucked off her bra and panties, kicking free of her heels a moment before she crawled into bed. She moved until she was in the centre of the expanse, and she slid under the quilt that covered it.

"Well, it has been a lovely evening and it's turning into a bright day. I am getting some rest."

Smith sighed. "Nothing else?" He put his hand on her thigh above he quilt.

She reached out and patted his hand. "Nothing else for eight hours."

Tremble chuckled and moved to lie against her left side.

Argyle was already settling in for his deep rest on the far left edge of the bed. He didn't need contact as he slept. He wouldn't wake up looking for anyone.

Smith eased her to her side and snuggled up against her back. Tremble wove his fingers around her hands and gave her a soft kiss.

"Good night, Benny."

She ducked her head so she wasn't yawning in his face, and she exhaled. "Good night, guys. When we wake up, I have a question to ask you."

Argyle said slowly, "Ask now."

She looked at Tremble and felt the slight squeeze of Smith's arms. "Fine. Would you guys be willing to wear a mark of our bonding?"

Argyle chuckled. "If you can get it to stick, I am in."

Tremble grinned. "Me, too."

Smith whispered in her ear, "Just tell me where you want it."

Benny sighed. "Good. A friend told me it would be a good idea."

Tremble smiled. "Which friend?"

Benny snuggled into the sheets and enjoyed her sensation of being surrounded. "Giltine."

Her partners were awake for a while after that, but Benny slept like a log.

Four hours later, Benny was up, Smith was on his back and Tremble was nowhere to be found. Argyle was still and silent on his corner of the bed.

She eased up and out of the collection of tumbled bedding and headed for her wardrobe. A blue cotton robe with a bright and sprightly pattern on the back was waiting for her. She slipped it on and pattered downstairs.

Tremble smiled at her over his shoulder as she entered the kitchen. "Have a seat. The fridge is fully stocked."

She paused for a moment to enjoy the view of him standing there chopping fruit wearing his shorts and his hair in a long braid. Nothing else. She sighed and rejoined the sane and smut-free world.

"Of course it is." She smirked and glanced around. Her small purse was still on the corner of the counter, and she opened it, fishing her phone out.

The message light was flashing, and when she flicked her fingers across the screen, she noted the email waiting.

The subject was *Design Approval* and the sender was Minerva. The image that opened made her laugh.

"What is it?"

"Minerva found someone to design our tattoo. It sums all of us up in the oddest way. Here. Take a look."

The base was a lion, the fangs and widow's peak were obviously a reference to Argyle, the brilliant platinum mane and the vivid rainbow eyes were all Tremble. The deer horns that the lion sported were Benny's contribution to the pattern.

"How large will it be?"

She wrinkled her nose. "It will be small. Less than one inch high and wide. If you approve this, we will have the artist here before dinner."

"What about the others?"

She grinned. "They snooze, they lose."

He raised his eyebrows in surprise and then smiled. "I like it. If they can create something that will stick to all our flesh, I will gladly wear it."

Benny looked at what he had been preparing. "Can I have some fruit salad?"

Tremble grinned and returned to his project. He served her a bowl of fruit with a dollop of thickened cream on top.

"So, Benny, what is on the agenda today?"

He sat on one of the chairs at the countertop and took one of her hands in his.

"Today, my dear Tremble, we do nothing. We relax, and if all goes well, we get our tattoos."

"Did a goddess of death really tell you to do it?"

"She said if I wanted to keep you all alive, you needed to be marked."

He paused and poured her a cup of coffee. "Then, I am pretty sure we should do it."

She answered the email with, *Looks good, ready when you are.*

A few seconds later. *Ink will be ready at 4. See you at five. Bringing Tomlin with me.*

Great. At the dower house.

Benny smiled. "She will be here at five with the tattoo artist."

"I look forward to it. What shall we do about placement?" Tremble raised his brows.

She patted her ribs on her left-hand side. "I want mine here. I can see it when I want to and hide it when it would be obvious."

"Would you want to hide it?"

"When I go out for karaoke? Of course."

"Why do you enjoy it so much?" He propped his head up on

his fist and smiled.
"That is an awkward story."
"We are bound. Time to start leaking the secrets."
She sipped at her coffee and wondered where to start.

Chapter Two

"Demon blood is a funny thing. Each manifestation requires a different sort of food to keep the demon healthy. Succubi and incubi feed on sex, warrior demons feed on battle and, of course, scholar demons like you and my grandfather, feed on knowledge." She sighed and stared into her coffee cup.

"What about high kings?" Tremble had a wary look in his eyes.

She sipped her coffee and mumbled into the cup.

"What?"

She enunciated. "Attention. We feed on attention and worship. It was one of the reasons I never considered myself to follow in my father's or great grandmother's footsteps, they need physical contact. I don't need much attention, but I do require some to stay healthy."

Tremble's mouth was open. "You are not kidding."

"I am not. It isn't a fun thing. I had to engage in every after-school activity that involved public performance. I was a freaking cheerleader for pities sake!"

She got up and poured another cup of coffee, resettling in her spot. "It doesn't do anything to my audience, but it gives me what I need to keep the magical batteries charged."

"And the more you perform..."

"I currently have enough of a charge going to last me for the next ten years. It is a mirror effect. The stronger the power of my audience members, the more energy I take in. Last night..."

He caught on. "You were in the presence of some of the most powerful beings on the continent."

"Yup. It is why my parents always had family parties during the months and weeks that I wasn't at school. I would be admired by the crowd and that would be enough."

"So, will we have to begin habits that feed our inner demon?"

Benny dug into her fruit salad and laughed. "You already have them. Your demon tailored itself to match your existing inclinations. Argyle likes to fight though he holds back, Smith has an interest in sex that he has never let out and you just about orgasmed when you saw my parents' library. Now that you have demon blood, you can read half of the tomes that were previously off limits."

He perked up. "Really?"

She snickered. "See? Just the thought of knowledge and you want to run over there."

Tremble blinked and rubbed the back of his neck. "Fair point."

"How long does it take you to braid your hair in the morning?" She smiled and propped her head on her fist.

"Five minutes if it is cooperating. Lately, it has been slightly recalcitrant." He grinned and flipped the braid to lie over his shoulder across his chest.

She reached out and stroked her fingers over the thick rope of silk. "How difficult of it."

He leaned in to kiss her, and they had a moment to enjoy the contact before a low and persistent buzzing broke the mood.

Tremble sighed and leaned back. "One of our phones. I will find it."

He got up and left her, so she worked on her second cup of coffee and enjoyed the noon sunlight coming through the glass.

Jessamine floated up and fanned herself. "I thought that being with your parents was unpredictable. You have half-naked men all over this place."

"Get used to it, Jess." Benny could hear Tremble talking, and she smiled at her ghostly friend. "Did you hide all night?"

"Until the moaning and laughter stopped, then I snuck over here. I have to say, I expected more of the same, but it was blissfully quiet."

Benny laughed. "We are all tuckered out after our eventful evening. Mom and Dad were delighted, and the relatives had a great time."

Tremble came back in, and he was scowling at the phone in his hand. "We have been recalled to duty as of tomorrow."

"Did they say why?"

He shook his head. "I warned the captain that we are all going to pop positive for demon blood, but he didn't care. He said we needed to get back on the roster. The team with Tearago suffered an accident last night. They showed up at a scene and a group of beta wolves decided to attack. They are all in hospital."

Benny wrinkled her nose. "Ouch. So what—" Her phone went off.

"Hello?"

"Hello, Ms. Ganger. This is Captain Matheson of the Redbird City XIA."

"Uh, hello, Captain."

"You are being put onto active duty beginning tomorrow. Your team takes to the streets at dusk, and you will be pulling overtime until just before dawn. Are you prepared to act as an Agent of the XIA?"

"Yes, Captain. Um, Captain?"

"Yes, Ms. Ganger?"

"What about the security scanner? My demon side has been a little frisky lately."

He cleared his throat, and Tremble covered his eyes as he listened, peeping in between.

"Um, right. Well, you will be issued a special dispensation, given your particular circumstances. Simply report to the officer on the scanner if you set it off."

"Yes, Captain. Thank you."

"Arrive and gear up for your first day with your team. Welcome to the XIA, Agent Ganger."

The phone call ended, and she fought to keep the blissful expression off her face.

"What did he say?"

She sashayed up to him and put her phone on the counter. "You may address me as Agent Ganger."

He put his hands on her waist and pulled her up for a kiss that got wild and ended up with her seated on the countertop, her robe open.

She wrapped her legs around his waist and growled lightly as she rocked against him. When he reached between them to stroke her, she moaned and bit at his lip.

He joined them quickly, and she held tight as he jerked against her with a strong rhythm. Pleasure spiralled inside her until it broke, and she groaned into his mouth a moment before he shook and held himself against her.

Panting, he pressed his forehead to her shoulder. "I did not mean to do that."

She blinked. "Were you reaching for the salad spinner and slipped?"

He laughed softly and bit at her shoulder. "That wasn't what I meant and you know it. I had meant to have a quiet day without sexual tension."

"I feel nice and relaxed." She nuzzled his neck with her lips.

"You feel wonderful." He slowly straightened and slipped out of her.

She patted the backs of his thighs with the soles of her feet. "You feel good, too."

He glanced down and behind him. "And you are far more limber than I would have given you credit for."

She grinned. "Cheerleader. It wasn't a proud moment in my life, but it taught me some necessary skills."

"I can't imagine you as a cheerleader. It seems off personality."

Benny adjusted her robe and winked at him. "Says the elf who hasn't even seen the pics of me in my Mage Guides uniform."

He backed away and adjusted himself, resuming the appearance of sexy respectability. "If I were interested in that, it would be pervy."

She snorted. "Not really. I go in as a guest speaker every now and then. I have an outfit that fits."

His eyes lit with delight. "You still have a costume?"

"It is called a uniform. And, yes, I have one. It is at the big house."

She wrinkled her nose at him, and she smiled as Smith came in.

"You two were having sex?"

Benny became aware that she was still sitting on the counter and Tremble was very close.

Smith looked hurt that he had missed it. His tousled hair stuck out at strange angles and his golden eyes were still sleepy.

She beckoned to him. "Good morning, Smith."

He covered his mouth as he yawned and stumbled toward her. "Call me Andrew."

He tumbled into her arms, and she caught him with an *oof* of air escaping. He was solid muscle, all warm and hard.

He nuzzled her neck and licked her, dragging the rough expanse of his tongue up to her earlobe.

She shivered wildly. "And good morning to you, again."

"I missed you when you weren't next to me."

Benny grabbed a handful of his hair and tugged at him until he was facing her. "You knew I was in the house, and there was nothing to worry about. We all belong to each other; I don't belong to all of you."

Tremble poured Andrew a cup of coffee. "That said, she knows you need sex more than the rest of us."

Andrew smiled slowly. "You do?"

She kept a blank expression on her face. "I do. I am just making the point that I am a person first and something to screw, second."

The lion in her grasp showed his understanding. "Of course, Benny. Sorry. I wake up after my cock does."

She stared at him for a while before her stern look cracked. "Right. I should have noticed. Everybody now gets three asinine statements before I take them seriously, every day. Beware when the three are over though, because I bite."

Tremble chuckled. "Tell him the news."

She blinked and then realised what he meant. "Oh, right. You can address me tomorrow night as Agent Ganger. We have all been recalled to duty."

"You get to come with us and work?"

She grinned. "And draw a paycheque."

Tremble leaned against the counter next to them. "How do you support yourself? Your job as a food writer couldn't have paid much?"

She smirked. "Trust fund. Very large trust fund. It began with the introduction of vampire blood, and Beneficia put money in it the moment I was born, as I was her namesake."

Tremble nodded.

Benny sighed and ran her hands through Andrew's hair. "The funny thing is that I don't need the money. My food and lodgings are taken care of, as is my transportation. All I buy is clothing and junk food."

It was fun to stroke the mane of gold and brown into thick

waves.

"Have some breakfast, Andrew. I need to grab a shower."

Tremble chuckled.

Andrew perked up. "Shower?"

She laughed. "Come on."

He didn't let her get on her feet; he held her against him and bolted for the stairs.

Tremble called out, "I am going exploring."

Held like a dolly, Benny simply hoped that Andrew didn't drop her.

It was a relief to stand in the shower and have him take her against the wall. At least she wasn't being dangled over the stairs anymore.

Pleasure rushed in on her a moment before she heard his deep groan. She was on the edge, but she didn't have a chance to reach down to stroke her clit; his hand beat her to it.

He was careful and precise, finding the motion that made her clench around him and then repeating it. She cried out in high moans faster and faster until she gasped and her body gripped him, milking him into another spasm.

When they had finished the physical exertion and were both limp and lazy with satiation, they rinsed off and returned to the outside world.

Argyle was leaning up on one elbow. "You know, I haven't been woken from sleep by folks having sex in centuries. Benny, you have quite the set of lungs."

She blushed and shrugged. "I figured there was freedom to let go in our home."

He grinned. "I am not objecting. I am just surprised to be awake while the sun is still out."

Damp and tired, Benny kissed Smith and crawled over to Argyle, lying with her head at a right angle to him, on his belly, while she looked up toward his face.

"You are all wet, Benny."

She grinned. "Not right now. Give me a few minutes."

Laughing, he stroked her head.

Smith tweaked her toes and found his wardrobe. "I am going to go and find the gym."

Benny didn't ask how he knew about the gym; she could hear Tremble on the machines downstairs.

Argyle stroked her hair and smiled. "How are you enjoying your first lazy day with us?"

She wrinkled her nose. "It is a lot more acrobatic than I planned on. How are you feeling?"

He grinned. "I feel like I could take a walk in the sunlight."

She snorted. "Give it a few weeks. Do you need to eat?"

His eyes grew heavy-lidded. "You are offering?"

"I am. As I told the other two, you belong to me and I belong to you. It goes around."

He grinned and his teeth were extended. She lifted a hand toward him, and he stroked the smooth skin of her wrist.

She chuckled as he licked her slowly. "This is also because we are all back on duty tomorrow night. We might not have time for a few days."

"Then, I had better make this count." He pressed his lips to her wrist and worked his way down her forearm.

When he slid his teeth into her, she bit back a moan. Her blood leaped, and he sucked lightly at her, drinking as she slid her thighs together with the restlessness of a cricket.

One would think she had had enough, but the prickly pain and the slow throbbing suction of his mouth were really working for her. It served her right for being only partially human.

The moment he finished, she was left hot and bothered.

After he made sure her wound was closed, he shifted under her and lifted her, draping her on him, face up with her groin inches from his mouth.

She was worried about slipping away, but he held her tight as his lips closed around her clit before he lapped at her. Wet heat resumed, and she was panting as another release crept up on her. She groaned and shuddered as her body jerked in Argyle's grasp.

When he pulled his mouth away from her, he moved her until she was curled against him, her head next to his.

"I still love the taste of you."

Benny sighed. "I am glad. You are going to be with me for a very long time."

"I certainly hope so."

She sighed and relaxed with him until the moment Tremble and Smith came back in, demanding to try out the hot tub.

A day of nothing was a lot of activity.

Chapter Three

Getting the tattoo had the same feeling as touching a chunk of dry ice. It was so cold that it burned.

Benny's ribs throbbed from the point where she had gotten her tattoo, and she held Tremble's hand as he got his.

Argyle had gotten his without any visible reaction, Andrew had passed out, and Benny had gritted her teeth with her demon eyes flaring into life as she kept her breathing even.

The artist, Sokor Tomlin, was a gargoyle who had an appreciation of skin that was evident with every stroke of his needle. Minerva had only given him their first names, but he had gotten suspicious as they approached the Ganger property.

When he was introduced to Benny, his eyes went wide, but he kept himself professional, arranging his tools and inks on the kitchen table while Benny arranged a chair to get her at the right angle for the application.

Sokor finished the final details on Tremble's ribs, and he finally asked, "So, Minerva said you were a bonded group?"

Minerva stood nearby with a stressed look on her face that faded when Benny made eye contact.

"Yes, we are. Minny, did you get the inks set?"

Minerva nodded and fished out another vial. "Yes, the inks are primed. This is the activator."

Sokor leaned back, and Tremble exhaled while the new design was wiped and cleaned. "What activator?"

Benny released her hand from Tremble's grip, and she collected all of the gloves and gauze, putting them in a copper bowl that she set on a trivet. With a few muttered words, she washed the blood off with cool fire.

Sokor nodded and collected his tools. "Minerva, I will be in the foyer."

Minerva nodded. "I will be with you in a moment. All right,

you four, line up."

Minerva arranged them in a wide circle; each of them had the liquid on their fingers that were over the mark on the next member of their group. "All right. Go ahead and put the activator on."

Benny closed her eyes at the moment of impact on her ribs and with the fingers of her right hand she touched Argyle's mark. Their group dropped to their knees as power ran through their hands and connected the circle. It wasn't fire, it wasn't pain, but it was a bonding that went deeper than the blood she had used the previous week. Their power bound and blended.

When it was over, Minerva was gone, as was Sokor. Benny knew that something was up in her friend's life, but right now, she was too exhausted to force her to answer questions she obviously didn't want to answer.

Benny pulled her fingers away from Argyle's ribs and flexed her hands. "Is everyone all right?"

Tremble glanced at her with a tired smile, paused and leaned forward. "Your eyes changed."

"What?" She looked at him in confusion. "Am I demoning out?"

"No. Fey. Your eyes are definitely fey."

Benny looked over at the live herbs on the kitchen counter. They were growing and sprouting wildly. She sucked in a deep breath and closed her eyes, willing their normal colour back into place.

She opened one eye and looked at all three of the men staring at her. "Better?"

Smith nodded. "Nice and normal. What happened?"

Benny rubbed her ribs where the small icon was now sealed into her skin. "All the power zipping around in here sifted through me, and the last energy to touch me was Tremble's."

Tremble smiled weakly. "And you have fey blood, so the eye shift was in there the whole time."

"Probably, though my relatives tend to end up on the gold and green end of the spectrum and it is usually nearly human." She trailed her fingers over the tattoo again. Her sports bra left her midriff exposed, but she couldn't stop touching it.

She looked at Argyle and blinked. "It's gone."

He shook his head and put his fingers over it. "It is still there.

I can feel it."

Everyone got to their feet and started checking. While they could feel their tattoos, they could not see them.

Andrew scowled. "Why did we get the markings?"

Tremble smiled. "A friend of Benny's said that we would need them, and I am pretty sure that we will."

Argyle tilted his head. "What friend?"

Benny blinked and started walking toward the door to the deck. "My godmother. We had a conversation during my song."

That sentence got her two curious men following her and one who already knew what she was going to say.

Smith wanted to know the mechanics how she had spoken to someone while singing.

She sat in a chair on the deck and watched the rising moon. "Once upon a time, a little girl was born and her name was Benny. Now, Benny had issues and her mother knew she would need help one day, so she cast about for the best possible godmother for little Benny, and she came across something that scared her."

The guys gathered around and listened to the story.

"With spells and summoning, not to mention begging, Benny's mother managed to get the godmother to agree."

She flattened her hands on the table. "Now, this godmother was gracious and generous with her gifts. But she was fearsome and no one was comfortable around her, for who really invites death to a baby shower?"

"She did."

The vampire was the only one who was completely at ease with the situation. Tremble looked nervous and Andrew looked queasy.

"So, Argyle, why are you so relaxed with this?"

He grinned. "We live with death. It is something that is at our side day in and day out. Death is nothing to fear, only respect."

Tremble shrugged. "I already knew, but it is still enough to shake me a little. Elves have very little exposure with death."

Andrew shuddered. "Shifters have a close association with death. We don't really like it."

Benny chuckled. "I take the vampire method of thinking. It is all around us so accept and embrace it. It will not take us before our time."

Silence wrapped around them, and she ran her fingers over her tattoo once again. With it hidden under her skin, she was free to soak it as long as she wanted. "Well, as much as I love this silence, I am going to test out the hot tub."

Benny got to her feet and wandered over to the wide pool of gently churning water. She peeled off her jeans and wrestled out of her sports bra. Her panties were flicked off and set aside.

With a relaxed groan, she slid into the hot tub and settled onto one of the formed seats. It felt wonderful just to let the water suspend her for a minute. She didn't have any mermaid in her, but she still loved the water.

Bodies entered the water with her, and everyone leaned back for a nice, long soak.

Heavy sighs and low groans filled the air as they all settled. It was a nice family moment.

It was a nice family moment right up until Harcourt and Lenora wandered onto the deck and pulled chairs up so they could sit near the quartet.

Benny waved at her parents. "Hello, Mom. Hello, Dad."

Her father was looking more human by the day. He smiled and said, "Good evening, Benny. Thank you for helping with the party last night."

"It was fun."

Lenora sighed. "What he is getting at is that we are the ones who now want to plan a party. Namely, your wedding."

Benny wanted to sink below the bubbling surface, but she had nowhere to go. "Nice timing."

Lenora grinned. "Jessamine tipped us off that you were all in one place and trapped by good manners."

Tremble cleared his throat. "When would you like the event to take place?"

Andrew nodded. "How many folk from our prides or clans can we invite?"

"Well, our side of the family tends to run around three hundred or so, so one hundred from each of you should be a suitable number?" Lenora materialized a notebook and started to make out details.

The men looked at each other and then turned accusing eyes to Benny.

"I can't rein her in. I am her daughter, not her jockey."

Her dad pitched in. "She is also an only daughter. She will have the best we can give her, and that is quite considerable."

Andrew asked, "What kind of a timeline are we looking at?"

"Well, it has to be during a full moon, protective spells have to be laid in and invitations need to be issued with all of your full names and ranks mentioned. We could wait for the blue moon, but who really wants to?"

Lenora slid the paperwork toward Andrew. "Damp or not, I need everything. And then, the rest of you." She flicked her fingers around the tub.

Tremble gave her a salute and Argyle inclined his head.

Benny smiled at her mother. "Can you fill mine in?"

"Of course, baby."

She beamed at her partners, as they all had to fill out the paperwork with their names on it.

"Thanks, Mom."

The guys turned one by one and filled out their details.

When the paperwork was filled out, Lenora took it back and smiled. "Let me know if there is anyone in particular you wish to invite. I will offer each of your leaders ninety spaces that must include all relatives willing to travel. Nobility and anyone else comes second."

The guys all nodded.

Benny quirked her lips. "So, when do you think?"

"One month from Wednesday. We can get it all done."

Benny cleared her throat. "You will be on your own for most of it. I start work as an Agent of the XIA tomorrow night."

Her father looked worried, but he always did when he thought about her being in any dangerous situation. He didn't stop her from doing what she needed to, but he didn't encourage her to take unnecessary chances. Only the absolutely most necessary ones.

Lenora sighed. "Well, I will simply keep the meetings with the seamstress and tailors to the appropriate hours. Argyle, how are you doing with sunset?"

He shrugged. "I am even waking up early afternoons now."

She laughed and nodded. "Good. I can get the formal wear preferred by your court and work from there."

Andrew cleared his throat. "My pride simply engages with

human formal wear."

"We can do better than that."

He nodded. "Excellent."

Tremble piped up. "I included my king's court and my top ten guest choices." He smiled.

Benny muttered, "Kiss ass."

He grinned. "Maybe later."

Lenora chuckled. "Benny, you have to pick the flowers and the dress."

Benny nodded. "Right. Moon silk and blue irises with pink roses."

Lenora grinned. "Good choices. I will get the family to volunteer your dowry."

The men looked at each other, and Andrew scowled. "I don't understand."

Tremble smirked. "Old tradition of families paying for the upkeep of the woman across her lifespan. The longer the lifespan, the greater the dowry."

Argyle grinned. "Vampires used to pay the dowry in human servants. I am not advocating it, but the idea was to keep strain off the mate and the local economy, not to mention the population."

Andrew snorted. "The lioness bring the territory and the alpha protects it. There is no other exchange of properties."

Harcourt smiled. "We do things a little differently. There has been a financial calculation of every habit and projected interest that Benny could develop in the next few decades. Being a mage is an expensive proposition, and Benny is one of the best."

Benny was suddenly the focus of three pairs of eyes. "What? Do you think exotic plants and geological samples are the kind of thing to be given for birthdays? It takes quite a bit of time and money to gain a useful collection. For now, I have depended on my mother's collection as well as Minerva's, but I will have to work on my own."

Lenora smiled. "The house started her lab off with the basics, but for anything more exotic, Benny will need to buy or trade for the objects she needs."

Harcourt chuckled. "Hence the dowry."

Benny shrugged. "You knew that this wasn't going to be easy

when we first bonded, guys. I am about to become a very expensive lady."

Tremble smiled. "I would never have guessed that a ride-along would have turned into a life sentence."

The gathering laughed, and Benny was content for that one moment. Everything felt right.

Chapter Four

The next afternoon, Benny and the guys arrived at the XIA building and walked through security.

One by one, they walked through the scanners and none of them set off the demon sensors. They each picked up new identification packs at security, just in case. Benny made a face at her identification, but she smiled at the badge. It was always weird to see her full name spelled out.

She folded the identification into the leather cover and headed for the locker room with the rest of her group.

The quartermaster gave her the uniforms and her locker key. When she was changed, she would get her gear, but she wasn't being given weapons for a while.

Locker seventy-six was in the far corner of the change room. Benny stripped off her t-shirt and jeans before sliding on the matte black of the XIA t-shirt and the matching loose trousers. The belt snugged in her waist, and she put on her calf-high boots.

Benny pulled a marker from her purse and slipped it into a pocket of the jacket. As she slipped her identification into the interior pocket, she also grabbed her cash wallet. Everything else was going to be locked and sealed in the locker room. Her cuffs were snugged at the base of her back. As she latched the locker, she took the marker out and traced a small line. The itty-bitty bit of magic would keep anyone from messing with her locker.

She met the guys on the other side of the locker room, and Agent Smith whistled low.

Agent Argyle smiled. "Looking good, Agent Ganger."

"Thank you, Agent Argyle."

Agent Tremble finished wrapping his hair into a tight braid, and he flicked it behind him. "Ready when you are."

They left the room and were heading for the hall that led to the parking lot when Captain Matheson stepped in front of them. "Come with me."

Bemused, Benny led her group into a boardroom and they had a seat in the chairs across from the captain.

The captain sat down and then got up again, pacing. "How did you do it?"

They looked at each other and shrugged. Tremble asked, "What?"

"How did you dampen the traces of demon blood? We know about the demon blood, but the scanners didn't pick it up."

Benny scratched the side of her nose. "From what I have observed, the scanners don't look for the blood; they look for what could be called a demon tie. A bond to a demon king. I no longer have that."

The captain paused. "How is that possible?"

Smith chimed in, "It wasn't easy."

Argyle snickered.

The captain ran his hands through his hair. "Damn. Well, unfortunately, it is well known that Agent Ganger has strong demon blood. The security officer was a little confused when none of you popped positive."

Benny leaned forward. "If you want to know how to design a demon detector, ask my dad. He designed the original systems, but as long as you are still looking for connections to a high king demon, you will be finding people who can be influenced by blood."

"And that is no longer the case with you."

"Nope. There was a spell and ritual that managed to release all of my family line from the high king's influence. From his blood to my blood and beyond, we are now free."

Captain Matheson pinched the bridge of his nose. "I do not want to know what was involved in that particular manoeuvre, do I?"

"Not particularly. Simply know that my father, mother and myself are no longer susceptible to demon influence, though my father and I may manifest the physical traits now and then."

Matheson looked at her partners. "You all are okay with this?"

They looked at each other and shrugged before stating, "Yes."

Benny didn't smirk, though she did want to. She straightened her shoulders.

Captain Matheson inhaled, "Well, as you are our only mage-equipped team, you will have to take over the crossover calls. The seers have been going crazy, and we think another wave is building. The city is on alert."

Benny leaned forward. "Is there any idea of the location of the incoming wave?"

Matheson grimaced. "We don't know where, we don't know when, we just know it is close in all respects. It is why we needed you back so quickly. We need you on duty when and if it happens on a night shift."

Argyle nodded. "Right. Not a problem."

Benny looked at him with her brows raised. "Glad you have confidence, Argyle."

The other two laughed.

Matheson's expression turned from tense to amazed. "You are all bound together." He thudded into his chair again, obviously picking up on the mingled scents through is senses.

Benny shrugged. "My contract says we could, so we did."

Tremble chuckled. "I am sure that you will be invited to the wedding."

The captain leaned back. "So, that kind of binding."

Benny nodded. "Yes, Captain. Are we cleared for duty this evening?"

"Yes. By the way, Argyle, I am surprised to see you here so early."

Argyle got to his feet. "Benny has brought light back to my life, in several ways. My new tolerance for sunlight is one of them."

The rest of them got to their feet, and the captain remained seated. "Have a good shift."

They all nodded and filed out of the boardroom.

Smith signed out the vehicle, and they all signed out a black bag filled with replacement clothing and, for the guys, additional weaponry.

Benny had her singular weapon tucked into the top of her boot. The folds of her trousers hid the small, narrow hilt and grip.

She put her bag next to theirs in the back of the SUV, and

she headed for the rear seat on the driver's side.

Smith stopped her. "Agent Ganger, you are going to be manning the computer."

She grinned and headed for the front passenger seat, buckling in. The computer was on a support, and she opened it up, searching the system for any active calls.

Smith was smiling at her.

She sighed. "Nothing yet. Drive. Head for the waterfront. It usually goes off as soon as the sun goes down."

"Yes, Agent Ganger."

He backed out of the parking spot and headed to the waterfront. When the ping came, they were almost on top of it.

"Agatha's Charm School. They have an incursion."

He hit the gas and came to a halt in front of one of the weather-beaten buildings on the waterfront.

She slipped in an earpiece and listened to the emergency call. "Two eagle shifters are looking for money and protection spells. The owner is confined in her office."

Smith and Argyle moved quickly, Benny unbuckled and kept listening to the call. The woman was panicked. The shifters had threatened to come in and abuse her if they didn't find what they sought.

She left the car and spoke to Tremble. "I am going in for the shopkeeper."

He nodded and followed her. "Stay out of the way. If they come at you, duck."

Benny nodded and slipped into the shop, the dim light caused her to blink for a few seconds, but the scent of blood and magic pulled her onward. She heard the collision of bodies in the rear of the school, but she turned toward the office.

The soft sobbing in her ear continued and that in itself was wrong. The caller had been informed that there were XIA agents in the building, but she hadn't stopped weeping.

Tremble nodded when Benny gestured for them to be silent as they approached the office door.

The door had a chair in front of it, a theoretical blockade. The problem was that the door opened inward.

Tremble pushed past Benny, and he drew his weapon. He silently moved the chair away and prepared to enter.

When he nodded, he opened the door and rolled to one side

an instant before a fireball blazed outward. Benny ducked in after the flame receded and threw herself to the floor.

She heard a startled cry, but the sobs continued in her earpiece. The blood scent led her to a bottle where a two-inch tall Miss Agatha was crouched and hiding. The glyphs on the bottle made it impervious to damage.

Benny looked to the right and saw the third member of the break-in team. A young woman had a recorder next to the phone and left it playing while she took aim at Tremble.

Benny whispered a communication spell and called for a pickup wagon in a matter of seconds. As the woman prepared to attack, Benny whistled sharply to draw her attention. Tremble came through the door, and the woman was struck with enough glamour to knock her off her feet and have her licking her lips while crawling toward him.

Benny grabbed her cuffs and locked the woman's hands behind her back.

Tremble chuckled. "Nice work with the cuffs."

"Thanks. Getting in and out of them took practice."

The woman's body started to change shape under Benny's hands.

"Tremble, get me a length of leather from the third shelf to the left of the door."

He got up and was back in a moment with the thin leather tie.

"What good will this do?"

Benny straddled the fighting shifter. "This is a charm shop, dumbass."

She laced the leather around the woman's neck and wrapped it around her biceps, pulling them tight and whispering the constriction spell.

The attempt to shift stopped, and the young woman shrieked.

"Clear!" Argyle and Smith called out as they hauled their opponents to the door.

"Clear here." Tremble called out.

Benny got up and let Tremble take the shifter. "I will get the proprietor."

Benny walked over to the bottle in the corner of the office, and she bowed. "Your business is clear."

The woman nodded and started chanting. She went from two

inches tall inside the bottle to five feet tall outside the bottle. Benny was unprepared for the hug.

"Oh, thank you. Thank you. I wasn't able to finish making the call."

"What your automated charms did was enough. I am sure your insurance can handle any damage that was caused by the break-in."

Miss Agatha leaned back. "Do I know you?"

Benny patted her on the shoulder. "I am Agent Ganger with the XIA. I came here once with the Mage Guides."

Miss Agatha nodded and straightened her tunic. "I thought you looked familiar. Good work on that short-range will-casting. You have a knack for it."

She escorted the woman out of the shop to where the thieves were being loaded into the transport under the care of some nulls.

"What charms were they after?" Benny whispered to Agatha.

"Persuasion and affection. I don't keep many in stock, but they can be useful in their particular line of work."

Benny quickly went to the nulls and spoke to the driver. "When they are searched, look for small squares of paper or pearls or any combination thereof. They may have gotten some persuasion or affection charms in their heist."

"Understood, Agent. Have a good night."

Benny turned to her partners. Smith and Argyle were a little clawed up, but otherwise fine. Tremble gave Miss Agatha a business card and gestured for Benny to get back in the SUV.

She slid into her spot next to the computer and keyed in their completion of the dispatch order. Once they were confirmed as back on duty, the screen refreshed and the guys piled in.

"So, how did you know that the call was fake?" Smith was keeping his voice casual.

"I wasn't sure, but I have met Agatha, and she is not the type to sob uncontrollably." Benny watched the screen and she identified another position. "Sixteenth and Harcourt. A neighbourhood party has turned into a brawl. Goblin and giant."

The guys groaned, and they started to loosen up in preparation for the match.

It was quite the start to her first day.

Chapter Five

Giant drinking songs were not for the faint of heart, but since the fight had broken up before Smith had gotten them there, it was a good sign.

XIA relationships with the community were sometimes tense, but tonight, Benny played rock-paper-scissors with one of the goblin children. She had to play it two handed, and it was best three out of five. She lost and rubbed the goblin at the base of her skull for a few minutes.

Argyle was having an in-depth conversation with the combatants, and Smith was answering questions on what it meant to be a shifter.

Tremble was staying at a polite distance from the goblins. Not all of the fey got along with them, and it was better for him not to cause an incident.

After admonishing the group to keep things to community standards, they returned to their vehicle.

Benny filed them as complete, and the system refreshed again.

As they pulled away from the gathering, she sighed. "Stop."

Smith stopped the vehicle, and Benny got out. She untied the balloon from the antenna and walked it back to the laughing giants. "Here you go."

She winked and headed back to the SUV. The laughter increased in volume, and she didn't glance back.

She slid into the car again and buckled up. "It wouldn't do to have a hot pink balloon on the antenna."

She heard giggling, but she didn't look around. "Next call is up on Gravemercy Way. We have an unlicensed rising. The mages should take it, but they are bogged down. They won't make it in time to stop it, and we need to stop it."

Smith hit the gas, and she confirmed that they were on their way.

"Gentlemen, we have a student necromancer attempting to raise her twin. The twin died in a drinking incident at the school, and it has taken Miaka this long to gain the necessary spells in order to raise him."

Argyle grunted. "I have to hang back."

"Of course. That is the one kind of magic you are sensitive to."

"I will be there if the ghoul rises. Even if she manages to put in both soul and consciousness, the degradation will have caused some rather nasty changes." He was grim. "If he rises, I will come in fast and question him later."

Smith nodded. "We are going in to..."

"We need to hold down the necromancer. Stop the power and keep her engaged until the mages can come to collect her. Just restraint. No blood. The blood of a new necromancer is one of the easier methods of controlling the undead." Benny grimaced. "But only after her first rising and before her locking in her power. If any of the dark mages know what is going on, they are going to be out for her blood."

Tremble sighed. "Why couldn't this just be simple?"

Benny grinned and put the computer away after sending the confirmation of arrival signal.

She flexed her fingers. "This is where I earn my keep."

Argyle handed her a set of cuffs. "You forgot to take yours off your last collar."

Benny sighed. "Sorry. There is so much I need to get used to."

The last flecks of sunset disappeared. Benny adjusted her eyesight and nodded to Smith and Tremble.

She left the vehicle and felt for the magic. It flared and popped all over the cemetery. A very bad sign.

Tremble asked, "What am I sensing?"

"Unfocused magic. She is all over the place. We need to call in more undead. She is going to raise the entire block if they aren't anchored."

"Right. So find her, find her fast, and you stop her before she tangles the living and the dead."

Benny nodded. "Right. Smith, can you shift and sniff her out? She will smell like girl and blood."

He nodded and his features shifted into feline, his hair wild and shaggy. His head lifted, and he led them into the darkness.

Argyle kept well back, but Benny could feel him in the shadows.

Candles flickered up ahead, and Benny eased up next to Smith. She touched his shoulder, and he waited in the darkness.

Tremble came in closer, but he left her to take point.

Dealing with unstable college girls wasn't really her forte, but she focused on the young woman who was frantically consulting a notebook as she chanted and sprinkled herbs around.

"Miaka." Benny whispered it, coming closer.

The girl nearly jolted out of her protective circle. "Who are you? I can't see you."

Benny moved into the circle of light, just on the edge of the chalk outline. "Hello, Miaka."

The girl peered at her through lank hair and blinked furiously. "I have to finish this. We will talk when Mike is with us. He always enjoyed talking to women."

"You can't raise him, Miaka. He won't come back whole."

Miaka scowled. "How do you know about it? He will be fine. I love him and he is my twin and he will be fine."

Benny hunkered down next to the headstone, reading the name and wincing at the youth of the deceased, with the barrier in front of her toes. "He will not be fine. Why didn't you apply for resurrection when he died?"

Miaka stuck her lower lip out. "I did. I wanted him back again, even if I would live on, but the resurrection guild wouldn't do it. My grandmother is a zombie, and she wouldn't die to let Mike have his turn."

Benny closed her eyes. Only one undead was allowed per family. It kept things from getting messy when it came to inheritance.

"So, how long has he been buried?"

"A year and ninety days. Today is our birthday. I brought him a cupcake with a candle. He can blow it out when he comes back."

Benny asked, "Have you given any thought to just bringing back his ghost? If he wants to communicate, it is very easy. If you bring him back in his body, he won't be the same."

"He said...he said Mike would be fine."
"Who said?"
"The demon. A demon gave me this spell, and he said Mike would come back fine."

Benny fought her instinctive hiss. "The demon lied. Demons make puppets out of the dead; they don't give them their lives back. He wouldn't belong to you; he would be the demon's creature."

"You are lying! He said you would lie!" Miaka hissed at her with madness in her eyes.

"Did he? What if I came through your wards and took your books?"

She cackled wildly, her stained sweatshirt and jeans exposed as she leaned back. "No human mage can get through those wards. He promised me. No mage could stop me."

Benny sighed and stepped across the demon-cast ward. "He lied."

Benny wrapped the book in a spell of confusion and the woman in a sleep spell. There was a bit of power stirring in the area, so she focused it upward and turned it into fire.

The form that solidified in the fire was a young man with a mop of dark hair and kind eyes. "Is she all right?"

"Hello, Michael. She is asleep. I can wake her if you like."

He smiled and shook his head. "No. If she needs me back, I will come as a ghost. Do you think that will help?"

Benny nodded. "I think she feels incomplete without you."

"And me without her, but I did something stupid and here I am. I never meant to split us apart, but sometimes these things just happen."

"What artifact would you like to be anchored to?"

He smiled. "My mom gave me a fountain pen when I entered college. I just wanted a business degree."

Benny looked at the objects on the ground. "Is this it?"

"That is the one. She can keep me with her always."

Benny picked it up and used the summoning magic to bind his soul to the object.

"I thought it was more complicated than that." He smiled.

"It is for most mages. I am not most mages."

She reinforced his connection and kept an anchoring and protective spell on it. No one would dislodge him from the pen until Miaka wanted him to go.

"She might cling to you for the rest of her life, Michael."

He leaned down and brushed a phantom hand over his sister's brow. "I know. I am still willing to do it. I never could be the family zombie. I had a heart transplant when I was nine. My organs were shot from the anti-rejection drugs."

Benny sighed and looked at Miaka. She glanced back, and Tremble was pounding his fists against the barrier.

Michael cocked his head. "How did you get through?"

"Oh, family secret."

She took her knife and sliced through the barrier. Tremble stumbled forward.

"The Mage Guild operatives have arrived."

She sat with Miaka as the operatives came to her and stumbled to a halt.

"This is Miaka Horrocks. She tried to raise her brother Michael. I managed to stop her, but his soul was already loosened and with us. I have anchored it to this pen. Please, please, keep the pen within twenty feet of her at all times. She is in an extremely vulnerable mental state."

The male mage looking at her nodded with a kind expression. "We will take care of her."

"Good, because I am going to check in on her. She has suffered a loss that was unexpected. She has wounds that will never heal." As an aside, Benny added, "She has also been influenced by a demon, so keep an eye out for that."

The mage carried her off with his partner. Benny waited for the next team to come in. She explained all the components and left them to take the bits apart.

Argyle was working with the team putting down the ghouls that had risen without souls.

Smith stayed near her, and he asked slowly, "Is she out of danger?"

Benny nodded. "I used her own magic to anchor her brother's ghost, so it should be fine. There was also the touch of a demon in the area, and my magic pushed his out of the way. He won't come sniffing around her again. The Mage Guild will be watching her constantly."

Smith nodded. "So, after this...dinner?"

She laughed. "Excellent idea, love."

Tremble came up on them, and he cupped her elbow. "You did very well."

"I am glad you think so. I want to check on Miaka at the Guild holding facility before we go home."

"Of course, darling."

She grinned at him. "That is Agent Darling to you."

The undead XIA officers had finished with the ghouls, and there was a Mage Guild necromancer standing by to anchor those who had been disturbed.

It was definitely time for dinner.

Chapter Six

It wasn't a night for tacos. They pulled into a small diner parking lot and filed in to scrub their hands before settling into a booth and thumbing through the menu.

Benny was in the mood for soup and a BLT. The coffee she ordered with it was habit more than anything.

The guys ordered a wide variety of foods, and they even had a crimson smoothie for Argyle.

Tremble had to ask, "How do you know to do all that?"

Benny grinned. "You have met my parents. Do you think I didn't want to learn all they had to offer me? I had tutors from every species, was enrolled in every basic instruction that they could manage, taught by the best in their fields. I am not a true necromancer, but I am better than many trained necromancers. There are so many butterflies around our property in winter it isn't even funny."

Smith snorted.

The food was hot and filled the hole that hanging around the cemetery had generated.

The bacon on her sandwich was pleasantly crispy, and it definitely hit the spot.

"So, what do we talk about now that all the sly flirting has been put aside?" She winked.

Tremble grinned. "I suppose that we will have to engage in innuendo and seduction from now on."

"Ohh, seduce me. That would be different. Usually, I am in the mood and I just find a target." She waggled her eyebrows.

Smith put his hand on her thigh under the table and slowly moved it to her groin. He held her for a moment before his fingers began flicking randomly. That had an effect.

She focused on her sandwich, and when it was gone, she said, "I hope that the rest of the night doesn't involve mages. It feels so weird."

Tremble nodded. "You're telling me. I couldn't get through that ward and that is unusual."

"It was demon-based. We have different rules, and since you haven't had time to study yet, you won't know them. Scholar."

Argyle had healed from his scuffle with the undead. "What was I again?"

She leaned over and stroked his cheek. "You were all warrior."

Smith looked at her with a slow smile. "Me?"

"Hello, lover."

He looked extremely pleased with that.

They paid their bill and got to their feet. They only had enough time for a dinner break. Benny got the feeling that there was more to come.

Back in the car, she found their next destination. "Back to the docks. Someone has caught a mermaid in a net, and folks are drunk and abusive. We have to rescue the damsel and get her back in the water."

Smith hit the gas, and she answered the notice with an affirmative that they were on their way.

On hour later, Benny was covered in mer-slime and wishing that she had let Smith grapple with the flailing mermaid. Benny sighed and flicked the coating off her arms.

Argyle grinned. "This is why we bring a change of clothing."

She glared at him and looked at Smith. "Can you go to that convenience store and get me a canister of bleach wipes?"

He nodded. "Back in a minute."

Smith trotted across the street, and she heard him chuckling the moment he thought he was out of earshot.

She sighed and checked to make sure her butt hadn't gotten any of the slime.

Argyle leaned next to her. "So, how are you enjoying being an active agent?"

She ran her hands up and over her breasts then flicked the mermaid slime a few feet away. Tremble was still speaking with those who had captured the bitchy mermaid because she had wrecked a local bar.

The slime creature in question was being hauled toward XIA

holding as they spoke.

"It has its moments. This is one of them."

He chuckled. "You are handling it well. The first time I grappled with a mermaid, she got away."

"The lake maids have always been cranky. It must come with being unable to have sex."

Smith came back brandishing the wipes. Benny took them gratefully and started to get the worst of the coating off herself.

When she had amassed a large collection of spent wipes, she was down to being damp all over. "Pretend you didn't see this."

She summoned a ring of cleansing fire that started at her boots and flared upward with a smooth spread. Her hair fluffed out again, and she felt clean.

Smith sighed. "Why didn't you just do that? I didn't have to get the wipes."

Tremble filled him in. "Mermaid slime can short out magic. We are also being watched by a few locals. Watching her flare into flame might have caused more problems than it solved."

Smith nodded. "Oh. I have never had to deal with one before."

Argyle chuckled. "Thanks to Benny, you didn't have to deal with one today. It would have locked you in human form for two or three days."

Benny asked, "Don't you have to take a test or something regarding other species?"

Smith shrugged. "We all specialise. Tremble knows more about stuff because he is simply so old."

Benny looked at him and smiled. "Would you have an objection to learning?"

A slow spark bloomed in his gaze. "Would you make it worth my while?"

Benny chuckled. "We will discuss it at home."

He shrugged. "Fair enough."

Argyle chortled. "That is one way to get him interested in higher education."

"It is that or hand him over to my father. Either way, he is going to learn. We have a paranormal census back home, so it will be easy to focus on species he may actually interact with."

Smith sighed. "I am not an idiot. I am just more interested in the physical effects of transformation."

She sighed. "I don't want to nag you, but we really do have an excellent library if you are interested."

"I will think about it."

It was fair enough. "Well, if everyone is ready, I will finish the reports and we can be on our way to the Mage Guild holding centre."

The SUV was loaded up, and they were on their way.

Smith grinned. "You type faster than Argyle does."

Benny nodded and kept her focus on the screen. "I used to write for a living. It rubs off after a while."

Each time they completed an incident, a blank report was generated with the time the encounter was started and ended. She had to recap all of the events including the agents who enacted the control action. Benny then had to sign each report, and it was time stamped with the filing time.

She nodded at the amount of reports she had filed. "Busy night."

Tremble patted her on the shoulder. "You did well for your first night out participating as an agent."

She smiled and kept typing up the mermaid report. "Thanks. I did try. There is just something about that poor girl being influenced by a demon that bothers me."

Argyle nodded. "Like Jennifer Langstrom."

"Yes and no. But that is what has me worried. Demon influence is insidious. It won't end just because she didn't manage the raising. He will come after her again."

Tremble asked, "How do you know that?"

"Because demons seek out the weak-willed and vulnerable who contain power that they haven't realised. Just because she is in custody doesn't mean that she will be safe from him. Her existence tempts him, and as we know, demons don't believe in self-discipline unless there is sex involved. Even then, it is easier with a partner to do the disciplining."

Smith scowled. "You think she has been sexually interfered with?"

Benny shook her head. "Nothing like that. She was given hope, and now that it has been removed, she will be looking to replace that vacancy of need and want that drove her forward. She will be more vulnerable than before."

Smith asked, "Can her brother's ghost be turned?"

She sighed. "No. That I can be confident of. Demon magic repels demon magic. If anyone tries to hack through that spell, I will feel it."

"Can they trace it back to you?"

She snorted and completed the arrest report on the mermaid.

"Yes. He can definitely trace the spell back to me, but he won't. As strong as his spells were, I could pass through them without trouble. He is a manipulator and I am way past being susceptible to that kind of bullshit." She watched the streets flow past.

Argyle broke the silence. "Were you susceptible once?"

She nodded. "I kept the silence for a while, but eventually, I told my parents. It was the last demon incident recorded in Redbird City before my parents' abduction."

"What did he offer you?"

"Normality. He said he could take my power and leave me a nice, normal, teenage girl. My father had changed, and my mother...well, she was still my mother, but it was different. Her illness had changed us all. Since they were sharing a soul, I felt lost, out of the loop. He said he could change it, make it like it was before. It was my lowest moment and I agreed, but not before I told my dad."

Tremble reached forward again and squeezed her shoulder.

"Harcourt intervened, and I found the motives of Jimhal the demon as they were brought into the open."

Smith asked, "Could this be Jimhal?"

Benny closed her eyes and remembered the blood and dismemberment. "No. Jimhal will never appear on this plane again. He is extremely dead. Dad offered him a chance to give up the prize he was seeking. Jimhal wanted to fight Dad for the territory of my mind and body; he lost." Benny chuckled weakly. "I don't think he ever realised that he was facing my father. If he did, he realised it too late."

Smith hissed. "That would be a mistake. Harcourt looks like he can take a hit."

"You have no idea."

She glanced back at Argyle, and he was opening and closing his fists.

"We are here."

Her attention was brought around to the building in front of them. "I don't know how long I will be. If I am too late, head for the agency and send Pooky to bring me home."

"We will wait for you. We are a team, Benny. We won't leave you behind."

She flashed a smile and left the car, covering herself in human-based magic.

She showed her credentials to the desk sergeant. "I am here to see a woman arrested earlier this evening. Miaka Horrocks."

He flicked through his records and nodded. "She is in holding."

"I need to speak with her. I am concerned for her wellbeing."

He blinked. "We know how to treat our own here."

"She may well be a target for a demon, and I am better equipped to deal with that than you are."

"Why is that?" His smug look told her that he wasn't going to let her in.

"I was raised by one." She let her eyes flare demon green, and then, she flicked them into brilliant fey colours.

By the time his startled shout brought backup, she looked like a half-elf.

It was easy to get his superior to let her in. The desk sergeant was obviously in need of a break if he couldn't tell the difference between fey eyes and demon eyes.

She was escorted in to the holding area, and she sought the pen. "Excuse me. She was brought in with a pen."

"It has been logged into evidence."

"Unlog it. It has her brother's soul in it, and he will be able to keep her calm. Consider him a second witness."

"She didn't mention it."

Benny sighed. "She didn't know, but I explained things in detail to the transporting officers. I am guessing that they just got busy and didn't mean to drive her mad. Please bring it and put it outside the cell."

Benny was let into Miaka's cell, and the woman was rocking violently, pulling on her hair.

"Oh, Miaka. What are you doing?"

"He's gone; he's gone. He's lost and it is all my fault."

Benny touched Miaka's cheek to get the young woman to look at her. "He isn't gone. He is nearby. Wait just a moment."

Benny waited until the officer opened the door for her, and she smiled politely. "Where is the pen?"

"There is no record of it."

"Do you mind if I find it?"

The officer smirked. "Go for it. The officers who brought her in are back on the street."

Benny held out her hand and summoned the pen, and just to be nasty, she pulled the uniform of the officer who had it on him. Dark fabric landed in her palm, and with a little investigation, she found the pen.

The officer across from her was staring. "You took their uniform?"

"Oh, you know XIA magic. It is messy."

"Can you put the clothing back?"

Benny sighed. "I am afraid not. I don't know who it came from. I just tracked the pen and pulled everything around it to keep it safe. I didn't want it to snag on anything."

She looked at the pen and whispered, "Michael, she needs you."

The ghost appeared and walked through the door to his sister.

The sobbing turned from panicked to delighted. Miaka was coming back to herself and swirling into her new reality.

The conversation between the twins began, and Benny looked around for a safe place to put the pen.

The officer was digging through the clothing and found the identity badge. The call was immediately placed and the nearly naked officer located.

When the officer questioned why the pen had been on his person, Benny could clearly hear him say that he wasn't going to take orders from an XIA agent.

Benny raised her eyebrows at the officer on this side of the call. Colour crept into his face.

Benny used a small charm to stick the pen to the wall next to the cell.

"I will be checking in with her later, and I will file paperwork to get her transferred to the XIA. We actually do know how to handle our own, and we have compassion for those who end up in a place that their genetic inheritance put them in."

She checked on Miaka again, and the woman was eagerly

speaking to her brother.

Michael glanced at Benny and inclined his head. She nodded back and left them to their reunion.

A small enchantment to tie Miaka to the pen was the same one that Lenora used to use so that Benny didn't lose her homework.

Benny inclined her head to the officer walking her around, and she left the building. One more batch of paperwork was in her future, and the sooner she got to the SUV, the better.

Chapter Seven

The guys saw her coming and straightened from their positions loitering on the SUV. Tremble summed it up. "Uh, oh."

Benny got into the seat and fired up the computer, writing a scathing report and request for prisoner transfer. When it came to the reasoning, she smirked and wrote that as the XIA agents had had to fend off the ghouls, it was their jurisdiction that had been impinged.

The rest of the prisoner torture was recorded, including the name of Mage Guild Officer Ambrican, who had removed the pen and kept it for his own purposes.

She outlined her summoning of the pen and the uniform that came with it, culminating with her attaching the pen to the prisoner via spell work, while the others climbed into the vehicle.

"What happened in there?" Argyle asked cautiously.

Smith pulled away from the parking spot and headed around the block to the XIA.

"They had her in an isolated cell and didn't put the pen close enough for activation. She was going insane at an accelerated rate, and the break in her spell only made it worse."

Tremble's voice was soft. "So, you are angry."

"Furious. I would have taken her out of there if she hadn't been on record with all agencies." Benny kept typing until she had assembled a complete assessment of the situation and her actions. When she sent the file, she closed the computer and her hands formed fists in her lap.

Cautiously, Argyle asked, "Why are you so angered by this?"

Benny worked at calming herself. Her eyes were flicking between glowing demon green and rainbow fey with rapid cycling. She could feel it.

The new change to her social structure was a source of stress. She hadn't found a normal balance and now something was hitting one of her hot buttons. Too much too soon.

Tremble put his hand on her shoulder again, and she breathed slowly, using his aura to calm herself. Between him and Argyle, she could probably anchor her mood to theirs and keep herself stable, but if either of them pitched a mood, she would go along for the ride. It was better to figure out a way to calm herself.

When they returned to the agency, she headed inside with her team and changed back into her normal clothing. Her locker hadn't been tampered with while she was gone, and it was one relief in a messed-up evening.

"Ganger. In my office."

The captain's voice rapped out. She turned and headed to the sound of the irritated commanding officer.

"Close the door."

She stood in front of the captain's desk. "Yes, Captain."

He looked at her and cocked his head. "Why did you do that? The Horrocks woman was off our books."

"She was going insane. In a matter of hours, she would have been catatonic, and from there, she would have been prime psychic fodder for the demon who was sponsoring her."

Matheson leaned back in his chair. "How do you know that?"

"I was once the target of a similar pattern of attack. Demons go with what works."

"How was it resolved in your case?"

She stared straight ahead. "My father intervened."

"And you intervened in the case of Miss Horrocks. Well, since you have legitimate reason to believe that a demon is involved and the Mage Guild does not want to draw the attention of one unless necessary, we are taking possession of the woman and her brother."

Benny nearly collapsed with relief. "I can help with warding a safe spot for her. She will need help developing mental skills and defenses to keep him out."

Captain Matheson held up a hand. "We call in specialists for that sort of thing, but it has been so long since there was a demon on the books that I will have to dig out the contact information."

"She will get help?"

"You can come in early and check on her tomorrow. For tonight, just put a ward around the room we are putting her in. Is that acceptable?"

Benny nodded. "Yes, Captain. Thank you."

Matheson sighed and ran a hand through his hair. "You were very careful to not incriminate your partners."

"I was doing my part as the mage-humanish part of the grouping."

"Well, you filled a position that we didn't even know was lacking."

"Argyle and Tremble managed to keep the ghouls confined. Smith located the mage and watched my back."

"So, a well-rounded team. Good work for your first night; now, come on and ward that cell."

Benny followed him, and her team followed her. They went down to the cells, and Benny eyed the sparse room with a wrinkled nose.

"Can I make it more comfortable?"

Matheson raised his brows. "Can you?"

She stepped in and thickened the pad of the bed with a whispered enchantment. The floor was sealed with a glyph that she drew with her shoe. It was warmed to a comfortable temperature, and when she had made it as physically comfortable as she could, she walked up to Argyle. "Bite my thumb, please."

He blinked, but obliged.

She hissed as her skin was punctured and cupped her hand so as not to waste the blood.

"Smith, can you give me a boost?"

He came in after her and offered his cupped hands. She awkwardly got up and hands cupped her backside to steady her. "Thanks, Tremble."

Wards could be made of anything, but if you were trying to keep out a demon, it had to be blood. She pressed a dot to the corner and jerked her head to the right. They carried her to the next corner, and she marked it as well. When all four were treated, they set her down and she went to where the wall met the floor and repeated the anointing. She washed her thumb and was about to stick it in her mouth when Argyle grabbed her hand and sucked it like a lollipop.

She knew the moment the puncture sealed. He withdrew her finger and gave her a tiny kiss and a wink.

"Wait out there." Benny faced the room and sent magic out to cast a web across the walls, floor and ceiling. No demon but Benny could cross the boundary, and no hostile intent could pass through the door.

She was a little dizzy when she was done, but it was a solid piece of enchantment.

Captain Matheson looked at her and nodded. "Smith, you had better get her home. She looks exhausted."

"Yes, Captain."

They were on their way out when Miaka and her spectral brother were on the way in. When Miaka saw her, the woman broke free and collided bodily with Benny. Her cuffs were still in place, but she whispered, "Thank you."

Benny teared up, and she pressed her head to Miaka's. "You will be safe here. I will talk with you when I come back on shift."

"Michael can stay with me?"

"He can. He can be with you as long as you need him."

The agent behind Miaka nodded and patted his pocket where the pen resided. "It will remain in an active distance."

Benny smiled. "Thanks."

She didn't mention that the pen would move on its own now, that wasn't something she wanted to announced considering that she had just gotten the very unstable girl into a place that respected the trauma that had created the illegal activity. She would get a fair run at justice.

Benny backed off, and Miaka was taken down the hall to her room. She should be comfortable enough until the following day.

Benny was in dire need of a nap. She had used a lot of magic, and since it was coming from her alone, it was taking its toll.

Her crew was waiting for her, and they all stumbled out into the pinking dawn. Pooky was waiting, and he shepherded them home in no time. They all needed to rest, and it was no surprise that they all chose her bed to climb into. The discomfort of a jumble of limbs took second place to the need to sleep.

Benny woke with a jolt that sent Tremble and Andrew into high alert. Argyle leaned up on an elbow and raised his eyebrows. "What is it, Benny? Something wrong?"

The other two were looking around as if preparing for an incursion, but Argyle had it right. Something was pulling her.

She got up and put on a robe, heading downstairs to check her phone. "I will be back in a minute."

The impulse that pulled her downstairs was a new one.

Her phone was hovering above the counter where she had left it, and all the lights it had available were flashing.

When Benny reached the phone, it quieted and settled against her palm.

Two lines of text from an unexpected source was displayed on the screen.

I need to speak with you about the pending case. Meet me at the Wicked Brew; I will be there all day.

Benny blinked. "Right. I need a shower."

The origin of the text was unknown to her phone, but the feel of the power was eerily familiar. Jennifer Langstrom had the unusual distinction of having a mind and aura patterned like Benny's, without the power. Benny had attempted to strip the soul copy off of Jennifer, but the layer underneath had taken to the imprint.

One short phone call had been all they had been allowed before her lawyers had told her to stop talking to Benny. If she wanted to meet in person, it had to be important. During her training, the XIA had recommended that Benny not meet her, but something was up.

She trotted upstairs and headed into the shower, locking out any of her companions. She didn't want company and definitely no shenanigans before she left.

Wrapped in a towel, she returned to the bedroom and filled in her collection. "I got a text from a friend. I have to meet her for coffee."

Tremble stood and headed for the shower. "I am coming with you."

She twisted her head toward him and followed him into the bathroom. "Why?"

"That was way too much power for a simple request." He smirked and pushed her out of the bathroom, closing and locking the door.

Sighing, she headed for her wardrobe, and she pulled out her normal collection of jeans, t-shirt and underwear. When she was dry and dressed, she pulled a brush through her hair in time to see Tremble emerge from the bathroom with his hair braided for the day.

She walked to the side of the bed where Andrew was watching her, and she rubbed her cheek against his. "See you in a few hours."

He blinked and rubbed his eyes. "What time is it?"

Argyle snorted. "It is ten in the morning."

Benny winced. "Sorry. If it wasn't a friend, I wouldn't go, but she needs to talk and we can't discuss things over the phone."

Andrew sighed. "Talk to you later."

He dropped back into the pillows, and she laughed.

Argyle beckoned to her, and she walked around the bed to cuddle with him for a moment before Tremble cleared his throat.

"Ready."

Argyle leaned back and slept instantly with a slight smile on his face.

There was only time for a glass of water before she hauled Tremble out and into the sunlight. Pooky galloped around and became his normal sports-car configuration.

"Sorry for the sudden need, Pooky. I got a call." She settled her small purse between the front seats.

Tremble slid and glanced at her. "Are you going to tell me where we are going and who we are meeting?"

Pooky started to roll down the driveway.

"We are going to Wicked Brew, and I am going to have a conversation with Jennifer Langstrom. She has information about the pending lawsuit."

He blinked. "What lawsuit?"

"Oh. Damn. I forgot this hit the fan when I was in training and you guys were on leave. Um...My parents are being sued for the wilful neglect that led to the death of the other girls and the endangerment of Jennifer."

Tremble cleared his throat. "You did forget to mention that."

"Sorry. I got distracted with the demon thing and all."

He sighed and closed his eyes. "Why are you going to meet with her today? I would think her lawyer would have told her to stay away."

Benny shrugged. "I have no idea. That is what we are going to find out."

Tremble sighed. "This is a bad idea."

She chuckled and squeezed his hand. "Like many others I have had, I am sure things will turn out fine...eventually."

He gave her a wry look through his rainbow eyes. "Don't think that wearing fey eyes will make me soften on this. It is not a good idea."

She let Pooky drive, he was doing it anyway, and looked at her face in the driver's mirror for an instant. "I didn't mean to. I am guessing that things are shifting. Let's wait and see how they work out."

Chapter Eight

Jennifer was sitting with a cup between her palms in a quiet corner of the busiest coffee shop in town.

Benny placed her order and moved to sit across from Jennifer. "You rang?"

Jennifer's eyes were hollow and haunted. She reached out and touched Benny's hand, sighing in relief. "I have missed that."

Benny's eyes teared up. "I am sorry, but I had to pull the copy off you."

Jennifer nodded and swallowed. "I understand. I didn't want to file charges, but my parents took over."

"It is fine. We will get through it, I am sure."

Jennifer nodded, and the foam on her cappuccino began to stir.

"I needed to speak with you in order to give you a warning or instruction. I am not sure."

Benny looked into the face of what had obviously become a seer. "I am listening."

Jennifer squeezed her hand. "See the fey first. Call the wild and see the fey first. Wear all that you have when you see them. It is important. All of you must wear all that you are."

The cryptic nature of the reading didn't bug Benny. She had been seered before.

Jennifer blinked and sighed, looking into her cup warily. "You know, I used to drink my coffee black, but now, I see too much in it. Is it the template?"

"No. It is the print of magic laid on your mind. You are now pulling wild magic into you, and it is coming in the form of time. Every seer is born to pull one wavelength."

"How do you know mine is time?"

"It feels like time."

Jennifer rubbed her forehead. "Why won't it shut off?"

Benny grabbed a napkin with her free hand and started writing with a pen groped from her purse. "Call this guy and tell him two things. One, I sent you, and two, you are a time seer. He will help train you. Your mind no longer has the automatic structure to process power. You are going to have to go into training or go insane."

Jennifer took the napkin with a shaking hand. "It's a man?"

Benny grinned. "He is the best trainer for you. Female seers grow into their powers. He acquired his, and he can help you start from the basics. He has gone through it himself."

Jennifer nodded and seemed content to ignore the lack of direct answer. "Right. One more thing. What is his name?"

Benny chuckled. "I am not authorised to use it. He is a name seer. That is how he looks forward and back. You use time and follow the magic, he uses names and sees where they go and where they have been, forward and backward in time. I think you two will get along."

"Thank you. I know things are about to hit the fan. Thank you for coming when I called."

Benny smiled. "It is the least I can do for what was done to you, but you saved my life."

Jennifer smiled. "You saved mine. I am just beginning to know my own mind, so when I know how I feel about the whole thing, I will let you know."

"Be sure you do. If you want to attack, I am ready for it."

Benny got to her feet and took her mochachino from the server and gripped the takeaway cup. "Thank you."

The server nodded and smiled.

She turned back to Jennifer. "Take care and call if you need anything."

Jennifer smiled and held up the napkin. "This feels like what I needed."

They parted ways without saying goodbye.

Benny beckoned to Tremble, and he pried himself away from the ladies sighing over him.

Tremble murmured outside, "She doesn't look good."

"No, she is going mad."

Benny didn't look back, but she could feel Jennifer's gaze on them as they got into Pooky and she gave the order to go to the

XIA so she could check on Miaka.

Tremble and Benny passed through security and got authorisation to visit Miaka. He went to check their schedule while she headed to holding.

Miaka was with Michael in an interview room, and a necromancer was interviewing her.

Benny tapped on the door, and Miaka smiled, asking quickly if Benny could enter. The bemused necromancer nodded.

Benny entered and moved to put her hand on Miaka's shoulder. "How are you feeling?"

"Much better. Officer Demorak was just having me walk through the rituals of last night. I had to confess that you were the one who handled Michael."

Michael grinned. "I was hardly handled."

"Agent Ganger, perhaps you could tell me what spell you used?"

Benny nodded to Officer Demorak and smiled. "Miaka raised her twin, and I anchored him to the pen using an association connection. As long as he wants to manifest, he will be bound to that pen."

The officer blinked. "You gave the ghost the choice?"

"Of course. It is his afterlife he is delaying. When he and Miaka decide she no longer needs him with her every day, they will discuss it and he can be released, by his own will or hers."

"How did you manage that?"

Benny snorted at the obvious answer. "They are twins. Joined in blood and soul."

The officer struck his forehead with his palm. "Right. Not necromancy, binding magic."

Benny winked at Miaka. "I have a knack for muddling magics."

Miaka smiled. "I am glad for it."

"Well, you seem to be doing fine. I just wanted to check on you."

Miaka sighed. "Thank you. You kept your word."

Benny winked again. "Now, I have to get the elf back to bed. He is getting all grouchy."

Officer Demorak stared. "You are the agents who dealt with that demon issue."

Benny grinned. "We are. Now, I will be leaving. I will be back this evening and check on you again before dawn, Miaka, Michael."

Michael smiled and put his hand on his sister's shoulder. It was a spectral effort, but Miaka relaxed at the phantom contact. "We look forward to the visit."

Benny left, and when she was outside the room, the door opened and closed behind her. Officer Demorak grabbed her arm. "How did you do it?"

"What?"

"How did you anchor him like that?"

Tremble was moving toward them with a scowl on his elegant features. His gaze was fixed on the hand on her arm.

"If you have to know, it was demon magic. Soul manipulation to achieve a purpose. There was a touch of vampire reanimation, a dash of fey energy and a binding of elemental touches to the metal of the pen."

She could feel her power try to rise, but she held it in. His threatening display was waking all of her instincts, and her instincts were to pound him into the floor.

Tremble came up and snarled at the officer. "Remove your hand or I remove your arm."

Benny shifted when she was free and patted Tremble's arm. "Nice. You gave him a choice."

The necromancer glanced around for help and surprise flickered on his face when he noted that none of the day shift were on his side. The day shift was primarily made up of shifters and fey with a smattering of actual monsters. No one was going to help the officer against one of their own.

The duty agent came to them. "Anything else you need, Agent Ganger?"

"Nope. We are all checked out. She is in great shape. Well done." Benny grinned.

The duty agent nodded and smiled. "We do our best to keep them sane and alive."

Tremble put his arm around her waist and escorted her out of the building.

When they were inside the car and headed home, he turned to her. "What was that about?"

"What?"

"Seeing Jennifer, visiting Miaka?"

Benny looked at him and took in his obvious irritation. "Magic leaves a mark. It stamps those who have touched it or have been touched by it. Miaka is vulnerable, she needs to feel safe; Jennifer is unstable and losing her mind. She needs a tutor."

"You know a tutor for insanity?" He took one of her hands and stroked her palm with his thumb.

"No. I know a man who had to master his own development as a seer. He came into it as a teen and came up with techniques to manage his vision. He can teach Jennifer what she needs to know to keep her mind from being torn apart by the magic it is hunting for because of the residue of the imprint."

"Your father did that to her. Not you."

Benny sighed. "She was printed with my mind and aura. I know how she thinks. She doesn't trust anyone right now."

"You are still not stable. You are not recovered from your trip to the demon zone. I can feel it."

She sighed and gripped his hand. "I can rest when things are settled. I am pretty sure it will happen eventually."

He chuckled and leaned in to kiss her. The soft kiss of his lips quickly turned into something more heated and unsuitable for the front seat of a car.

When Pooky stopped moving and revved the engine, she reluctantly stopped the make-out session and yawned. "Time to catch up on more sleep."

They walked through the house and up the stairs, removing their clothing as quietly as they could. They settled in Tremble's bed, and he held her while they caught up on a bit more sleep.

She wished she hadn't finished her coffee.

Andrew hauled her out of bed and bullied her into the bathroom. "Come on, Benny. We need to eat and get to work in an hour. Don't want to be late."

She used the toilet and brushed her teeth again, brushing her hair into a more socially acceptable configuration that wouldn't frighten children before she left and retrieved her clothing.

Everybody was downstairs, and she heard the sounds of food being prepared when she went in search of her partners.

Omelettes were assembling in three skillets, and Andrew was

watching them with a focused eye.

Tremble was checking his phone, and he smiled when she came into the kitchen. "We are going to be doing a road trip tonight."

Benny took the coffee that Argyle handed to her with a smile. "Where to?"

Tremble sighed. "We are doing a centaur transport. One of them manifested in a downtown club last night, so we are taking him to the preserve tonight."

She wrinkled her nose. "The one species I don't get along with."

The three men occupying her kitchen stared at her.

Andrew said, "You are kidding, right?"

"Nope. The magic that mixed the men and horses is a little too weird for me. I find the creepy." She shrugged and chuckled at their expressions. "Come on. There had to be a species I didn't get along with sooner or later."

Centaurs had a tendency to pursue females relentlessly, and it got tiring to be on guard all the time. She wanted to kill them and that wasn't a good frame of mind to be in for any period of time. It was even worse when murder was an actual option.

She smiled and leaned back as Argyle slid her plate in front of her. "Thanks."

He nodded. "Tremble mentioned that you had already visited Miaka and that you met with Jennifer."

She gave the elf a dark look. "Squealer."

"They needed to know."

She made a face and explained her reasoning for meeting with Jennifer. When she had detailed as much as she could, she sat and waited.

Andrew frowned. "Well, it doesn't seem that you did anything that would skew the case against your father. It should be fine."

Benny arched a brow. "You are a legal expert?"

He shrugged. "I dabble."

Argyle chuckled. "He was pre-law before he entered the XIA."

Andrew sighed. "Fine. I have studied law. But I have no idea how this case will turn out. There has never been another one like it. Demonic influence over infants is not a common occurrence."

Benny nodded and kept her mouth shut. The letter in the potion book had explained far more than she had ever imagined. If that knowledge could save her father from a life of incarceration, she would use it, but only if she had to.

They settled down to eat with Argyle supervising, and when the dishes were done, they set out to return to duty and haul a horse-boy off to the collective where other centaurs could control him.

Yay.

Chapter Nine

The centaur was named Steve, and he started making moves on her the moment he scented her. She didn't take it personally; he had also hit on the troll woman who had loaded him into the transport.

Since Steve got aggressive when any of the guys were around, it was Benny's duty to sit in the back of the transport with the shackled centaur and keep him calm.

"So, how many of those guys do you take at a time?" Steve shifted his hooves in their booted cuffs.

Benny sighed and glared at him. "One at a time. We don't need to pile onto each other to show affection."

He inhaled, and his sharply hooked nostrils flared. "You look human and smell like fey. Were you two doing each other before you had to pick me up?"

She gave him a bland look and whispered a small volume spell. He could still talk, but it was a tiny whisper.

"Benny, what is going on in there; I felt magic." Tremble's voice was a little nervous through the earpiece.

She chuckled. "Nothing. I just turned down the volume in here. It will return to normal when he is outside again."

"Okay. We did promise the colony that we would deliver him intact."

"I know. I won't neuter him. I promise. Tempting though it is."

"Great. Hang in there, Benny."

"Tremble, one more thing."

"What is it?"

"Are we there yet?"

His muffled snort sounded in her ear, and she heard the others chortling in the background.

It was an hour later when the vehicle stopped moving and

the sound of hoof beats approached the transport.

She waved the spell away and smiled. "Looks like this is your stop."

She felt power on the other side of the doors. Fey power.

Remembering what Jennifer had said, she let her control slip and let her body take what it recognised as its natural form.

A human-looking woman had stepped into the transport, a demon king walked out with the shocked centaur in tow. The trip down the ramp was slow, and she caught Steve when he stumbled, but he jerked away from her touch.

"Don't move away from a helping hand." She steadied him with a hand on his shoulder, and soon, they were on soft grass with a semi-circle of centaurs watching and a few lithe and pale fey in the background.

"What are you?"

She gave the appalled male a smirk. "Agent Ganger of the XIA."

The rest of her team was nearby, and they followed her lead, wrapping themselves in power.

Tremble waved to one of the men behind the centaurs, and the stunned elf made his way toward them.

"Cousin, it is good to see you."

Tremble inclined his head. "My prince. May I do you the honour of introducing my comrades?"

The elegant man who looked carved of moonlight smiled slightly. "I believe that would be wise as you are on our territory."

Introductions were made amongst the men, and finally, Benny faced Prince Emrick Brightleaf, ruler of the local lands.

He took her hand. "Beneficia Ganger? You cannot be. She has a human aspect."

Benny inclined her horned head. "I am indeed she. My aspect is what I wish it to be. I am currently displaying something more akin to my fey ancestors than is normally apparent."

Her words were slow and formal. She didn't want to flash the sharp teeth that didn't quite match the elegant deer horns.

"You are a woman with much power." His lips grazed her skin.

Smith stiffened next to her, but she accepted the caress.

"I am indeed. You are showing a remarkable lack of good

sense, dear prince."

He raised his white eyebrows and smiled with his lips quirked to one side as he rose. "I am?"

"My partners are my partners in all things. As enchanting as your presence is, it will not be wise for the contact with you to continue."

He released her hand and took in the strange assembly. Smith had released Steve to the centaurs, and they had reluctantly left with their new member in tow.

Now, it was just the XIA and the fey.

Tremble moved to her side. "We were going to formally present ourselves, but we are joining in a union that is equal across our four bloodlines."

Prince Emrick could not have looked more shocked. "A union?"

"Married. The Ganger family is making the arrangements, but in our traditions, we were going to introduce ourselves to the fey community."

Benny blinked and smiled as her mind spun with the ramifications of this meeting. Normally, they would have started with the lowest members of the fey society and work their way to the prince if they had gained approval. Now, they only needed to get Emrick's authorisation and the rest had to follow.

"The Ganger family has authorised this union?" Prince Emrick was hesitant.

Benny inclined her head. "Yes. It is a little bulky, but hardly the strangest mating in my family line."

He looked ill at ease. "What of children?"

Ah, so that was it. "They will be raised as Gangers with the family affiliation made clear when paternity has been established. That will not be for a few years. I am enjoying my new life in the XIA. My family has never kept any distinctly blooded member from their people."

"In that case, I give you my blessing and await the invitation to the event. I am sure it will be a party to remember."

She inclined her head, and he backed away before slipping onto a horse that appeared from the shadows, and he and his party rode away.

She shook her head and resumed her human shape. "That was unexpected."

Benny held still as she was suddenly hugged from all sides.

Tremble was shaking as he held onto her. "You really mean to wed us all."

She caught on to what he said. She had changed them; they were no longer what they had been and their places in their own society were not assured.

"Of course. You are all Gangers now. You can even take the family name if you like. I am not fussy." She laughed as they kissed her in turn.

Finally, she called a halt. "We are on duty. Grab the boots and we will be on our way."

Argyle chuckled. "Ride next to me. I promise not to get grabby on the way home."

Benny leaned against him and sighed. "Sounds restful."

It was. The other two were busy trying to determine who would arrive at the altar first on the big day, and Benny had to throw a wrench into the works. "Smith, we still have to meet your alpha, and we need to meet Argyle's maker or king."

That thought seemed to shut him up for a while until they re-entered the city.

She dozed with her head against Argyle's shoulder until they pulled up to the XIA headquarters. Argyle's phone was in his hand, and he winked. "We have an hour."

She blinked. "What?"

"The king is waiting for us to present ourselves at his home. As this was our only assignment tonight, we are now free to attend at his pleasure."

Benny groaned. "We are so not dressed for that."

Argyle opened the door and slid out, extending his hand to hers. "I am sure you will think of something."

After they were logged out and changed, she did indeed think of something and her companions' clothing was changed from denim into leather with a few choice bits of spell work.

Andrew sighed. "I suppose that my family is last."

Benny chuckled as Pooky took them through the calm and old neighbourhood where the vampire king mayor resided.

"You had a chance to pounce. You didn't pounce, so now we are going to see the vampires first." She wrinkled her nose at him as her clothing shifted around and under her in the car.

Pooky entered the long, sweeping drive, and Argyle spoke into the security camera, gaining them access to the surprisingly understated home.

"We are lucky in Mathias. He is a calm and understanding ruler." Argyle seemed to be making a point to both Tremble and Andrew.

When the car settled in front of the home, two shadows emerged from beside the doors to the house and stepped down to open their vehicle.

As Benny slid out of the car, her dress flowed into configuration around her—a leather overdress and trousers in contrasting black. Argyle took her hand, and they led the other two into the mayor's home.

Miss Leonora Wicks was waiting in the frame of the doorway as it opened at their approach. "Miss Ganger. I am delighted to see you again."

"Thank you, Leo. It is good to see you as well."

The woman still had the grey cast to her skin that had been there on their first meeting at the crime scene a few weeks earlier.

Once again, she smiled and her face went from blank and sober, to beautiful and welcoming. "He is waiting in the gardens. Your timing was perfect."

Argyle cleared his throat. "Allow me to introduce our bound companions."

Leo gave him another sweeping smile. "I don't care. This way."

She moved silently; her chiffon gown gave her the appearance of a floating spectre as they moved through the modest mansion and into the floral-scented darkness of the back garden.

The vampire king was tending his flowers and checking out his peach tree. "Leo, come here and taste this."

Miss Wicks rolled her eyes. "If I had a nickel for every time I heard that."

With a grin, the woman stepped toward the mayor, and he held out the fruit to her in a reverse of a biblical moment.

Benny watched as Leo reached for it with her hand, but Mathias held it so that she had to take it from his grip with her teeth.

Her face wasn't visible from that angle, but Benny knew that sound. Leo chewed furiously. "Not ripe!"

Mathias grinned and nodded. "I thought that was the case, but you know, I can't really tell."

Leo wrinkled her nose at him. "Your guests are here."

Mathias nodded and the peach arced through the air. Benny caught it and ripened it in her hand. She took a bite. "Thank you, Mayor Mathias."

He grinned. "It is good to see you again, Benny."

She released Argyle's hand and walked up to her family friend. "It is nice to see you so happy, Uncle Matt."

"It is good to feel it, Benny. Now, what can I do for you and the good Argyle?"

Benny looked toward her vampire, and she smiled. "I wish to have him for my own, Uncle. We are bound, and now, I wish it to be formal in the eyes of the vampire nation."

"It will not be easy. He will outlive you if he does not suffer an injury."

She wrinkled her nose. "He is not quite one of yours anymore."

Mathias moved past her, and he grabbed Argyle by the chin and turned his head from side to side. "What did you do to him?"

Benny twisted her lips before biting into the peach again. "Nothing that he didn't consent to. They are mine; I am theirs; we are bound."

Mathias moved faster than she could track, examining Tremble and Smith as well. "All of them have a touch of demon in them."

"My blood."

Smith's teeth extended in surprise when the vampire king was suddenly in front of him. Mathias calmed him down.

"Easy, beast. I am just looking into...and there he is." Mathias looked into Tremble and nodded when he found the traces of Argyle he was seeking.

Benny blinked when Leo took the peach out of her hand and finished it. "Sorry. I had to get that sour taste out of my mouth."

A moment later, Mathias was next to her. "Well, you have given me three more subjects, so giving you one is fair enough."

Argyle came forward. "You are authorising our union?"

Mathias smiled. "Of course, Cairbre. I know what I am looking at and am both glad that I can call upon it and am willing to come if you call."

Leo took a call and walked into the house; Mathias watched her go.

Benny looked from the doorway to the ancient power standing next to her. "Love?"

"As close as I can come. She has been through much, sacrificed much, and is always willing to give more. She is a woman to be admired, and I have not met one such as her before."

Benny nudged him with her arm. "Fire and ice under one skin."

He nodded. "Precisely. Now, dawn approaches and your companions look exhausted. Take them to bed."

She wrinkled her nose at him and gathered the men around her, ushering them back to Pooky and, from there, back home.

Chapter Ten

As sweat dried on their bodies, Andrew asked her. "What exactly is passing between you and the heads of our clans?"

Their fingers were tangled together, and she rested her head against his shoulder. "Each one we speak to is acknowledging that your first duty is to our group, and each one knows that they are obligated to come to our defense, just as I am agreeing to come to their defense."

"I still don't get it."

"If your pride tangles with another, we will stand on the side of your pride, for the purpose of increasing numbers and to bring power. For Tremble's family, we bring fresh blood and energy, not to mention my family ties. That gives them added political clout when it comes to dealing with other principalities on the continent. They can get higher-ranking brides and husbands from other groups now."

"What do the vampires get?"

Argyle answered. "Protection. Protection from Benny's namesake. She can no longer hunt here unless Mathias requests it."

Benny yawned and snuggled against Andrew. "I am quite a catch."

Argyle reached out and patted her hip. "Yes, you are."

Tremble was reading a book across the room, and as she watched, he put the book down and crawled into bed.

She smiled as he curled around her. Given a choice, they preferred to be together. It was starting to feel like a family.

"Hey, Benny. We have a court date for an inquest." Her father's voice came through the phone as if he was next to her.

"When?" Benny finished brushing her teeth and held the phone to her cheek.

"Because of the publicity, we are going in tomorrow. They

want to get everything settled and have me punished as quickly as they can." Harcourt laughed.

"You are sounding...better?"

"I am. The cut ties to Yomra have done wonders for my aspect. Your uncle Imriod is my counsel. I am sure things will turn out as well as they can."

"You know that they don't have call to be charging you."

"I know that they feel they have reason. The spell would have been passive if not for someone coming after you, but if you were not in danger, it would not have been needed."

Benny nodded, though he couldn't see her. "Right. Keep me posted. I want to be there."

"I believe you are being named as a witness of some sort. You will be there, love." She could hear the smile in his voice.

"Good. Glad that is out of the way."

"Now, finish your teeth and get to work. We are hearing good things about how you are handling yourself."

"You have spies watching me?"

"Of course. Just because you are an adult doesn't mean we will stop trying to take care of you or make sure you are safe. It just means we do it from a distance. Have a good shift."

The call was over in that light rush of speech, and she chuckled and spit out the foam. It was nice to know that she was still being cared for, even in her own place with her own family starting up. It was creepy, but nice, just like her parents.

Andrew was grilling ham steaks and Tremble was on waffles. Argyle was slicing fruit.

Benny checked her messages and texted a reply to Freddy that everything seemed to be going fine. Freddy demanded details, but Benny told her to get bent.

A plate slid in front of her, and she glanced up to see Andrew's smirk. "We have a half-hour appointment with my brother-in-law before work. Most of the pride won't be there, so it will be a little less tense than it would be on a weekend afternoon."

"Won't that be a little weird? I mean, it is usually a formal introduction for a mate from outside the pride."

"Well, when I mentioned that you had already met the other portions of our unit, he accelerated things to save face."

Tremble chuckled. "That shows he is more than an alpha; he

is a politician."

Argyle nodded. "Very nice. Do you need us to do anything before we go?"

Andrew grinned. "Rub up against Benny and myself a few times. We still scent cue, so it will be faster if you smell like us."

Benny's fork froze halfway to her mouth as Argyle hugged Andrew without any delay. He stroked his cheek along the tanned skin of his partner, and Andrew's eyes closed for a moment.

When the embrace was over, Tremble stepped in and bent his head to repeat the caress on the other side of Andrew's face and neck.

The shudder that went through their lion was hard to miss.

Benny had to admit to being turned on by the sight of so much male muscle pressing together before parting. It was as if their clothing wasn't even there.

Argyle chuckled. "Benny. You might want to give us our shirts back."

She looked at him and blinked slowly. "Hmm?"

He lifted her free hand and pressed it to his cool, bare chest. "Shirts. Back."

She sat up and blushed. "Right. Sorry. Got caught up in the moment."

She sent the spell to clothe them through the air, and magic wrapped around them. Part of her sighed and kept replaying the scene over and over again. It was going into her foreplay memory file.

Benny made a mental note to figure out why her instincts had stripped them without any conscious direction. Unconscious magic could get dangerous very quickly.

She finished breakfast quickly and loaded the dishes into the dishwasher. Andrew pinned her against the counter.

"I just need your scent on me now." Andrew leaned in and brushed his cheek against hers.

Benny shook and reached up, looping her arms around his neck. "Done."

She leaned and pressed her lips to the column of his neck, exhaling against his skin.

He pressed firmly against her, and a low, rumbling purr sounded deep in his chest.

She nibbled, licked and stroked the hair at the back of his

neck while she worked. When Andrew was vibrating under her touch, she relaxed and leaned back.

The husky tone in her voice was unmistakable as she said, "I believe we have an appointment with your alpha?"

His glare said a thousand words. "If he says one wrong thing, this is going to get very ugly."

The guys jostled each other as they headed for the door; the XIA would be their first stop, to check on Miaka and then the trip to Andrew's family seat would be next.

Spirits were high, but there was an underlying tension that hadn't been there before.

Miaka was sitting with a notebook and a necromancer when Benny arrived.

The necromancer got to her feet and smiled. "Good afternoon, Agent Ganger. I have heard wonderful things about you."

The woman extended her hand, and Benny reached out to shake it. The contact was a little startling, but the shock of cold didn't stop Benny from shaking the hand of the self-animating woman in front of her.

"I am glad to know it. You have the advantage of me."

"Ah, I am Kima Remiller. I specialise in instructing those who have specific talents, like Miaka here. I will be her private tutor during her time in the restricted facility, and when she is released, she will join us at a school specialising in the arts of the undead."

Benny released Kima's hand and glanced over at Miaka. "You have been sentenced?"

She nodded, and Michael gave a thumbs-up behind her head. "I was sentenced under the magical-stress provision. Michael testified for me. Your statement on the matter carried some weight."

Benny paused before she realised that Miaka was referring to the report she had written in the car and the follow-up report when they had brought Miaka into the XIA.

"I am glad it helped. Grief can make folk do extraordinary things."

Kima nodded wisely. "It can indeed. She has a lot of potential, and it needs to be directed so that she and society can feel the benefit."

Benny felt an unfurling sense of relief. She couldn't hug Miaka, but she patted her on the shoulder and promised to keep in touch as much as was feasible.

Kima sat down again, and they continued their lesson with both Michael and Miaka paying close attention. It was yet another wonderful mental image to walk away with.

Today was turning into quite an encouraging day.

"So, Dornan will come out of the house with my sister, Emily. The betas might be behind them, and the attached alphas will be outside on guard. Everybody will be watching Dornan. If he goes on alert, we will all be in for it." Andrew spoke grimly.

Argyle had his sunglasses on, and he glanced over at Andrew. "What happens if he goes on alert?"

Andrew sighed. "We will have to fight for our place in the pride."

Tremble grinned. "Do we want a place in the pride?"

Benny elbowed him. "Shush. Of course. This is even all the way around. Elves, vamps and now lions. Everybody is going to have all the backup we can manage."

Tremble took her hand and raised it to his lips. "Yes, Benny."

Andrew turned down the long drive and jerked his head toward the sprawling ranch house with high spires at every corner. "Felines love a high perch. We are no exception. They saw us on the highway. You can see them gathering on the grounds and emerging from the woods. Huh. There are more off today than I thought."

Benny didn't comment that it didn't seem to be a good thing. A yard full of lion shifters was setting her senses on edge.

Argyle was flexing his hands, and Tremble's ears were as alert as she had ever seen them. Even Andrew was on alert.

Meeting a swirling and evolving family was definitely different from the cold greeting of the fey and the relaxed moments with the vampires. Benny braced for anything.

Andrew pulled in at a safe distance from the house, and he glanced at them. "Okay, you have been briefed and we are all ready for a fight. I don't think that there is anything else to cover."

Benny nodded. "We are going to follow your lead, Andrew. We are going to take our cues from you."

"Got it. Well, here we go."

In a rehearsed move, three of them opened their doors while Benny unbuckled. When they gathered outside her door, Andrew opened it and took her hand to guide her out. She was the alpha female to their gathering of alphas, and they were exhibiting their protection. It was odd, but since the lionesses owned the property, they were entitled to protection. Benny was their ersatz lioness.

They stepped toward the front doors of the home and paused a safe distance from the threshold. The doors opened, and Dornan and Emily came out, with Emily's heavy belly leading the way.

Dornan gave a formal nod. "Andrew You bring members of your pride here to greet us?"

Andrew jerked his head slightly. "I have. They are my pride and my family. I would like to introduce you."

Emily nodded her head. "Come, brother. I need a hug and your nieces are going out of their heads waiting until this is safe."

Andrew nodded and stepped forward. "Dornan Bearing, Emily Smith-Bearing, I would introduce you to my partners. Tremble, Argyle and Agent Ganger are my chosen life bonds. They are my family and now yours."

Dornan stepped forward, and they could feel the eyes on them from every angle. He walked up to Andrew and inhaled the scent off his body. He shuddered slightly and then came over to greet them in precisely the same ways.

Emily came up behind him and repeated the actions, rubbing Benny's cheek with her own in greeting. Tension eased and everyone relaxed. The members of the pride slowly walked in to greet and accept the newcomers in their midst. One small moment turned from tense to warm, and it made Benny smile.

Emily pulled her aside as the little girls rushed out to meet their new uncles and aunty. "I think he is where he is supposed to be."

Benny watched Andrew move through his family and pride members accepting congratulations for his bravery and the power that his new pride exhibited.

"I think so, too. We just all fit. The odds were against it, but there it is. We fit together and nowhere else."

Argyle had a three year old on his shoulders and Tremble was holding the toddler with aplomb.

Emily linked arms with her, indicating her instant comfort. "I think they would make great fathers."

"I think so, too, but I am waiting until I have a few years in the XIA under my belt. We have joined more than lodgings; we have linked lifespans. I have a bit more time than most humans are granted."

"So, you are thinking of having kids?" Emily tried to be sly.

"Of course. Tremble has already volunteered to be the house husband, but none of us are in a rush. We can't be. We have no idea who the father of the first would be."

Emily blushed. "So you.. all together?"

"No. But it is fairly serial. One sets off the others and so on."

A sly female voice from behind Benny murmured, "It sounds like a circus."

Emily stiffened and turned with Benny. "Maggie, you were not invited to speak."

The woman was beautiful, golden and had the sly look of an ex-girlfriend.

If Benny didn't have such a good opinion of her own worth as a female, she would have been intimidated. As it was, she smiled slightly and extended her hand. "Pleased to meet you."

Maggie narrowed her eyes and sneered. "I don't shake hands with mongrels."

Emily's shoulders stiffened. "You are speaking to my soon-to-be sister-in-law."

"Madam Alpha, you are going to have to choose between pride and family. You can't have both. Eric deserves better."

Benny lowered her hand; her brain was smug in the knowledge that Maggie didn't call him Andrew. That was the name he preferred, and if she didn't use it, she didn't know him all that well.

Benny smiled. "He does deserve better. He chose better. He has three loyal partners, and we would all fight to the death for him."

Maggie's features shifted for battle, and she lunged forward. "Prove it."

Chapter Eleven

Benny shifted to keep Emily out of the line of attack, and she let her other form out.

The half-shifted, charging lioness's eyes widened in shock as she was facing a demon king with fey eyes and vampire calm.

It was almost comical to see the woman go from aggressive to grovelling as Benny grabbed her, flipped her and pinned her to the ground with one hand in her hair and her head back. It was a submission pose and Maggie didn't fight it.

Emily cleared her throat. "Well, that was unexpected."

Benny looked at her new sister. "Apologies. I had hoped to ease you into this particular manifestation."

Emily waved it off. "Not you. Them."

Benny looked over to where the guys were standing and the demon manifestations were exceedingly obvious.

"What did you do to my brother?"

Benny wrinkled her nose. "We are all bound together. It was necessary, but we now share portions of all the others in our odd little unit. The demon manifestation is me, fey is Tremble, and Argyle's teeth and calm come in handy. We get enhanced senses and claws from Andrew."

Emily hugged her belly. "All that is just inside you?"

Benny held Maggie in the twisted position and smiled. "Of course. I only let it out on special occasions. It was important for Andrew's family to know what we had become, together."

Emily exhaled. "Well, you don't seem like a ravening beast, and you don't seem evil."

Benny didn't mention that she wanted to snap Maggie's neck as casually as you would swat a fly. She smiled and looked down at her prisoner. "Are you going to behave?"

Maggie nodded slowly and as much as should was able to. "Yes."

Benny whispered a charm to lock Maggie in her half-shifted form for a day. "Now, you are going to have to deal with having your furry face on display for a day. Twenty-four hours from now, you will regain control. Never attack me or mine again. It is not worth your life to try and gain position by aggression."

Maggie scuttled back the moment that Benny let her go.

Benny looked at Emily and slowly receded back into her normal skin. It was a little disturbing that it was coming so easily when she wanted extra power. Reaching for her demon side wasn't her favourite means of defense.

Andrew came up to her and wrapped her in his arms. "Are you all right?"

She nodded. "I am fine. She didn't lay a claw on me."

Maggie was sitting on the ground with her hands on her face, her claws a little too near her eyes for Benny's liking.

Emily sighed. "I will look after her. Thank you for not killing her."

Benny nodded toward Emily. "It was a near thing...wait how did you know?"

He chuckled and rubbed his chin on the top of her head. "When you change, we can feel what you feel through our binding. It is definitely not the way we imagine you normally think. It is far more aggressive."

She sighed. "Sorry."

Dornan cleared his throat. "Well, since I have seen the power that you bring to our pride, welcome once again, Beneficia Ganger."

She gave Andrew a quick look before turning in his arms and opening his embrace.

"We bring you power, allies and magic. What does your pride offer us?"

Dornan blinked. "We offer you companionship, allies and family."

Benny stepped forward. "Right answer. Welcome to the family, Alpha."

He bent his head, and they rubbed cheeks for a moment. He smelled like dry oak leaves and musk with a hint of sunshine.

"Welcome, sister."

"Thank you, brother." Benny smiled and returned to Andrew's embrace, tucking his arms around her. They had some time to formally meet the rest of the available pride, but then, work called. Benny was looking forward to taking on the minutia of the XIA. Tomorrow was going to be stressful, so she wanted to bury herself in the boring details of extranatural law enforcement.

When a little girl tapped at her leg demanding an introduction, Benny grinned. She was now an aunty. Today was definitely a distraction.

Back in the SUV, Benny enjoyed the sucker that little Melody had given her. Benny had responded by enchanting a few strands of braided grass into a flower that would change its appearance every six hours. The little girl had hugged her and immediately taken off to show every lion on the premises her new flower.

Andrew chuckled. "I am getting all kinds of ideas watching you with that sucker."

She opened her mouth and crunched down on the candy.

Three voices said, "Ouch."

Argyle had a strange expression not accounted for by her candy assassination.

"Argyle, what's up?"

He smiled slightly. "I haven't been out like this in actual daylight in an extremely long time."

He had been wearing a hood that sat on his shoulders at the moment, but his skin hadn't burned or even heated up. Even his eyes didn't show their normal irritation from the sun.

"Oh. I am guessing you have gotten better?"

He grinned. "I got something."

Tremble chuckled. "You sound like it is an STD."

They all laughed at that.

Argyle shrugged. "I suppose I will have to get used to being nearly human again, so to speak."

Benny smiled. "Consider it adjusting to daylight and leave it at that. I don't think any of us qualify for human anymore."

Tremble snorted. "I never was human, nor was Andrew."

Andrew turned and gave Tremble a look. "I was for a few years. I mean I was raised in the pride, but shifting didn't kick in until puberty."

Argyle cleared his throat. "I was twenty-six. I was human. I remember human. I don't know what to do with it now."

Benny blinked. "If you want it changed, I am sure that we could supress the humanity."

He shook his head. "No. I am just wondering where the nearest beach is."

The occupants of the vehicle chuckled and pulled into the XIA. In ten minutes, they were logged in, changed and armed for the evening. The skies were red and the shenanigans were about to start.

Benny cuffed the nymph that had been seducing her way through the park in an effort to find her way home. It was an odd means of location, but it worked for nymphs. Someone would eventually help her get home.

The boys had to hang back on this one. The nymph could seduce simply by looking into a man's eyes. Benny was going to have to hang onto her until the collection wagon arrived.

"This isn't really fair." Benny kept her grip on the nymph while the others interviewed participants in the unlawful sex acts. They were all going to get a summons to appear.

Tremble shrugged. "Sorry. It is you or us. I think your odds at resisting her are greater."

Benny snorted and waited for the pickup.

Two female officers were driving the collection vehicle tonight. One of the females was a porcupine shifter, and she wasn't going to take any guff from a lonely nymph looking for directions. It was the public sex that had been the problem, all six times.

Benny made sure that her charge was tucked away and her cuffs were retrieved before the transport left.

"Are you guys finished with your gawking?"

Tremble shrugged. "You are best suited to dealing with females with seduction on their minds."

She snorted and winked as she slid into the passenger seat to type in an incident report. "I thought that was your job."

Argyle leaned against the doorframe next to her. "Only when we are allowed to act on it and only with you."

Agent Smith got behind the wheel. "He isn't wrong. Aside from the enjoyment your wrestling with the nymph provided, it was your body we wanted."

Blushing and concentrating were difficult things to do at the same time, but she managed to get the report details down to the transport vehicle number and agent designations.

"Right. Done. What's next?"

Argyle cleared his throat. "Since I am riding shotgun today, let me check."

She blushed and got out of the passenger seat and waved him in. "Apologies, Agent Argyle."

He stroked her arm and settled in his position. Benny scampered around the car and headed for her position behind the driver.

A moment later, they were in motion and Argyle was sending them to the park where they had entered the demon zone. Apparently, the goblin fires were still burning.

Tremble gave her a side-glance. "What can we do about the goblin fires?"

Benny shrugged. "We will see when we get there."

Argyle looked at her. "What does that mean?"

She wrinkled her nose. "I said we will see. I can't guess until I see the actual blazes. I do know we need to go out with fangs and claws."

Smith glanced at her in the rear-view mirror. "Why?"

"Goblins only pay attention if you are scary. It is what they are wired for. Demon aspects are too scary, so we just need to be pointy."

Everyone in the car chuckled. It seemed that the demon aspects were something that they were getting used to. It would set them apart for the rest of their lives, but now, they were apart, together.

Chapter Twelve

Benny checked her watch, and at the minute mark, she stepped into the flames. Around the park, her team did the same.

Ah, mistress, what do you wish of me?

Oh, fire djinn, element of the burning desert, we wish for you to cease your flickering flame and take yourself to where the population isn't.

The focus of the wish was the important thing. When you dealt with magical, living flame that you had only read about in books, it was best to stick to the formalities.

This place provides plenty of magic and a new wave of it is nearly upon us. I like it here.

You are disturbing the population and frightening children. They do not know what or who you are. There is no place for you here.

The flame wreathed her hands and arms. *Where will I go? It was magic that summoned me here.*

From across the park, Benny felt an idea blossom in Argyle's mind.

I accept your offer.

What? What offer?

To reside at your home until the wave comes and I can take a body again.

The flame rose up, and the dozens of fires across the park wove together into a column that swirled away and streaked through the sky.

Benny knelt on the scorched ground and caught her breath. Her fumbling hand pulled out her phone, and she made a quick call.

"Hiya, Mom."

Her mother's voice was amused. "Hello, Benny."

"Argyle offered our family property to a fire djinn as a resting place. It is on the way."

"It is already here, Benny. He is very polite and has accepted the ruin at the back of the property as his domain for the time being."

"That was quick."

"He is fire, Benny. He moves quickly."

She paused, "Are you ready for tomorrow night?"

Her mother sighed. "They are offering me immunity from prosecution as an accessory if I testify against him."

"Are you going to take it?"

"Your father wants me to, and he has that look in his eyes that he knows something I don't, so I think I will."

"Good. Well, I had better get back to work. Take care of our new companion."

Her mother laughed. "I will use him to clear the poplar cluster at the back of the property."

"Thanks, Mom. Night."

"Night, baby."

Benny hung up, put her phone away and got back to her feet. The other three were staggering toward her.

Smith shook his head. "Why am I so tired?"

Tremble answered him, "Because all of your body heat was consumed by the djinn. I have never met one before, but it was just as described."

Argyle looked from one of them to the other. "Shouldn't that have killed you?"

Benny studiously brushed dirt from her knees.

Three voices said, "Benny?"

She looked at her nails and then flicked glances at them. "It was Tremble's contribution to our group. Fey are immune to the effect of the djinn."

Tremble blinked. "What?"

Benny wrinkled her nose. "I will show you the book when we get home. There is a reason that fey are in my family line; aside from being pretty, you are surprisingly sturdy."

Tremble blushed, and they all returned to the vehicle. Argyle gestured for Benny to sit behind the computer. "I have no idea how to describe what we just did."

She settled in behind the computer and started typing. "Big

words from the guy who offered to let a djinn settle in our back yard."

"I don't know why I suggested that."

She chuckled and patted his shoulder. "He planted the idea. Djinn are known to grant wishes, but most of those wishes are their own."

Argyle watched the words flow from her tapping fingers, and he chuckled as she outlined the very basics of what had occurred, including requesting the elemental being to leave. She did not fill in the departure details or where it was currently located.

When she was done, she sent the report and slid past Argyle, patting him on the arm. She wanted desperately to kiss him, but they were on duty.

She settled in her spot and leaned back with her eyes closed as they started moving.

A hand shook her gently, and the scent of tacos brought her all the way around. Benny sat up and blinked at Tremble's face.

"Come on, Benny. This should wake you up. We had him make it to your standard requirements."

Benny moved slowly and exited the vehicle, leaning on Tremble as he supported her to the picnic tables in the empty lot.

Argyle and Smith were waiting and drawing a bit of a crowd. Apparently, the locals were not yet used to XIA agents finding their little out-of-the-way taco truck.

Tremble supported her to the seat, and Argyle slid the tacos practically under her nose. She picked up her first target and started to eat.

Smith and Tremble started in on their own food, and Argyle kept watch over the whispering crowd.

Benny barely registered the food as she made her way into her serving. Normally, she should have been sweating, but her guess was that the djinn took more heat than she had been aware of. She was in thermal shock.

She had no sooner realised it than Tremble pressed against her left side and Smith on her right. Argyle didn't have any body heat to contribute.

When she finished four brain-meltingly hot tacos, Tremble

got her a refill. She kept eating until the final drop of grease hit the paper. Warmth was returning.

She drank her peppered soda and sighed. "Thanks. I needed that."

Tremble nudged her with his thigh. "We could feel it."

"It was probably why the djinn left so suddenly. He knew he had taken too much." Smith's voice was grim.

She nodded. "Probably."

"It is nearly dawn. We were in that fire for three hours."

Benny groaned and flexed her hands. "That would explain it."

Tremble nudged her again. "The captain wants to speak with us before we go off shift."

She nodded and balled up the remains of the food wrappers. "Ready when you are."

Argyle tidied up, and they headed back to the vehicle.

No one spoke during their trip. Benny suspected that the meeting had to do with her family troubles, but she couldn't be sure until they actually talked to Matheson.

The XIA was surprisingly calm when they arrived. They made it through security and were knocking on the captain's door without anyone speaking to them.

When "Come in" sounded, they walked into the office where four chairs were arranged in front of the captain's desk. He was sitting and scribbling notes in a book.

"Good. Sit."

Bemused, they took seats with Benny sitting across from the captain and the others to the left and right with Argyle nearest the door.

The captain leaned back in his chair and sighed. "Your little team is weird but effective, even for the XIA."

They waited.

"With Agent Ganger's parents' inquest beginning tomorrow, I am afraid that that effectiveness will be compromised during the proceedings. You are suspended from active duty until the matter is closed."

Smith leaned forward. "Why?"

The captain grimaced. "It is a demand from the administrators. If you are on active duty and something is disseminated during the inquest, you may be at risk, and if anyone attacks you, the risk will transfer to them. It is to protect the public as well as your team."

Benny wrinkled her nose. "Didn't we already do this?"

Captain Matheson chuckled. "We did, and we will do it again if it is necessary. I want you focused on the job. The team is getting amazing results, and it has caused the mages to consider offering a few of their staff members to us while you are gone. I had no idea that you were a member of the guild."

She scratched her chin. "I had inherited membership. I was a Mage Guide when I was younger, and apparently, that is a gateway to full guild status. I never bothered pursuing it as I would have had to have formal education in the magical arts."

He gave her a surprised look.

She pointed at her chest. "When it came to magic, I was home schooled. No diploma, so no guild status."

He nodded. "Right. Well. That aside, you have made enough of an impression in their magical circles to get us additional staff, so we are not going to be shorthanded while you are on leave."

Tremble cocked his head. "Is there any idea how long this leave will be?"

Matheson shrugged. "That is up to the courts, but I don't want you back until Agent Ganger's family is stable in whatever position that they settle. Guilt or innocence will be determined, and we will arrange matters after we know how the public has reacted."

Benny felt the emotions running through the binding that held them together. She didn't say anything.

Tremble cleared his throat. "If the public comes out against Benny, what happens then?"

Matheson rubbed the back of his neck. "We will deal with it if it happens. I cannot guess what is being planned for you, but there are options being considered, no matter what the court decides."

Benny nodded tightly. "Wonderful. Well, I suppose that is that."

"You are hereby dismissed on suspension of duties with full pay." Captain Matheson nodded. "Use the time wisely."

Argyle nodded and got to his feet. He extended his hand to Benny, and the others got up as well. There was nothing else to say.

They headed to the change room and got back into their civilian clothing.

Benny's mood was dark as they headed to the parking lot, but when Tremble exclaimed in delight, she smiled. Pooky had brought some friends. Pooky was standing in equine form with three horses of the Wild Hunt in full view of all the XIA and two reporters who were nearby.

Argyle smiled and escorted her to her steed. "Well, this will be interesting."

When they were all mounted and smirking foolishly, the beasts wheeled and galloped across the lot and down the highway in a heady beat of hooves. The number of flashes that had caught them as they rode out meant that they were going to be appearing in some sort of news report in the next day.

Benny enjoyed the wind in her hair and the feel of Pooky under her. They reached speeds that a normal vehicle would have had trouble keeping up with, until they thundered into the wide meadow behind the dower house.

Tremble's eyes were glowing, and his hair was a wild wave down his back. Argyle looked like a blood king, and Smith's own gleaming golden skin was alive with the last of the night. Even Benny felt more awake and encouraged by the gallop through the night.

When the steeds pulled up, even with the dower house, Tremble dismounted and walked toward her, putting his hands on her waist and pulling her over his shoulder. Instead of heading toward the house, he strode into the woods, and she only caught a glimpse of the other two heading for the house.

Her clothing turned into a silk robe, and he tore the silk down the centre as he lifted her to a tree. The bark went from rough to silken against her back while he pinned her and moved into her with energy.

Benny surrendered to her senses, and when Tremble shouted his release, her power joined his and spread through the forest in waves.

She was holding tight to his shoulders, and the pearl of his skin gleamed in the last shreds of moonlight. Her heart was thudding in her chest, and she fought to get her breath.

Tremble pressed soft kisses to her shoulder and up her neck.

Benny smiled and threaded her fingers through the loose mane of his hair. "You need to go for a ride more often."

He grinned against her neck. "You will always be my favourite steed."

Her giggle rippled through the forest, and she heard a laughing answer in the trees.

"Uh oh."

He raised his head. "What?"

"Why did you pick the forest?"

He frowned. "It was close."

"Was it, or did something call you?"

She unlocked her legs and tried to slide down his body, but he caught her before she could touch the mossy ground. A silken robe wrapped around him and hers reformed to cover her.

Tremble held her against him so that her feet still didn't touch the ground. "Why are you worried?"

"I think we may be waking something. The whispers in the woods are turning into laughter. Something in there is excited."

He smiled and stroked her cheek. "I think that was us."

She frowned and smacked his arm. "Something else. I can hear it."

He nuzzled her cheek. "I can hear it as well. Don't worry about it. It isn't harmful. The woods here have just gotten old enough to have a dryad. The forest here is in labour. It needs more power to bring her out."

"Uh, how long is that going to take?"

"A few decades."

Benny raised her head. "What?"

"What we just did was an early contraction. The labour is just starting."

"Do you know which tree it is?"

He grinned. "Not yet. We will all be invited when it is time."

"So, I am guessing that we are now tied to the land."

He swung her fully into his arms and carried her across the meadow. "You manifest as a forest lord in your demon form and you are only now accepting your tie to the land? I thought you were smarter than that."

She smacked his chest, and he chuckled all the way to the house. The sounds of clanking weights told her what the other two were up to. While Tremble had worked his invigoration off with her, they had chosen the ancient method of physical exertion.

Tremble carried her up the stairs and cuddled with her in the bizarrely large bed. It was still going to take some getting used to, but when he curled around her and held her against him, she was willing to try.

A few hours later, hands on her body and a blindfold over her eyes wakened her. She tried to determine who was touching her by the temperature of their skin. After a few minutes, she gave up trying to figure out what was who, and she simply enjoyed it.

If this was what suspension had in store for her, she hoped that her parents took up a life of petty crime after the inquest.

Chapter Thirteen

"Harcourt Emile Ganger, we are here to determine whether charges should be laid on you for the soul interference with eight infants thirty years ago."

The occupants of the chamber murmured, but Benny sat with her partners in silence. Her mother was sitting in the row ahead of her, and her father was in a separate section, under guard.

The judge finished the explanation of why everyone was there and sat back. "Prosecution, proceed to make your case."

The prosecution stood up and outlined the case. Benny had been born and her parents had been worried about her. Her father had crept to the nursery and copied her aura and soul on to the other baby girls.

It was that selfish act to defend his own daughter that had led Harcourt Emile Ganger into the path of endangering the newborns that were next to her. That danger had come to roost in the last two years, resulting in seven deaths.

The use of demonic energy in the alteration of the life patterns of eight babies was the charge. Using them as bait carried a relatively minor sentence, but the soul tampering was the major infraction.

Jennifer was called as a witness to the assault due to her imprint of Benny's patterns.

"He grabbed me and I don't remember much after that. The energy felt weird and greasy. I vaguely heard shouting, but I didn't wake until I was in hospital. I had no idea why I had been marked for death until I was briefed by my parents' counsel." Jennifer looked more rested than she had the last time they ran into each other.

The prosecutor nodded. "What did you think about what had been done to you?"

"I was shocked. I have always enjoyed a normal if oddly successful life. To hear that the way I think was a copy of someone else...it was a shock." Jennifer swallowed.

The prosecutor nodded sympathetically. "Understandable. Has it impacted your life?"

"Before, I don't know. But after the imprint was removed, I definitely felt different. My brain has changed."

"So, the trauma has sent you into a downward spiral?"

Jennifer sat up and blinked. "No. It just changed my direction. I am doing much better now."

Benny tried not to crack a smile, but she felt her lips twitch. Her smirk faded as the prosecutor listed the names of the dead women.

Each of the women had lived full and vibrant lives. None had a husband or child and all were at the top of their field.

Finally, the prosecutor pointed out that even Harcourt's wife was willing to speak against him. He couldn't bring up the demon issue as Benny's dad was firmly in control of his human form once again.

The prosecutor rested their petition.

"I now call the defense to make the case to deny a court date." The judge nodded.

The defense counsel got to his feet and cleared his throat. "I call Beneficia Ganger to the stand, as per my client's request."

Benny got up and sat in the witness box, facing the families of the deceased and her parents. Her mom smiled weakly and waved briefly. Benny inclined her head.

"Beneficia Ganger, do you swear to tell the truth in this matter?" The gargoyle snapped his wings, and she focused on him.

"I do so swear."

The counsel brought out a glowing orb. "Do you agree to hold this orb for the entire portion of questioning?"

She knew that orb. It would sting like hell if she lied. "I do."

The orb was placed in her palms, and she balanced her hands on the edge of the box in front of her.

"What is your relation to this case?"

Benny blinked. "Oh, I am Beneficia Ganger, the daughter of Harcourt and Lenora Ganger. I was the baby that they made the copy of."

The orb tingled.

"That they copied the signature of."

"Why did they do this?"

She inhaled and exhaled before stating it for the record. "I come from a family with demon bloodlines, and my mother's bloodline had its own power. My parents wanted to protect me, so since they couldn't hide my birth, they hid my location."

The gargoyle smiled. "Your father doesn't seem like a demon."

"We have only recently cut the ties that bind our family to the patriarch of our bloodline. It has caused a ripple effect in all of us, but now, my dad looks like he did when I was little."

"What do you mean? How did he change?"

Benny twisted her lips. "Which time are you referring to? I want to be precise."

"The first time. When did he change and why?"

Benny cleared her throat. "He changed when my mother died. He had to take on his demon form to bring her back. He didn't regain a human form until recently."

The gargoyle nodded, "So, the statement from the nurse that a male demon came into the nursery and bewitched her could not have been an accurate statement of events from three decades ago."

Benny chuckled. "No. He looked just like he does now. We have family pictures, school pictures and articles from the universities where he used to teach. His green and scaly form didn't manifest until after my mother's illness."

The judge was making notes and he asked the prosecution, "How did the nurse identify the defendant?"

The prosecutor scowled. "From a lineup of demon photos."

The judge nodded. "Thank you."

The defense attorney nodded his head and asked, "You said you had demon blood. How does it manifest for you?"

"I am strong, fast and can access magic across all boundaries."

"Do you have a demon shape?"

"I got one recently, yes."

"May we see it?"

"I do not see how it is pertinent to what we are here for."

The judge nodded. "Please oblige."

Benny shrugged and she shifted. A few humans and mages recoiled, but far more leaned forward, fascinated. There were not many chances to see a demon in public.

"Now, can you tell me what you did when you came upon the form of Jennifer Langstrom?"

"After we drove off the murderer, I removed the template on her mind. I had just learned of the serial murders and had located Jennifer via my ride-along with the XIA."

"Were you with them when they figured out she was in danger?"

Benny bit her lip. "I was the one who figured out what was going on once my parents told me about the other babies. I told the XIA, and we all worked to track and find the remaining woman. We found her just in time."

"Who was hunting her?"

Benny had to be honest. "No one. They were hunting me. My great grandfather, the demon king Yomra had manipulated a human into killing the women in an effort to concentrate my power."

The gargoyle blinked. "What? What do you mean?"

"The spell that was cast on the babies wasn't a demon construct, it was a soul split. The girls each became part of me, and when they died, those parts came flooding back."

"Didn't you notice?"

Benny blushed. "I thought I had finally finished puberty."

The courtroom erupted in laughter and snickers. Even Harcourt laughed.

When the room was quiet again, the gargoyle asked, "Your mother offered her testimony against her husband in this case and received full immunity for it. Do you know why that would be?"

"Because she knows he didn't do it."

"How do you know that?"

"Because I know who did."

The prosecutor got to his feet. "Objection."

The judge tapped his desk. "This is an inquest, not a trial. Object all you like, we are still hearing it."

The gargoyle smiled. "Now, Miss Ganger, who did this terrible deed?"

Benny looked at her mom and smiled. "My mother."

Lenora gave her a thumbs-up.

The courtroom was in an uproar again, and the gallery shifted restlessly. The judge called a halt to the inquest, and a recess with the public banned from the resumption of the proceedings. It didn't sit well, but the courtroom was cleared via a herding spell. She handed the gargoyle the orb and returned to her people.

Benny was wrapped in Tremble, Argyle and Smith as the crowd pushed in. She belatedly shifted back to human and held onto Smith's back as he used his broad shoulders to keep them from the crowd.

Tremble whispered, "How long have you known?"

"The binding spell. My mom put a confession between the pages of her potion book, thinking that she would be dead before I ever found it. Dad never brews potions, so he wasn't able to destroy it. When she came back from hospital, she was missing a few months before her stay there, so I am guessing she never knew that she confessed."

The defense counsel met them outside the doors and escorted them to a small waiting room with guards to make sure that no one spoke to the attorneys.

The break was only fifteen minutes, but it was enough time for Benny to cuddle up to each of her partners and relax in their embrace.

Argyle whispered, "You are doing great, Benny."

She smiled, and when the bell chimed, they filed back to the courtroom, which was now exceedingly empty.

The judge gestured for Benny to retake the witness box, and the orb was back in her hands.

The attorney fluttered his wings and cleared his throat. "You had just stated that your mother was the one who had cast the spell in the hospital nursery."

"I did."

"Why should we believe that you are not simply trying to save your father as you share your demon nature with him?"

She held up the orb. "This object was created to shock anyone who is telling what their mind acknowledges as an untruth."

"Demons lie."

She cocked her head. "They don't actually; they simply act in their own best interests and pursue their own pleasure. They lack a conscience, not common sense. And I am only partially demon. I have far more fey in me than I do demon blood, but no one is commenting on the rainbow eyes."

"Why do you think that your mother cast the spell?"

Benny quirked her lips. "She wanted to hide me and to keep my power at a reasonable level. The splitting of my power managed it. With only a trickle of demon energy, all of those girls grew up with bright minds and a drive to learn and succeed. It defied their upbringing in several cases."

"How are you so aware of them?"

She blinked. "After I learned they existed, I wanted to find their points of commonality. I researched them after they had passed on. Jennifer is the only one I have seen in person."

He nodded and checked his notes. "You mentioned that your mother had passed. Is this your stepmother?"

"No. She is the one who bore me, wiped my nose and applied first aid when I did something stupid. That happened a lot."

The orb remained stubbornly quiet, and Benny settled in for a long interrogation.

Chapter Fourteen

Benny filled in about her parents and home life growing until the moment her mother got ill.

"I don't like to speak of it, but she lost a few months of memory after she came home. She recovered, but never got the memory of the worst time of her illness back."

"Were there any other changes at that time?"

"Dad turned green and scaly with horns. Is that enough?"

"Thank you, Miss Ganger. You may return to your seat."

Benny got up and handed him the orb on her way down. She resumed her seat with Argyle on one side and Smith on the other.

The defense spoke to her dad. "Mister Ganger, how is it that the soul of your daughter came to be split into nine pieces?"

The gargoyle handed the orb over to Harcourt. He sighed.

"I had marking to do for my class, and I went home to finish it so I could get back to the hospital to be with my wife and daughter. At that time, I was teaching at two local universities and consulting at five colleges." He sighed and ran a hand through his hair.

"Lenora was agitated when I left. It had not been an easy birth, and Benny had not been strong when she made it into the world. Lenora was worried, and I left her anyway." He flexed his hands and his face showed his regret.

"When I came back, she was in bed, her hands tight together and her lips white. She said she had done what she had to, to protect our baby. Benny was safe and her godmother would look after her if Lenora didn't make it. I told her she was being silly, but she was haunted. We brought Benny home, and Lenora got better, but I always remembered what she had said. She had kept them from finding her so Benny would be safe." Harcourt's voice broke and he gather himself.

"When she was dying, she told me what she had done. I had told her I was worried about Benny's slow development in the magical arts. With us as her parents, I was expecting her to show more power at an earlier stage. The spell for division of power explained it all. Benny could get by on one-ninth of the power she was born with, and the others would benefit greatly."

The attorney nodded. "What happened to your wife?"

"She got cancer, and there was nothing that we could do. We had to wait until it ran its course, and then, I was able to put demon magic to use. Unfortunately, using the magic left the stain on my body."

"What did you do?"

"I used demon venom to key her to my body and burned the cancer out of her body. I brought her back using the control I had to spark her life, and from there, her own magic took over. I lost my human aspect, but I kept my love."

"Did you resume teaching?"

"No. Lenora and I continued consulting as researchers, but we didn't walk out of the house much. Our friends came to us, and those that didn't mind my new appearance became regular visitors."

Benny held Argyle's hand as her father was asked to show his demon aspect. The familiar features came and went.

Harcourt was dismissed, and Lenora was called to testify. She confirmed all of what had already been said.

"When I first held Benny in my arms, I was terrified of what the world would deliver to her. I wanted her safe, but I remembered how hard it was for me growing up. I wanted a better life for her and less power was the way to do it, at least at the time." Lenora sniffled. "It was all I could think of."

The gargoyle nodded and seemed at a loss for words. "Thank you, Missus Ganger. You may be seated."

The prosecutor looked befuddled, but the judge had a serious expression. "Court is in recess while I assess the testimony of those here today."

They all rose and left, the waiting room was quiet and Benny walked over to hug her parents. "I love you both."

Lenora stroked her cheek. "Thank you for understanding, Benny."

Her dad gave her a firm bear hug. "You did well, Benny. It is better that we get things out in the open. Time to stop hiding."

"One way or another?"

"Precisely."

They waited for two hours until the chime rang again. When it pealed, they got up and walked back to the courtroom.

The judge sat, and he stared at everyone, slowly making eye contact with the defense and the prosecution. "This decision has not been an easy one. At this time, given the statute of limitations, there are no charges that would be relevant to the case at hand. While the families may pursue punitive damages, there are no criminal charges to be laid.

"Harcourt Emile Ganger is free to return to his home. His only crime is not investigating the actions of his wife when they were still at the hospital. Once the infants had left the building, there was nothing else to be done." The judge looked over those assembled.

"As the prosecution granted immunity to Lenora Ganger, there are no charges to pursue. If we were inclined to do so, the spell was cast on her own flesh and blood out of a post-partum protective instinct and therefore is not one that can legally be pursued. She has recovered, and her daughter was not materially harmed by the spell, the side effect has worn off with the death of the other women. All has reset to the point at which fate would have had it.

"I dismiss all culpability in this case on behalf of all the Gangers and wish them a more serene future. Case dismissed."

The prosecutor nodded, and his shoulders slumped with relief. The defense attorney smiled, and his wings opened as he stood. Her parents had paperwork to fill out, but they would be home before dawn.

Benny let the guys escort her out, and she braced herself for the court of public opinion. The courthouse steps were covered with folk waiting to see what was happening.

Jennifer was waiting with her family, and when Benny smiled at her, she rushed forward and hugged her. "I am so relieved."

"Your parents are free to sue mine if they choose to."

"I don't care. The tutor you set me up with is amazing." Jennifer mumbled it in Benny's ear.

"I am glad. He knows what he is talking about."

"We are looking into going into business together."

"Really?" Benny leaned back in surprise.

Jennifer grinned. "A coffee shop. We are thinking of naming it the Patchwork Dragon."

"I swear to be there on opening day."

"I will hold you to it. At this point, it is a few months away. It should be up and running just after winter holidays."

Benny was surprised. "Why so long?"

"I need to get my seer's license. A coffee shop run by a licensed seer would have had a certain cachet, and it means I can use my talent without going anywhere. All the magic will come to me."

"Good. If there is anything I can do, let me know."

"I will. Thanks for this new start. Good luck with your own." Jennifer winked and let her go.

Freddy came up and hugged her as they walked down to the sidewalk. The thud of hoof beats rang through the parking lot. They got on their steeds and took off for home. Folk may have been staring, but nothing was thrown. It was hard to hate the Wild Hunt. They were such beautiful horses.

A gallop through the wilds outside of town was just what she needed. When they got to the meadow, she was feeling soft satisfaction in the events of the night and far less panic.

News reports went over the bits of the case that were recorded and reported, as well as images of all of the Gangers were spread across the news and websites.

Benny spent time with her family, greeting old friends at the big house and introducing them to her new partners. Family came by, friends, acquaintances and a few curious folk who managed to work their way through the wards at the end of the street.

The new portions of their family also came by. The lions arrived and enjoyed a backyard barbeque as well as space to run around in whatever form they chose.

The vampires came with their own food and spent time socialising with the Gangers.

When the fey arrived, it was a party. Magic flared, enchantments spun and it was an experiment in who could make the most indecent-decent outfit. The combinations got peculiar.

As Tremble's sister pulled her aside, Benny knew what was coming.

"When are you going to have a wedding?"

"We are trying for the next full moon, but we might have to wait until we can find a way to make it legal. My parents are in full research mode."

She laughed, a light, lilting sound. "So, we are not the only eager parties?"

"Nope. Anyone who isn't in our party wants to know when we are getting married, and we have to wait for legal matters to catch up. We need a blood-bound dispensation, but for now, we are bonded and know it."

"True enough. Well, you are an interesting sister-in-law. I have never felt so much magic in such a small package."

Benny had come to grips with being short next to the other races. It was the most human thing about her.

"Does he really ride a member of the Wild Hunt?" His sister's tone was sly.

"Sure. Did you want to meet one?"

And so, the rest of Benny's night turned into arranging pony rides for elegant fey. It was not what she had expected, but it was something to kill time.

Arranging weddings with more than four distinct traditions was going to take some time. Lenora threw herself into it and into the new requests for both her and Harcourt to lecture at a number of nearby schools.

The lawsuits were also pending for using the babies as camouflage, but they could ask for what they wanted. If the families didn't have a history of financial success before the soul split, they would have to deduct all of the wages earned since their deceased daughters had begun working.

It was the same for the other young women. The pattern of success was a stain for those suing. Benny made money in a very specific way, and if her counterparts made money in the same method, their earnings belonged to her.

It was way too complicated.

Benny just wanted to get back to work, but they had to wait for the call. She hoped like hell that the call came soon.

Planning a wild wedding and defending a lawsuit at the same

time was bizarre, and she desperately wanted a small sliver of normal back. *Pretty please.*

Epilogue

The assembled XIA commanders and councillors kept their eyes fixed on the group.

In uniform, with her new badge highly polished, Benny stood with her partners and waited to find out what would happen next. Their little gathering had already had a number of job offers, consulting for a variety of species in regards to law enforcement and investigation, but they had all agreed that if they could, they would remain with the XIA.

The chairman of the meeting folded his hands in front of him. "Agents Smith, Tremble, Argyle and Ganger, this council has come to a decision regarding your continued employment by this agency."

Benny felt the tension fill her partners, and she mentally confessed to her own. They had not been asked for their opinion so—for once—Benny didn't offer it.

"While the circumstances of Agent Ganger's bloodline are unusual, they do provide us with an opportunity that the XIA has never had before."

Benny could feel Argyle perk up. His attention was well and fully captured. The other two were wary. She was willing to hear what was being offered.

"Since all charges against you and your family have been dropped as time served and there is still a bit of public unrest with your demon status, we have worked out an alternative."

A female councillor cleared her throat. "We are in need of a liaison to travel to cities and towns where new creatures are not being welcomed or are committing offenses. We need a gathering that can look human, go in and do what is necessary to secure the peace."

Benny blinked. "You want us...to look human?"

The councillor smiled. "We are aware that you can manage it

and have managed it. The sharing of characteristics that you and your companions can engage in is on the record."

Benny wrinkled her nose. "Fair enough. May we discuss this for a moment?"

The council nodded and the woman said, "Of course."

Benny consulted her partners for a moment. They must have seemed strange to the watchers, but a heated debate raged across their joined thoughts. When they had a consensus, Argyle spoke.

"We agree to the arrangement on principle, but we will need to see a document outlining our available courses of action. It will be held in confidence, but we wish to have the backing of this council when we act against the laws of a local area."

The serious folk looked at each other, and the councillor cleared her throat. "That is what we were attempting to tell you. While we will be able to offer you protection once you have entered the XIA territories, we are not welcome everywhere, and in those areas, you will have to protect yourselves. With that stipulation, will you consider this a new branch for investigations?"

Tremble eased forward. "When would we commence our new branch of investigations?"

The captain leaned down and heaved up a box of files. "Each of these files contains a person or persons in a settlement who is hiding who they are from a town or family that would persecute or destroy them. The extra-naturals need to be removed, rescued or arrested, and the locals are not able to manage it. If you accept this arrangement, you begin immediately."

After another silent consultation, Benny smiled, "Show us the contract and let's get this started."

One by one, they signed a contract that was hiring them as investigative consultants under the banner of the XIA. There were new extra-naturals coming into power that needed their help, and there was nothing like a well-balanced team to help out when it was needed. It would get them out, let them travel and give the steeds a chance to run.

Benny put her signature and a spot of blood beneath that of her partners. She was doing it for the steeds, really.

After all, Benny had all the opportunities to exert herself that she could want.

Author's Note

Whew! Well, I did it. I planned for the first three books in the Obscure Magic series and they were done.

Personally, I had a problem during this book. My father passed away suddenly, halfway through. I tried my best to keep it going, but my heart wasn't in it.

An Obscure Magic returns Jan. 1, 2016. We will delve into the lives of some of the ladies we have met on the way...and Benny and the boys will pop up when you least expect them.

Ritual Space, Hell in a Handbag, Defying Eternity, Chosen and Slain, are a few of the titles lying in wait.

In the meantime, there is a holiday series of nine books beginning on Oct 26 and culminating on Dec. 24. The first book is titled *Dear Santa, Get Bent.* When the reindeer have had enough of enforced celibacy, they break out and make a run for the human world in an effort to...socialise. The elves of the Naughty and Nice list are sent out in *Operation Reindeer Retrieval,* to bring the ladies home by whatever means necessary.

Thanks for reading,

Viola Grace

www.violagrace.com
http://www.violagrace.com

About the Author

Viola Grace (aka Zenina Masters) is a Canadian sci-fi/paranormal romance writer with ambitions to keep writing for the rest of her life. She specialises in short stories because the thrill of discovery, of all those firsts, is what keeps her writing.

An artist who enjoys a story that catches you up, whirls you around and sets you down with a smile on your face is all she endeavours to be. She prefers to leave the drama to those who are better suited to it; she always goes for the cheap laugh.

Made in the USA
Charleston, SC
16 January 2016